Emily Sarah Holt

Out in the Forty Five

Or Duncan Keith's Vow

Emily Sarah Holt

Out in the Forty Five
Or Duncan Keith's Vow

ISBN/EAN: 9783337267414

Printed in Europe, USA, Canada, Australia, Japan

Cover: Foto ©Andreas Hilbeck / pixelio.de

More available books at **www.hansebooks.com**

Out in the Forty-five

Or

Duncan Keith's Vow

BY

EMILY SARAH HOLT

AUTHOR OF "MISTRESS MARGERY," "ASHCLIFFE HALL,"
"THE LORD MAYOR," "SISTER ROSE," ETC.

"Yes, Thou shalt answer for me, righteous Lord!
Thine all the merit, mine the great reward;
Thine the sharp thorns, and mine the golden crown;
Mine the life won, and Thine the life laid down."
REV. S. J. STONE.

NEW EDITION

John F. Shaw & Co., Ltd.,
Publishers,
3, Pilgrim Street, London, E.C.

CONTENTS.

CHAPTER VIII.

CHAPTER IX.

CHAPTER X.

CHAPTER XI.

CHAPTER XII.

CHAPTER XIII.

CHAPTER XIV.

OUT IN THE FORTY-FIVE.

CHAPTER I.

WE ALIGHT AT BROCKLEBANK FELLS.

" Sure, there is room within our hearts good store ;
For we can lodge transgressions by the score :
Thousands of toys dwell there, yet out of door
        We leave Thee."
                        —GEORGE HERBERT.

"GIRLS !" said my Aunt Kezia, looking round
at us, " I should just like to know what is
going to come of the whole four of you !"
My Aunt Kezia has an awful way of looking round
at us. She begins with Sophy—she is our eldest—then
she goes to Fanny, then to Hatty, and ends up with
me. As I am the youngest, I have to be ended up
with. She generally lays down her work to do it, too ;
and sometimes she settles her spectacles first, and that
makes it feel more awful than ever. However, when
she has gone round, she always takes them off—

—spectacles, I mean—and wipes them, and gives little solemn shakes of her head while she is doing it, as if she thought we were all four going to ruin together, and had got very near the bottom.

This afternoon, when she said that, instead of sitting quiet, as we generally do, Hatty—she is the pert one amongst us—actually spoke up.

"I should think we shall be married, Aunt Kezia, one of these days—shan't we?"

"My dear, if you *are*," was my Aunt Kezia's reply, more solemn than ever, "the only wedding present that I shall be conscientiously able to give to those four misguided men will be a rope a-piece to hang themselves with."

"Oh dear! I do wish she would not!" said Fanny in a plaintive whisper behind me.

"Considering who brought us up, Aunt Kezia," replied impertinent Hatty, "I should have thought they would have had better bargains than that."

"Hester, you forget yourself," said my aunt severely. Then, though she had only just finished wiping her spectacles, she took them off, and wiped them again, with more little shakes of her head. "And I did not bring you all up, neither."

My cheeks grew hot, for I knew that meant me. My Aunt Kezia did not bring me up, as she did the rest. I was thought sickly in my youth, and as Brocklebank Fells is but a bleak place, I was packed off to Carlisle, where Grandmamma lived, and there I have been with her until six weeks back, when she went to live with Uncle Charles down in the South, and I came home to Brocklebank, being thought to have now outgrown my sickliness. My Aunt Kezia is Father's sister, and has kept house for him since Mamma died, so of course she is no kin to Grandmamma at all. I know it sounds queer to say "Father and Mamma," instead of "Father and Mother," but I cannot help it. Grandmamma would never let me say "Mother;" she said it was old-fashioned and vulgar: and now, when I come back, Father will not hear of my calling him "Papa," which he says is new-fangled finnicking nonsense. I did not get used, either, to saying "Papa," as I did "Mamma," for Grandmamma never seemed to care to hear about him; I don't believe she liked him. She never seemed to want to hear about anything at Brocklebank. I don't think she ever took even to the girls, except Fanny. They all came to see me in turns, but Grandmamma said Sophy was only fit to be a country parson's wife; she knew nothing except things about the house and sewing and mending: she said fine breeding would be thrown away upon her. She might do very well, Grandmamma said, with her snuff-box elegantly held in her left hand, and taking a pinch out of it with the mittened fingers of her right—that is, Grandmamma, not Sophy—she said Sophy might do very well for a country squire's eldest daughter and some parson's wife, to cut out clothes and roll pills and make dumplings, but that was all she was good for. Then

Hatty's pert speeches she could not bear one bit. Grandmamma said it was perfectly dreadful, and that her great glazed red cheeks—that is what she called them—were insufferably vulgar; she wouldn't like anybody to hear that such a creature was her granddaughter. She wanted Hatty to take a lot of castor oil or some such horrid stuff, to bring down her red cheeks and make her slender and ladylike; she was ever so much too fat, Grandmamma said, and she thought it so vulgar to be fat. She wanted to pinch her in with stays, too, but it was all of no use. Hatty would not be pinched, and she would not take castor oil, and she would eat and drink—like a ploughboy, Grandmamma said—so at last she gave her up as a bad job. Then Fanny came, and she is more like Grandmamma in her ways, and she did not mind the castor oil, but swallowed bottles of it; and she did not mind the stays, but let Grandmamma pinch her anyhow she pleased, so I think she rather liked Fanny. I was pale and thin enough without castor oil, so she did not give me any, for which I am thankful, for I could not have swallowed it as meekly as Fanny.

It looked very queer to me, after Grandmamma's houseful of servants, to come home and find only four at Brocklebank, and but three of those in the house, and my Aunt Kezia doing half the work herself, and expecting us girls to help her. Grandmamma would hardly let me pick up my kerchief, if I dropped it; I had to call Willet, her woman, to give it to me. And here, my Aunt Kezia looks as if she thought I ought to want no telling how to dust a table or make an apple pie. She has only cookmaid and chambermaid, —Maria and Bessy, their names are,—and Sam the serving man. There is the old shepherd, Will, but he only comes into the house by nows and thens. Grandmamma had a black man who waited on us. She said it gave the place an air, and that there were gentlewomen in Carlisle who would scarce have come to see her if she had not had a black man to look genteel. I don't fancy I should care much for people who would not come to see me unless I had a black servant. I should think they came to visit him, not me. But Grandmamma said that my old Lady Mary Garsington, in the Close, never came to see anybody who had less than a thousand a year, and did not keep a black. She was the grandest person Grandmamma knew at Carlisle, for most of her friends live in the South.

I do not know exactly where the South is, nor what it is like. Of course London is in the South; I know that. But Grandmamma used to talk about the South as if she thought it so fine; and my Uncle Charles once said nobody could be a gentleman who had not lived in the South. They were all clod-hoppers up here, he said, and you could only get any proper polish in the South. Fanny was there then, and she was quite hurt with it. She did not like to think Father a clodhopper; and I am sure he is not. Besides, our ancestors did come from the South. Our grandfather, William Courtenay, who bought the land and built Brocklebank, belonged [1] Wiltshire, and his father was a Devonshire man, and a Courtenay of Powderham, whatever that may mean : Father knows more about it than I do, and so, I think, does Fanny.

Grandmamma once told me she would never have thought of allowing Mamma to marry Father, if he had not been a Courtenay and a man of substance. She said all his other relations were so very mean and low, she could not have condescended so far as to connect herself with them. Why, I believe one of them was only a farmer's daughter: and I think, from what I have heard Grandmamma and my Uncle Charles say, that another of them had something to do with those low people called Dissenters. I don't suppose she really was one—that would be too shocking ; but Grandmamma always went into the clouds when she mentioned these vulgar ancestors of mine, so I never heard more than "that poor wretched mother of your grandfather's, my dear," or "that dreadful farming creature whom your grandfather married." I once asked my Aunt Dorothea—that is, Uncle Charles's wife—if this wretched great-grandmother of mine had been a very bad woman. But she said, "Oh no, not *bad*"—and I think she might have told me something more, but my Uncle Charles put in, in that commanding way he has, "Could not have been worse, my dear Dorothea—connected with those Dissenters,"—so I got to know no more, and I was sorry.

---

[1] This and similar expressions are Northern provincialisms.

Father once had two more sisters, who were both married, one in Derbyshire, and one in Scotland. They both left children, so we have two lots of cousins on Father's side. Our cousins in Derbyshire are both girls; their names are Charlotte and Amelia Bracewell: and there are two of our Scotch cousins, but they are a boy and a girl, and they have queer Scotch names, Angus and Flora Drummond. At least, they were boy and girl, I suppose; for Angus Drummond must be over twenty now, and Flora is not far off it. It is more than ten years since we saw the Drummonds, but the Bracewells have been to visit us several times. Amelia Bracewell is Fanny made hotter, or Fanny is Amelia and water—which you like. She makes me laugh, and my Aunt Kezia sniff. The other day, my Aunt Kezia came into the room while we were talking about Amelia, and she heard Fanny say,—

"She is so full of sympathy. She always comes and wants you to sympathise with her. She just lives upon sympathy."

"So full of sympathy!" said my Aunt Kezia, turning round on Fanny. "So empty, child, you mean. What poor weak thing are you talking about?"

"Cousin Amelia Bracewell," answered Fanny. "She is such a charming creature. Don't you think so, Aunt Kezia? Such a dear sympathetic darling!"

"It is well you told me whom you meant, Fanny," said my Aunt Kezia, pursing up her lips. "I should never have guessed you meant Amelia Bracewell, from what you said. Well, how differently two people can see the same thing, to be sure!"

"Don't you like her, Aunt Kezia?" returned Fanny in an astonished tone.

"If I am to speak the full truth, my dear," said my Aunt Kezia, "I am afraid I come as near to despising her as a Christian woman and a communicant has any business to do. I never had any fancy for birds of prey."

"Birds of prey!" exclaimed Fanny, blankly.

"Birds of prey," repeated my aunt in a very different tone. "She is one of those folks who are for ever drawing twopenny cheques upon your feelings, and there are no funds in my bank to meet them. I can stand a bucketful of feeling drawn out of me, but I hate to let it waste away in a drop here and a driblet there about nothing at all. Now I will just tell you, girls—I once went to see a woman who had lost fifteen hundred a year, all at a blow, without a bit of warning. What she had to say was—'The Lord has taken it, and He knows best. I can trust Him to care for me.' Well, about a week afterwards, I had a visit from another woman, who had let a pan boil over, and had spoilt a lot of jam. She wanted me to say she was the most tried creature since Adam. And I could not, girls—I really could not. I have not the slightest doubt there have been a million women worse tried since the battle of Prague, never mention Adam. As to Amelia Bracewell, who carries her fan as if it were a sceptre, and slurs her *r*'s like a Londoner, silly chit! I have hardly any patience with her. Charlotte's bad enough, but Amelia! My word, she takes some standing, I can tell you!"

Now, I always admired the way Amelia sounds her *r*'s, or, I suppose I ought to say, the way she does not sound them. It is so soft and pretty. Then she writes poetry,—all about the blue sea and the silver moon, or else the gleaming sunbeams and the hoary hills—so grand! I never read anything so beautiful as Amelia's poetry. She told me once that a gentleman from London, who was fourth cousin to a peer of some sort, had told her she wrote as well as Mr. Pope. Only think!

Charlotte is as different as she can be. Her notion of things is to go down to the stable and saddle her own horse, and scamper all over the country, all by herself. Father says she is a fine girl, but she will break her neck some day. My Aunt Kezia says, St. Paul told women to be keepers at home, and she thinks that page must have dropped out of Charlotte's Bible. She does some other things, too, that I do not fancy she would care for my Aunt Kezia to hear. She calls her father " the old gentleman," and sometimes " the old boy." I do not know what my Aunt Kezia would say, if she did hear it.

I wonder what Flora Drummond is like now. I used to think she had not much in her. Perhaps it was only that she did not let it come out. However, I shall have a chance of finding out soon ; for she and Angus are coming to stay with us, on his way to

York, where his father is sending him on some kind of business. I do not know what it is, and I don't care. Business is always dry, uninteresting stuff. Flora will stay with us while Angus goes on to York, and then he will pick her up again as he comes back. I wish the Bracewells might be here at the same time. I should like Flora and Amelia to know one another, and I do not think they do at all.

It is shocking dull here at Brocklebank. I dare say I feel it more than my sisters, having lived in Carlisle all my life, so to speak: and as to my Aunt Kezia, I do believe, if she had her garden, and orchard, and kitchen, and dairy, and her work-box, and a Bible, and Prayer-book, and *The Compleat Gentle-woman*, she would be satisfied to live at the North Pole or anywhere. But I am perfectly delighted when anybody comes to see us, if 'tis only Ephraim Hebble-thwaite. He is the son of Farmer Hebblethwaite, lower down the valley, and I believe he admires Fanny. Fanny cannot bear him; she says he has such an ugly name. But I think he is very pleasant, and I suppose he could change his name, though I can't see why it signifies. Beside him, and Ambrose Catterall, and Esther Langridge, we know no young people except our cousins. Father being Squire of Brocklebank, we cannot mix with the common folks.

Old Mr. Digby is the Vicar, and I do not think he is far short of a hundred years old. He is an old bachelor, and has nobody to keep his house but our

Sam's mother, a Scotchwoman — old Elspie they call her. He does not often preach of late years— except on Good Friday and Easter Sunday, and such high days. A pleasant old man he used to be, but he grows forgetful now, for the last time we met him, he patted my head just as if I were still a little child, and I shall be seventeen in March. He has been Vicar over sixty years, and christened Father and married my grand-parents.

I do wish we had just a few more friends. It really is too bad, for we might have known the family at Seven Stones, only two miles off, if they had not been Whigs, and there are five sons and four daughters there. Father would no more think of shaking hands with a Whig (if he knew it) than he would eat roast beef on Good Friday. I should not care. Why should one not have some fun, because old Mr. Outhwaite is a Whig?

I shall have to keep my book locked up if I tell it all I think, as I have been doing now. I would not have Hatty get hold of it for all the world. And as to my Aunt Kezia—I believe she would whip me and send me to bed if she read only the last page.

Here comes Ambrose Catterall up the walk, and I must go down, though I do not expect there will be any fun. He will stay supper, I dare say, and then he and Father will have a game of whist with Sophy and Fanny, and I shall sit by with my sewing, and Hatty will knit and whisper into my ear things that I want to laugh at and dare not. If I did, Father would look up over his cards with a black brow and say "Silence!" in such a tone that I shall wish I was somebody else. Who I don't know — only not Caroline Courtenay.

Father does not like our names—at least mine and Sophy's. Mamma named us, and he says we have both fine romantic silly names. Hatty was called after his mother, and that he likes; and Fanny is after a sister of Mamma's who died young. But Father never gives over growling because one of us was not a boy.

"Four girls!" he says: "*four* girls, and never a lad! Who on earth wants four girls? I'll sell one or two of you cheap, if I can find him."

But I don't think he would, if it came to the point. I know, for all his queer speeches sometimes, he is proud of Fanny's good looks, and Sophy's good house-keeping, and even Hatty's pert sayings. I know by the way he chuckles now and then when she says anything particularly smart. I don't know what he is proud of in me, unless it is my manners. Of course, having lived in Carlisle with Grandmamma, I have the best manners of any. And I speak the best, I know. Sophy talks shockingly broad; she says, "Aw wanted him to coom, boot he would not." Fanny has found that will not do, so she tries to imitate my Aunt Dorothea and Amelia Bracewell, but she goes on the other side of her pattern, and does not sound the *u* full where she ought to do it, but says, "The basin is fell of shegar." Hatty laughs at them both, and lets her *u* go where it likes, but she is not so bad as Sophy.

I think I shall try and put the notion into my Aunt Kezia's head to have the Bracewells here for Christmas. I know Angus and Flora will be here then, and later. That would make a decent party, if we got Ephraim Hebblethwaite, and Ambrose Catterall too.

After all, I went on writing so late, that I only got downstairs in time to see Ambrose Catterall's back as he went down the drive. He could not stay for some reason—I did not hear what. Father growled as he heard him go off, singing, down the walk.

"Where on earth did the fellow get hold of that piece of whiggery?" said he. "Just listen to him!"

I listened, and heard the refrain of the Whigs' favourite song,—

> " Send him victorious,
> Happy and glorious,
> Long to reign over us—"

"Disgusting stuff!" said Father, with some stronger words which I know my Aunt Kezia would not let me put down if she were looking. "Where did the fellow get hold of it? His father is a decent Tory enough. What is he at now? Listen, girls."

Ambrose's tune had changed to,—

> " King George he was born in the month of October,—
> 'Tis a sin for a subject that month to be sober ! "

"I'll forbid him my house!" cries Father, starting up. "I'll send a bullet through his head! I'll

October him, and sober him too, if he has not a care!
Fan! Where's Fan? Go to the spinnet, girl, and
sing me a right good Tory song, to take the taste of
that abominable stuff out of my mouth."

"Nay, Brother," saith my Aunt Kezia, who was
pinning a piece of work on the table, "surely a man
may use respect to the powers that be, though they be
not the powers he might wish to be?"

"'Powers that be!'" saith Father. "Powers that
shouldn't be, you mean. I'll tell you what, Kezia,—
you may have been bred a Tory, but you were born
a Puritan. Where on earth you got it——! As for
that fellow, I'll forbid him my house. 'King George,'
forsooth! Let me hear one of you call the Elector
of Hanover by that name, and I'll—I'll——. Come
along, Fan, and give me a Tory song."

So Fanny sat down to the spinnet, and played the
new song that all the Tories are so fond of. How
often she made Britain arise from out the azure
waves, I am sure I don't know, but she, and Father
with her, sang it so many times that all that day I
had "Britons never shall be slaves!" ringing in my
ears till I heartily wished they would be slaves and
have done with it.

At night, when we were going to bed, after Father
had blessed us, Hatty runs round to his back and
whispers in his ear.

"Don't send Ambrose Catterall away, there's a
good Father!" says she: "there will be two of us
old maids as it is."

Father laughed, and pinched Hatty's ear. So I saw my gentlewoman had been thinking the same thing I had. But I don't think she ought to have said it out.

Stay, now! Why should it be worse to say things than to think them? Is it as bad to think them as to say them? Oh dear! but if one were for ever sifting one's thoughts in that way,—why, it would be just dreadful! Not many people are careful about their words, but one's thoughts!

No, I don't think I could do it, really. I suppose my Aunt Kezia would say I ought. I do so dislike my Aunt Kezia's oughts. She always thinks you ought to do just what you do not want. If only people would say, now and then, that you ought to eat plum-pudding, or you ought to dance, or you ought to wear jewels! But no! it is always you ought to sew, or you ought to carry some broken victuals to old Goody Branscombe, or you ought to be as sweet as a rosebud when Hatty says things at you.

Stop! would it be so if I always wanted to do the things I ought? I suppose not. Then why don't I?

But why *ought* I? There's another question.

I wish we either wanted to do what we ought, or else that we ought to do what we want!

I was obliged to stop last night all at once, because I heard Hatty coming up the garret stairs. I always write in the garret, and keep my book there, so that none of the girls shall get hold of it—Hatty particularly. She would make such shocking game of it. I had only just put my book away safely when in she came.

"What on earth are you doing up here?" cried she.

"What are you doing?" said I.

"Looking for you," she says.

"Then why should not I be looking for you?" said I.

"Because you weren't, Miss Caroline Courtenay!" and she makes a swimming courtesy. "Oh yes, you don't need to tell *me* you have a secret, my young gentlewoman. I know as well as if I had seen it. O Pussy, have you come too? Do you know what it is, Pussy? Does she come up here to read her love-letters—does she? Oh, how charming! Wouldn't I like to see them! How does she get them, Pussy? She has been rather fond of going to see Elspie this past week or two; is that it, Pussy? Won't you tell me, my pretty, pretty cat?"

"Hatty, don't be so absurd!" cried I.

"We know, don't we, Pussy?" says Hatty in a provoking whisper to the cat in her arms. "I thought there would be somebody at Carlisle that she would be sorry to leave—didn't you, Pussy-cat? What is he like, Pussy? Tall and dark, I'll wager, with a pair of handsome mustachios, and the most beautiful black eyes you ever saw! Won't that be about it, Pussy?"

I could have thrown the cat at her. How could any mortal creature be sweet, or keep quiet, talked to in that way? I flew out.

"Hatty, you are the most vexatious tease that ever lived! Do, for pity's sake, go down and let me alone. You know perfectly well it is all stuff and nonsense!"

"Oh, how angry she is, my pretty pussy!" says Hatty, hiding her laughing face behind the cat. "It *was* all nonsense, you know; but really, when she gets into such a tantrum, I begin to think I must have hit the white. What do you say, Pussy?"

I stamped on the garret floor.

"Hatty, will you take that hideous cat down and be quiet?" cried I.

"Dear, dear! To think of her calling you a hideous cat! Doesn't that show how angry she is? People should not get angry—should they, Pussy? She will box our ears next. I really think we had better go, my darling tabby."

So off went Hatty with the cat in her arms, but as she was going down the stairs, she said, I am sure for me to hear,—

"We will come some other time, won't we, Pussy? when the dragon is out of her den: and we will have a quiet rummage, you and I; and we'll find her love-letters!"

Now is not that too bad? What is one to do? Job could not have kept his temper if he had lived with Hatty. I wish she would get married—I do! Fanny never interferes with any one—she just goes her way and lets you go yours. And when Sophy interferes, it is only because something is left untidy, or you have not done something you promised to do.   She does not tease for teasing's sake, like Hatty.

And then, when I came down, after having composed my face, and passed Hatty on my way into the parlour, what should she say but,—

" Didn't you wish I was in Heaven just now ? "

" I should not have cared where you were, if you had kept out of the garret ! " said I.

Hatty gave one of her odious giggles, and away she went.

Now, how *can* I live at peace with Hatty, will anybody tell me ?

I am so delighted ! My Aunt Kezia has come into my plan for having the Bracewells here at Christmas, along with the Drummonds.

" It might be as well," said she, " if we could do some good to that poor frivolous thing Amelia ; but don't you get too much taken up with her, Caroline, my dear.   She is a silly maid at best."

" Oh, Amelia is Fanny's friend, not mine, Aunt Kezia," said I.   " And Charlotte is Sophy's."

" And is Flora to be yours ? " said Aunt Kezia.

" I have not made one yet," I answered.   " I do not know what Flora is like."

" As well to wait and see, trow," says my Aunt Kezia.

Sam was bringing in breakfast while this was said ; and as soon as he had set down the cold beef he turned to my Aunt Kezia and said,—

" Then she's just a braw lassie, Miss Flora, nae

mair and nae less ; and she'll bring ye a' mickle gude, and nae harm."

"Why, how do you know, Sam ?" asked my Aunt Kezia.

"Hoots! my mither's sister's daughter was her nurse," said he. "Helen Raeburn they ca' her, and her man's ane o' the Macdonalds. Trust me, but I ha'e heard monie a tale o' thae Drummonds,—their faither and mither and their gudesire and minnie an' a'."

"What is Angus like, Sam ?" said I.

"Atweel, he's a bonnie laddie; but no just——"

Sam stopped short and pulled a face.

"Not just what ?" says my Aunt Kezia.

"Ye'll be best to find oot for yersel, Mrs. Kezia, I'm thinkin'."

And off trudged Sam after jelly, and we got no more out of him.

I wonder where the living creature is that could stand Hatty! There was I at work this morning in the parlour, when in she came—there were Sophy and Fanny too—holding up something above her head.

"'Busk ye, busk ye, my bonnie, bonnie bride!'" sang Hatty. "Look what I've found, just now, in the garret! Oh yes, Miss Caroline, you can look too."

"Hatty, if you don't give me that book this minute——!" cried I. "I did think I had hidden it out of search of your prying fingers."

"Dear, yes, and of my bright eyes, I feel no doubt," laughed Hatty. "You are not quite so clever as you fancy, Miss Caroline. Carlisle is a charming city, but it does not hold all the brains in the world."

"What is it, Hatty?" said Sophy. "Don't tease the child."

"Wait a little, Miss Sophia, if you please. This is a most interesting and savoury volume, wherein Miss Caroline Courtenay sets down her convictions on all manner of subjects in general, and her unfortunate sisters in particular. I find——"

"Hatty, do be reasonable, and give the child her book," said Fanny. "It is a shame!"

"Oh, you keep one too, do you, Miss Frances?" laughed Hatty. "I had my suspicions, I will own."

"What do you mean?" said Fanny, flushing.

"Only that the rims of your pearly ears would not be quite so ruddy, my charmer, if you were not in like case. Well, I find from this book that we are none of us perfect, but so far as I can gather, Fanny comes nearest the angelic world of any of us. As to——"

"Hatty, you ought to be ashamed of yourself if you have been so dishonourable as to read what was not meant for any one to see."

"My beloved Sophy, don't halloo till you are out of the wood. And *you* are not out, by any means. You are vulgar and ill-bred, my dear; you say 'coom' and 'boot,' and you are only fit to marry a country curate, and cut out shirts and roll pills."

"I say *what?*" asked Sophy, disregarding the other particulars.

"You say 'coom' and 'boot,' my darling, and it

ought to be ' kem ' and ' bet,' " said Hatty, with such an affected pronunciation that Sophy and Fanny both burst out laughing.

" What *do* you mean?" said Sophy amid her laughter.

" Then—Fanny, my dear, you are not to escape ! You are better bred than Sophy, because you take castor oil——"

" Hatty, what nonsense you are talking !" I cried, unable to endure any longer. But Hatty went on, taking no notice.

" But you drop your *r*'s, deah, and say deah Ca'oline, —(can't manage it right, my dear !)—and you are slow and affected."

" Hatty, you know I never said so !" I screamed.

" Then as to *me*," pursued Hatty, casting her eyes up to the ceiling, " as to poor me, I am—well, not one of the angels, on any consideration. I tease my sweetest sister in the most cruel manner——"

" Well, that is true, Hatty, if nothing else is," said Fanny.

" I have ' horrid glazed red cheeks,' and I eat like a ploughboy ; and I don't take castor oil. Castor oil is evidently one of the Christian graces."

" How can you be so ridiculous !" said Sophy. " See, you have made the poor child cry."

" With passion, my dear, which is a very wicked thing, as I am sure my Aunt Kezia would tell her. A little castor oil would——"

" What is that about your Aunt Kezia ? " came in another voice from the doorway.

Oh, I was so glad to see her !

"Hoity-toity! why, what is all this, girls?" said she, severely.   "Hester, what are you doing?   What is Cary crying for?"

"Hatty is teasing her, Aunt," said Fanny.   "She is always doing it, I think."

"Give me that book, Hester," said my Aunt Kezia ; and Hatty passed it to her without a word.   "Now, whom does this book belong?"

"It is mine, Aunt Kezia," I said, as well as my sobs would let me ; "and Hatty has found it, and she is teasing me dreadfully about it."

"What is it, my dear?" said my Aunt Kezia.

"It is my diary, Aunt Kezia ; and I did not want Hatty to get hold of it."

"She says such things, Aunt Kezia, you can't imagine, about you and all of us."

"I am sure I never said anything about you, Aunt Kezia," I sobbed.

"If you did, my dear, I dare say it was nothing worse than all of you have thought in turn," saith my Aunt Kezia, drily.   "Hester, you will go to bed as soon as the dark comes.   Take your book, Cary ; and remember, my dear, whenever you write in it again, that God is looking at every word you write."

Hatty made a horrid face at me behind my Aunt Kezia's back ; but I don't believe she really cared anything about it. She went to bed, of course; and it is dark now by half-past five.   But she was not a bit daunted, for I heard her singing as she lay in bed, " Fair Rosalind, in woful wise,"[1] and afterwards, "I ha'e nae kith, I ha'e nae kin."[2] If Father had heard that last, my Aunt Kezia would have had to forgive her and let her off the rest of her sentence.

I have found a new hiding-place for my book, where I do not think Hatty will find it in a hurry. But when I sit down to write now, my Aunt Kezia's words come back to me with an awful sound. "God is looking at every word you write!" I suppose it is so: but somehow I never rightly took it in before. I hardly think I should have written some words if I had. Was that what my Aunt Kezia meant?

[1] "Fair Rosalind, in woful wise,
Six hearts has bound in thrall ;
As yet she undetermined lies
Which she her spouse shall call."

[2] Perhaps the most plaintive and poetical of all the popular Jacobite ballads.

CHAPTER II.

TAWNY EYES.

" She has two eyes so soft and brown,
Take care !
She gives a side-glance and looks down,—
Beware ! Beware !
Trust her not,
She is fooling thee ! "
—LONGFELLOW.

ERE they all are at last, and the house is as full as it will hold. The Bracewells came first in their great family coach and four —Charlotte and Amelia, and a young friend whom they had with them. Her name is Cecilia Osborne, and she is such a genteel-looking girl ! She moves about, not languidly like Amelia, but in such a graceful, airy way as I never saw. She has dark hair, nearly black, and brown eyes with a sort of tawny light in them,—large eyes which gleam out on you just when you are not expecting it, for she generally looks down. Amelia appears more listless and affected than ever by the side of her, and Charlotte's hoydenish romping seems worse and more vulgar.

The Drummonds did not come for nearly a week

afterwards. I was rather afraid what Cecilia would think of them, for I expected they would talk Scotch —I know Angus used to do—and Cecilia is from the South, and I thought she would be quite shocked. But I find they talk just as we do, only with a little Scots accent, as if they were walking over sandhills in their throats—as least that is how it sounds to me. Flora has rather more of it than Angus, but then her voice is so clear and soft that it sounds almost pretty. A young gentleman came with them, named Duncan Keith, who was going with Angus about that business he has to do. They only stayed one night, didn't[1] Mr. Keith and Angus, and then went on about their business; but Father was so pleased with Mr. Keith, that he invited him to come back when Angus does, which will be in about three weeks or a month. So here we are, eight girls instead of four, with never a young man among us. Father says, when Angus and Mr. Keith come back, we will have Ephraim Hebble-thwaite and Ambrose Catterall to spend the evening, and perhaps Esther Langridge too. I don't feel quite sure that I should like Esther to come. She is not only as bad as Sophy with her "buts" and her "comes," but she does not behave quite genteelly in some other ways: and I don't want Cecilia Osborne to fancy that we are a set of vulgar creatures who do not know how to behave. I don't care half so much what Flora thinks.

---

[1] This provincialism is correct for Lancashire, and as far as I know for Cumberland.

Cecilia has not been here a fortnight, and yet I keep catching myself wondering what she will think about everything. It is not that I have made a friend of her: in fact, I am not sure that I quite like her. She seems to throw a sort of spell over me, does Cecilia, as if I were afraid of her and must obey her. I don't half like it.

My Aunt Kezia has put us into rooms in pairs, while they are here. In Sophy's chamber, where I generally sleep, are Sophy and Charlotte. In Fanny's, which she and Hatty have when we are by ourselves, are Fanny and Amelia. In the green spare chamber are Hatty and Cecilia; and in the blue one, Flora and me. My Aunt Kezia said she thought we should find that the pleasantest arrangement; but I do wish she had given Flora to Hatty, and put Cecilia with me. I am sure I should have understood Cecilia much better than Hatty, who will persist in calling her Cicely, which she says she does not like because it is such a vulgar name—and so common, too. Cecilia says she wishes she had not been called by a name which had a vulgar short one to it: she would like to have been either Camilla or Henrietta. She thinks my name sweetly pretty; but she wonders why we cal: Hester, Hatty, which she says is quite low and ugly, and hardly. is the proper short for Hester. She says Hatty and Gatty are properly short for Harriet, and Hester should be Essie, which is much prettier. But then we call Esther Langridge, Essie, and we could not do with two Essies. I know Father used to call Mamma, Gatty, but Grandmamma said she always thought it so vulgar.

Grandmamma was always talking about things being vulgar, and so is Cecilia. I notice that some people—for instance, my Aunt Kezia and Flora—never seem to think whether things are vulgar or not. Cecilia says that is because they are so vulgar they don't know it. I wonder if it be. But Cecilia says—she said I was not to repeat it, though—that my Aunt Kezia and Sophy are below vulgarity. When we were dressing one morning, I asked Flora what she thought. She is as genteel in her manners as Cecilia herself, only in quite a different way. Cecilia behaves as if she wanted you to notice how genteel she is. Flora is just herself: it seems to come natural to her, as if she never thought about it. So I asked Flora what she thought "vulgarity" meant, and if people could be below vulgarity.

"I should not think they could get below it," said she. "It is easy to get above it, if you only go the right way. How can you get below a thing which is down at the bottom?"

"But how would you do, Flora, not to be vulgar?"

"Learn good manners, and then never think about them."

"But you must keep up your company manners," said I.

"Why have any?" said she.

"What, always have one's company manners on!" cried I, "and be courtesying and bowing to one's sisters as if they were people one had never seen before?"

"Nay, those are ceremonies, not manners," said Flora. "By manners, I do not understand ceremonies, but just the way you behave to anybody at any time. It is not a ceremony to set a chair for a lame man, nor to shut a door lest the draught blow on a sick woman. It is not a ceremony to eat with a knife and fork, or to see that somebody else is comfortable before you make yourself so."

"Why, but that is just kindness!" cried I.

"What are manners but kindness?" said Flora. "Let a maiden only try to be as kind as she can to every creature of God, and she will not find much said in reproof of her manners."

"Are you always trying to be kind to everybody, Flora?"

"I hope so, Cary," she said, gravely.

"Flora, have you any friend?" said I. "I mean a particular friend—a girl friend like yourself."

"Yes," she said. "My chief friend is Annas Keith."

"Mr. Duncan Keith's sister?"

"Yes," said Flora.

"Do tell me what she is like," said I.

"I am not sure that I could," said Flora. "And if I did, it would only be like looking at a map. Suppose somebody showed you a map of the British Isles, and put his finger on a little pink spot, and told you that was Selkirk. How much wiser would you be? You could not see the Yarrow and Ettrick, and breathe the caller air and gather the purple heather. And I don't think describing people is much better than to show places on a map. Such different things strike different people."

"How?" said I. "I don't see how they could, in the same face."

"As we were coming from Carlisle with Uncle Courtenay," said Flora, smiling, "I asked him to tell me what you were like, Cary."

"Well, what did Father say?" I said, and I felt very much amused.

"He said, 'Oh, a girl with a pale face and a lot of light thatch on it, with fine ways that she picked up in Carlisle.' But when I came to see you, I thought that if I had had to describe you, those were just the things I should not have mentioned."

"Come, then, describe me, Flora," said I, laughing. "What do you see?"

"I see two large, earnest-looking blue eyes," she said, "under a broad white forehead; eyes that look right at you; clear, honest eyes,—not—at least, the sort of eyes I like to look at me. Then I see a small nose——"

"Let my nose alone, please," said I: "I know it turns up, and I don't want to hear you say so."

Flora laughed. "Very well; I will leave your nose alone. Underneath it, I see two small red lips, and a little forward chin; a rather self-willed little chin, if you please, Cary—and a good figure, which has learned to hold itself up and to walk gracefully. Will that do for a description?"

"Yes," I said, looking in the glass; "I suppose that is me."

"Is it, Cary? That may be all I see; but is it *you?* Why, it is only the morocco case that holds you. You are the jewel inside, and what that is, really and fully, I cannot see. God can see it; and you can see some of it. But I can see only what you choose to show me, or, now and then, what you cannot help showing me."

"Do you know that you are a very queer girl, Flora? Girls don't talk in that way. Cecilia Osborne told me yesterday she thought you a very curious girl indeed."

"I think my match might be found," said Flora, rather drily. "For one thing, Cary, you must remember I have had nothing to do with other girls except Annas Keith. Father and Angus have been my only companions; and a girl who has neither mother nor sisters perhaps gets out of girls' ways in some respects."

"But you are not the only 'womankind,' as Father calls it, in the house?" said I.

"Oh, no, there is Helen Raeburn," answered Flora: "but she is an old woman, and she is not in my station. She would not teach me girls' ways."

"Then who taught you manners, Flora?"

"Oh, Father saw to all that Helen could not," she said. "Helen could teach me common decencies, of course; such as not to eat with my fingers, and to shake hands, and so forth: but the little niceties of

ladylike behaviour that were beyond her—Father saw
to those."

"Well, I think you have very pleasant manners,
Flora. I only wish you were not quite so grave."

"Thank you for the compliment, Miss Caroline
Courtenay," said Flora, dropping me a courtesy. "I
would rather be too grave than too giddy."

That very afternoon, Cecilia Osborne asked me to
walk up the Scar with her. Somehow, when she
asks you to do a thing, you feel as if you must do it.
I do not like that sort of enchanted feeling at all.
However, I fetched my hood and scarf, and away we
went. We climbed up the Scar without much talk—
in fact, it is rather too steep for that: but when we
got to the top, Cecilia proposed to sit down on the
bank. It was a beautiful day, and quite warm for the
time of the year. So down we sat, and Cecilia pulled
her sacque carefully on one side, that it should not
get spoiled—she was very charmingly dressed in a
sacque of purple lutestring, with such a pretty bonnet,
of red velvet with a gold pompoon in front—and
then she began to talk, as if she had come for
that, and I believe she had. It was not long before
I felt pretty sure that she had brought me there to
pump me.

"How long have you known Miss Drummond?"
she began.

"Well, all my life, in a fashion," I said; "but it
is nearly ten years since we met."

"Ten years is a good deal of your life, is it not?"

said Cecilia, darting at me one of those side-glances from her tawny eyes.

I tried to do it last night, and made my eyes feel so queer that I was not sure they would get right by morning.

"Well, I suppose it is," said I; "I am not quite seventeen yet."

"You dear little thing!" said Cecilia, imprisoning my hand. "What is Miss Drummond's father?"

"A minister," said I.

"A Scotch Presbyterian, I suppose?" she said, turning up her nose. I did not think she looked any prettier for it.

"Well," said I, "I suppose he is."

"And Mr. Angus—what do they mean to make of him, do you know?"

"Flora hopes he will be a minister too. His father wishes it; but she is not sure that Angus likes the notion himself."

"Dear me! I should think not," said Cecilia. "He is fit for something far better."

"What can be better?" I answered.

"You have such charming ideas!" replied Cecilia. She put in another word, which I never heard before, and I don't know what it means. She brought it with her from the South, I suppose. Unso—unsophy—no, unsophisticated—I think that was it. It sounded uncommon long and fine, I know.

"I suppose Scotch ministers have not much money?" continued Cecilia.

“I don’t know—I think not,” I answered. “But I rather fancy my Uncle Drummond has a little of his own.”

Cecilia darted another look at me, and then dropped her eyes as if she were studying the grass.

“And Mr. Keith?” she said presently, “is he a relation?”

“I don’t know much about him,” said I, “only what I have heard Flora say. He is no relation of theirs, I believe. I think he is the squire’s son.”

“The squire’s son!” cried Cecilia, in a more interested tone. “And who is the squire?—is he rich?—where is the place?”

“As to who he is,” said I, “he is Mr. Keith, I suppose. I don’t know a bit whether he is rich or poor. I forget the name of the place—I think it is Abbotsmuir, or something like that. Either an abbot or a monk has something to do with it.”

“And you don’t know if Mr. Keith is a rich man?” said Cecilia, I thought in rather a disappointed tone.

“No, I don’t,” said I. “I can ask Flora, if you want to know.”

“Not for the world!” cried Cecilia, laying her hand again on mine. “Don’t on any account let Miss Drummond know that I asked you such a question. If you like to ask from yourself, you know— well, that is another matter; but not from me, on any consideration.”

“I don’t understand you, Miss Osborne,” said I.

“No, you dear little thing, I believe you *don’t* understand me," said Cecilia, kissing me. "What pretty hair you have, and how nice you keep it, to be sure! —so smooth and glossy! Come, had we not better be going down, do you think?"

So down we came, and found dinner ready; and I do not think I ever thought of it again till I was going to bed. Then I said to Flora,—"Do you like Cecilia Osborne?"

"I——think we had better not talk about people, Cary, if you please."

But there was such a pause where I have drawn that long stroke, that I am sure that was not what she intended to say at first.

"Then you don't," said I, making a hit at the truth, and, I think, hitting it in the bull's eye. "Well, no more do I."

Flora looked at me, but did not speak. Oh, how different her look is from Cecilia's sudden flashes!

"She has been trying to pump me, I am sure, about you and Angus, and Mr. Keith," said I; "and I think it is quite as well I knew so little."

"What about?" said Flora.

"Oh, about money, mostly," said I. "Whether Uncle had much money, and if Mr. Keith was a rich man, and all on like that. I can't bear girls who are always thinking about money."

Flora drew a long breath. "That is it, is it?" she said, in a low voice, as she tied her nightcap, but it was rather as if she were speaking to herself than to me. "Cary, perhaps I had better answer you. I am afraid Miss Osborne is a very dangerous girl; and she would be more so than she is if she were a shade more clever, so as to hide her cards a little better. Don't tell her anything you can help."

"But what shall I say if she asks me again? because she wanted me not to tell you that she had asked, but to get to know as if I wanted it myself."

"Tell her to ask me," said Flora, with more spirit than I had expected from her.

When Cecilia began again (as she did) asking me the same sort of things, I said to her, "Why don't you ask Cousin Flora instead of me? She knows so much more about it than I do."

Cecilia put her hands on my shoulders and kissed me.

"Because I like to ask you," said she, "and I should not like to ask her."

My Aunt Kezia was just coming into the room.

"Miss Cecilia, my dear," said she, "do you always think what you like?"

"Of course, Mrs. Kezia," said Cecilia, smiling at her.

"Then you will be a very useless woman," said my aunt, "and not a very happy one neither."

"Happy—ah!" said Cecilia, with a long sigh. "This world is not the place to find happiness."

"No, it isn't," said my Aunt Kezia, "for people who spend all their time hunting for it. It is a deal better to let happiness hunt for you. You don't go the right way to get it, child."

"I do not, indeed!" answered Cecilia, with a very sorrowful look. "Ah, Mrs. Kezia, 'the heart knoweth his own bitterness.' That is Scripture, I believe."

"Yes, it does," said my aunt, "and it makes a deal of it, too."

"Oh dear, Mrs. Kezia!" cried Cecilia. "How could anybody make unhappiness?"

"If you don't, you are the first girl I have met of your sort," saith my Aunt Kezia, turning down the hem of a kerchief. Then, when she came to the end of the hem, she looked up at Cecilia. "My dear, there is a lesson we all have to learn, and the sooner you learn it, the better and happier woman you will be. The end of selfishness is not pleasure, but pain. You don't think so, do you? Ah, but you will find as you go through life, that always you are not only better, but happier, with God's blessing on the thing you don't like, than without it on the thing you do. Ay, it always turns to ashes in your mouth when you will have the quails instead of the manna. I've noted many a time—for when I was a girl, and later than that, I was as self-willed as any of you—that sometimes when I have set my heart upon a thing, and would have it, then, if I may speak it with reverence, God has given way to me. Like a father with an obstinate child, He has said to me, as it were, 'Poor foolish child! You will have this glittering piece of mischief. Well, have your way: and when you have cut yourself badly with it, and are bleeding and smarting as I did not wish to see you, come back to your Father and tell Him all about it, and be healed and comforted.' Ah dear me, the dullest of us is quite as clever as she need be in making rods for her own back. And then, if our Father keep us from hurting ourselves, and won't let us have the bright knife to cut our fingers with, how we do mewl and whine, to be sure! We are just a set of silly babes, my dear—the best of us."

"My Aunt Dorothea once told me," said I, "that the Papists have what they call 'exercises of detachment.' Perhaps you would think them good things, Aunt Kezia. For instance, if an abbess sees a nun who seems to have a fancy for any little thing particularly, she will take it from her and give it to somebody else."

"Eh, poor foolish things!" said Aunt Kezia. "Bits of children playing with the Father's tools! They are more like to hurt themselves a deal than to get His work done. Ay, God has His exercises of detachment, and they are far harder than man's. He knows how to do it. He can lay a finger right on the core of your heart, the very spot where it hurts worst. Men can seldom do that. They would sometimes if they could, I believe; but they cannot, except God guides them to it. Many's the time I've been asked, with a deal of hesitation and apology, to do a thing that did not cost me a farthing's worth of grief or labour; and as lightly as could be, to do another which would have gone far to break either my back or my heart. Different folks see things in such different ways. I'll be bound, now, if each of us were asked to pick out for one another the thing in this house that each cared most about, we should well-nigh all of us guess wrong. We know so little of each other's inmost hearts. That little kingdom, your own heart, is a thing that you must keep to yourself; you can't let another into it. You can bring him to the gate, and let him peep in, and show him a few of your treasures; but you cannot give him the freedom of the city. Depend upon it, you would think very differently of me from what you do, and I should think differently of each of you, if we could see each other's inmost hearts."

"Better or worse, Mrs. Kezia?" said Cecilia.

"May be the one, and may be the other, my dear. It would hang a little on the heart you looked at, and a great deal on the one who looked at it. I dare say we should all get one lesson we need badly—we might learn to bear with each other. 'Tis so easy to think, ' Oh, she cannot understand me! she never had this pain or that sorrow.' Whereas, if you could see her as she really is, you would find she knew more about it than you did, and understood some other things beside, which were dark riddles to you. That is often a mountain to one which is only a molehill to an:ther. And trouble is as it is taken. If there were no more troubles in this world than what we give each other in pure kindness or in simple ignorance, girls, there would be plenty left "

"Then you think there were troubles in Eden?" said Cecilia, mischievously.

"I was not there," said my Aunt Kezia. "After the old serpent came there were troubles enough, I'll warrant you. If Adam came off scot-free for saying, 'The woman whom Thou gavest to be with me,' Eve must have been vastly unlike her daughters."

I was quite unable to keep from laughing, but Cecilia did not seem to see anything to laugh at. She never does, when people say funny things; and she never says funny things herself. I cannot understand her. She only laughs when she does something; and, nine times out of ten, it is something in which I cannot see anything to laugh at—something which—well, if it were not Cecilia, I should say was rather silly and babyish. I never did see any fun in playing foolish tricks on people, and worrying them in all sorts of ways. Hatty just enjoys it; but I don't.

However, before anything else was said, Father came in, and a young gentleman with him, whom he introduced as Mr. Anthony Parmenter, the Vicar's nephew (He turned out to be the Vicar's grand-nephew, which, I suppose, is the same thing.) I am sure he must have come from the South. He did not shake hands, nor profess to do it. He just touched the hand you gave him with the tips of his fingers, and then with his lips, as if you were a china tea-dish that he was terribly frightened of breaking. Cecilia seemed quite used to this sort of thing, but I did not know what he was going to do; and, as for my Aunt Kezia, she just seized his hand, and gave it a good old-fashioned shake, at which he looked very much put out. Then she asked

him how the Vicar was, and he did not seem to know;
and how long he was going to stay, and he did not
know that; and when he came, to which he said
Thursday, in a very hesitating way, as if he were not
at all sure that it was not Wednesday or Friday. One
thing he knew—that it was hawidly cold—there, that
is just how he said it. I suppose he meant horribly.
My Aunt Kezia gave him up after awhile, and went
on sewing in silence. Then Cecilia took him up, and
they seemed to understand each other exactly. They
talked about all sorts of things and people that I never
heard of before; and I sat and listened, and so did my
Aunt Kezia, only that she put in a word now and
then, and I did not.

Before they had been long at it, Fanny and Amelia
came in from a walk, in their bonnets and scarves, and
Mr. Parmenter bowed over their hands in the same
curious way that he did before. Amelia took it as she
does everything—that is, in a languid, limp sort of way,
as if she did not care about anything; but Fanny
looked as if she did not know what he was going to do
to her, and I saw she was puzzled whether she ought
to shake hands or not. Then Fanny went away to
take her things off, but Amelia sat down, and pulled
off her scarf, and laid it beside her on the sofa, not
neatly folded, but all huddled up in a heap, and there
it might have stayed till next week if my Aunt Kezia
(who hates Amelia's untidy ways) had not said to her,—

" My dear, had you not better take your things
upstairs ? "

Amelia rose with the air of a martyr, threw the scarf on her arm, and carrying her bonnet by one string, went slowly upstairs. When they came down together, my Aunt Kezia said to Fanny,—

"My dear, you had better take a shorter walk another time."

"We have not had a long one, Aunt," said Fanny, looking surprised. "We only went up by the Scar, and back by Ellen Water."

"I thought you had been much farther than that," says my Aunt Kezia, in her dry way. "Poor Emily [1] seemed so tired she could not get upstairs."

Fanny stared, and Amelia gave a faint laugh. My Aunt Kezia said no more, but went on running tucks: and Amelia joined in the conversation between Cecilia and Mr. Parmenter. I hardly listened, for I was trying the new knitting stitch which Flora taught me, and it is rather a difficult one, so that it took all my mind: but all at once I heard Amelia say,—

"The beauty of self-sacrifice!"

My Aunt Kezia lapped up the petticoat in which she was running the tucks, laid it on her knee, folded her hands on it, and looked full at Amelia.

"Will you please, Miss Emily Bracewell, to tell me what you mean?"

"Mean, Aunt?"

"Yes, my dear, mean."

"How can the spirit of that sweet poetical creature,"

[1] Emily was used during the last century as a diminutive for Amelia. There is really no etymological connection between the two names.

murmured Fanny, behind me, "be made plain to such a mere thing of fact as my Aunt Kezia?"

"Well," said Amelia, in a rather puzzled tone, "I mean—I mean—the beauty of self-sacrifice. I do not see how else to put it."

"And what makes it beautiful, think you?" said my Aunt Kezia.

"It is beautiful in itself," said Amelia. "It is the fairest thing in the moral world. We see it in all the analogies of creation."

"My dear Emily," said my Aunt Kezia, "you may have learned Latin and Greek, but I have not. I will trouble you to speak plain, if you please. I am a plain English woman, who knows more about making shirts and salting butter than about moral worlds and the analogies of creation. Please to explain yourself—if you understand what you are talking about. If you don't, of course I wouldn't wish it."

"Well, a comparison, then," answered Amelia, in a slightly peevish tone.

"That will do," said my Aunt Kezia. "I know what a comparison is. Well, let us hear it."

"Do we not see," continued Amelia, with kindling eyes, "the beauty of self-sacrifice in all things? In the patriot daring death for his country, in the mother careless of herself, that she may save her child, in the physician braving all risks at the bedside of his patient? Nay, even in the lower world, when we mark how the insect dies in laying her eggs, and see the fresh flowers of the spring arise from the ashes of the withered blossoms of autumn, can we doubt the loveliness of self-sacrifice?"

"How beautiful!" murmured Fanny. "Do listen, Cary."

"I am listening," I said.

"Charming, Madam!" said Mr. Parmenter, stroking his mustachio. "Undoubtedly, all these are lessons to those who have eyes to see."

I did not quite like the glance which was shot at him just then out of Cecilia's eyes, nor the look in his which replied. It appeared to me as if those two were only making game of Amelia, and that they understood each other. But almost before I had well seen it, Cecilia's eyes were dropped, and she looked as demure as possible.

"Some folk's eyes don't see things that are there," saith my Aunt Kezia, "and some folk's eyes are apt to see things that aren't. My Bible tells me that God hath made everything beautiful in its season. Not out of its season, you see. Your beautiful self-sacrifice is a means to an end, not the end itself. And if you make the means into the end, you waste your strength and turn your action into nonsense. Take the comparisons Amelia has given us. Your patriot risks death in order to obtain some good for his country; the mother, that she may save the child; the physician, that he may cure his patient. What would be the good of all these sacrifices if nothing were to be got by them? My dears, do let me beg of you not to be caught by clap-trap. There's a deal of it in the world just now. And silly stuff it is, I assure you. Self-sacrifice is as beautiful

as you please when it is a man's duty, and as a means
of good; but self-sacrifice for its own sake, and without
an object, is not beautiful, but just ridiculous nonsense."

"Then would you say, Aunt Kezia," asked Amelia,
"that all those grand acts of mortification of the early
Christians, or of the old monks, were worthless and
ridiculous? They were not designed to attain any object,
but just for discipline and obedience."

"As for the early Christians, poor souls! they had
mortifications enough from the heathen around them,
without giving themselves trouble to make troubles,"
said my Aunt Kezia. "And the old monks, poor
misguided dirty things! I hope you don't admire them.
But what do you mean by saying they were not means
to an end, but only discipline? If that were so, discipline was the end of them. But, my dear, discipline
is a sharp-edged tool which men do well to let alone,
except for children. We are prone to make sad blunders
when we discipline ourselves. That tool is safer in
God's hands than in ours."

"But there is so much poetry in mortification!"
sighed Amelia.

"I am glad if you can see it," said my Aunt Kezia.
"I can't. Poetry in cabbage-stalks, eaten with all the
mud on, and ditch water scooped up in a dirty panni-
kin! There would be a deal more poetry in needles and
thread, and soap and water. Making verses is all very
well in its place; but you try to make a pudding of
poetry, and you'll come badly off for dinner."

"Dinner!" said Amelia, contemptuously.

"Yes, my dear, dinner. You dine once a day, I believe."

"Dear, I never care what I eat," cried Amelia. "The care of the body is entirely beneath those who have learned to prize the superlative value of the mind."

My Aunt Kezia laughed. "My dear," said she, "if you were a little older I might reason with you. But you are just at that age when girls take up with every silly notion they come across, and carry it ever so much farther, and just make regular geese of themselves. 'Tis a comfort to hope you will grow out of it. Ten years hence, if we are both alive, I shall find you making pies and cutting out bodices like other sensible women. At least I hope so."

"Never!" cried Amelia. "I never could demean myself to be just an every-day creature like that!"

"I am sorry for your husband," said my Aunt Kezia, bluntly, "and still more for yourself. If you set up to be an uncommon woman, the chances are that instead of rising above the common, you will just sink below it, into one of those silly things that spend their time sipping tea and flirting fans, and making men think all women foolish and unstable. And if you do that —well, all I have to say is, may God forgive you!— Cary, I want some jumballs for tea. Just go and see to them."

So away I went to the kitchen, and heard no more of the talk. But what was I to do? I knew how to eat jumballs very well indeed, but how to make them I knew no more than Mr. Parmenter's eyeglass. She forgets, does my Aunt Kezia, that I have lived all my life in Carlisle, where Grandmamma would as soon have thought of my building a house as making jumballs.

"Maria," said I, "my Aunt Kezia has sent me to make jumballs, and I don't know how, not one bit!"

"Don't you, Miss Cary?" said Maria, laughing: "well, I reckon I do. Half a pound of butter—will you weigh it yourself, Miss?—and the same of white sugar, and a pound of flour, and three ounces of almonds, and three eggs, and a little lemon peel—that's what you'll want."[1]

We were going about the buttery, as she spoke, gathering up and weighing these things, and putting them together on the kitchen table. Then Maria tied a big apron on me, which she said was Fanny's, and gave me a little pan in which she bade me melt the butter. Then I had to beat the sugar into it, and then came the hard part—breaking the eggs, for only the yolks were wanted. I spoiled two, and then I said,—

"Maria, do break them for me! I shall never manage this business."

"Oh yes, you will, Miss Cary, in time," says she, cheerily. "It comes hard at first, till you're used to it. Most things does. See now, you pound them almonds —I have blanched 'em—and I'll put the eggs in."

So we put in the yolks of eggs, and the almonds, and the flour, and the lemon peel, till it began to smell

---

[1] In and about London, the name of jumbles is given to a common kind of gingerbread, to be obtained at the small sweet-shops; but these are not the old English jumball of the text.

uncommon good, and then Maria showed me how to make coiled-up snakes of it on the baking-tin, as jumballs always are: and I washed my hands, and took off Fanny's apron, and went back into the parlour.

I found there all whom I had left, and Hatty and Flora as well. When tea came, and my jumballs with it, my Aunt Kezia says very calmly,—

"Pass me those jumballs, my dear, will you? Amelia won't want any; she is an uncommon woman, and does not care what she eats. You may give me some, because I am no better than other folks."

"O Aunt Kezia, but I like jumballs!" said Amelia.

"You do?" says my Aunt Kezia. "Well, but, my dear, they don't grow on trees. Somebody has to make them, if they are to be eaten; and 'tis quite as well we are not all uncommon women, or I fear there would be none to eat.—Cary, you deserve a compliment, if you made these all by yourself."

I hastened to explain that I deserved none at all, for Maria had helped me all through; but my Aunt Kezia did not seem at all vexed to hear it; she only laughed, and said, "Good girl!"

"Isn't it horrid work?" said Cecilia, who sat next me, in a whisper.

"Oh no!" said I; "I rather like it."

She shrugged her shoulders in what Hatty calls a Frenchified way. "Catch me at it!" she said.

"You can come to the kitchen and catch me at it, if you like," said I, laughing. "But it is all as new to me as to you. Till a few months ago, I lived with my grandmother in Carlisle, and she never let me do anything of that sort."

" What was her name ? " said Cecilia.

" Desborough," said I ; " Mrs. General Desborough."

" Oh, is Mrs. Desborough your grandmother ? " cried she.   " I know Mrs. Charles Desborough so well."

" That is my Aunt Dorothea," said I.   " Grand-mamma is gone to live with my Uncle Charles."

" How pleasant ! " said Cecilia.   " You are such a sweet little darling ! " and she squeezed my hand under the table.

I began to wonder if she meant it.

" O Cary ! " cried Cecilia the next morning, " do come here and tell me who this is."

" Who what is ? " said I, for I looked out of the window, and could see nobody but Ephraim Hebble-thwaite.

" Oh, that handsome young man coming up the drive," returned she.

" That ? " I said.   " Is he handsome ?   Why, 'tis but Ephraim Hebblethwaite."

" Whom ? " cried Cecilia, with one of her little shrieking laughs.   " You never mean to say that fine young man has such a horrid name as Ephraim Hebblethwaite ! "

Hatty had come to look over my shoulder.

" Well, I am afraid he has," said I.

" Just that exactly, my dear," returned Hatty, in her teasing way.   " Poor creature !   He is sweet on Fanny."

"Is he?" asked Cecilia, in an interested tone. "Surely she will not marry a man with such a name as that?"

"Well, if you wish to have my private opinion about it," said Hatty, in her coolest, that is to say, her most provoking manner, "I rather—think—she—will."

"I wouldn't do such a thing!" disdainfully cried Cecilia.

"Nobody asked you, my dear," was Hatty's answer. "I hope you would not, unless you are prepared to provide another admirer for Fanny. They are scarce in these parts."

"I cannot think how you can live up here in these uncivilised regions!" cried Cecilia. "The country people are all just like bears——"

"Do they hug you so very hard?" said Hatty.

"They are so rough and unpolished," continued Cecilia, "so—so—really, I could not bear to live in Cumberland or any of these northern counties. It is just horrid!"

"Then hadn't you better go back again?" said Hatty, coolly.

"I am sure I shall be thankful when the time comes," answered Cecilia, rather sharply. "Except you in this family, I do think——"

"Oh, pray don't except us!" laughed Hatty, turning round the next minute to speak to Ephraim Hebblethwaite. "Mr. Ephraim Hebblethwaite, this is Miss Cecilia Osborne, a young lady from the South Pole or somewhere on the way, who does not admire us

Cumbrians in the smallest degree, and will be absolutely delighted to turn her back upon the last of us.”

“You know I never said that!” said Cecilia, rather affectedly, as she rose and courtesied to Ephraim.

Ephraim is the only person I know who can get along with Hatty.   He always seems to see through what she says to what she means; and he never answers any of her pert speeches, nor tries to explain things, nor smooth her down, as many others do.

“Miss Osborne must stay and learn to like us a little better,” said he, good-humouredly. “Where is Fanny?”

“Looking in the glass, I imagine,” said Hatty, calmly.

“Hatty!” said I. “She is in the garden with Sophy.”

“You are the Nymphs of the Winds,” laughed Ephraim, “and Hatty is the North Wind.”

“Are you sure she is not the East?” said I, for I was vexed.   And as I turned away, I heard Hatty say, laughing,—

“I do enjoy teasing Cary!”

“For shame, Hatty!” answered Ephraim, who speaks to us all as if we were his sisters.

“I assure you I do,” pursued Hatty, in a voice of great glee, “particularly when my lady puts on her grand Carlisle air, and sweeps out of the room as she did just now. It is such fun!”

I had slipped into the next window, where they could not see me, and I suppose Hatty thought I had gone out of the door beyond. I had not the least idea of eaves-dropping, and what I might hear when they fancied me gone never came into my head till I heard it.

"You see," Hatty went on, "there is no fun in teasing Sophy, for she just laughs with you, and gives you as good as you bring; and Fanny melts into tears as if she were a lump of sugar, and Father wants to know why she has been crying, and my Aunt Kezia sends you to bed before dark—so teasing her comes too expensive. But Cary is just the one to tease; she gets into a tantrum, and that is rich!"

Was it really Cecilia's voice which said, "She is rather vain, certainly, poor thing!"

"She is just as stuck-up as a peacock!" replied Hatty: "and 'tis all from living with Grandmamma at Carlisle—she fancies herself ever so much better than we are, just because she learned French and dancing."

"Well, if I had a sister, I would not say things of that sort about her," said Ephraim, bluntly. "Hatty, you ought to be ashamed."

"Thank you, Mr. Hebblethwaite, I don't feel so at all," answered laughing Hatty.

"And she really has no true polish—only a little outside varnish," said Cecilia. "If she were to be introduced at an assembly in Town, she would be set down directly as a little country girl who did not know anything. It is a pity she cannot see herself better."

"There are some woods that don't take polish nearly so well as others," said Ephraim, in a rather curious tone. I felt hurt; was he turning against me too?

"So there are," said Cecilia. "I see, Mr. Hebblethwaite, you understand the matter."

"Pardon me, Miss Osborne," was Ephraim's dry

answer. "I am one of those that do not polish well. Compliments are wasted on me—particularly when the shaft is pointed with poison for my friends. And as to seeing one's self better—I wish, Madam. we could all do that."

As Ephraim walked away, which he did at once, I am sure he caught sight of me. His eyes gave a little flash, and the blood mounted in his cheek, but he kept on his way to the other end of the room, where Fanny and Amelia sat talking together. I slipped out of the door as soon as I could.

That wicked, deceitful Cecilia! How many times had she told me that I was a sweet little creature—that my life at Carlisle had given me such a polish that I should not disgrace the Princess's drawing-room![1] And now——! I went into my garret, and told my book about it, and if I must confess the truth, I am afraid I cried a little. But my eyes do not show tears, like Fanny's, for ever so long after, and when I had bathed them and become a little calmer, I went down again into the parlour. I found my Aunt Kezia there now, and I was glad, for I knew that both Cecilia and Hatty would be on their best behaviour in her presence. Ephraim was talking with Fanny, as he generally does, and there was that "hawid" creature Mr. Parmenter, with his drawl and his eyeglass and all the rest of it.

"Indeed, it is very trying!" he was saying, as I came in; but he never sounds an *r*, so that he said, "vewy

---

[1] There was no Queen at this time. Augusta of Saxe Gotha was Princess of Wales, and the King had three grown-up unmarried daughters.

twying." I don't know whether it is that he can't, or that he won't. "Very trying, truly, Madam, to see men give their lives for a falling cause. Distressing—quite so."

"I don't know that it hurts me to see a man give his life for a falling cause," saith my Aunt Kezia. "Sometimes, that is one of the grandest things a man can do. But to see a man give his life up for a false cause—a young man especially, full of hope and fervency, whose life might have been made a blessing to his friends and the world—that is trying, Mr. Parmenter, if you like."

"Are we not bound to give our lives for the cause of truth and beauty?" asked Amelia, in that low voice which sounds like an Eolian harp.

"Truth—yes," saith my Aunt Kezia. "I do not know what you mean by beauty, and I am not sure you do. But, my dear, we do give our lives, always, for some cause. Unfortunately, it is very often a false one."

"What do you mean, Aunt?" said Amelia.

"Why, when you give your life to a cause, is it not the same thing in the end as giving it for one?" answered my Aunt Kezia. "I do not see that it matters, really, whether you give it in twenty minutes or through twenty years. The twenty years are the harder thing to do—that is all."

"Duncan Keith says——" Flora began, and stopped.

"Let us hear it, my dear, if it be anything good," quoth my Aunt Kezia.

"I cannot tell if you will think it good or not, Aunt," said Flora. "He says that very few give their lives to or for any cause. They nearly always give them for a person."

"Mr. Keith must be a hero of chivalry," drawled Mr. Parmenter, showing his white teeth in a lazy laugh.

(Why do people always simper when they have fine teeth?)

"Chivalry ought to be another name for Christian courage and charity," saith my Aunt Kezia. "Ay, child—Mr Keith is right. It is a pity it isn't always the right person."

"How are you to know you have found the right person, Aunt?" said Hatty, in her pert way.

My Aunt Kezia looked round at her in her awful fashion. Then she said, gravely, "You will find, Hatty, you have always got the wrong one, unless you aim at the Highest Person of all."

I heard Cecilia whisper to Mr. Parmenter, "Oh, dear! is she going to preach a sermon?" and he hid a laugh under a yawn. Somebody else heard it too.

"Mrs. Kezia's sermons are as short as some parsons' texts," said Ephraim, quietly, and not in a whisper.

"But you would not say," observed Mr. Parmenter, without indicating to whom he addressed himself, "that this cause, now—ha—of which we were speaking,— that the lives, I mean—ha—were sacrificed to any particular person?"

"I never saw one plainer, if you mean me," said my Aunt Kezia, bluntly. "What do nine-tenths of the men care about monarchy or commonwealth—absolute kings or limited ones—Stuart or Hanoverian? They just care for Prince Charles, and his fine person and ringing voice, and his handsome dress: what else? And the women are worse than the men. Some men will give their lives for a cause, but you don't often see a woman do it. Mostly, with women, it is father or brother, lover or husband, that carries the day: at least, if you have seen women of another sort, they haven't come my way."

"But, Aunt, that is so ignoble a way of acting!" cried Amelia, as though she wanted to show that she was one of the other sort. "Love and devotion to a holy or chivalrous cause should be free from all petty personal considerations."

"You can get yours free, my dear, if you like—and find you can manage it," said my Aunt Kezia. "I couldn't. As to ignoble, that hangs much on the person. When Queen Margaret of Scotland was drowning in yonder border river, and the good knight rode into the water and held forth his hand to her, and said, 'Grip fast!' was that a petty, ignoble consideration? It was a purely personal matter."

"Oh, of course, if you——" said Amelia, and did not go on.

"Things look very different, sometimes, according to the side on which you see them," saith my Aunt Kezia.

I could not help thinking that people did so.

CHAPTER III.

THE HUNT SUPPER.

BEFORE he went away, Ephraim came up into the window where I sat with my knitting. Mr. Parmenter was gone then, and Cecilia was upstairs with Fanny and Amelia.

"Cary," said he, "may I ask you a question ? "

"Why, Ephraim, I thought you did that every day," I said, feeling rather diverted at his saying such a thing.

"Ah, common questions that do not signify," said he, with a smile. "But this is not an insignificant question, Cary ; and it is one that I have no right to ask unless you choose to give it me."

"Go on, Ephraim," said I, wondering what he meant.

"Are you very fond of Miss Osborne ? "

"I never was particularly fond of her," I said, rather hotly, and I felt my cheeks flush ; "and if I had been, I think this morning would have put an end to it."

"She is not true," he said. "She rings like false metal. Those who trust in her professions will find the earth open and let them in. And I should not like you to be one, Cary."

"Thank you, Ephraim," said I. " I think there is no fear."

" Your Cousin Amelia is foolish," he went on, " but I do not think she is false. She will grow out of most of her nonsense. But Cecilia Osborne never will. It is ingrain. She is an older woman at this moment than Mrs. Kezia."

" Older than my Aunt Kezia!" I am afraid I stared.

" I do not mean by the parish register, Cary," said Ephraim, with a smile. " But she is old in Satan's ways and wiles, in the hard artificial fashions of the world, in everything which, if I had a sister, I should pray God she might never know anything about. Such women are dangerous. I speak seriously, Caroline."

I thought it had come to a serious pass, when Ephraim called me Caroline.

" It is not altogether a bad thing to know people for what they are," he continued. " It may hurt you at the time to have the veil taken off; and that veil, whether by the people themselves or by somebody else, is often pulled off very roughly. But it is better than to have it on, Cary, or to see the ugly thing through beautiful coloured glass, which makes it look all kinds of lovely hues that it is not. The plain white glass is the best. When you do come to something beautiful, then, you see how beautiful it is." Then, changing his tone, he went on,—" Esther Langridge sent you her love, Cary, and told me to say she was coming up here this afternoon."

I did not quite wish that Esther would keep away, and yet I came very near doing it. She is not a beautiful thing—I mean in her ways and manners. She speaks more broadly than Sophy, and much worse than the rest of us, and she eats her peas with a knife, which Grandmamma used to say was the sure sign of a vulgar creature. Esther is as kind-hearted a girl as breathes; but—oh dear, what will Cecilia say to her! I felt quite uncomfortable.

And yet, why should I care what Cecilia says? She has shown me plainly enough that she does not care for me. But somehow, she seemed so above us with those dainty ways, and that soft southern accent, and all she knew about etiquette and the mode, and the stories she was constantly telling about great people. Sir George Blank had said such a fine thing to her when she was at my Lady Dash's assembly; and my Lady Camilla Such-an-one was her dearest friend; and the Honourable Annabella This carried her to drive, and my Lord Herbert That held her cloak at the opera. It was so grand to hear her!

Somehow, Cecilia never said things of that kind when my Aunt Kezia was in the room, and I noted that her grand stories were always much tamer in Flora's or Sophy's presence. She did not seem to care about Hatty much either way. But when there were only Amelia, Fanny, Charlotte and me, then, I could not help seeing, she laid the gilt on much thicker. Char-

lotte used to sit and stare, and then laugh in a way that
I thought very rude; but Cecilia did not appear to
mind it. When Father came into the parlour, she did
so change. Oh, then she was so sweet and amiable!—
so delicately attentive!—so anxious that he should be
made comfortable, and have everything just as he liked
it! I did think, considering that he had four daughters,
she might have left that to us. To Ephraim Hebblethwaite she was very attentive and charming, too, but in
quite a different way. But she wasted no attention at
all on Mr. Parmenter, except for those side-glances now
and then out of the tawny eyes, which seemed to say
that they perfectly understood one another, and that no
explanations of any sort were necessary between them.

I cannot make out what Mr. Parmenter does for his
living. He is not a man of property, for the Vicar told
Father that his nephew, Mr. Parmenter's father, left
nothing at all for his children. Yet Mr. Anthony never
seems to do anything but look through his eyeglass,
and twirl his mustachios, and talk. I asked Amelia
if she knew, for one of the Miss Parmenters, who
is married now, lives not far from Bracewell Hall.
Amelia, however, applied to Cecilia, saying she would
be more likely to know.

"Oh, he does nothing," said Cecilia; "he is a beau."

"Now what does that mean?" put in Hatty.

"I'll tell you what it means," said Charlotte. "Emily,
you be quiet. It means that his income is twenty pence
a year, and he spends two thousand pounds; that he is
always dressed to perfection, that he is ready to make

love to anybody at two minutes' notice—that is, if her fortune is worth it; that he is never at home in an evening, nor out of bed before noon; that he spends four hours a day in dressing, and would rather ten times lose his wife (when he has one) than break his clouded cane, or damage his gold snuff-box. Isn't that it, Cicely?"

"You are so absurd!" said Amelia, languidly.

"I told you to keep quiet," was Charlotte's answer. "Never mind whether it is absurd; is it true?"

"Well, partly."

"But I don't understand," I said. "How can a man spend two thousand pounds, if he have but twenty pence?"

"Know, ignorant creature," replied Charlotte, with mock solemnity, "that lansquenet can be played, and that tradesmen's bills can be put behind the fire."

"Then you mean, I suppose, that he games, and does not pay his debts?"

"That is about the etiquette,[1] my charmer."

"Well, I don't know what you call that down in the South," said I, "but up here in Cumberland we do not call it honesty."

"The South! Oh, hear the child!" screamed Charlotte. "She thinks Derbyshire is in the South!"

"They teach the children so, my dear, in the Carlisle schools," suggested Hatty.

"I don't know what they teach in the Carlisle schools," I said, "for I did not go there. But if Derby-

---

[1] The word "ticket" was still spelt "etiquette."

shire be not south of Cumberland, I haven't learned much geography."

"Oh dear, how you girls do chatter!" cried Sophy, coming up to us. "I wish one or two of you would think a little more about what wants doing. Cary, you might have made the turnovers for supper. I am sure I have enough on my hands."

"But, Sophy, I do not know how," said I.

"Then you ought, by this time," she answered. "Do not know how to make an apple turnover! Why, it is as easy as shutting your eyes."

"When you know how to do it," put in Hatty.

"That is more than you do," returned Sophy, "for you are safe to leave something out."

Hatty made her a low courtesy, and danced away, humming, "Cease your funning," just as we heard the sound of horses' feet on the drive outside. There were all sorts of guesses as to who was coming, and none of them the right one, for when the door opened at last, in walked Angus Drummond and Mr. Keith.

"Well, you did not expect us, I suppose?" said Angus.

"Certainly not to-night," was Sophy's answer.

"We finished our business sooner than we expected, and now we are ready to begin our holiday," said he.

Father came in then, and there was a great deal of kissing and hand-shaking all round; but my Aunt Kezia and Flora were not in the room. They came in together, nearly half an hour later; but I think I never saw such a change in any girl's face as in Flora's, when she saw what had happened. She must be very fond

of Angus, I am sure.   Her cheeks grew quite rosy—she
is generally pale—and her eyes were like stars.   I did
not think Angus seemed nearly so glad to see her.

Essie Langridge was very quiet all the evening; I fancy
she was rather frightened of Cecilia. She said very little.

Father had a long day's hunting yesterday, and
Angus Drummond went with him.   Mr. Keith would
not go, though Father laughed about it, and asked
if he were afraid of the hares eating him up.   Neither
would he go to the hunt supper, afterwards.   There
were fourteen gentlemen at it, and a pretty racket
they made.   My Aunt Kezia does not like these hunt
suppers a bit ; she would be glad if they were anywhere
else than here ; but Father being the squire, of course
they cannot be.   She always packs us girls out of the
way, and will not allow us to show our heads.   So we
sat upstairs, in Sophy's chamber, which is the largest
and most out of the way ; and we had some good fun,
first in finding seats, for there were only two chairs in
the room, and then in playing hunt the slipper and all
sorts of games.   I am afraid we got rather too noisy
at last, for my Aunt Kezia looked in with,—

" Girls, are you daft ?   I protest you make nigh as
much racket as the gentlemen themselves ! "

What Mr. Keith did with himself I do not know.   I
think he went off for a walk somewhere.   I know he
tried to persuade Angus to go with him, but Angus
said he wanted his share of the fun.   I heard Mr. Keith
say, in a low voice,—

" What would your father say, Angus ? "

"Oh, my father's a minister, and they are bound to be particular," said Angus, carelessly. "I can't pretend to make such a fash as he would."

I did not hear what Mr. Keith answered, but I believe he went on talking about it. When I got upstairs with the rest, however, I missed Flora; and going to our room to look for her, I found her crying. I never saw Flora weep before.

"Why, Flora!" said I, "what is the matter with you?"

"Nothing with me, Cary," she said, "but a great deal with Angus."

"You do not like his being at the supper?" I said. I hardly knew what to say, and I felt afraid of saying either too much or too little. It seems so difficult to talk without hurting people.

"Not only that," she said. "I do not like the way he is going on altogether. I know my father would be in a sad way if he knew it."

I told Flora what I had heard Angus say to Mr. Keith.

"Ah!" she said, with another sob, "Angus would not have said that three months ago. I was sure it must have been going on for some time. He has been in bad company, I feel certain. And Angus always was one to take the colour of his company, just as a glass takes the colour of anything you pour in. What can I do? Oh, what can I do? If he will not listen to Duncan——"

"Ambrose Catterall says that young men must always sow their wild oats," I said, when she stopped thus.

"That is one of the Devil's maxims," exclaimed Flora, earnestly. "God calls it sowing to the flesh : and He says the harvest of it is corruption. Some flowers seed themselves : thistles do. Did you ever know roses grow from thistle seed? No: 'whatsoever a man soweth, that shall he reap.' Ah me, for Angus's harvest!"

"Well, I don't see what you can do," said I.

"There is the sting," she replied. "It would be silly to weep if I did. No, in such cases, I think there is only one thing a woman can do—and that is to cry mightily unto God to loose the bonds of the oppressor, and let the oppressed go free. I don't know—I may be mistaken—but I hardly think it is of much use for women to talk to such a man. It is not talking that he needs. He knows his own folly, very often, at least as well as you can tell him, and would be glad enough to be loosed from his bonds, if only somebody would come and tear them asunder. He cannot: and you cannot. Only God can. Some evil spirits can be cast out by nothing but prayer. Cary ——" Flora broke off suddenly, and looked up earnestly in my face. "Don't mention this, will you, dear? I should not have said a word to you nor any one if you had not surprised me."

I promised her I would not, unless somebody first spoke to me. She would not come to Sophy's room.

"Tell the girls," she said, "that I want to write home; for I shall do it presently, when I feel a little calmer."

Something struck me as I was turning away. "Flora," I said, "why do you not tell my Aunt Kezia all about it? I am sure she would help you, if any one could."

"Yes, dear, I think she would," said Flora, gently; "but you see no one could. And remember, Cary!" she called me back as I was leaving the chamber, and came to me, and took both my hands; and her great sorrowful eyes, which looked just like brown velvet, gazed into mine like the eyes of a dog which is afraid of a scolding: "remember, Cary, that Angus is not wicked. He is only weak. But how weak he is!"

She broke down with another sob.

"But men should be stronger than women," said I, "not weaker."

"They are, in body and mind," replied Flora: "but sex, I suppose, does not extend to soul. There, some men are far weaker than some women. Look at Peter. I dare say the maid who kept the door would have been less frightened of the two, if he had taunted her with being one of ' this man's disciples.' "

"Well, I should feel ashamed!" I said.

"I am not sure if women do not feel moral weakness a greater shame than men do," replied Flora. "Men seem to think so much more of want of physical bravery. Many a soldier will not stand an ill-natured laugh, who would want to fight you in a minute if you hinted that he was afraid of being hurt. Things seem to look so different to men from what they do to women; and, I think, to the angels, and to God."

I did not like to leave her alone in her trouble: but she said she wanted nothing, and was going to write to her father; so I went back to Sophy's room, and gave Flora's message to the girls.

"Dear! I am sure we don't want her," said Hatty: and Charlotte added, "She is more of a spoil-sport than anything else."

So we played at "Hunt the slipper," and "Questions and commands," and "The parson has lost his cloak," and "Blind man's buff": and then when we got tired we sat down—on the beds or anywhere—Hatty took off the mirror and perched herself on the dressing-table, and Charlotte wanted to climb up and sit on the mantel-shelf, but Sophy would not let her—and then we had a round of "How do you like it?" and then we went to bed.

In the middle of the night I awoke with a start, and heard a great noise, and Sam's voice, and old Will's, and a lot of queer talking, as if something were being carried upstairs that was hard to pull along; and there were a good many words that I am sure my Aunt Kezia would not let me write, and—well, if He do look at what I am writing, I should not like God to see them neither. I felt sure that the gentlemen were being carried up to bed—such of them as could not walk— and such as could were being helped along. I rather wonder that gentlemen like to drink so much, and get themselves into such a queer condition. I do not think they would like it if the ladies began to do such things. I could not help wondering if Angus were among them. Flora, who had lain awake for a long while, and had only dropped asleep, as she told me afterwards, about half an hour before, for she heard the clock strike one, slept on at first, and I hoped she would not awake. But as the last lot were being dragged past our door, Flora woke up with a start, and cried,—

" What is that ? O Cary, what can be the matter ? "

I wanted to make as light of it as I could.

"Oh, go to sleep," I said; "there is nothing wrong."

" But what is that dreadful noise ? " she persisted.

" Well, it is only the gentlemen going to bed," said I.

Just then, sounds came through the door, which showed that they were close outside. Somebody—so far as I could guess from what we heard—was determined to sit down on the stairs, and Sam was trying to prevail upon him to go quietly to bed. All sorts of queer things were mixed up with it—hunting cries, bits of songs, invectives against Hanoverians and Dissenters, and I scarcely know what else.

" Who is that wretched creature ? " whispered Flora to me.

I had recognised the voice, and was able to answer.

"It is Mr. Bagnall," said I, "the Vicar of Dornthwaite."

" A minister ! " was Flora's answer, in an indescribable tone.

"Oh, that does not make any difference," I replied, "with the clergy about here. Mr. Digby is too old for it now, but I have heard say that when he was a younger man, he used to be as uproarious as anybody."

At last Sam's patience seemed to be exhausted, and he and Will between them lifted the reverend gentleman off his feet, and carried him to bed despite his struggles.

At least I supposed so from what I heard.   About ten minutes later, Sam and Will passed our door on their way back.

"Yon's a bonnie loon to ca' a minister," I heard Sam say as he went past.   "But what could ye look for in a Prelatist?"

"He gets up i' t' pu'pit, and tells us our dooty, of a Sunda', but who does hisn of a Monda', think ye?" was old Will's response.

The footsteps passed on, and I was just going to relieve my feelings by a good laugh, when I was stopped and astonished by Flora's voice.

"O Cary, how dreadful!"

"'Dreadful!'" said I, "what is dreadful?"

"That wretched man!" she said, in a tone which matched her words.

"He does not think himself a wretched man, by any means," I said.   "His living is worth quite two hundred a year, and he has a little private property beside. They say he does not stand at all a bad chance for a deanery.   His wife is not a pleasant woman, I believe; she has a temper: but his son is carrying all before him at college, and his daughters are thought to be among the prettiest girls in the county."

"Has he children?   Poor things!" sighed Flora.

"Why, Flora, I cannot make you out," said I. "I could understand your being uncomfortable about Angus; but what is Mr. Bagnall to you?"

"Cary!" I cannot describe the tone.

"Well?" said I.

" Is the Lord nothing to me ? " she said, almost passionately ; " nor the poor misguided souls committed to that man's charge, for which he will have to give account at the last day ? "

" My dear Flora, you do take things so seriously ! " I said, trying to laugh ; but her tone and words had startled me, for all that.

" It is well to take sin seriously," said she. " Men are serious enough in Hell ; and sin is its antechamber."

" You don't suppose poor Mr. Bagnall will be sent there, for a little too much champagne at a hunt supper ? " said I. I did not like it, for I thought of Father. I have heard him singing " Old King Cole " and half a dozen more songs, all mixed up in a heap, after a hunt supper. " Men always do it there. And I can assure you Mr. Bagnall is thought a first-class preacher. People go to hear him even from Cockermouth."

" That is worse than ever," said Flora. " A man who preaches the truth and serves the Devil—that must be awful ! "

" Flora, you do say the queerest things ! " said I. " Does your father never do so ? "

" My father ? " she answered in an astonished, indignant voice. " *My father !* Cary ! but "—with a change in the tone—" you do not know him, of course. Why, Cary, if he knew that Angus had been for once in the midst of such a scene as that, I think it would break my father's heart."

I wondered how Angus had fared, and if he were singing snatches of Scotch songs in some bedchamber at the other end of the long gallery, but I had not the cruelty to say it to Flora.

When we came down the next morning, I was curious to peep into the dining-room, just to see what it was like. The wreck of a ship is the only thing I can think of, which might look like it. Half the chairs were flung over in all directions, and two broken to pieces; a quantity of broken glass was heaped both on the floor and the table ; dark wine stains on the carpet, and pools upon the table, not yet dry, were sufficient signs of what the night had been. Bessy stood in the window, duster in hand, picking up the chairs, and setting them in their places.

"Didn't the gentlemen enjoy theirselves, Miss Cary?" said she. "My word, but they made a night on't! I'd like to ha' been wi' 'em, just for to see!"

I made no answer beyond nodding my head. Flora's words came back to me,—"It is well to take sin seriously." I could not laugh and jest, as I dare say I should have done but for them.

When I came into the parlour, I only found three of all the gentlemen in the house,—Father, Mr. Keith, and Ambrose Catterall. I thought Father seemed rather cross, and he was finding fault with everybody for something. Sophy's hair was rough, and Hatty had put on a gown he did not like, and Fanny's ruffle had a hole in it; and then he turned round and scolded my Aunt Kezia for not having us in better order. My Aunt Kezia said never a word, but I felt sure from her drawn brow and set lips, as she stood making tea, that she could have said a great many.   Mr. Keith was silent and grave.   Ambrose Catterall seemed to think it his duty to make fun for everybody, and he laughed and joked and chattered away finely.   I asked where old Mr. Catterall was.

"Oh, in bed with a headache," laughed Ambrose, "like everybody else this morning."

"Speak for yourself," said Mr. Keith.   "I have not one."

"Well, mine's going," returned Ambrose, gaily.   "A cup of Mrs. Kezia's capital tea will finish it off."

"Finish what off?" asked my Aunt Kezia.

"My last night's headache," said he.

"That tea must have come from Heaven, then, instead of China," replied she.   "Nay, Ambrose Catterall; it will take blood to finish off the consequence of your doings last night."

"Why, Mrs. Kezia, are you going to fight me?" asked he, laughing.

"Young man, why don't you fight the Devil?" answered my Aunt Kezia, looking him full in the face. "He does not pay good wages, Ambrose."

"Never saw the colour of his money yet," said Ambrose, who seemed extremely amused.

"I wish you never may," quoth my aunt.   "But I sadly fear you are going the way to do it."

The more Ambrose laughed, the graver my Aunt Kezia seemed to grow.   Before we had finished breakfast, Angus came languidly into the room.

"What ails you, old comrade?" said Ambrose; and

Flora's eyes looked up with the same question, but I think there were tears on the brown velvet.

"Oh, my head aches conf——I mean—abominably," said Angus, flushing.

"Take a hair of the dog that bit you," suggested Ambrose; "unless you think humble pie will agree with you better. I fancy Miss Drummond would rather help you to that last."

I saw a flash in Mr. Keith's eyes, which gave me the idea that he might not be a pleasant person to meet alone in a glen at midnight, if he had no scruples as to what he did.

"You hold your tongue!" growled Angus.

"By all means, if you prefer it," said Ambrose, lightly.

One after another, the gentlemen strolled in,—all but two who stayed in bed till afternoon, and of these Mr. Catterall was one. Among the last to appear was Mr. Bagnall; but he looked quite fresh and gay when he came, like Ambrose.

"We had to say grace for ourselves, Mr. Bagnall," said Father. "Sit down, and let me help you to some of this turkey pie."

"Thanks—if you please. What a lovely morning!" was Mr. Bagnall's answer. "The young ladies look like fresh rosebuds with the dew on them."

"We have not you gentlemen to thank for it, if we do," broke in Hatty. "Our slumbers were all the less profound for your kind assistance. Oh yes, you can look, Mr. Bagnall! I mean *you.* I heard 'Sally in our Alley' about one o'clock this morning."

"No, was I singing that, now ? " said Mr. Bagnall, laughing. " I did not know I got quite so far. But at a hunt supper, you know, everything is excusable."

" Would you give me a reference to the passage which says so, Mr. Bagnall ? " came from behind the tea-pot. " I should like to note it in my Bible."

Mr. Bagnall laughed again, but rather uncomfortably.

" My dear Mrs. Kezia, you do not imagine the Bible has anything to do with a hunt supper ? "

" It is to be hoped I don't, or I should be wofully disappointed," she answered. " But I always thought, Mr. Bagnall, that the Word of God and the ministers of God should have something to do with one another."

" Kezia, keep your Puritan notions to yourself !" roared Father from the other end of the table ; and he put some words before it which I would rather not write. " I can't think," he went on, looking round, " wherever Kezia can have picked up such mad whims as she has. For a sister of mine to say such a thing to a clergyman—I declare it makes my hair stand on end ! "

" Your hair may lie down again, Brother. I've done," said my Aunt Kezia, coolly. " As to where I got it, I should think you might know. It runs in the blood. And I suppose Deborah Hunter was your grandmother as well as mine."

Father's reply was full of the words I do not want to write, but it was not a compliment to his grandmother.

" Come, Mrs. Kezia," said Mr. Bagnall, " let us make it up by glasses all round, and a toast to the sweet Puritan memory of Mrs. Deborah Hunter."

"No, thank you," said my Aunt Kezia. "As to Deborah Hunter, she has been a saint in Heaven these thirty years, and finely she'd like it (if she knew it) to have you drinking yourselves drunk in her honour. But let me tell you—and you can say what you like after it—she taught me that 'the chief end of man was to glorify God, and to enjoy Him for ever.' Your notion seems to be that the chief end of man is to glorify himself, and to enjoy *him* for ever. I think mine's the better of the two : and as to yours, the worst thing I wish any of you is that you may get mine instead of it. Now then, Brother, I've had my say, and you can have yours."

And not another word did my Aunt Kezia say, though Father stormed, and the other gentlemen laughed and joked, and paid her sarcastic compliments, all the while breakfast lasted. There were two who were silent, and those were Angus and Mr. Keith. Angus seemed too poorly and unhappy to take any interest in the matter; and as to Mr. Keith, I believe in his heart (if I read it right in his eyes) that he was perfectly delighted with my Aunt Kezia.

"The young ladies did not honour us by riding to the meet," said Mr. Bagnall at last, looking at that one of us who sat nearest him—which, by ill luck, happened to be Flora.

"No, Sir. I do not think my aunt would have allowed it; but——" Flora stopped, and cast her eyes on her plate.

"But if she had, you would have been pleased to come?" suggested Mr. Bagnall, rubbing his hands.

He spoke in that disagreeable way in which some men do speak to girls—I do not know what to call it. It is a condescending, patronising kind of manner, as if—yes, that is it!—as if they wanted to amuse themselves by hearing the opinion of something so totally incapable of forming one. I wish they knew how the girls long to shake the nonsense out of them.

But Flora did not lose her temper, as I should have done: she held her own with a quiet dignity which I envied, but could never have imitated.

"Pardon me, Sir. I was about to say the direct contrary—that if my aunt had allowed it, I for one would rather not have gone."

"Afraid of a fall, eh?" laughed Mr. Bagnall. "Well, ladies are not expected to be as venturesome as men."

Now, why do men always fancy that it is a woman's duty to do what men expect her? I cannot see it one bit.

"I was not afraid of that, Sir," said Flora.

Father, with whom Flora is a favourite, was listening with a smile. I believe Aunt Drummond was his pet sister.

"No? Why, what then?" said Mr. Bagnall, shaking the pepper over his turkey pie until I wondered what sort of a throat he would have when he had finished it.

"I am afraid of hardening my heart, Sir," said Flora, in her calm decisive way.

"Hardening your heart, girl! What do you mean?" said Father. "Hardening your heart by riding to hounds!"

"A little puzzling, certainly," said Sir Robert Dacre,

who sat opposite. "We must ask Miss Drummond to explain."

He did not speak in that disagreeable way that Mr. Bagnall did; but Flora flushed up when she found three gentlemen looking at her, and asking her for an explanation.

"I mean," she answered, "that one hardens one's heart by taking pleasure in anything which gives another creature pain. But I beg your pardon; indeed I did not mean to put myself forward."

"No, no, child; we drew you forward," said Father, kindly. He gets over his tempers in a moment, and he seemed to have quite forgotten the passage at arms with my Aunt Kezia.

"Still, I do not quite understand," said Sir Robert, not at all unkindly. "Who is the injured creature in this case, Miss Drummond?"

Flora's colour rose again. "The hare, Sir," she said.

"The hare!" cried Mr. Bagnall, leaning back in his chair to laugh. "Well, Miss Flora, you are quixotic."

"May I quote my father, Sir?" was her reply. "He says that Don Quixote (supposing him a real person, which I take it he was not) was one of the noblest men the world ever saw, only the world was not ready for him."

"The world not ready for him? No, I should think not!" laughed Father. "Not just yet, my little lady-errant."

Flora smiled quietly. "Perhaps it will be, some day, Uncle Courtenay," she said.

"When the larks fall from the sky — eh, Miss Flora?" said Mr. Bagnall, rubbing his hands again in that odious way he has.

"When ' they shall not hurt nor destroy in all My holy mountain,' " was Flora's soft answer.

"Surely you don't suppose that literal?" replied Mr. Bagnall, laughing. "Why, you must be as bad —I had nearly said as *mad*—as my next neighbour, Everard Murthwaite (of Holme Cultram, you know," he explained aside to Father). "Why, he has actually got a notion that the Jews are to be restored to Pales· tine! Whoever heard of such a mad idea? Only think—the Jews!"

"Ridiculous nonsense!" said Father.

"Is it not usually the case," asked Mr. Keith, who till then had hardly spoken, "that the world counts as mad the wisest men in it?"

"Why, Mr. Keith, you must be one of them!" cried Mr. Bagnall.

"Of the wise men? Thank you!" said Mr. Keith, drily.

There was a laugh at this.

"But I can tell you of something queerer still," Mr. Bagnall went on. "Old Cis Crosthwaite, in my parish, says she knows her sins are forgiven."

Such exclamations came from most of the gentlemen at that! "Preposterous!" said one. "Ridiculous!" said another. "Insufferable presumption!" cried a third.

"Cis Crosthwaite!" said Sir Robert Dacre, more quietly.

"Yes, Cis Crosthwaite," repeated Mr. Bagnall; "an old wretch of a woman who has never been any better than she should be, and whom I met sticking hedges only last winter. Her son Joe is the worst poacher in the parish."

All the gentlemen seemed to think that most dreadful. I do not know why it is they always appear to reckon snaring wild game which belongs nobody a more wicked thing than breaking all the Ten Commandments. Would it not have been in them if it were?

Only Sir Robert Dacre said, "Poor old creature! don't let us saddle her with Joe's sins. I dare say she has plenty of her own."

"Plenty? I should think so. She is a horrid old wretch," answered Mr. Bagnall. "And do but think, if this miserable creature has not the arrogance and presumption to say that her sins are forgiven!"

"I suppose Christ died that somebody's sins might be forgiven?" said Mr. Keith, in his quiet way.

"Of course, but those are respectable people," Mr. Bagnall said, rather indignantly.

"Before or after the forgiveness?" asked Mr. Keith.

"Sir," said Mr. Bagnall, rather stiffly, "I am not accustomed to discuss such matters as these at table."

"Are you not? I am," said Mr. Keith, quite simply.

"But," continued Mr. Bagnall, "I thought every one understood the orthodox view—namely, that a man must do his best, and practise virtue, and lead a proper sort of life, and then, when God Almighty sees you a decent and fit person, and endeavouring to be good, He helps you with His grace." [1]

"Of course!" said the Vicar of Sebergham — I suppose by way of Amen.

"Men are to do their best, then, and practise these virtues, in the first instance, without any assistance from God's grace? That Gospel sounds rather ill tidings," was Mr. Keith's answer.

Everybody was listening by this time. Sir Robert Dacre, I thought, seemed secretly diverted; and Hatty's eyes were gleaming with fun. Father looked uncomfortable, and as if he did not know what Mr. Keith would be at. From my Aunt Kezia little nods of satisfaction kept coming to what he said.

"Sir," demanded Mr. Bagnall, looking his adversary straight in the face, "are you not orthodox?"

He spoke rather in the tone in which he might have asked, "Are you not honest?"

"May I ask you to explain the word, before I answer?" was Mr. Keith's response.

"I mean, are you one of these Methodists?"

"Certainly not. I belong to the Kirk of Scotland."

Mr. Bagnall's "Oh!" seemed to say that some at any rate of Mr. Keith's queer notions might be accounted for, if he were so unfortunate as to have been born in a different Church.

"But," pursued Mr. Keith, "seeing that the Church of England, and the Kirk of Scotland, and the Methodists,

---

[1] These exact expressions are quoted in Whitefield's sermons.

all accept the Word of God as the rule of faith, they should all, methinks, be sound in the faith, if that be what you mean by ' orthodox.' "

" By ' orthodox,' " said the Vicar of Sebergham, after a sonorous clearing of his throat, " I understand a man who keeps to the Articles of the Church, and does not run into any extravagances and enthusiasm."

" Hear him !" cried Mr. Bagnall, as if he were at a Tory meeting. Hatty burst out laughing, but immediately smothered it in her handkerchief.

" I do hear him, and with pleasure," said Mr. Keith. " I am no friend to extravagance, I assure you. Let a Churchman keep to the Bible and the Articles, and I ask no more of him. But excuse me if I say that we are departing from the question before us, which was the propriety, or impropriety, of one saying that his sins were forgiven. May I ask why you object to that ?—and is the objection to the forgiveness, or to the proclamation of it ? "

" Sir," said Mr. Bagnall, warmly, " I think it presumption—arrogance—horrible self-conceit."

" To have forgiveness ?—or to say so ? "

" I cannot answer such a question, Sir !" said Mr. Bagnall, getting red in the face, and seizing the pepperbox once more, with which he dusted his pie recklessly. " When a man sets himself up to be better than his neighbours in that way, it is scandalous—perfectly scandalous, Sir !"

" ' Better than his neighbours !' " repeated Mr. Keith, as if he were considering the question. " If a pardoned criminal be better than his neighbours, I suppose the neighbours are worse criminals ? "

" Sir, you misunderstand me. They fancy themselves better than others." Mr. Bagnall was getting angry.

" But seeing all are criminals alike, and they own it every Sunday," was Mr. Keith's answer, " does it not look rather odd that an objection should be made to one of them stating that he has been pardoned? Is it because the rest are unpardoned, and are conscious of it ? "

" Come, friends!" said Sir Robert, before Mr. Bagnall could reply. " Let us not lose our tempers, I beg. Mr. Keith is a Scotsman, and such are commonly good reasoners and love a tilt; and 'tis but well in a young man to keep his wits in practice. But we must not get too far, you know."

" Just so! just so!" saith Father, who I think was glad to have a stop put to this sort of converse. " Mr. Bagnall, I am sure, bears no malice. Sir Robert, when do the Holme Cultram hounds meet next ? "

Mr. Bagnall growled something, I know not what, and gave himself up to his pie for the rest of the time. Mr. Keith smiled, and said no more. But I know in whose hands I thought the victory rested.

CHAPTER IV.

THINGS BEGIN TO HAPPEN.

THIS afternoon I went up the Scar by myself. First I climbed right to the top, and after looking round a little, as I always like to do on the top of a mountain, I went down a few yards to the flat bit where the old Roman wall runs, and sat down on the grass just above. It was a lovely day. I had not an idea that any one was near the place but myself, and I was just going to sing, when to my surprise I heard a voice on the other side of the Roman wall. It was Angus Drummond's.

"Duncan Keith, why don't you say something?" He broke out suddenly, in a petulant tone—rather the tone of a child who knows it has been naughty, and wants to get the scolding over which it feels sure is coming some time.

"What do you wish me to say?"

Mr. Keith's tone was cold and constrained, I thought.

"Why don't you tell me I am an unhanged reprobate, and that you are ashamed to be seen walking with me? You know you are thinking it."

"No, Angus. I was thinking something very different."

"What, then?" asked Angus, sulkily.

"'Doth He not leave the ninety and nine in the wilderness, and go after that which is lost, *until He find it?*'"

There was no coldness in Mr. Keith's tone now.

"What has that got to do with it?" growled Angus in his throat.

"Angus," was the soft answer, "the sheep sometimes makes it a very hard journey for Him."

I know I ought to have risen and crept away long before this : but I did not. It was not right of me, but I sat on. I knew they could not see me through the wall, nor could they get across it at any place so near that I could not be gone far enough before they could catch sight of me.

"I suppose," said Angus, in the same sort of sulky murmur, "that is your way of telling me, Mr. Keith, that I am a miserable sinner."

"Are you not?"

"Miserable enough, Heaven knows! But, Duncan, I don't see why you, and Flora, and Mrs. Kezia, and all the good folks, or the folks who think themselves extra good, which comes to the same thing——"

"Does it? I was not aware of that," said Mr. Keith.

"I can't see," Angus went on, "why you must all turn up the whites of your eyes like a duck in thunder, and hold up your hands in pious horror at me, because I have done just once what every gentleman in the land does every week, and thinks nothing of it. If you had not been brought up in a hen-coop, and ruled like a copy-book, you would not be so con—— so hideously strict and particular! Just ask Ambrose Catterall whether there is any weight on his conscience; or ask that jolly parson, who tackled you and Flora at breakfast, what he has to say to it. I'll be bound he will read prayers next Sabbath with as much grace and unction as if he had never been drunk in his life. And because I get let in just once, why——"

Angus paused as if to consider how to finish his sentence, and Mr. Keith answered one point of his long speech, letting all the rest go.

" Is it just this once, Angus ? "

" I suppose you mean that night at York, when I got let in with those fellows of Greensmith's," growled Angus, more grumpily than ever. " Now, Duncan, that's not generous of you. I did the humble and penitent for that, and you should not cast it up to me. Just that time and this ! "

" And no more, Angus ? "

Angus muttered something which did not reach me.

" Angus, you know why I came with you ? "

" Yes, I know well enough why you came with me," said Angus, bitterly. " Just because that stupid old meddler, Helen Raeburn, took it into her wooden head that I could not take care of myself, and talked my father into sending me with you now, instead of letting me go the other way round by myself! Could not take care of myself, forsooth!"

"Have you done it?"

"I hadn't it to do. Mr. Duncan Keith was to take care of me, just as if I had been a baby—stuff! There is no end to the folly of old women!"

"I think young men might sometimes match them. Well, Angus, I have taken as much care as you let me. But you deceived me, boy. I know more about it than you think. It was not one or two transgressions that let you down to this pitch. I know you had a private key from Rob Greensmith, and let yourself in and out when I believed you asleep."

Angus sputtered out some angry words, which I did not catch.

"No. You are mistaken. Leigh did not tell of you or his brother. Your friend Robert told me himself. He wanted to get out of the scrape, and he did not care about leaving you in it. The friendship of the wicked is not worth much, Angus. But if I had not known it, I should still have felt perfectly sure that there had been more going on than you ever confessed to me. Three months since, Angus, you would not have used words which you have used this day. You would not have spoken so lightly of being 'let in'—let into what? Just stop and think. And twice to-day—once in Flora's presence—you have only just stopped your tongue from a worse word than that. Would you have said such a thing to your father before we left Abbotscliff?"

" Uncle Courtenay was as drunk as any of them last night," Angus blurted out.

I did not like to hear that of Father. Till now I never thought much about such things, except that they were imperfections which men had and women had not, and the women must put up with them. Sins?—well, yes, I suppose getting drunk is a sin, if you come to think about it ; but so is getting into a passion, and telling falsehoods, and plenty more things which one thinks little or nothing about, because one sees everybody do them every day. It is only the extra good people, like my Aunt Kezia, and Flora, and Mr. Keith, that put on grave faces about things of that kind.

But stay! God must be better than the extra good people. Then will He not think even worse of such things than they do?

It was just because those three seemed to think it so awful, and to be inclined to make a fuss over it, that I did not like to hear what Angus said about Father. Grandmamma never thought anything about it ; she always said drinking and gaming were gentlemanly vices, which the King himself—(I mean, of course, the Elector, but Grandmamma said the King)—need not be ashamed of practising.

I listened rather uneasily for Mr. Keith's answer. I am beginning to feel a good deal of respect for his opinion and himself, and I did not want to hear him say anything about Father that was not agreeable. But he put it quietly aside.

" If you please, Angus, we will let other people alone.

Both you and I shall find our own sins quite enough to repent of, I expect. You have not answered my question, Angus."

"What question?" grumbled Angus. I fancy he did not want to answer it.

"Would you, three months since, have let your father see and hear what you have let me do within even the last week?"

Angus growled something in the bottom of his throat which I could not make out.

Mr. Keith's tone changed suddenly.

"Angus, dear old fellow, are you happier now than you were then?"

"Duncan, I am the most miserable wretch that ever lived! I want no preaching to, I can tell you. That last text my father preached from keeps tolling in my ear like a funeral bell—and it is all the worse because it comes in his voice: 'Remember from whence thou art fallen!' Don't I remember it? Do I want telling whence I have fallen? Haven't I made a thousand resolves never, *never* to fail again, and the next time I get into company, all my resolves melt away and my hard knots come undone, and I feel as strong as a spoonful of water, and any of them can lead me that tries, like an animal with a ring through his nose?"

"Water is not a bad comparison, Angus, if you look at both sides of it. What is stronger than water, when the wind blows it with power? And you know who is compared to the wind. 'Awake, O North Wind, and come, Thou South; blow upon my garden, that the spices thereof may flow out.'   It is the wind of God's Spirit that we want, to blow the water—powerless of itself—in the right direction.   It will carry all before it then."

"Oh, yes, all that sounds very well," said Angus, but in a pleasanter tone than before—not so much like a big growling dog. "But you don't know, Duncan—you don't know! You have no temptations. What can you know about it?   I tell you I *can't* keep out of it. It is no good talking."

" 'No temptations!'   I wish that were true.   But you are quite right as to yourself; you cannot keep out of it.   Do you mean to add that God cannot keep you?"

I did not hear Angus's reply, and I fancy it came in a gesture, and not in words. But Mr. Keith said, very softly,—

"Angus, will you let Him keep you?"

Instead of the answer for which I was eagerly listening, another sound came to my ear, which made me jump up in a hurry, almost without caring whether I was heard or not.   That was the clock of Brocklebank Church striking twelve.   I should be ever so much too late for dinner; and what would my Aunt Kezia say? I got away as quietly as I could for a few yards, and then ran down the Scar as fast as I dared for fear of falling, and came into the dining-room, feeling hot and breathless, just as Cecilia, looking fresh and bright as a white lily, was entering it from the other end.   The rest were seated at the table.   Of course Mr. Keith and Angus were not there.

"Caroline, where have you been ? " saith my Aunt Kezia.

I trembled, for I knew what I had to expect when my Aunt Kezia said Caroline in full.

"I am very sorry, Aunt," said I. "I went up the Scar, and—— well, I am afraid I forgot all about the time."

My Aunt Kezia nodded, as if my frank confession satisfied her, and Father said, " Good maid!" as I slipped into the chair where I always sit, on his left hand. But Cecilia, who was arranging her skirts just opposite, said in that way which men seem to call charming, and women always see through and despise (at least m" Aunt Kezia says so),——

" Am I a little late ? "

" Don't name it !" said Father.

" Dear, no, my charmer ! " cried Hatty. " Cary's shockingly late, of course : but you are not—quite impossible."

Cecilia gave one of her soft smiles, and said no more.

I really am beginning to wish the Bracewells gone. Yet it is not so much on their own account. Amelia is vain and silly, and Charlotte rude and romping ; but I do not think either of them is a hypocrite. Charlotte is not, I am sure; she lets you see the very worst side of her: and Amelia's affectation is so plain and unmistakable, that it cannot be called insincerity. It is on account of that horrid Cecilia that I want them to go, because I suppose she will go with them. Yes, truth is truth, and Cecilia is horrid. I am getting quite frightened of her. I do not know what she means to do next:

but she seems to me to be always laying traps of some sort, and for somebody.

I wonder if people ever do what you expect of them? If somebody had asked me to make a list of things that could not happen, I expect that I should have put on it one thing that has just happened.

Sophy and I went up this morning to Goody Branscombe's cot, to take her some wine and eggs from my Aunt Kezia. Anne Branscombe thinks she is failing, poor old woman, and my Aunt Kezia told her to beat up an egg with a little wine and sugar, and give it to her fasting of a morning: she thinks it a fine thing for keeping up strength. We came round by the Vicarage on our way back, and stepped in to see old Elspie. We found her ironing the Vicar's shirts and ruffles, and she put us in rocking-chairs while we sat and talked.

Old Elspie wanted to know all we could tell her about Flora and Angus, and I promised I would bring Flora to see her some day. She says Mr. Keith—Mr. Duncan Keith's father, that is—is the squire of Abbotscliff, a very rich man, and a tremendous Tory.

"You're vara nigh strangers, young leddies," said Elspie, as she ironed away. "Miss Fanny, she came to see me a twa-three days back, and Miss Bracewell wi' her; and there was anither young leddy, but I disremember her name."

"Was it Charlotte Bracewell?" said Sophy.

"Na, na, I ken Miss Charlotte ower weel to forget her, though she has grown a deal sin' I saw her afore.

This was a lassie wi' black hair, and e'en like the new wood the minister has his dinner-table, wi' the fine name—what ca' ye that, now?"

"Mahogany?" said I.

"Aye, it has some sic fremit soun'," said old Elspie, rather scornfully. "I ken it was no sae far frae muggins.[1] Mrs. Sophy, my dear, ha'e ye e'er suppit muggins in May? 'Tis the finest thing going for keeping a lassie in gude health, and it suld be drinkit in the spring. Atweel, what's her name wi' the copper-colourit e'en?"

"Cecilia Osborne," said I. "What did you think of her, Elspie?"

The iron went up and down the Vicar's shirt-front, and I saw a curious gathering together of old Elspie's lips—still she did not speak. At last Sophy said,—

"Couldn't you make up your mind about her, Elspie?"

"I had nae mickle fash about *that*, Mrs. Sophy," said Elspeth, setting down her iron on the stand with something like a bang. "And gin I can see through a millstane a wee bittie, she'll gi'e ye the chance to make up yourn afore lang."

"Nay, mine's made up long since," answered Sophy "I shall see the back of her with a deal more pleasure than I did her face a month ago. Won't you, Cary?"

"I don't like her the least bit," said I.

"Ye'll be wiser lassies, young leddies, gin ye're no

---

[1] Mugwort.

ower ready to say it," said Elspie, coolly. "It was no ane o' *your* white days when she came to Brocklebank Fells. Aye, weel, weel! The Lord's ower a'."

As we went down the road, I said to Sophy, "What did old Elspie mean, do you suppose?"

"I am afraid I can guess what she meant, Cary."

Sophy's tone was so strange that I looked up at her; and I saw her eyes flashing and her lips set and white.

"Sophy! what is the matter?" I cried.

"Don't trouble your little head, Cary," she said, kindly enough. "It will be trouble in plenty when it comes."

I could not get her to say more. As we reached the door, Hatty came dancing out to meet us.

> "'The rose is white, the rose is red,'—
> The sun gives light, Queen Anne is dead :
> Ladies with white and rosy hues,
> What will you give me for my news?"

"Hatty, you must have made that yourself!" said Sophy.

"I have, just this minute," laughed Hatty. "Now then, who'll bid for my news?"

"I dare say it isn't worth a farthing," said Sophy.

"Well, to you, perhaps not. It may be rather morti-fying. My sweet Sophia, you are the eldest of us, but your younger sister has stolen a march on you. You have played your cards ill, Miss Courtenay. Fanny is going to be the first of us married, unless I contrive to run away with somebody in the interval. I don't know whom—there's the difficulty."

" Well, I always thought she would be," said Sophy, quite good-humouredly. " She is the prettiest of us, is Fanny."

"So much obliged for the compliment ! " gleefully cried Hatty. " Cary, don't you feel delighted ? "

" Is Ephraim here now ? " I said, for of course I never thought of anybody else.

"Ephraim !" Hatty whirled round, laughing heartily. " Ephraim, my dear, will have to break his heart at leisure. Ambrose Catterall has stolen a march on *him.*"

" You don't mean that Fanny and Ambrose are to be married !" cried Sophy, with wide-open eyes.

" I do, Madam ; and my Aunt Kezia is as mad as a hatter about it. She would have liked Ephraim for her nephew ever so much better than Ambrose."

" Well, I do think !" exclaimed Sophy. "If Ephraim did really care for Fanny, she has used him shamefully."

"So *I* think !" said Hatty. " I mean to present him on his next birthday with a dozen pocket-handkerchiefs, embroidered in the corner with an urn and a willow-tree."

" An urn, you ridiculous child ! " returned Sophy. "That means that somebody is dead."

" Don't throw cold water on my charming conceits !" pleaded Hatty. " Now go in and face my Aunt Kezia —if you dare."

We found her cutting out flannel petticoats in the parlour. My Aunt Kezia's brows were drawn together, and my Aunt Kezia's lips were thin ; and I trembled. However, she took no note of us, but went on tearing up flannel, and making little piles of it upon the table end.

Sophy, with heroic bravery, attacked the citadel at once.

"Well, Aunt, this is pretty news!"

"What is?" said my Aunt Kezia, standing up straight and stiff.

"Why, this about Fanny and Ambrose Catterall."

"Oh, that!   I wish there were nothing worse than that in *this* world."   My Aunt Kezia spoke as if she would have preferred some other world, where things went straighter than they do in this.

"Hatty said you were put out about it, Aunt."

"That's all Hatty knows.   I think 'tis a blunder, and Fanny will find it out, likely enough.   But if that were all—— Girls, 'tis nigh dinner-time.   You had better take your bonnets off."

"What is the matter with my Aunt Kezia?" said I to Sophy, as we went upstairs.

"Don't ask *me*!" said that young lady.

Half-way upstairs we met Charlotte.

"Oh, what fun you have missed, you two!" cried she.   "Why didn't you come home a little sooner?   I would not have lost it for a hundred pounds."

"Lost what, Charlotte?"

"Lost *what?*   Ask my Aunt Kezia—now just you do!"

"My Aunt Kezia seems unapproachable," said Sophy.

Charlotte went off into a fit of laughter, and then slid down the banister to the hall—a feat which my Aunt Kezia has forbidden her to perform a dozen times at least. We went forward, made ourselves ready for dinner, and came down to the dining-parlour.

In the dining-room we found a curious group. My Aunt Kezia looked as stiff as whalebone; Father, pleased and radiant; Flora and Mr. Keith both seemed rather puzzled. Angus was in a better temper than usual. Charlotte was evidently full of something very funny, which she did not want to let out; Cecilia, soft, serene, and velvety; Fanny looked nervous and uncomfortable; Hatty, scornful; while Amelia was her usual self.

When dinner was over, we went back to the parlour. My Aunt Kezia gathered up her heaps of flannel, gave one to Flora and another to me, and began to stitch away at a third herself. Amelia threw herself on the sofa, saying she was tired to death; and I was surprised to see that my Aunt Kezia took no notice. Fanny sat down to draw; Hatty went on with her knitting; Charlotte strolled out into the garden; and Cecilia disappeared, I know not whither.

For an hour or more we worked away in solemn silence. Hatty tried to whisper once or twice to Fanny, making her blush and look uncomfortable; but Fanny did not speak, and I fancy Hatty got tired. Amelia went to sleep.

At last, and all at once, Flora—honest, straightforward Flora—laid her work on her knee, and looked up at my Aunt Kezia's grim set face.

" Aunt Kezia, will you tell me, is something the matter ?"

“ Yes, my dear,” my Aunt Kezia seemed to snap out. “ Satan’s the matter.”

“ I don’t know what you mean, Aunt,” said Flora.

“ ’Tis a mercy if you don’t. No, child, there is not much the matter for you. The matter’s for me and these girls here. Well, to be sure! there’s no fool like an old f—— Caroline! (I fairly jumped) can’t you look what you are doing? You are herring-boning that seam on the wrong side!”

Alas! the charge was true. I cannot tell how or why it is, but if there are two seams to anything, I am sure to do one of them on the wrong side. It is very queer. I suppose there is something wanting in my brains. Hatty says—at least she did once when I said that— the brains are wanting.

However, we sat on and sewed away, till at last Amelia woke up and went upstairs; Flora finished her petticoat, and my Aunt Kezia told her to go into the garden. Only we four sisters were left. Then my Aunt Kezia put down her flannel, wiped her spectacles, and looked round at us.

I knew something was coming, and I felt quite sure that it was something disagreeable; but I could not form an idea what it was.

“ Girls,” said my Aunt Kezia, “ I think you may as well hear at once that I am going to leave Brocklebank.”

I fairly gasped in astonishment. Brocklebank without my Aunt Kezia! It sounded like hearing that the sun was going out of the sky. I could not imagine such a state of things.

"Is Sophy to be mistress, then?" said Fanny, blankly.

" Aunt Kezia, are you going to be married?" our impertinent Hatty wanted to know.

" No, Hester," said my Aunt Kezia, shortly. " At my time of life a woman has a little sense left; or if she have not, she is only fit for Bedlam. I do not think Sophy will be mistress, Fanny. Somebody else is going to take that place. Otherwise, I should have stayed in it."

"What do you mean, Aunt Kezia?" said Fanny, speaking very slowly, and in a bewildered sort of way.

Sophy said nothing. I think she knew. And all at once it seemed to come over me—as if somebody had shut me up inside a lump of ice—what it was that was going to happen.

" I mean, my dear," my Aunt Kezia replied quietly, " that your father intends to marry again."

Sophy's face and tongue gave no sign that she had heard anything which was news to her. Fanny cried, " Never, surely!" Hatty said, " How jolly!" and then in a whisper to me, "Won't I lead her a life!" I believe I said nothing. I felt shut up in that lump of ice.

" But, Aunt Kezia, what is to become of us all? Are we to stay here, or go with you?" asked Fanny.

" Your father desires me to tell you, my dears," said my Aunt Kezia, " that he wishes to leave you quite free to please yourselves. If you choose to remain here, he will be glad to have you; and if any of you like to come with me to Fir Vale, you will be welcome, and you know what to expect."

“What are we to expect if we stop here?” asked Sophy, in a hard, dry voice.

“That is more than I can say,” was my Aunt Kezia’s answer.

“But who is it?” said Fanny, in the same bewildered way.

“O Fanny, what a bat you are!” cried Hatty.

“I wonder you ask,” answered Sophy. “I have seen her fishing-rod for ever so long. Cecilia, of course.”

“Cecilia!” screamed Fanny. “I thought it was some middle-aged, respectable gentlewoman.”

Hatty burst out laughing. I never felt less inclined to laugh. My Aunt Kezia had taken off her spectacles, and was going on with her tucks as if nothing had happened.

“Well, I will think about it,” said Sophy. “I am not sure I shall stay.”

“*I* shall stay,” announced Hatty. “I expect it will be grand fun. She will fill the house with company— that will suit me; and I shall just look sharp after her and keep her in order.”

“Hatty!” cried Fanny, in a shocked tone.

“I hope you will keep yourself in order,” said my Aunt Kezia, drily. “Little Cary, you have not spoken yet. What do you want to do?”

Her voice softened as I had never heard it do before when she spoke to me. It touched me very much; yet I think I should have said the same without it.

“O Aunt Kezia, please let me go with you!”

“Thank you, Cary,” said my Aunt Kezia in the same

tone. "The old woman is not to be left quite alone, then? But it will be dull, child, for a young thing like you."

"I would rather have it dull than lively the wrong way about," said I; and Hatty broke out again.

"Would you!" said she, when she had done laughing. "I wouldn't, I promise you. Sophy, don't you know a curate you could marry? You had better, if you can find one."

"Not one that has asked me," was Sophy's dry answer. "You don't want me, then, Miss Hatty?"

"You would be rather meddlesome, I am afraid," said Hatty, with charming frankness. "You would always be doing conscience."

"Don't you intend to keep one?" returned Sophy.

"I mean to lay it up in lavender," said Hatty, "and take it out on Sundays."

"Hatty, if you haven't a care——"

"Please go on, Aunt Kezia. Unfinished sentences are always awful things, because you don't know how they are going to end."

"*You'll* end in the lock-up, if you don't mind," said my Aunt Kezia; "and if I were you, I wouldn't."

"I'll try to keep on this side the door," said Hatty, as lightly as ever. "And when is it to be, Aunt Kezia?"

"The month after next, I believe."

"Isn't Cecilia going home first, to see what her friends say about it?"

"She has none belonging to her, except an uncle and his family, and she says they will be delighted to hear it.　Hatty, you had better get out of the way of calling her Cecilia.　It won't do now, you know."

"But you don't mean, Aunt Kezia, that we are to call her Mother!" cried Fanny, in a most beseeching tone.

"My dear, that must be as your father wishes.　He may allow you to call her Mrs. Courtenay.　That is what I shall call her."

"Isn't it dreadful!" said poor Fanny.

"One thing more I have to say," continued my Aunt Kezia, laying down her flannel again and putting on her spectacles.　"Your father does not wish you to be present at his marriage."

"Aunt Kezia!" came, I think, from us all—indignantly from Sophy, sorrowfully from Fanny, petulantly from Hatty, and from me in sheer astonishment.

"I suppose he has his reasons," said my Aunt Kezia; "but that being so, I think Sophy had better go home for a while with the Bracewells, and Hatty, too.　You, Cary, may go with Flora instead, if you like.　Fanny, of course, is arranged for already, as she will be married by then, and will only have to stop at home."

I thought I would very much rather go with Flora.

"I have had a letter from your Aunt Dorothea lately," my Aunt Kezia went on, "in which she asks for Cary to pay her a visit next June.　But now we are only in March.　So, as Cary must be somewhere between times, and I think she would be better out of the way, she will go to Abbotscliff with Flora—unless, my dear," she added, turning to me, "you would rather be at Bracewell Hall?　You may, if you like."

"I would rather be at Abbotscliff, very much, Aunt Kezia," said I ; and I think Aunt Kezia was pleased.

"Aunt Kezia, don't send me away !" pleaded Sophy. "Do let me stay and help you to settle at Fir Vale. I should hate to stay at Bracewell, and I should just like bustling about and helping you in that way. Won't you let me ?"

"Well, my dear, we will see," said my Aunt Kezia ; and I think she was pleased with Sophy too. Hatty declared that Bracewell would just suit her, and she would not stay at any price, if she had leave to choose. So it seems to be settled in that way. Fanny will be married on the 30th,—that is three weeks hence ; and the week after, Hatty goes with the Bracewells, and I with Flora, to their own homes; and my Aunt Kezia and Sophy will remain here, and only leave the house on the evening before the marriage.

It seems very odd that Father should have wished not to have us at his wedding. Was it Cecilia who did not wish it ? But I am not to call her Cecilia any more.

When my cousins came in for tea, they were told too. Charlotte cried, " Well, I never !" for which piece of vulgarity she was sharply pulled up by my Aunt Kezia. Amelia fanned herself—she always does, whatever time of year it may be—and languidly remarked, " Dear !" Angus said, "Castor and Pollux !" for which he also got rebuked. And after a sort of "Oh!" Flora said nothing, but looked very sorrowfully at us. Cec—I mean Miss Osborne—did not appear at all until tea was nearly over, and then she came in from the garden, and M.

Parmenter with her, that everlasting eyeglass stuck in his eye. I do so dislike the man.

Father never comes to tea. He says it is only women's rubbish, and laughs at Ephraim Hebblethwaite because he says he likes it. I fancy few men drink tea. My Uncle Charles never does, I know; but my Aunt Dorothea says she could not exist a day without tea and cards.

I wonder if it will be pleasant to stay with my Aunt Dorothea. I believe she and my Uncle Charles are living in London now. I should like dearly to see London, and the fine shops, and the lions in the Tower, and Ranelagh, and all the grand people. And yet, somehow, I feel just a little bit uneasy about it, as if I were going into some place where I did not know what I should find, and it might be something that would hurt me. I do not feel that about Abbotscliff. I expect it will be pleasant there, only perhaps rather dull. And I want to see my Uncle Drummond, and Flora's friend, Annas Keith. I wonder if she is like her brother. And I never saw a Presbyterian minister, nor indeed a minister of any sort. I do hope my Uncle Drummond will not be like Mr. Bagnall, and I hope all the gentlemen in the South are not like that odious Mr. Parmenter.

Flora seems very much pleased about my going back with her. I do not know why, but I fancied Angus did not quite like it. Can he be afraid of my telling his father the story of the hunt-supper? He knows nothing of what I heard up on the Scar.

I do hope Ephraim Hebblethwaite is not very unhappy about Fanny. I should think it must be dreadful, when you love any one very much, to see her go and give herself quite away to somebody else. And Ambrose thinks of going to live in Cheshire, where his uncle has a large farm, and he has no children, so the farm will come to Ambrose some day; and his uncle, Mr. Minshull, would like him to come and live there now. Of course, if that be settled so, we shall lose Fanny altogether.

Must there always be changes and break-ups in this world? I do not mean the change of death: that, we know, must come. But why must there be all these other changes? Why could we not go on quietly as we were? It seems now as if we should never be the same any more.

If that uncle of Cecilia's would only have tied her to the leg of a table, or locked her up in her bed-chamber, or done something to keep her down there in the South, so that she had never come to torment us!

I suppose I ought not to wish that, if she makes Father happier. Ay, but will she make him happy? That is just what I am uncomfortable about! I don't believe she cares a pin for *him*, though I dare say she likes well enough to be the Squire's lady, and queen it at Brocklebank. Somehow, I cannot trust those tawny eyes, with their sidelong glances. Am I very wicked, or is she?

Will things never give over happening?
This morning, just after I came down—there were

only my Aunt Kezia, Mr. Keith, Flora, and me in the dining-parlour—we suddenly heard the great bell of Brocklebank Church begin to toll. My Aunt Kezia set down the chocolate-pot.

"It must be somebody who has died suddenly, poor soul!" cried she. "Maybe, Ellen Armathwaite's baby: it looked very bad when I saw it last, on Thursday. Hark!"

The bell stopped tolling, and we listened for the sound which would tell us the sex and age of the departed.

"One!" Then silence.

That meant a man. Ellen Armathwaite's baby girl it could not be. Then the bell began again, and we counted. It tolled on up to twenty—thirty—forty: we could not think who it could be.

"Surely not Farmer Catterall!" said my Aunt Kezia. "I have often felt afraid of an apoplexy for him."

But the bell went on past sixty, and we knew it was not Farmer Catterall.

"Is it never going to stop?" said Flora, when it had passed eighty.

My Aunt Kezia went to the door, and calling Sam, bade him go out and inquire. Still the bell tolled on. It stopped just as Sam came in, at ninety-six.

"Who is it, Sam?—one of the old bedesmen?"

"Nay, Mrs. Kezia; puir soul, 'tis just the auld Vicar!"

"Mr. Digby!" we all cried together.

"Ay; my mither found him deid i' his bed early this morrow. She's come up to tell ye, an' to ask gin' ye can spare me to go and gi'e a haun', for that puir witless body, Mr. Anthony Parmenter, seems all but daft."

Miss Osborne and Amelia came in together, and I saw Cecilia turn very white. (Oh dear! how shall I give over calling her Cecilia?) My Aunt Kezia told them what had happened, and I thought she looked relieved.

"What ails Mr. Parmenter?" asked my Aunt Kezia.

"'Deed, and what ails a fule onie day?" said Sam, always more honest than soft-spoken. "He's just as ill as a bit lassie—fair frichtened o' his auld uncle, now he is deid, that ne'er did him a bawbee's worth o' harm while he was alive. My mither says she's vara sure he'll be here the morn, begging and praying ye to tak' him in and keep him safe frae his puir auld uncle's ghaist. Hech, sirs! I'll ghaist him, gin' he comes my way."

"Now, Sam, keep a civil tongue in your head," quoth my Aunt Kezia, "and don't let me hear of your playing tricks on Mr. Parmenter or any one else. You should be old enough to have some sense by this time. I will come out and speak to your mother in a moment. Yes, I suppose we must let you go. What cuckoos there are in this world, to be sure!"

But Mr. Parmenter did not wait till to-morrow—he came up this afternoon, just as Sam said he would. Father was not at home, and to my surprise my Aunt Kezia would not take him in, but sent him on to Farmer Catterall's. I do not think the tawny eyes liked it, for though they were mostly bent on the ground, I saw them give one sidelong flash at my Aunt Kezia which did not look to me like loving-kindness.

I feel to-night what I think Angus means when he says that he is flat. Everything feels flat. Fanny is gone—she was married on Saturday. Amelia, Charlotte, and Hatty set forth on Tuesday, and they are gone. I thought that Ce——Miss Osborne would have gone with them, and have returned by-and-by; but she stays on, and will do so, I hear, almost till my Aunt Kezia goes, when Mrs. Hebblethwaite has asked her to stay at the Fells Farm for the last few days before the wedding. It is settled now that my Aunt Kezia and Sophy stay here till the day before it. It does seem so queer for Sophy to be here till then, and not be at the wedding ! I don't believe it is Father's doing. It is not like him. Flora, Angus, Mr. Keith, and I are to start to-morrow ; but Mr. Keith only goes with us as far as Carlisle—that is, the first day's journey ; then he leaves us for Newcastle, where he has some sort of business (that horrid word !), and I go on with my cousins to Abbotscliff. We shall be met at Carlisle by a Scots gentleman who is travelling thence to Selkirk, and is a friend of my Uncle Drummond. He goes in his own chaise, with two mounted servants, and both he and they are armed, so I hope we shall get clear of freebooters on the Border. He has nobody with him, and says he shall have plenty of room in the chaise. It is very lucky that this Mr. Cameron should just be going at the same time as we are. I don't think Angus would be much protection, though I should not wish him to know I said so.

If Ephraim Hebblethwaite have broken his heart, he

behaves very funnily. He was not only at Fanny's wedding, but was best man; and he looks quite well and happy. I begin to think that we must have been mistaken in guessing that he cared for Fanny. Perhaps it only amused him to talk to her.

Fanny's wedding was very smart and gay, and everybody came to it. The bridesmaids were we three, Esther Langridge, and two cousins of Ambrose's, whose names are Annabel Catterall and Priscilla Minshull. I rather liked Annabel, but Priscilla was horrid. (Sophy says I say "horrid" too often, and about all sorts of things. But if people and things are horrid, how am I to help saying it?) I am sure Priscilla Minshull was horrid. She reminded me of Angus's saying about turning up one's eyes like a duck in thunder. I never watched a duck in thunder, and I don't know whether it turns up its eyes or it does not: only Priscilla did. She seemed to think us all (my Aunt Kezia said) no better than the dirt she walked on. And I am sure she need not be so stuck up, for Mr. James Minshull, her father, is only a parson, and not only that, but a chaplain too: so Priscilla is not anybody of any consequence. I said so to Flora, and she replied that Priscilla would be much less likely to be proud if she were.

I was dreadfully tired on Sunday. We had been so hard at work all the fortnight before, first making the wedding dress, and then dressing the wedding dinner; and when I went to bed on Saturday night, I thought I never wanted to see another. Another wedding, of course, I mean. However, everything went off very well; and Fanny looked charming in her pink silk brocaded with flowers, with white stripes down it here and there, and a pink quilted slip beneath. She had pink rosettes, too, in her shoes, and a white hood lined with pink and trimmed with pink bows. Her hoop came from Carlisle, and was the biggest I have seen yet. The mantua-maker from Carlisle, who was five days in the house, said that hoops were getting very much larger this year, and she thought they would soon be as big as they were in Queen Anne's time. We had much smaller hoops—of course it would not have been seemly to have the bridesmaids as smart as the bride—and we were dressed alike, in white French cambric, with light green trimmings. Of course we all wore white ribbons. I think Father would have stormed at us if we had put on any other colour. I should not like to be the one to wear a red ribbon when he was by![1] We wore straw milk-maid hats, with green ribbon mixed with the white; and just a sprinkle of grey powder in our hair. Cecilia would not be a bridesmaid, though she was asked. I don't think she liked the dress chosen; and indeed it would not have suited her. But wasn't she dressed up! She wore—I really must set it down—a purple lutestring,[2] over such a hoop that she had to lift it on one side when she went in at the church door; this was guarded with gold lace and yellow feathers. She had a white laced apron, purple velvet slippers with red heels,

---

[1] The white ribbon, like the white cockade, distinguished a Jacobite; the red ribbon and the black cockade were Hanoveriar

[2] A variety of silk then fashionable.

and her lace ruffles were something to look at! And wasn't she patched! and hadn't she powdered her hair, and made it as stiff with pomatum as if it had been starched! Then on the top of this head went a lace cap—it was not a hood—just a little, light, fly-away cap, with purple ribbons and gold embroidery, and in the middle of the front a big gold pompoon.

What a contrast there was between her and my Aunt Kezia! She wore a silk dress too, only it was a dark stone-colour, as quiet as a Quakeress, just trimmed with two rows of braid, the same colour, round the bottom, and a white silk scarf, with a dark blue hood, and just a little rosette of white lace at the top of it. Aunt Kezia's hood *was* a hood, too, and was tied under her chin as if she meant it to be some good. And her elbow-ruffles were plain nett, with long dark doe-skin gloves drawn up to meet them. Cecilia wore white silk mittens. I hate mittens; they are horrid things. If you want to make your hands look as ugly as you can, you have only to put on a pair of mittens.

The wedding-dinner, which was at noon, was a very grand one. It should have been, for didn't my arms ache with beating eggs and keeping pans stirred! Hatty said we were martyrs in a good cause. But I do think Fanny might have taken a little more trouble herself, seeing it was her wedding. Now, let us see, what had we? There was a turkey pie, and a boar's head, chickens in different ways, and a great baron of roast beef; cream beaten to snow (Sophy did that, I am glad to say), candied fruits, and ices, and several sorts of pudding, for dessert. Then for drink, there were wine, and mead, purl, and Burton ale.

Well! it is all over now, and Fanny is gone. There will never be four of us any more. There seems to me something very sad about it. Poor dear Fanny, I hope she will be happy!

"I dare guess she will, in her way," says my Aunt Kezia. "She does not keep a large cup for her happiness. 'Tis all the easier to fill when you don't; but a deal more will go in when you do. There are advantages and disadvantages on each side of most things in this world."

"Is there any advantage, Aunt Kezia, in my having just pricked my finger shockingly?"

"Yes, Cary. Learn to be more careful in future."

CHAPTER V.

LEAVING THE NEST.

" I've kept old ways, and loved old friends,
  Till, one by one, they've slipped away ;
Stand where we will, cling as we like,
  There's none but God can be our stay.
'Tis only by our hold on Him
  We keep a hold on those who pass
Out of our sight across the seas,
  Or underneath the churchyard grass."
                    —Isabella Fyvie Mayo.

CARLISLE, *April the 5th,* 174⅘.

I REALLY feel that I must put a date to my writing now, when this is the first time of my going out into the great world. I have never been beyond Carlisle before, and now I am going, first into a new country, and then to London itself, if all go well.

News came last night, just before we started, that my Lord Orford is dead—he that was Sir Robert Walpole, and the Elector's Prime Minister. Father says his death is a good thing for the country, for it gives more hope that the King may come by his own. I don't know what would happen if he did. I suppose it would not make much difference to us. Indeed, I rather wish things would not happen, for the things that happen are so often disagreeable ones. I said so this evening, and Mr. Keith smiled, and answered, "You are young to have reached that conviction, Miss Caroline."

"Oh, rubbish!" said Angus. "Only old women talk so!"

"Angus, will you please tell me," said I, "whether young men have generally more sense than old women?"

"Of course they have!" replied he.

"The young men are apt to think so," added Flora.

"But have young women more sense than old ones?" said I. "Because I see, whenever people mean to speak of anything as particularly silly, they always say it is worthy of an old woman. Now why an *old* woman? Have I more common sense now than I shall have fifty years hence? And if so, at what age may I expect it to take leave of me?"

"You are not talking sense now, at any rate," replied Angus—who might be my brother, instead of my cousin, for the way in which he takes me up, whatever I say.

"Pardon me," said Mr. Keith. "I think Miss Caroline is talking very good sense."

"Then you may answer her," said Angus.

"Nay," returned Mr. Keith. "The question was addressed to you."

"Oh, all women are sillies!" was Angus's flattering answer. "They're just a pack of ninnies, the whole lot of them."

“It seems to me, Angus,” observed Mr. Keith, quite gravely, “that you must have paid twopence extra for manners.”

Flora and I laughed.

“I was not rich enough to go in for any,” growled Angus. “*I'm* not a laird’s son, Mr. Duncan Keith, so you don’t need to throw stones at me.”

“Did I, Angus? I beg your pardon.”

Angus muttered something which I did not hear, and was silent. I thought I had better let the subject drop.

But before we went to bed, something happened which I never saw before. Mr. Keith took a book from his pocket, and sat down at the table. Flora rose and went to the sofa, motioning to me to come beside her. Even Angus twisted himself round, and sat in a more decorous way.

“What are we going to do?” I asked of Flora.

“The exercise, dear,” said she.

“Exercise!” cried I. “What are we to exercise?”

A curious sort of gurgle came from Angus’s part of the room, as if a laugh had made its way into his throat, and he had smothered it in its cradle.

“The word is strange to Miss Caroline,” said Mr. Keith, looking round with a smile. “We Scots people, Madam, speak of exercising our souls in prayer. We are about to read in God’s Word, and pray, if you please. It is our custom, morning and evening.”

“But how can we pray?” said I. “There is no clergyman.”

"Though I am not a minister," replied Mr. Keith, "yet I trust I have learned to pray."

It seemed to me so strange that anybody not a clergyman should think of praying before other people! However, I sat down, of course, on the sofa by Flora, and listened while Mr. Keith read something out of the Gospel of St. John, about the woman of Samaria, and what our Lord said to her. But I never heard such reading in my life! I thought I could have gone on listening to him all night. The only clergymen that I ever heard read were Mr. Bagnall and poor old Mr. Digby, and the one always read in a high sing-song tone, which gave me the idea that it was nothing I need listen to; and the other mumbled indistinctly, so that I never heard what he said. But Mr. Keith read as if the converse were really going on, and you actually heard our Lord and the woman talking to one another at the well. He made it seem so real that I almost fancied I could hear the water trickling, and see the cool wet green mosses round the old well. Oh, if clergymen would always read and preach as if the things were real, how different going to church would be!

Then we knelt down, and Mr. Keith prayed. It was not out of the Prayer-Book. And I dare say, if I were to hear nothing but such prayers, I might miss the dear old prayers that have been like sweet sounds floating around me ever since I knew anything. But this even-ing, when it was all new, it came to me as so solemn and so real! This was not saying one's prayers; it was talking to one's Friend. And it seemed as if God really were Mr. Keith's Friend—as if they knew each other, and were not strangers at all, but each understood what the other would like or dislike, and they wanted to please one another. I hope I am not irreverent in writing so, but really it did seem like that. And I never saw anything like it before.

I suppose, to the others, it was an old worn-out story —all this which came so new and fresh to me. When we rose up, Angus said, without any pause,—

"Well! I am off to bed. Good-night, all of you."

Flora went up to him and offered him a kiss, which he took as if it were a condescension to an inferior creature; and then, without saying anything more to Mr. Keith or me, lighted his candle and went away. Flora sighed as she looked after him, and Mr. Keith looked at her as if he felt for her.

I shall be glad to get him home," said Flora, answering Mr. Keith's look, I think. "If he can only get back to Father, then, perhaps——"

"Aye," said Mr. Keith, meaningly, "it is all well, when we do get back to the Father."

Flora shook her head sorrowfully. "Not that!" she answered. "O Duncan, I am afraid, not that, yet! I feel such terrible fear sometimes lest he should never come back at all, or if he do, should have to come over sharp stones and through thorny paths."

"'*So* He bringeth them unto their desired haven,'" was Mr. Keith's gentle answer.

"I know!" she said, with a sigh. "I suppose I

ought to pray and wait. Father does, I am sure. But it is hard work!"

Mr. Keith did not answer for a moment; and when he did, it was by another bit of the Bible. At least I think it was the Bible, for it sounded like it, but I should not know where to find it.

"'Wait on the Lord; be of good courage, and He shall strengthen thine heart; wait, I say, on the Lord.'"

CASTLETON, *April the sixth.*

Mr. Keith left us so early this morning that there was not time for anything except breakfast and good-bye. I feel quite sorry to lose him, and wish I had a brother like him. (Not like Angus—dear me, no!) Why could we four girls not have had one brother?

About half an hour after Mr. Keith was gone, the Scots gentleman with whom we were to travel—Mr. Cameron—came in. He is a man of about fifty, bald-headed and rosy-faced, pleasant and chatty enough, only I do not quite always understand him. By six o'clock we were all packed into his chaise, and a few minutes later we set forth from the inn door. The streets of Carlisle felt like home; but as we left them behind, and came gradually out into the open country, it dawned upon me that now, indeed, I was going out into the great world.

We sleep here to-night, where Flora and I have a little bit of a bed-chamber next door to a larger one where Mr. Cameron and Angus are. On Monday we expect to reach Abbotscliff. I am too tired to write more.

ABBOTSCLIFF MANSE, *April the ninth.*

I really could not go on any sooner. We reached the manse—what an odd name for a vicarage!—about four o'clock yesterday afternoon. The church (which Flora calls the kirk) and the manse, with a few other houses, stand on a little rising ground, and the rest of the village lies below.

But before I begin to talk about the manse, I want to write down a conversation which took place on Monday morning as we journeyed, in which Mr. Cameron told us some curious things that I do not wish to forget. We were driving through such a pretty little village, and in one of the doorways an old woman sat with her knitting.

"Oh, look at that dear old woman!" cries Flora. "How pleasant she looks, with her clean white apron and mutch!"

"Much, Flora?" said I. "What do you mean?" I thought it such an odd word to use. What was she *much?*

Flora looked puzzled, and Mr. Cameron answered for her, with amusement in his eyes.

"A mutch, young lady," said he, "is what you in the South call a cap."

"The South!" cried I. "Why, Mr. Cameron, you do not think we live in the South?"

I felt almost vexed that he should fancy such a thing. For all that Grandmamma and my Aunt Dorothea used to say, I always look down upon the South. All the people I have seen who came from the South seemed to me to have a great deal of wiliness and foolishness, and no common sense. I suppose the truth is that there are agreeable people, and good people, in the South, only they have not come my way.

When I cried out like that, Mr. Cameron laughed.

"Well," said he, " north and south are comparative terms. We in Scotland think all England 'the South,'—and so it is, if you will think a moment. You in Cumberland, I suppose, draw the line at the Trent or the Humber ; lower down, they employ the Thames ; and a Surrey man thinks Sussex is the South. 'Tis all a matter of comparison."

"What does a Sussex man call the South ? " said Angus.

"Spain and Portugal, I should think." said Mr. Cameron.

"But, Mr. Cameron," said I, " asking your pardon, is there not some difference of character or disposition between those in the North and in the South—I mean, of England ? "

"Quite right, young lady," said he. " They are different tribes ; and the Lowland Scots, among whom you are now coming, have the same original as yourself. There were two tribes amongst those whom we call Anglo-Saxons, that peopled England after the Britons were driven into Wales—namely, as you might guess, the Angles and the Saxons. The Angles ran from the Frith of Forth to the Trent ; the Saxons from the Thames southward. The midland counties were in all likelihood a mixture of the two. There are, more-over, several foreign elements beyond this, in various counties. For instance, there is a large influx of Danish blood on the eastern coast, in parts of Lancashire, in Yorkshire and Lincolnshire, and in the Weald of Sussex; there was a Flemish settlement in Lancashire and Norfolk, of considerable extent; the Britons were left in great numbers in Cumberland and Cornwall; the Jutes—a variety of Dane—peopled Kent entirely. Nor must we forget the Romans, who left a deep impress upon us, especially amongst Welsh families. 'Tis not easy for any of our mixed race to say, I am this, or that. Why, if most of us spoke the truth (supposing we might know it), we should say, ' I am one-quarter Saxon, one-eighth British, one-sixteenth Iberian, one-eighth Danish, one-sixteenth Flemish, one-thirty-secondth part Roman,'—and so forth. Now, Miss Caroline, how much of that can you remember?"

"All of it, I hope, Sir," said I; "I shall try to do so. I like to hear of those old times. But would you please to tell me, what is an Iberian?"

"My dear," said Mr. Cameron, smiling, "I would gladly give you fifty pounds in gold, if you could tell me."

"Sir!" cried I, in great surprise.

He went on, more as if he were talking to himself, or to some very learned man, than to me.

"What is an Iberian? Ah, for the man who could tell us! What is a Basque?—what is an Etruscan?—what is a Magyar?—above all, what is a Cagot? Miss Caroline, my dear, there are deep questions in all arts

and sciences; and, without knowing it, you have lighted
on one of the deepest and most interesting. The most
learned man that breathes can only answer you, as I
do now (though I am far from being a learned man)—
I do not know. I will, nevertheless, willingly tell you
what little I do know; and the rather if you take an
interest in such matters. All that we really know of
the Iberii is that they came from Spain, and that they
had reached that country from the East; that they
were a narrow-headed people (the Celts or later Britons
were round-headed); that they dwelt in rude houses in
the interior of the country, first digging a pit in the
ground, and building over it a kind of hut, sometimes
of turf and sometimes of stone; that they wore very
rude clothing, and were generally much less civilised
than the Celts, who lived mainly on the coast; that
they loved to dwell, and especially to worship, on a
mountain top; that they followed certain Eastern ob-
servances, such as running or leaping through the fire
to Bel,—which savours of a Phœnician or Assyrian
origin; and that it is more than likely that we owe
to them those stupendous monuments yet standing—
Stonehenge, Abury, the White Horse of Berkshire,
and the White Man of Wilmington."

"But what sort of a religion had they, if you please,
Sir?" said I; for I wanted to get to know all I could
about these strange fathers of ours.

"Idolatry, my dear, as you might suppose," answered
Mr. Cameron. "They worshipped the sun, which they
identified with the serpent; and they had, moreover, a

sacred tree—all, doubtless, relics of Eden. They would appear also to have had some sort of woman-worship, for they held women in high honour, loved female sovereignty, and practised polyandry—that is, each woman had several husbands."

" I never heard of such queer folks ! " said I. " And what became of them, Sir ? "

" The Iberians and Celts together," he answered, "made up the people we call Britons. When the Saxons invaded the country, they were driven into the remote fastnesses of Wales, Cumberland, and Cornwall. Some antiquaries think the Picts had the same original, but this is one of the unsettled points of history."

" I wish it were possible to settle all such questions ! " said Flora.

" So do the antiquaries, I can assure you," returned Mr. Cameron, with a smile. " But it is scarce possible to come to a conclusion with any certainty as to the origin of a people of whom we cannot recover the language."

" If you please, Sir," said I, " what has the language to do with it ? "

" It has everything to do with it, Miss Caroline. You did not know that languages grew, like plants, and could be classified in groups after the same manner ? "

" Please explain to us, Mr. Cameron," said Flora. " It all sounds so strange."

" But it is very interesting," I said. " I want to know all about it."

" If you want to know *all* about it," answered our

friend, " you must consult some one else than me, for I do not know nearly all about it. In truth, no one does. For myself, I have only arrived at the stage of knowing that I know next to nothing."

"That's easy enough to know, surely," said Angus.

"Not at all, Angus. It is one of the most difficult things to ascertain in this world. No man is so ready to give an off-hand opinion on any and every subject, as the man who knows absolutely nothing. But we must not start another hare while the young ladies' question remains unanswered. Languages, my dears, are not made; they grow. The first language—that spoken in Eden—may have been given to man ready-made, by God; but I rather imagine, from the expressions of Holy Writ, that what was granted to Adam was the inward power of forming a tongue which should be rational and consistent with itself; and, if so, no doubt it was granted to Eve that she should understand him—perhaps that she should possess a similar power."

"The woman made the language, Sir, you may be sure," said Angus. "They are shocking chatterers."

"Unfortunately, my boy, Scripture is against you. 'Whatsoever Adam'—not Eve—'called the name of every living creature, that was the name thereof.' To proceed:—The confusion of tongues at Babel seems, from what we can gather, to have called into being a number of languages quite separate from each other, yet all having a certain affinity. The structure differs; but some of the words are alike, or at least so nearly alike that the resemblance can be traced. Take the word for 'father' in all languages: cut down to its root, there is the same root found in all. *Ab* in Hebrew, *abba* in Syriac, *pater* in Greek and Latin, *vater* in Low Dutch, *père* in French, *padre* in Spanish and Italian, *father* in English—ay, even the child's *papa* and the infant's *daddy*—all come from one root. But this cutting away of superfluities to get at the root, is precisely what a 'prentice hand should not attempt; like an unskilled gardener, he will prune away the wrong branches."

"Then, Sir," I asked, "what are the languages which belong to the same class as ours?"

"Ours, young lady, is a composite language. It may almost be said to be made up of bits of other languages. German or Low Dutch is its mother, and the Scandinavian group—Swedish, Danish, and so forth—may be termed its aunts. It belongs mostly to what is called the Teutonic group; but there are in it traces of Celtic, and though more dimly perceptible, even of Latin and Oriental tongues. We are altogether a made-up nation —to which fact some say that we owe those excellences on which we are so fond of priding ourselves."

"Please, Sir, what are they?" I asked.

Mr. Cameron seemed much amused at the question.

"What are the excellences we have?" said he; "or, what are those on which we pride ourselves? They are often not the same. And—notice it, young ladies, as you go through life—the virtue on which a man plumes himself the most highly is very frequently one which he possesses in small measure. (I do not say, in *no* measure.) Well, I suppose the qualities on which we English——"

"We are not English!" cried Angus, hotly.

"For this purpose we are," was Mr. Cameron's answer. "As I observed before, the Lowland Scots and the northern English are one tribe. But I was going to say, when you were so rude as to interrupt me, English *and* Scots, young gentleman."

Angus growled out, "Beg your pardon."

"Take it," said Mr. Cameron, pleasantly. "Now for the question. On what good qualities do we plume ourselves? Well, I think, on steadiness, independence, loyalty, truthfulness, firmness, honesty, and love of fair play. How far we are justified in doing so, perhaps other nations are the better judges. They, I believe, generally regard us as a proud and surly race—qualities on which there is no occasion to plume ourselves."

"Much loyalty we have got to glory in!" said Angus.

"We have always tried," replied Mr. Cameron, "to run loyalty and liberty together; and when the two pull smoothly, undoubtedly the national chaise gets along the best. Unhappily, when harnessed to the same chariot, one of those steeds is very apt to kick over the traces. But we will not venture on such delicate ground, seeing that our political colours differ; nor is this the time to do it, for here is the inn where we are to dine."

When we drove up to the manse on Wednesday, the door stood open, and in the doorway was Helen Raeburn, who had evidently seen our chaise, and was waiting for us. Flora was out the first, and she and Helen flew into one another's arms, and hugged and kissed each other as if they could never leave off. I was surprised to find Helen so old. I thought Elspie's niece would have been between thirty and forty; and she looks more like sixty. Then Flora flew into the house to find her father, and Helen turned to me.

"You're vara welcome, young leddy," said she, "and the Lord make ye a blessin' amang us. Will ye come ben the now? Miss Flora, she's aff to find the minister, bless her bonnie face!—but if ye'll please to come awa' wi' me, I'll show ye the way.—Maister Angus, my laddie, welcome hame!—are ye grown too grand to kiss your auld nursie, my callant?"

Angus gave her a kiss, but not at all like Flora; rather as if he had it to do, and wanted to get it over.

"Well, Helen!" said Mr. Cameron, as he came down from the chaise, "and how goes the world with you, my woman?"

"I wish ye a gude evening, Mr. Alexander," said she. "The warld gaes vara weel wi' me, thanks to ye for speirin'. No that the warld's onie better, but the Lord turns all to gude for His ain. The minister's in his study, and he'll be blithe to see ye. Now, my lassie—I ask your pardon, but ye see I'm used to Miss Flora."

"Please call me just what you like," I said, and I followed Helen up a little passage paved with stone, and into a room on the right hand, where I found Flora standing by a tall fine-looking man, who had his arm round her shoulders, and who was so like her that he could only be her father. Flora's face was lighted up as I had seen it but once before—so bright and happy she looked!

"And here is our young guest, your cousin," said my Uncle Drummond, turning to me with a very kind smile. "My dear, may your stay be profitable and pleasant among us,—ay, and mayest thou find favour in the eyes of the God of Israel, under whose wings thou art come to trust!"

It sounded very strange to me. Did these people pray about everything? I had heard Father speak contemptuously of "praying Presbyters," and I thought Uncle Drummond must be one of that sort. But I could not see that a minister looked at all different from a clergyman. They seemed to me very much the same sort of creature.

Mr. Cameron was to stay the night at the manse, and to go on in the morning to his own home, which is about fourteen miles further. Flora carried me off to her chamber, where she and I were to sleep, and we changed our travelling dresses, and had a good wash, and then came down to supper. During the evening Mr. Cameron said, laughingly,—

"Well, my fair maid who objects to the South, have you digested the Iberii?"

"I think I have remembered all you told us, Sir," said I; "but if you please, I am very sorry, but I am afraid we do come from the South. Our family, I

mean. My father's father, I believe, belonged Wiltshire; and his father, who was a captain in the navy,
was a Courtenay of Powderham, whatever that means.
My sister Fanny knows all about it, but I don't understand it—only I am afraid we must have come from
the South."

Mr. Cameron laughed, and so did my Uncle Drummond and Flora.

"Don't you, indeed, young lady?" said the first.
"Well, it only means that you have half the kings of
England and France, and a number of emperors of the
East, among your forefathers. Very blue blood indeed,
Miss Caroline. I do not see how, with that pedigree,
you could be anything but a Tory. Mr. Courtenay is
rather warm that way, I understand."

"Oh, Father is as strong as he can be," said I. "I
should not dare to talk of the Elector of Hanover by
any other name if he heard me."

"Well, you may call that gentleman what you please
here," said Mr. Cameron; "but I usually style him
King George."

"Nay, Sandy, do not teach the child to disobey her
father," said my Uncle Drummond. "The Fifth Command is somewhat older than the Brunswick succession
and the Act of Settlement."

"A little," said Mr. Cameron, drily.

"Little Cary," said my uncle, softly, turning to me,
"do you know that you are very like somebody?"

"Like whom, Uncle?" said I.

"Somebody I loved very much, my child," he

answered, rather sadly; "from whom Angus has his blue eyes, and Flora her smile."

"You mean Aunt Jane," said I, speaking as softly as he had done, for I felt that she had been very dear to him.

"Yes, my dear," he replied; "I mean my Jeannie. You are very like her. I think we shall love each other, Cary."

I thought so too.

Mr. Cameron left us this morning. To-day I have been exploring with Flora, who wants to go all over the house and garden and village—speaks of her pet plants as if they were old friends, and shakes hands with every one she meets, and pats every dog and cat in the place. And they all seem so glad to see her—the dogs included; I do not know about the cats. As we went down the village street, it was quite amusing to hear the greetings from every doorway.

"Atweel, Miss Flora, ye've won hame!" said one.

"How's a' wi' ye, my bairn?" said another.

"A blessing on your bonnie e'en, my lassie!" said a third.

And Flora had the same sort of thing for all of them. It was, "Well, Jeannie, is your Maggie still in her place?" or, "I hope Sandy's better now?" or, "Have you lost your pains, Isabel?" She seemed to know all about each one. I was quite diverted to hear it all. They all appeared rather shy with me, only very kindly; and when Flora introduced me as "her cousin from England," which she did in every cottage, they had all something kind to say : that they hoped I was well after my journey, or they trusted I should like Scotland, or something of that sort. Two told me I was a bonnie lassie. But at last we came to a shut door—most were open—and Flora knocked and waited for an answer. She said gravely to me,—

"A King's daughter lies here, Cary, waiting for her Father's chariot to take her home."

A fresh-coloured, middle-aged woman came to the door, and I was surprised to hear Flora say, "How is your grandmother, Elsie ? "

" She's mickle as ye laft her, Miss Flora, only weaker; I'm thinkin' she'll no be lang the now. But come ben, my bonnie lassie ; you're as welcome as flowers in May. And how's a' wi' ye ? "

Flora answered as we were following Elsie down the chamber and round a screen which boxed off the end of it. Behind the screen was a bed, and on it lay, as I thought, the oldest woman on whom I ever set my eyes. Her face was all wrinkled up, yet there was a fresh colour in her cheeks, and her eyes, though much sunk, seemed piercingly bright.

" Ye're come at last," she said, in a low clear voice, as Flora sat down on the bed, and took the wrinkled brown hand in hers.

" Yes, dear Mirren, come at last," said she. " I'm very glad to get home."

" Ay, and that's what I'll be the morn."

" So soon, Mirren ? "

" Ay, just sae soon. I askit Him to let me bide

while ye came hame. I aye thocht I wad fain see ye ance mair—my Miss Flora's lad's lassie. He's gi'en me a' that ever I askit Him—but ane thing, an' that was the vara desire o' my heart."

"You mean," said Flora, gently, "you wanted Ronald to come home?"

"Ay, I wanted him to come hame frae the far country!" said old Mirren with a sigh. "I'd ha'e likit weel to see him come hame to Abbotscliff—vara weel. But I longed mickle mair to see him come hame to the Father's house. It's no for his auld minnie to see that. But if it's for the Lord to see some ither day, I'm content. And He has gi'en me sae monie things that I ne'er askit Him wi' ane half the longing that I did for that, I dinna think He'll say me nay the now."

"Is He with you, Mirren dear?"

I could not imagine how Flora thought Mirren was to know that. But she answered, with a light in those bright eyes,—

"Ay, my doo. 'His left haun' is under my heid, and His richt haun' doth embrace me.'"

I sat and listened in wonder. It all sounded so strange. Yet Flora seemed to understand. And I had such an unpleasant sense of being outside, and not understanding, as I never felt before, and I did not like it a bit. I knew quite well that if Father had been there, he would have said it was all stuff and cant. But I did not feel so sure of my Aunt Kezia. And suppose it were not cant, but was something unutterably real,— something that I ought to know, and must know some

day, if I were ever to get to Heaven! I did not like
it. I felt that I was among a new sort of people—
people who lived, as it were, in a different place from
me—a sort of whom I had never seen one before (that
did not come from Abbotscliff) except my Aunt Kezia,
and there were differences between her and them. My
Uncle Drummond and Flora, and Mr. Keith, and this
old Mirren, and I thought Helen Raeburn and Mr.
Cameron, all belonged this new sort of people. The
one who did not seem to belong them was Angus.
Yet I did not like Angus nearly so well as the rest.
And yet he belonged my sort of people. It was a
puzzle altogether, and not a pleasant puzzle. And
how anybody was to get out of the one set into the
other set, I could not tell at all.

Stop! I did know one other person at Brocklebank
who belonged this new sort of people. It was Ephraim
Hebblethwaite. He was not, I thought—well, I don't
know how to put it—he did not seem so far on the
road as the others; only he was on that road, and not
on this road. And then it struck me, too, whether old
Elspie, and perhaps Sam, were not on the road as well.
I ran over in my mind, as I was walking back to the
manse with Flora, who was very silent, all the people
I knew; and I could not think of one other who might
be on Flora's road. Father and my sisters, Esther
Langridge, the Catteralls, the Bracewells, Cecilia—oh
dear, no!—Mr. Digby, Mr. Bagnall (yet they were
parsons), Mr. Parmenter—no, not one. At all the four
I named last, my mind gave a sort of jump as if it

were quite astonished to be asked the question. But where did the roads lead? Flora and her sort, I felt quite sure, were going to Heaven. Then where were Angus and I and all the rest going?

And I did not like the answer at all.

But I felt that the two roads led in opposite ways, and they could not both go to one place.

As we walked up the path to the manse, Helen came out to meet us.

"My lassie," she said to Flora, "there's Miss Annas i' the garden, and Leddy Monksburn wad ha'e ye gang till Monksburn for a dish o' tea, and Miss Cary wi' ye."

Flora's face lighted up.

"Oh, how delightful!" she said. "Come, Cary— come and see Annas Keith."

I was very curious to see Annas, and I followed willingly. Under the old beech at the bottom of the garden sat a girl-woman—she was not either, but both —in a gown of soft camlet, which seemed as if it were part of her; I do not mean so much in the fit of it, as in the complete suitableness of it and her. Her head was bent down over a book, and I could not see her face at first—only her hair, which was neither light nor dark, but had a kind of golden shimmer. Her hat lay beside her on the seat. Flora ran down the walk with a glad cry of "Annas!" and then she stood up, and I saw Annas Keith.

A princess! was my first thought. I saw a tall, slight figure, a slender white throat, a pure pale face, dark grey eyes with black lashes, and a soul in them. Some people have no souls in their eyes. Annas Keith has.

Yet I could not have said then, and I cannot say now, when I try to recall her picture in my mind's eye, whether Annas Keith is beautiful. It does not seem the right word to describe her: and yet "ugly" would be much further off. She is one of those women about whose beauty or want of beauty you never think unless you are trying to describe them, and then you cannot tell what to say about it. She takes you captive. There is a charm about her that I cannot put into words. Only it is as different from the spell that Cecilia Osborne threw over me (at first) as light differs from darkness. The charm about Annas feels as if it lifted me higher, into a purer air. Whenever I had been long with Cecilia, my mind felt soiled, as if I had been breathing bad air.

When Flora introduced me, Miss Keith turned and kissed me, and I felt as if I had been presented to a queen.

"We want to know you," she said. "All Flora'friends are our friends. You will come, both of you?"

"I thank you, Miss Keith," said I. "I should like to come very much."

"Annas, please," she said quietly, with that sweet smile of hers. It is only when she smiles that she reminds me of her brother.

"And how are the Laird and Lady Monksburn?" said Flora.

I did not know that the Laird (as they always seem

to call the squires here) had been a titled gentleman :
and I said so.   Annas smiled.

"Our titles will seem odd to you," said she. "We call
a Scots gentleman by the name of his estate, and every
laird's wife is 'Lady'—only by custom and courtesy,
you understand.   My mother really is only Mrs. Keith,
but you will hear everybody call her Lady Monksburn."

"Then if my father were here, they would call
him——" I hesitated, and Flora ended the sentence
for me.

"The Laird of Brocklebank ; and if you had a mother
she would be Lady Brocklebank."

I thought it sounded rather pleasant.

"And when is Duncan coming home ?" asked Flora.

"To-morrow, or the day after, we hope," said Annas.

I noticed that she had less of the Scots accent than
Flora ; and Mr. Keith has it scarcely at all.   I found
after a while that Lady Monksburn is English, and that
Annas has spent much of her life in England.   I wanted
to know what part of England it was, and she said,
"The Isle of Wight."

"Why, then you do really come from the South !"
cried I.   "Do tell me something about it.   Are there
any agreeable people there ?—I mean, except you."

Annas laughed.   "I hope you have seen few people
from the South," said she, "if that be your impression
of them."

"Only two," said I ; "and I did not like either of
them one bit."

"Well, two is no large acquaintance," said Annas.

" Let me assure you that there are plenty of agreeable people in the South, and good people also; though I will not say that they are not different from us in the North. They speak differently, and their manners are more polished."

" But it is just that polish I feel afraid of," I replied. " It looks to me so like a mask. If we are bears in the North, at least we mean what we say."

" I do not think you need fear a polished Christian," said Annas. " A worldly man, polished or unpolished, may do you hurt."

" But are we not all Christians ? " said I. And the words were scarcely out of my lips when the thoughts came back to me which had been tormenting me as we walked up from old Mirren's cottage. Those two roads! Did Annas mean that only those were Christians who took the higher one ? Only, what was there in the air of Abbotscliff which seemed to make people Christians? or in that of Brocklebank, which seemed unfavourable to it ?

"Those are Christians who follow Christ," said Annas. "Do you think they who do not, have a right to the name ? "

" I should like to think more about it," I answered. " It all looks strange to me."

" Do think about it," replied Annas.

When we came to Monksburn, which is about a mile from the manse, I found it was a most charming place on the banks of the Tweed. The lawn ran sloping down to the river; and the house was a lovely old building of grey stone, in some places almost lost in ivy. Annas said it had been the Abbots' grange belonging to the old Abbey which gives its name to Abbotscliff and Monksburn, and several other estates and villages in the neighbourhood. Here we found Lady Monksburn in the drawing-room, busied with some soft kind of embroidered work; and I thought I could have guessed her to be the mother of Mr. Keith. Then when the Laird came in, I saw that his grey eyes were Annas's, though I should not call them alike in other respects.

Lady Monksburn is a dear old lady; and as she comes from the South, I must never say a word against Southerners again. She took both my hands in her soft white ones, and spoke to me so kindly that before I had known her ten minutes I was almost surprised to find myself chattering away to her as if she were quite an old friend—telling her all about Brocklebank, and my sisters, and Father, and my Aunt Kezia. I could not tell how it was,—I felt so completely at home in that Monksburn drawing-room. Everybody was so kind, and seemed to want me to enjoy myself, and yet there was no fuss about it. If those be southern manners, I wish I could catch them, like small-pox. But perhaps they are Christian manners. That may be it. And I don't suppose you can catch that like the small-pox. However, I certainly did enjoy myself this afternoon. Mr. Keith, I find, can draw beautifully, and they let me look through some of his portfolios, which was delightful. And when Annas, at her mother's desire, sat down to the harpsichord, and sang us some old

Scots songs, I thought I never heard anything so charming—until Flora joined in, and then it was more delicious still.

I think it would be easy to be good, if one lived at Monksburn!

Those grey eyes of Annas's seem to see everything. I am sure she saw that Flora would like a quiet talk with Lady Monksburn, and she carried me to see her peacocks and silver pheasants, which are great pets, she says; and they are so tame that they will come and eat out of her hand. Of course they were shy with me. Then we had a charming little walk on the path which ran along by the side of the river, and Annas pointed out some lovely peeps through the trees at the scenery beyond. When we came in, I saw that Flora had been crying; but she seemed so much calmer and comforted, that I am sure her talk had done her good. Then came supper, and then Angus, who had cleared up wonderfully, and was more what he used to be as a boy, instead of the cross, gloomy young man he has seemed of late. Lady Monksburn offered to send a servant with arms to accompany us home, but Angus appeared to think it quite unnecessary. He had his dirk and a pistol, he said; and surely he could take care of two girls! I am not sure that Flora would not rather have had the servant, and I know I would. However, we came safe to the manse, meeting nothing more terrific than a white cow, which wicked Angus tried to persuade us was a lady without a head.

CHAPTER VI.

NEW IDEAS FOR CARY.

> " O Jesu, Thou art pleading,
>   In accents meek and low,
> ' I died for you, My children,
>   And will ye treat Me so ?'
> O Lord, with shame and sorrow,
>   We open now the door :
> Dear Saviour, enter, enter,
>   And leave us never more ! "
>
> —BISHOP WALSHAM HOW.

AS we drank our tea, this evening, I said,—

" Uncle, will you please tell me something ? "

" Surely, my dear, if I can," answered my Uncle Drummond kindly, laying down his book.

" Are all the people at Abbotscliff going to Heaven ? "

I really meant it, but my Uncle Drummond put on such a droll expression, and Angus laughed so much, that I woke up to see that they thought I had said something very queer. When my uncle spoke, it was not at first to me.

" Flora," said he, " where have you taken your cousin ? "

" Only into the cottages, Father, and to Monksburn,"

said Flora, in a diverted tone, as if she were trying not to laugh.

"Either they must all have had their Sabbath manners on," said my Uncle Drummond, "or else there are strange folks at Brocklebank. No, my dear; I fear not, by any means."

"I am afraid," said I, "we must be worse folks at Brocklebank than I thought we were. But these seem to me, Uncle, such a different kind of people—as if they were travelling on another road, and had a different end in view. Nearly all the people I see here seem to think more of what they ought to do, and at Brocklebank we think of what we like to do."

I did not, somehow, like to say right out what I really meant—to the one set God seemed a Friend, to the other He was a Stranger.

"Do you hear, Angus, what a good character we have?" said my Uncle Drummond, smiling. "We must try to keep it, my boy."

Of course I could not say that I did not think Angus was included in the " we." But the momentary trouble in Flora's eyes, as she glanced at him, made me feel that she saw it, as indeed I could have guessed from what I had heard her say to Mr. Keith.

"Well, my lassie," my Uncle Drummond went on, "while I fear we do not all deserve the compliment you pay us, yet have you ever thought what those two roads are, and what end they have in view?"

"Yes, Uncle, I can see that," said I. "Heaven is at the end of one, I am sure."

" And of the other, Cary ? "

I felt the tears come into my eyes.

" Uncle, I don't like to think about that. But do tell me, for that is what I want to know, what is the difference?   I do not see how people get from the one road to the other."

I did not say—but I feel sure that my Uncle Drummond did not need it—that I felt I was on the wrong one.

" Lassie, if you had fallen into a deep tank of water, where the walls were so high that it was not possible you could climb out by yourself, for what would you hope?"

" That somebody should come and help me, I suppose."

" True. And who is the Somebody that can help you in this matter ? "

I thought, and thought, and could not tell. It seems strange that I did not think what he meant. But I had been so used to think of our Lord Jesus Christ as a Person who had a great deal to do with going to church and the Prayer-book, but nothing at all to do with me, that really I did not think what my uncle meant me to say.

" There is but one Man, my child, who can give you any help. And He longed to help you so much, that He came down from Heaven to do it. You know who I mean now, Cary ? "

" You mean our Lord Jesus Christ," I said. " But, Uncle, you say He longed to help?   I never knew that. I always thought——"

"You thought He did not wish to help you at all, and that you would have very hard work to persuade Him?"

'Well—something like it," I said, hesitatingly

Flora had left the room a moment before, and now she put her head in at the door and called Angus. My Uncle Drummond and I were left alone.

"My dear lassie," said he, as tenderly as if I had been his own child, "you would never have wished to be helped if He had not first wished to help you. But remember, Cary, help is not the right word. The true word is *save*. You are not a few yards out of the path, and able to turn back at any moment. You are lost. Dear Cary, will you let the Lord find you?"

"Can I hinder Him?" I said.

"Yes, my dear," was the solemn answer. "He allows Himself to be hindered, if you choose the way of death. He will not save you against your will. He demands your joining in that work. Take, again, the emblem of the tank: the man holds out his hands to you; you cannot help yourself out; but you can choose whether you will put your hands in his or not. It will not be his fault if you are drowned; it will be your own."

"Uncle, how am I to put my hands in *His?*"

"Hold them out to Him, Cary. Ask Him, with all your heart, to take you, and make you His own. And if He refuse, let me know."

"I will try, Uncle," I answered. "But you said— does God *never* save anybody against his will?"

My Uncle Drummond was silent for a moment.

" Well, Cary, perhaps at times He does. But it is not His usual way of working. And no man has any right to expect it in his own case, though we may be allowed to hope for it in that of another."

I wonder very much now, as I write it all down, how I ever came to say all this to my Uncle Drummond. I never meant it at all when I began. I suppose I got led on from one thing to another. When I came to think of it, I was very grateful to Flora for going away and calling Angus after her.

" But, Uncle," I said, recollecting myself suddenly, "how does anybody know when the Lord has heard him ? "

He smiled. " If you were lifted out of the tank and set on dry ground, Cary, do you think you would have much doubt about it ? "

" But I could see that, Uncle."

" Take another emblem, then. You love some people very dearly, and there are others whom you do not like at all. You cannot see love and hate. But have you any doubt whom you love, or whom you dislike ? "

" No," said I,—" at least, not when I really love or dislike them very much. But there are people whom I cannot make up my mind about; I neither like nor dislike them exactly."

" Those are generally people of whom you have not seen much, I think," said my Uncle Drummond ; " or else they are those colourless men and women of whom you say that they have nothing in them. You could not feel so towards a person of decided character, and one whom you knew well."

" No, Uncle ; I do not think I could."

" You may rest assured, my dear, that unless He be an utter Stranger, you will never feel so towards the Lord. When you come to know Him, you must either love or hate Him. You cannot help yourself."

It almost frightened me to hear my Uncle Drummond say that. It must be such a dreadful thing to go wrong on that road !

" Cary," he added suddenly, but very softly, " would you find it difficult to love a man who was going to die voluntarily instead of you ? "

" I do not see how I could help it, Uncle," cried I.

" Then how is it," he asked in the same tone, " that you have any difficulty in loving the Man who has died in your stead ? "

I thought a minute.

" Uncle," I said, " it does not seem real. The other would."

" In other words, Cary—you do not believe it."

" Do not believe it !" cried I. " Surely, Uncle, I believe in our Lord ! Don't I say the Creed every Sunday ? "

" Probably you do, my dear."

" But I do believe it !" cried I again.

" You do believe—what ? " said my Uncle Drummond.

" Why, I believe that Christ came down from Heaven,

and was crucified, dead, and buried, and rose again, and ascended into Heaven. Of course I believe it, Uncle—every bit of it."

" And what has it to do with you, my dear? It all took place a good while ago, did it not?"

I thought again. " I suppose," I said slowly, " that Christ died to save sinners; and I must be a sinner. But somehow, I don't quite see how it is to be put together. Uncle, it seems like a Chinese puzzle of which I have lost a piece, and none of the others will fit properly. I cannot explain it, and yet I do not quite know why."

" Listen, Cary, and I will tell you why."

I did, with both my ears and all my mind.

" Your mistake is a very common one, little lassie. You are trying to believe *what*, and you have got to believe *whom*. If you had to cross a raging torrent, and I offered to carry you over, it would signify nothing whether you knew where I was born, or if I were able to speak Latin. But it would signify a great deal to you whether you knew *me;* whether you believed that I would carry you safe over, or that I would take the opportunity to drop you into the water and run away. Would it not?"

" Of course it would," I said; " the whole thing would depend on whether I trusted you."

My Uncle Drummond rose and laid his hand on my head—not as Mr. Digby used to do, as though he were condescending to a little child; but as if he were blessing me in God's name. Then he said, in that low, soft, solemn tone which sounds to me so very high and holy, as if an angel spoke to me:—" Cary, dear child, the whole thing depends—your soul and your eternity depend—on whether you trust the Lord Jesus."

Then he went out of the room, and left me alone, as if he wanted me to think well about that before he said anything more.

I think something is coming to help me. My Uncle Drummond was late for supper last night—a thing which I could see was very unusual. And when he did come, he was particularly silent and meditative. At length, when supper was over, as we turned our chairs round from the table, and were sitting down again to our work, my Uncle Drummond, who generally goes to his study after supper, sat down among us.

" Young people," said he, with a look on his face which it seemed to me was partly grave and partly diverted, " considering that you are more travelled persons than I, I come to you for information. Have you—any of you—while in England, either seen or heard anything of one Mr. George Whitefield, a clergy-man of the Church of England, who is commonly reckoned a Methodist?"

Angus made a grimace, and said, " Plenty !"

Flora was doubtful ; she thought she had heard his name.

I said, "I have heard his name too, Uncle; but I do not know much about him, only Father seemed to think it a good joke that anybody should fancy him a wise man."

"Angus appears to be the best informed of you," said my uncle. "Speak out, my boy, and tell us what you know."

"Well, he is a queer sort of fellow, I fancy," said Angus. "He was one of the Methodists; but they say those folks have had a split, and Whitefield has broken with them. He travels about preaching, though, as they do; and they say that the reason why he took to field-preaching was because no church would hold the enormous congregations which gathered to hear him. He has been several times to the American colonies, where they say he draws larger crowds than John Wesley himself."

"A good deal of 'They say,'" observed Uncle Drummond, with a smile. "Do 'they say' that the bishops and clergy are friendly to this remarkable preacher, or not?"

"Well, I should rather think *not*," answered Angus. "There is one bishop who has stuck to him through thick and thin—the Bishop of Gloucester, who gave him his orders to begin with; but the rest of them look askance at him over their shoulders, I believe. It is irregular, you know, to preach in fields—wholly improper to save anybody's soul out of church; and these English folks take the horrors at anything irregular. The women like him because he makes them cry so much."

"Angus!" cried Flora and I together.

"That's what I was told, I assure you, young ladies," returned Angus. "I am only repeating what I have heard."

"Well, that you may shortly have an opportunity of judging," said my Uncle Drummond; "for this gentleman has come to Selkirk, and has asked leave of the presbytery to preach in certain kirks of this neighbourhood. There was some demur at first to the admission of a Prelatist; but after some converse with him this was withdrawn, and he will preach next Sabbath morning at Selkirk, and in the afternoon at Monks' Brae. You can go to Monks' Brae to hear him, if you will; I, of course, shall not be able to accompany you, but I trust to find an opportunity when he preaches in the fields, if there be one. I should like to hear this great English preacher, I confess. What say you?"

"They'll go, you may be sure, Sir," said Angus, before we could answer. "Trust a lassie to gad about if she has the chance. Mind you take all the pocket-handkerchiefs you have with you. They say 'tis dreadful the way this man gars you greet. 'Tis true, you English are more given that way than we Scots; but folks say you cannot help yourself,—you must cry, whether you will or no."

"I should like to go, I think, Uncle," said I. "Only—I suppose he is a real clergyman?"

"There goes a genuine Englishwoman!" said Angus. "If Paul himself were to preach, she would not go to hear him till she knew what bishop had ordained him."

"Yes, Cary," answered my Uncle Drummond, smiling; "he is a real clergyman. More 'real' than you think me, I fear."

"Oh, you are different, Uncle," said I; "but I am sure Father would not like me to hear any preacher who was not—at least—I don't know—he did not seem to think this Mr. Whitefield all right, somehow. Perhaps he did not know he was a proper person."

"'A proper person!'" sighed Angus, casting up his eyes.

"My dear," said my Uncle Drummond, kindly, "you are a good lassie to think of your father's wishes. Never mind Angus; he is only making fun, and is a foolish young fellow yet. Of course, not having spoken with your father, I cannot tell so well as yourself what his wishes are; and 'tis quite possible he may think, for I hear many do, that this gentleman is a schismatic, and may disapprove of him on that account only. If so, I can tell you for certain, 'tis a mistake. But as to anything else, you must judge for yourself, and do what you think right."

"You see no objection to our going, Father?" asked Flora, who had not spoken hitherto.

"Not at all, my dear," said my Uncle. "Go by all means, if you like it. You may never have another opportunity, and 'tis very natural you should wish it."

"Thank you," answered Flora. "Then, if Angus will take me, I will go."

"Well, I don't know," said Angus. "I am afraid some of my handkerchiefs are at the wash. I should not like to be quite drowned in my tears. I might wash you away, too; and that would be a national calamity."

"Don't jest on serious subjects, my boy," said Uncle; and Angus grew grave directly. "I am no enemy to honest, rational fun; 'tis human, and natural more especially to the young. But never, never let us make a jest of the things that pertain to God."

"I beg your pardon, Father," said Angus, in a low voice. "I'll take you, Flora. What say you, Cary?"

"Yes, I should like to go," I said. And I wondered directly whether I had said right or wrong. But I do so want to hear something that would help me.

I found that Monks' Brae was on the Monksburn road, but nearly two miles further on. 'Tis the high road from Selkirk to Galashiels, after you leave Monksburn, and pretty well frequented; so that Angus was deemed guard enough. But last night the whole road was so full of people going to hear Mr. Whitefield, that it was like walking in a crowd all the way. The kirk was crammed to the very doors, and outside people stood looking in and listening through the doors and the open windows. Mr. Lundie, the minister of Monks' Brae, led the worship (as they say here); and when the sermon came, I looked with some curiosity at the great preacher who did such unusual things, and whom some people seemed to think it so wrong to like. Mr. Whitefield is not anything particular to look at: just a young man in a fair wig, with a round face and rosy cheeks. He has a most musical voice, and he knows how to put it to the best advantage. Every word is as distinct as can be, and his voice rings out clear and strong, like a well-toned bell. But he had not preached ten minutes before I forgot his voice and himself altogether, and could think of nothing but what he was preaching about. And I never heard such a sermon in my life. My Uncle Drummond's are the only ones I have heard which even approach it, and he does not lift you up and carry you away, as Mr. Whitefield does.

All the other preachers I ever heard, except those two, are always telling you to do something. Come to church, and say your prayers, and take the Sacrament; but particularly, do your duty. Now it always seems to me that there are two grand difficulties in the way of doing one's duty. The first is, to find out what is one's duty. Of course there is the Bible; but, if I may say it with reverence, the Bible has never seemed to have much to do with me. It is all about people who lived ever so long ago, and what they did; and what has that to do with me, Cary Courtenay, and what I am doing? Then suppose I do know what my duty is —and certainly I do in some respects—I am not sure that I can express it properly, but I feel as if I wanted something to come and make me do it. I am like a watch, with all the wheels and springs there, ready to go, but I want somebody to come and wind me up. And I do not know how that is to be done. But Mr. Whitefield made me wish, oh so much! that that unknown somebody would come and do it. I never thought much about it before, until that talk with my Uncle Drummond, and now it feels to be what I want more than anything else.

I cannot write the sermon down: not a page of it.

I think you never can write down on paper the things that stir your very soul. It is the things which just tickle your brains that you can put down in elegant language on paper. When a thing comes close to you, into your real self, and grapples with you, and leaves a mark on you for ever hereafter, whether for good or evil, you cannot write or talk about that,—you can only feel it.

The text was, " What think ye of Christ ? "

Mr. Whitefield saith any man that will may have his sins forgiven, and may know it. I have heard Mr. Bagnall speak of this doctrine, which he said was shocking and wicked, for it gave men licence to live in sin. Mr. Whitefield named this very thing (whereby I saw it had been brought as a charge against him), and showed plainly that it did not tend to destroy good works, but only built them up on a safer and surer foundation. We work, saith he, not for that we would be saved by our works, but out of gratitude that we have been saved by Christ, who commands these works to such as would follow Him. And he quoted an Article of the Church,[1] saying that he desired men to see that he was no schismatic preaching his own fancies, but that the Church whereof he was a minister held the same doctrine. I wonder if Mr. Bagnall knows that, and if he ever reads the Articles.

[1] Art. XII. and XIII. All the members of the Church of England ought to be perfectly familiar with the Articles and Homilies, as the Reformers intended them to be. How else can they know what they profess to hold, when they call themselves members of the Church? If they do not share her opinions, they have no right to use her name.

He spoke much, also, of the new birth, or conversion. I never heard any other preacher, except Uncle, mention that at all. I know Mr. Digby thought it a fanatical notion only fit for enthusiasts. But certainly there are texts in the Bible that speak plainly of it. And Mr. Whitefield saith that we do not truly believe in Christ, unless we so believe as to have Him dwelling in us, and to receive life and nourishment from Him as the branch does from the vine. And St. John says the same thing. How can it be enthusiasm to say what the Bible says?

People seem so dreadfully frightened of what they call enthusiasm.[1] Grandmamma used to say there was nothing more vulgar. But the queer thing is that many of these very people will let you get as enthusiastic as ever you like about a game of cards, or one horse coming in before another in a race, or about politics, or poaching, and things of that sort that have to do with this world. It is about the things of real consequence—things which have to do with your soul and the next world—that you must not get enthusiastic!

May one not have too little enthusiasm, I wonder, as well as too much? Would it not be reasonable to be enthusiastic about things that really signify, and cool about the things that do not?

I want to write down a few sentences which Mr. Whitefield said, that I may not forget them. I do not

---

[1] "Enthusiasm" was the term then usually applied to the doctrines of grace, when the word was used in a religious sense.

know how they came in among the rest. They stuck to me just as they are.[1] He says :—

"Our senses are the landing-ports of our spiritual enemies."

"We must take care of healing before we see sinners wounded."

"The King of the Church has all its adversaries in a chain."

"If other sins have slain their thousands of professing Christians, worldly-mindedness has slain its ten thousands."

"How can any say, 'Lead us not into temptation,' in the morning, when they are resolved to run into it at night ?"

"How many are kept from seeing Christ in glory, by reason of the press!" (That is, he explained, that people are ashamed of being singularly good,[2] unless their acquaintances are on the same side.)

"Christ will thank you for coming to His feast."

When Mr. Whitefield came near the end of his sermon, I thought I could see why people said he made them cry so much. His voice sank into a soft, pleading, tender accent, as if he yearned over the souls before him. His hands were held out as if he were just hold ing out Jesus Christ to us, and we must take Him or turn away and be lost. And he begged us all so piti fully not to turn away. I saw tears running down the

---

[1] These sentences are not taken from any one of Whitefield's sermons exclusively, but are gathered from the gems of thought scattered through his works.

[2] *Singular* still meant *alone* in Whitefield's day.

cheeks of many hard-looking men and women. Flora cried, and so did I. But Angus did not. He did not look as though he felt at all inclined to do it.

This is one of the last sermons, we hear, that Mr. Whitefield will preach on this side the sea. He sails for the American colonies next month. He is said to be very fond of his American friends, and very much liked by them.[1]

As we were coming away, we came upon our friends from Monksburn, whom we had not seen before.

"This is preaching!" said Annas, as she clasped our hands.

"Eh, puir laddie, he'll just wear himself out!" said the Laird. "I hope he has a gude wife, for sic men are rare, and they should be well taken care of while they are here."

"He has a wife, Sir," observed Angus, "and the men of his own kidney think he would be rather better off if he had none."

"Hoots, but I'm sorry to hear it," said the Laird. "What ails her, ken ye, laddie?"

"As I understood, Sir, she had three grave drawbacks. In the first place, she is a widow with a rich jointure."

"That's a queer thing to call a drawback!" said the Laird.

"In the second place, she is a widow with a temper, and a good deal of it."

---

[1] He died at Newbury Port, in New England, in September 1770. America has no nobler possession than the grave of George Whitefield.

"Dinna name it!" cried the Laird, lifting up his hands. "Dinna name it! Eh, puir laddie, but I'm wae for him, gin he's fashed wi' ane o' that sort."

"And in the third place," continued Angus, "I have been told that he may well preach against worldly-mindedness, for he gets enough of it at home. Mrs. Whitefield knows what are trumps, considerably better than she knows where to look in the Bible for her husband's text."

"Dear, dear!" cried Lady Monksburn in her soft voice. "What could the good man be thinking of, to bind such a burden as that upon his life?"

"He thought he had converted her, I believe," said Angus, "but she came undone."

"I should think," remarked Mr. Keith, "that he acted as Joshua did with the Gibeonites."

"How was that?" said Angus.

"It won't hurt you to look for it," was the answer.

I don't know whether Angus looked for it, but I did as soon as I got in, and I saw that Mr. Keith thought there had been too much hastiness, and perhaps a little worldly-mindedness in Mr. Whitefield himself. That may be why he preaches so earnestly against it. We know so well where the slippery places are, when we have been down ourselves. And when we have been down once, we are generally very, very careful to keep off that slide for the future.

Mr. Whitefield said last night that it was not true to say, as some do, "that a man may be in Christ to-day, and go to the Devil to-morrow." Then if anybody is converted, how can he, as Angus said, "come undone"? I only see one explanation, and it is rather a terrible one: namely, that the conversion was not real, but only looked like it. And I am afraid that must be the truth. But what a pity it is that Mr. Whitefield did not find it out sooner!

"Well, Helen, and how did you like the great English preacher?" I said to Flora's nurse.

"Atweel, Miss Cary, the discourse was no that ill for a Prelatist," was the answer.

And that was as much admiration as I could get from Helen.

There was more talk about Mr. Whitefield this morning at breakfast. I cannot tell what has come to Angus. Going to hear Mr. Whitefield preach at Monks' Brae seems to have made him worse instead of better. Flora and I both liked it so much; but Angus talks of it with a kind of bitter hardness in his voice, and as if it pleased him to let us know all the bad things which had been said about the preacher. He told us that they said—(I wish they would give over saying!)—that Mr. Whitefield had got his money matters into some tangle, in the business of building his Orphan House in Georgia; and "they said" he had acted fraudulently in the matter. My Uncle Drummond put this down at once, with—

"My son, never repeat a calumny against a good man. You may not know it, but you do Satan's very work for him."

Angus made a grimace behind his hand, which I

fancy he did not mean his father to see. Then, he went on, "'They say' that **Mr.** Whitefield is so fanatical and extravagant in preaching against worldliness, that he counts it sinful to smell to a rose, or to eat anything relishing."

"Did he say so?" asked my Uncle: "or did 'they' say it for him?"

"Well, Sir," answered Angus with a laugh, "I heard Mr. Whitefield had said that he would give his people leave to smell to a rose and a pink also, so long as they would avoid the appearance of sin: and, quoth he, 'if you can find any diversion which you would be willing to be found at by our Lord in His coming, I give you free licence to go to it and welcome.'"

"Then we have disposed of that charge," saith my Uncle. "What next?"

"Well, they say he hath given infinite displeasure to the English gentry by one of his favourite sayings— that 'Man is half a beast and half a devil.' He will not allow them to talk of 'passing the time'—how dare they waste the time, saith he, when they have the devil and the beast to get out of their souls? Folks don't like, you see, to be painted in those colours."

"No, we rarely admire a portrait that is exactly like us," saith my Uncle Drummond.

"Pray, Sir, think you that is a likeness?" said Angus.

"More like, my son, than you and I think. Some of us have more of the one, and some of the other: but in truth I cannot contradict Mr. Whitefield. 'Tis a just portrait of what man is by nature."

"But, Sir!" cried Angus, "do you allow nothing for a man's natural virtues?"

"What are they?" asked my Uncle. "I allow that 'there is none that doeth good, no, not one.' You were not taught, Angus, that a man had virtues natural to him, except as the Spirit of God implanted them in him."

"No, Sir; but when I go forth into the world, I cannot help seeing that it is so."

"I wish I could see it!" said my Uncle. "It would be a much more agreeable sight than many things I do see."

"Well, Sir, take generosity and good temper," urged Angus. "Do you not see much of these in men who, as Mr. Whitefield would say, are worldly and ungodly?"

"I often see the Lord's restraining grace," answered my Uncle, quietly; "but am I to give the credit of it to those whom He restrains?"

"But think you, Sir, that it is wise——" Angus paused.

"Go on, my boy," said my Uncle. "I like you to speak out, like an honest man. By all means have courage to own your convictions. If they be right ones, you may so have them confirmed; and if they be wrong, you stand in better case to have them put right."

I did not think Angus looked quite comfortable. He hesitated a moment, and then, I suppose, came out with what he had meant to say.

"Think you not, Sir, that it is wise to leave unsaid such things as offend people, and make them turn away from preaching? Should we not be careful to avoid offence?"

"Unnecessary offence," saith my Uncle. "But the offence of the cross is precisely that which we are warned not to avoid. 'Not with wisdom of words,' saith the Apostle, 'lest the cross of Christ should be made of none effect.' In his eyes, 'then is the offence of the cross ceased,' was sufficient to condemn the preaching whereof he spoke. And that policy of keeping back truth is the Devil's policy; 'tis Jesuitical. 'Will ye speak wickedly for God, and talk deceitfully for Him?' 'Shall the throne of iniquity have fellowship with *Thee?*' Never, Angus: never!"

"But our Lord Himself seems to have kept things back from His disciples," pleaded Angus, uneasily.

"Yes, what they were not ready for and could not yet understand. But never that which offended them. He offended them terribly when He told them that the Son of Man was about to be crucified. So did the Jesuits to the Chinese: and when they found the offence, they altered their policy, and said the story of the crucifixion was an invention of Christ's enemies. Did He?"

Angus made no answer: and breakfast being over, we separated to our several work.

CHAPTER VII.

RUMOURS OF WAR.

"They've left their bonnie Highland hills,
Their wives and bairnies dear,
To draw the sword for Scotland's Lord,
The young Chevalier."
—CAROLINE, LADY NAIRN.

YESTERDAY, when Flora and I sat at our sewing in the manse parlour, something happened which has set everything in a turmoil. We had been talking, but we were silent just then: and I was thinking over what my Uncle Drummond and Mr. Whitefield had said, when all at once we heard the gate dashed open, and Angus came rushing up the path with his plaid flying behind him. Flora sprang up and ran to meet him.

"What is the matter?" she said. "'Tis so unlike Angus to come dashing up in that way. I do hope nothing is wrong with Father."

I dropped my sewing and ran after her.

"Angus, what is wrong?" she cried.

"Why should anything be wrong? Can't something be right?" cried Angus, as he came up, and I saw that his checks were flushed and his eyes flashing. "The Prince has landed, and the old flag is flying at Glenfinnan. Hurrah!"

And Angus snatched off his cap, and flung it up so high that I wondered if it would come down again.

"The Prince!" cried Flora; and looking at her, I saw that she had caught the infection too. "O Angus, what news! Who told you? Is it true? Are you quite sure?"

"Sure as the hills. Duncan told me. I have been over to Monksburn, and he has just come home. All the clans in Scotland will be up to-morrow. That was the one thing we wanted—our Prince himself among us. You will hear of no faint hearts now."

"What will the Elector do?" said Flora. "He cannot, surely, make head against our troops."

"Make head! We shall be in London in a month. Sir John Cope has gone to meet Tullibardine at Glenfinnan. I expect he will come back a trifle faster than he went. Long live the King, and may God defend the right!"

All at once, Angus's tone changed, as his eyes fell upon me. "Cary, I hope you are not a traitor in the camp? You look as if you cared nothing about it, and you rather wondered we did."

"I know next to nothing about it, Angus," I answered. "Father would care a great deal; and if I understood it, I dare say I might. But I don't, you see."

"What do I hear!" cried Angus, in mock horror, clasping his hands, and casting up his eyes. "The daughter of Squire Courtenay of Brocklebank knows next to nothing about Toryism! Hear it, O hills and dales!"

"About politics of any sort," said I. "Don't you know, I was brought up with Grandmamma Desborough, who is a Whig so far as she is anything—but she always said it was vulgar to get warm over politics, so I never had the chance of hearing much about it."

"Poor old tabby!" said irreverent Angus.

"But have you heard nothing since you came to Brocklebank?" asked Flora, with a surprised look.

"Oh, I have heard Father toast 'the King over the water,' and rail at the Elector; and I have heard Fanny chant that 'Britons never shall be slaves' till I never wanted to hear the tune again; and I have heard Ambrose Catterall sing Whig songs to put Father in a pet, and heard lots of people talk about lots of things which are to be done when the King has his own again. That is about all I know. Of course I know how the Revolution came about, and all *that:* and I have heard of the war thirty years ago, and the dreadful executions after it——"

"Executions! Massacres!" cried Angus, hotly.

"Well, massacres if you like," said I. "I am sure they were shocking enough to be called any ugly name."

Angus seemed altogether changed. He could not keep to one subject, nor stand still for one minute. I was not much surprised so long as it was only he; but I was astonished when I saw the change which came over my Uncle Drummond. I never supposed he could get so excited about anything which had to do with earth. And yet his first thought was to connect it with Heaven.[1]

I shall never forget the ring of his prayer that night. An exile within sight of home, a prisoner to whom the gates had just been opened, might have spoken in the words and tones that he did.

"Lord, Thou hast been gracious unto Thy land!" "Let them give thanks whom the Lord hath redeemed, and delivered from the hand of the enemy!" That was the key-note of every sentence.

I found, before long, that I had caught the complaint myself. I went about singing "The King shall ha'e his ain again," and got as hot and eager for fresh news as anybody.

"Oh dear, I hope the Prince will conquer the Elector before I go to London," I said to Flora: "for I do not know whatever Grandmamma will say if I go to her in this mood. She always says there is nothing so vulgar as to get enthusiastic over anything. You ought to be calm, composed, collected, and everything else which is cold and begins with C."

Flora laughed, but was grave again directly.

"I expect, Cary, your journey to London is a long way off," said she. "How are you to travel, if all the country be up, and troops going to and fro everywhere?"

"I am sure I don't care if it be," said I. "I would rather stay here, a great deal."

---

[1] The great majority of Scottish Jacobites were Episcopalians and "Moderates," a term equivalent to the English "High and Dry.' There were, however, a very few Presbyterians among them.

I thought we were tolerably warm about the Prince's landing, at Abbotscliff; but when I got to Monksburn, I found the weather still hotter. The Laird is almost beside himself; Mr. Keith as I never saw him before. Annas has the air of an inspired prophetess, and even Lady Monksburn is moved out of her usual quietude, though she makes the least ado of any. News came while we were there, that Sir John Cope had been so hard pressed by the King's army that he was forced to fall back on Inverness; and nothing would suit the Laird but to go out and make a bonfire on the first hill he came to, so as to let people see that something had happened. The Elector, we hear, has come back from Hanover, and his followers are in a panic. I hope they will stay there.

Everybody agrees that the army will march southwards at once after this victory, and that unless my journey could take place directly, I shall have to stay where I am, at least over the winter. The Laird wishes he could get Annas out of the way. If I were going, I believe he would send her with me, to those friends of Lady Monksburn in the Isle of Wight. I thought Lady Monksburn looked rather anxious, and wistful too, when he spoke about it. Annas herself did not seem to care.

"The Lord will not go to the Isle of Wight," she said, quietly.

Oh, if I could feel as they do—that God is everywhere, and that everywhere He is my Friend! And then, my Uncle Drummond's words come back upon me. But *how* do you trust Christ? What have you to do? If people would make things plain!

Well, it looks as if I should have plenty of time for learning. For it seems pretty certain, whatever else is doubtful, that I am a fixture at Abbotscliff.

I wonder if things always happen just when one has made up one's mind that they are not going to happen?

About ten o'clock this morning, Flora and I were sewing in the parlour, just as we have been doing every day since I came here. My Uncle Drummond was out, and Angus was fixing a white cockade in his bonnet. Helen Raeburn put in her head at the door.

"If you please, Miss Cary," said she, "my cousin Samuel wad be fain to speak wi' ye."

For one moment I could not think who she meant. What had I to do with her cousin Samuel? And then, all at once, it flashed upon me that Helen's cousin Samuel was our own old Sam.

"Sam!" I almost screamed. "Has he come from Brocklebank? Oh, is anything wrong at home?"

"There's naething wrang ava, Miss Cary, but a hantle that's richt—only ane thing belike—and that's our loss mair than yours. But will ye see Samuel?"

"Oh, yes!" I cried. And Flora bade Helen bring him in.

In marched Sam—the old familiar Sam, though he had put on a flowered waistcoat and a glossy green tie which made him look rather like a Merry Andrew.

"Your servant, ladies! Your servant, Maister Angus! I trust all's weel wi' ye the morn?"

And Sam sighed, as if he felt relieved after that speech.

"Sam, is all well at home?   Who sent you?"

"All's weel, Miss Cary, the Lord be thanked.   And Mrs. Kezia sent me."

"Is my Aunt Kezia gone to her new house?   Does she want me to come back?"

"Thank goodness, na!" said Sam, which at first I thought rather a poor compliment; but I saw the next minute that it was the answer to my first question. "Mrs. Kezia's gone nowhere.   Nor they dinna want ye back at Brocklebank nae mair.   I'm come to ha'e a care of ye till London town.   The Lord grant I win hame safe mysel' at after!"

"Is the country so disturbed, Sam?" said Flora.

"The country's nae disturbed, Miss Flora.   I was meanin' temptations and sic like.   Leastwise, ay—the country is a bit up and down, as ye may say; but no sae mickle.   We'll win safe eneuch to London, me and Miss Cary, if the Lord pleases.   It's the comin' hame I'm feared for."

"And is——" I hardly knew how to ask what I wanted to know.   Flora helped me.   I think she saw I needed it.

"Was the wedding very grand, Sam?"

"Whose wedding, Miss Flora?   There's been nae weddings at Brocklebank, but Ben Dykes and auld Bet Donnerthwaite, and I wish Ben joy on't.   I am fain he's no me."

"Nay, you are fain you are no he," laughed Angus.

"I'm fain baith ways, Maister Angus. The Laird 'd hae his table ill served gin Ben tried his haun'."

"But what do you mean, Sam?" cried I. "Has not——"

I stopped again, but Sam helped me out himself.

"Na, Miss Cary, there's nae been siccan a thing, the Lord be thanked! She took pepper in the nose, and went aff a gude week afore it suld ha'e been; and a gude riddance o' ill rubbish, say I. Mrs. Kezia and Miss Sophy, they are at hame, a' richt: and Miss Hatty comes back in a twa-three days, without thae young leddies suld gang till London toun, and gin they do she'll gang wi' 'em."

"Father is not married?" I exclaimed.

"He's better aff," said Sam, determinately. "I make na count o' thae hizzies."

How glad I felt! Though Father might be sorry at first, I felt so sure he would be thankful afterwards. As for the girl who had jilted him, I thought I could have made *her* into mincemeat. But I was so glad of his escape.

"The Laird wad ha'e had ye come wi' yon lanky loon wi' the glass of his e'e," went on Sam: "he was bound frae Carlisle to London this neist month. But Mrs. Kezia, she wan him o'er to send me for ye. An' I was for to say that gin the minister wad like Miss Flora to gang wi' ye, I micht care ye baith, or onie ither young damsel wha's freens wad like to ha'e her sent soothwards."

"O Flora!" I cried at once—"Annas!"

"Yes, we will send word to Monksburn," answered

Flora: and Angus jumped up and said he would walk over.

"As for me," said Flora, turning to Sam, "I must hear my father's bidding. I do not think I shall go—not if I may stay with him. But the Laird of Monksburn wishes Miss Keith to go south, and I think he would be glad to put her in your care."

"And I'd be proud to care Miss Annas," said Sam, with a pull at his forelock. "I mind her weel, a bit bonnie lassie. The Laird need nae fear gin she gangs wi' me. But I'd no ha'e said sae mickle for yon puir weak silken chiel wi' the glass in his e'e."

"Why, Sam, who do you mean?" said I.

"Wha?" said Sam. "Yon pawky chiel, the auld Vicar's nevey—Maister Parchmenter, or what ye ca' him—a bonnie ane to guard a pair o' lassies he'd be!"

"Mr. Parmenter!" cried I. "Did Father think of sending us with him?"

"He just did, gin Mrs. Kezia had nae had mair wit nor himsel'. She sent ye her loving recommend, young leddies, and ye was to be gude lassies, the pair o' ye, and no reckon ye kent better nor him that had the charge o' ye."

"Sam, you put that in yourself," said Angus.

"Atweel, Sir, Mrs. Kezia said she hoped they'd be gude lassies, and discreet—that's as true as my father's epitaph."

"Where is Miss Osborne gone, Sam?" asked Flora.

"Gin naebody wants to ken mair than me, Miss Flora, there'll no be mickle speiring. I'm only sure o' ane place where she'll no be gane, I'm thinkin', and that's Heaven."

"You don't seem to me to have fallen in love with her, Sam," said Angus, who appeared exceedingly amused.

"Is't me, Sir? Ma certie, but gin there were naebody in this haill warld but her an' me, I'd tak' a lodging for her in the finest street I could find i' London toun, an' I'd be aff mysel' to the Orkneys by the neist ship as left the docks. I wad, sae!"

Angus laughed till he cried, and Flora and I were not much better. He went at once to Monksburn, and came back with tidings that the Laird was very glad of the opportunity to send Annas southwards. And when my Uncle Drummond came in, though his lip trembled and her eyes pleaded earnestly, he said Flora must go too.

And to-night Mr. Keith brought news that men were up all over the Highlands, and that the Prince was marching on Perth.

My Uncle Drummond says we must go at once— there is not to be a day's delay that can be helped. Mr. Keith and Angus are both to join the Prince as soon as they can be ready. My Uncle will go with us himself to Hawick, and then Sam will go on with us to Carlisle, where we are to wait one day, while Sam rides over to Brocklebank to fetch and exchange such things as we may need, and if we can hear of any friend of Father's or my Uncle's who is going south, we are to join their convoy. The Laird of Monksburn sends one of his men with us; and both he and Sam will be well armed. I am sure I hope there will be no occasion for the arms.

Angus is in a mental fever, and dashes about, here, there, and everywhere, without apparent reason, and also without much consideration. I mean consideration in both senses—reflection, and forbearance. Flora is grave and anxious—I think, a little frightened, both for herself and Angus. Mr. Keith takes the affair very seriously; that I can see, though he does not say much. Annas seems (now that the first excitement is over) as calm as a summer eve. We are to start, if possible, on Friday, and sleep at Hawick the first night.

"Hech, Sirs!" was Helen's comment, when she heard it. "My puir bairns, may the Lord be wi' ye! It's ill setting forth of a Friday."

"Clashes and clavers!" cries Sam, turning on her. "Helen Raeburn, ye're just daft! Is the Lord no sae strang o' Friday as ither days? What will fules say neist?"

"Atweel, ye may lauch, Sam, an' ye will," answered Helen: "but I tell ye, I ne'er brake my collar-bone of a journey but ance, and that was when I'd set forth of a Friday."

"And I ne'er brake mine ava, and I've set forth monie a time of a Friday," returned Sam. "Will ye talk sense, woman dear, gin women maun talk?"

I do feel so sorry to leave Abbotscliff. I wish I were not going to London. And I do not quite like to ask myself why. I should not mind going at all, if it were only a change of place. Abbotscliff is very lovely, but there is a great deal in London that I should like to see. If I were to lead the same sort of life as here, and with the same sort of people, I should be quite satisfied to go. But I know it will be very different. Everything will be changed. Not only the people, but the ways of the people. Instead of breezy weather there will be hot crowded rooms, and instead of the Tweed rippling over the pebbles there will be noisy music and empty chatter. And it is not so much that I am afraid it will be what I shall not like. It will at first, I dare say: but I am afraid that in time I shall get to like it, and it will drive all the better things out of my head, and I shall just become one of those empty chatterers. I am sure there is danger of it. And I do not know how to help it. It is pleasant to please people, and to make them laugh, and to have them say how pretty, or how clever you are: and then one gets carried away, and one says things one never meant to say, and the things go and do something which one never meant to do. And I should not like to be another of my Aunt Dorothea!

I do not think there is half the fear for Flora that there is for me. She does not seem to get carried off her mind's feet, as it were: there is something solid underneath her. And it is not at all certain that Flora will be there. If she be asked to stay, Uncle says, she may please herself, for he knows she can be trusted: but if Grandmamma or my Aunt Dorothea do not ask her, then she goes on with Annas to her friends, who, Annas says, will be quite delighted to see her.

I do so wish that Flora might stay with me!

M

This afternoon we went over to Monksburn to say farewell.

Flora and Annas had a good deal to settle about our journey, and all the people and things we were leaving behind. They went into the garden, but I asked leave to stay. I did so want a talk with Lady Monksburn on two points. I thought, I hardly know why, that she would understand me.

I sat for a few minutes, watching her bright needles glance in and out among the soft wools: and at last I brought out the less important of my two questions. If she answered that kindly, patiently, and as if she understood, the other was to come after. If not, I would keep it to myself.

"Will you tell me, Madam—is it wrong to pray about anything? I mean, is there anything one ought not to pray about?"

Lady Monksburn looked up, but only for a moment.

"Dear child!" she said, with a gentle smile, "is it wrong to tell your Father of something you want?"

"But may one pray about things that do not belong to church and Sunday and the Bible?" said I.

"Everything belongs to the Bible," said she. "It is the chart for the voyage of life. You mean, dear heart, is it right to pray about earthly things which have to do with the body? No doubt it is. 'Give us this day our daily bread.'"

"But does that mean real, common bread?" I asked. "I thought people said it meant food for the soul."

"People say very foolish things sometimes, my dear.

It may include food for the soul, and very likely does. But I think it means food for the body first. ' Your Father knoweth that ye have need of all these things.' That, surely, was said of meat and drink and clothing."

I thought a minute. " But I mean more than that," I said; "things that one wishes for, which are not necessaries for the body, and yet are not things for the soul."

" Necessaries for the mind?" suggested Lady Monksburn. " My dear, your mind is a part of you as much as your body and spirit. And ' He careth for *you*,' body, soul, and spirit—not the spirit only, and not the spirit and body only."

" For instance," I said, "suppose I wanted very much to go somewhere, or not to go somewhere—for reasons which seemed good ones to me—would it be wicked to ask God to arrange it so ? "

Lady Monksburn looked up at me with her gentle, motherly eyes.

" Dear child," she said, " you may ask God for anything in all the world, if only you will bear in mind that He loves you, and is wiser than you. ' Father, if it be possible,—nevertheless, not My will, but Thine, be done.' You cannot ask a more impossible thing than that which lay between those words. If the world were to be saved, if God were to be glorified, it was not possible. Did He not know that who asked it with strong crying and tears ? Was not the asking done to teach us two things—that He was very man, like ourselves, shrinking from pain and death as much as the very weakest of us can shrink, and also that we

may ask anything and everything, if only we desire
beyond it that God's will be done?"

"Thank you," I said, drawing a long breath. Yes,
I might ask my second question.

"Lady Monksburn, what is it to trust the Lord
Jesus?"

"Do you want to know what trust is, Cary,—or what
He is? My child, I think I can tell you the first, but
I can never attempt to paint the glory of the second."

"I want to know what people mean by *trusting* Him.
How are you to trust somebody whom you do not
know?"

"It is hard. I think you must know a little before
you can trust. And by the process of trusting you learn
to know. Trust and love are very near akin. You
must talk with Him, Cary, if you want to know Him."

"You mean, pray, I suppose?"

"That is talking to Him. It is a poor converse
where all the talk is on one side."

"But what is the other side—reading the Bible?"

"That is part of it."

"What is the other part of it?"

Lady Monksburn looked up at me again, with a smile
which I do not know how to describe. I can only say
that it filled me with a sudden yearning for my dead
mother. She might have smiled on me like that.

"My darling!" she answered, "there are things
which can be described, and there are things which
can but be felt. No man can utter the secret of the
Lord—only the Lord Himself. Ask Him to whisper

it to you.   You will care little for the smiles or the frowns of the world when He has done so."

Is not that just what I want?   "But will He tell it to any one?" I said.

"He tells it to those who long for it," she replied. "His smile may be had by any who *will* have it.   It costs a great deal, sometimes.   But it is worth the cost."

"What does it cost, Madam?"

"It costs what most men think very precious, and yet is really worth nothing at all.   It costs the world's flatteries, which are as a net for the feet; and the world's pleasures, which are as the crackling of thorns under the pot; and the world's honours, which are empty air.   It often costs these.   There are few men who can be trusted with both."

There was a minute's silence, and then she said,—

"The Scottish Catechism, my dear, saith that 'Man's chief end is to glorify God, and to enjoy Him for ever.' Grander words were never penned out of God's own Word.   And among the most striking words in it are those of David, which may be called the response thereto—'When I awake up after Thy likeness, I shall be satisfied with it.'"

Then Annas and Flora came in.

But I had got what I wanted.

BLOOMSBURY SQUARE, LONDON,
September 23rd, 1745.

While we were travelling, I could not get at my book to write anything; and had I been able, I doubt whether I should have found time. We journeyed from early morning till late at night, really almost as though we were flying from a foe: though of course we should have had nothing to fear, had the royal army overtaken us. It was only the Elector's troops who would have meddled with us; and they were in Scotland somewhere. There is indeed a rumour flying abroad to-night (saith my Uncle Charles), that the Prince has entered Edinburgh: but we know not if it be true or no. If so, he will surely push on straight for London, since the rebellious troops must have been driven quite away, before he could do that. So my Uncle Charles says; and he saith too, that they are a mere handful of raw German mercenaries, who would never stand a moment against the courage, the discipline, and the sense of right, which must animate the King's army.

Oh dear! where shall I begin, if I am to write down all about the journey? And if I do not, it will look like a great gap in my tale. Well, my Uncle Drummond took us to Hawick—but stop! I have not left Abbotscliff yet, and here I am coming to Hawick. That won't do. I must begin again.

Mr. Keith and Angus marched on Thursday night, with a handful of volunteers from Tweedside. It was hard work parting. Even I felt it, and of course Angus is much less to me than the others. Mr. Keith said farewell to my Uncle and me, and he came last to Flora. She lifted her eyes to him full of tears as she put her hand in his.

" Duncan," she said, " will you make me a promise ? "

"Certainly, Flora, if it be anything that will ease your mind."

"Indeed it will," she said, with trembling lips. "Never lose sight of Angus, and try to keep him safe and true."

"True to the Cause, or true to God?"

"True to both. I cannot separate between right and right."

I thought there was just one second's hesitation—no more—before Mr. Keith gave his solemn answer.

"I will, so help me God!"

Flora thanked him amidst her sobs. He held her hand a moment longer, and I almost thought that he was going to ask her for something. But suddenly there came a setting of stern purpose into his lips and eyes, and he kissed her hand and let it go, with no more than—"God bless you, dear Flora. Farewell!"

Then Angus came up, and gave us a much warmer (and rougher) good-bye: but I felt there was something behind Mr. Keith's, which he had not spoken, and I wondered what it was.

We left Abbotscliff ourselves at six o'clock next morning. Flora and I were in the chaise; my Uncle Drummond, Sam, and Wedderburn (the Laird's servant) on horseback. At the gates at Monksburn we took up Annas, and Wedderburn joined us there too. The Laird came to see us off, and nearly wrung my hand off as he said, to Flora and me, "Take care of my bairn. The Lord's taking them both from their auld father. If I be bereaved of my children, I am bereaved."

" The Lord will keep them Himself, dear friend," said my Uncle Drummond. " Surely you see the need to part with them ?"

" Oh ay, I see the need clear enough ! And an auld noodle I am, to be lamenting to you, who are suffering the very same loss." Then he turned to Annas. " God be with thee, my bonnie birdie," he said : " the auld Grange will be lone without thy song. But thou wilt let us hear a word of thy welfare as oft as thou canst."

" As often as ever I can, dear Father," said Annas : and as he turned back, and we drove away, she broke down as I had never imagined Annas would do.

We slept that night at the inn at Hawick. On the Saturday morning, my Uncle Drummond left us, and we went on to Carlisle, which we reached late at night. Here we were to stay with Dr. and Mrs. Benn, friends of Father's, who made much of us, and seemed to think themselves quite honoured in having us : and Sam went off at once on a fresh horse to Brocklebank, which he hoped to reach by midnight. They would be looking for him. I charged him with all sorts of messages, which he said grimly that he would deliver if he recollected them when he got there : and I gave him a paper for my Aunt Kezia, with a list of things I would have sent.

On Sunday we went to the Cathedral with our hosts, and spent the day quietly.

But on Monday morning, what was my astonishment, as I was just going into the parlour, to hear a familiar voice say—

" Did you leave your eyes at Abbotscliff, my dear ?"

"Aunt Kezia!" I cried.

Yes, there stood my Aunt Kezia, in her hood and scarf, looking as if only an hour had passed since I saw her before. I was glad to see her, and I ventured to say so.

"Why, child, did you think I was going to send my lamb out into the wilderness, with never a farewell?"

"But how early you must have had to rise, Aunt Kezia!"

"Mrs. Kezia, this is an unlooked-for pleasure," said the Doctor, coming forward. "I could never have hoped to see you at this hour."

"This hour! Why, 'tis but eight o'clock!" cries my Aunt Kezia. "What sort of a lig-a-bed do you think me, Doctor?"

"Madam, I think you the flower of creation!" cries he, bowing over her hand.

"You must have been reading the poets," saith she, "and not to much good purpose.—Flora, child, you look but white! And is this Miss Annas Keith, your friend? I am glad to see you, my dear. Don't mind an old woman's freedom : I call all girls 'my dear.'"

Annas smiled, and said she was very pleased to feel as though my Aunt Kezia reckoned her among her friends.

"'My friends' friends are mine," saith my Aunt Kezia. "Well, Cary, I have brought you all the things in your minute, save your purple lutestring scarf, which I could not find. It was not in the bottom shelf, as you set down."

"Why, where could I have put it?" said I. "I always keep it on that shelf."

I was sorry to miss it, because it is my best scarf, and I thought I should want it in London, where I suppose everybody goes very fine. However, there was no more to be said—on my side. I found there was on my Aunt Kezia's.

"Here, hold your hand, child," saith she. "Your father sends you ten guineas to spend; and here are five more from me, and this pocket-piece from Sophy. You can get a new scarf in London, if you need it, or anything else you like better."

"Oh, thank you, Aunt Kezia!" I cried. "Why, how rich I shall be!"

"Don't waste your money, Cary: lay it out wisely, and then we shall be pleased. I will give you a good rule: Never buy anything without sleeping on it. Don't rush off and get it the first minute it comes into your head. You will see the bottom of your purse in a veek if you do."

"But it might be gone, Aunt Kezia."

"Then it is something you can do without."

"Is Hatty come home, Aunt?" said Flora.

"Not she," saith my Aunt Kezia. "Miss Hatty's gone careering off, the deer know where. I dare be bound you'll fall in with her. She is gone with Charlotte and Emily up to town."

I was sorry to hear that. I don't much want to meet Hatty—above all if Grandmamma be there.

CHAPTER VIII.

RULES AND RIBBONS.

" No fond belief can day and night
From light and darkness sever ;
And wrong is wrong, and right is right,
For ever and for ever."

AST evening, as we were drawing our chairs up for a chat round the fire in our chamber, who should walk in but my Aunt Kezia.

"Nay, I'll not hold you long," saith she, as I arose and offered my seat. " I come but to give a bit of good counsel to my nieces here. Miss Annas, my dear, it will very like not hurt you too."

" I shall be very glad of it, Mrs. Kezia," said Annas.

" Well,"——saith my Aunt, and broke off all at once. " Eh, girls, girls! Poor unfledged birds, fluttering your wings on the brim of the nest, and poohpoohing the old bird behind you, that says, 'Take care, my dears, or you will fall!' She never flew out of the nest, did she?—she never preened her wings, and thought all the world lay before her, and she could fly as straight as any lark of them all, and catch as many flies as any swallow ? Ay, nor she never tumbled off into the mire, and found she could not fly a bit, and all the insects went darting past her as safe as if she were a dead leaf? Eh, my lassies, this would be a poor world, if it were all. I have seen something of it, though you thought not, likely enough. But flowers are flowers, and dirt is dirt, whether you find them on the banks of the Thames or of Ellen Water. And I have not dwelt all my life at Brocklebank: though if I had, I should have seen men and women, and they are much alike all the world over."

I could not keep it in, and out it came.

"Please, Aunt Kezia, don't be angry, but what is become of Cecilia Osborne?"

"I dare say you will know, Cary, before I do. She went to London, I believe."

"Oh, I don't want to *see* her, Aunt Kezia."

"Then you are pretty sure to do it."

"But why did she not——" I was afraid to go on

"Why did she not keep her word? You can ask her if you want to know. Don't say I wanted to know, that's all. I don't."

"But how was it, Aunt Kezia?" said I, for I was on fire with curiosity. Flora made an attempt to check me.

"You are both welcome to know all I know," said my Aunt: "and that is, that she spent one evening at the Fells with us, and the Hebblethwaites and Mr. Parmenter were there: the next day we saw nothing of her, and on the evening of the third there came a little note to me—a dainty little pink three-cornered note, all over perfume—in which Miss Cecilia Osborne presented her compliments to Mrs. Kezia Courtenay, and begged to say that she found herself obliged to go to London, and would have set out before the note should reach me. That is as much as I know, and more than I want to know."

"And she did not say when she was coming back?"

"Not in any hurry, I fancy," said my Aunt Kezia, grimly.

"Going to stop away altogether?"

"She's welcome," answered my Aunt, in the same tone.

"Then who will live at Fir Vale?" asked Flora.

"Don't know. The first of you may that gets married. Don't go and do it on purpose."

Annas seemed much diverted. I wanted very much to know how Father had taken Cecilia's flight, but I did not feel I could ask that.

"Any more questions, young ladies?" saith my Aunt Kezia, quizzically. "We will get them done first, if you please."

"I beg your pardon, Aunt," said I. "Only I did want to know so much."

My Aunt Kezia gave a little laugh. "My dear, curiosity is Eve's legacy to her daughters. You might reasonably feel it in this instance. I should almost have thought you unfeeling if you had not. However, that business is all over; and well over, to my mind. I am thankful it is no worse. Now for what I want to say to you. I have been turning over in my mind how I might say to you what would be likely to do you good, in such a way that you could easily bear it in mind. And I have settled to give you a few plain rules, which you will find of service if you follow them. Now don't you go saying to yourselves that Aunt Kezia is an old country woman who knows nothing of grand town folks. As I was beginning to say when you interrupted me, Cary—there, don't look abashed, child; I am not angry with you—manners change, but natures don't. Dress men and women how you will, and let them talk what language you please, and have what outside ways you like, they are men and women still. Wherever you go, you will find human nature is unchanged; and the Devil that tempts men is unchanged; and the God that saves them is unchanged. There are more senses than one, lassies, in which the things that are seen are temporal; but the things that are not seen are eternal."

My Aunt Kezia began to feel in her bag—that great print bag with the red poppies and blue cornflowers, and the big brass top, by which I should know my Aunt Kezia was near if I saw it in the American plantations, or in the moon, for that matter—and out came three little books, bound in red sheepskin. Such pretty little books! scarcely the size of my hand, and with gilded leaves.

"Now, girls," she said, "I brought you these for keepsakes. They are only blank paper, as you see, and you can put down in them what you spend, or what you see, or any good sayings you meet with, or the like—just what you please: but you will find my rules written on the first leaf, so you can't say you had not a chance to bear them in mind. Miss Annas, my dear, I hope I don't make too free, but you see I did not like to leave you out in the cold, as it were. Will you accept one of them? They are good rules for any young maid, though I say it."

"How kind of you, Mrs. Kezia!" said Annas. "Indeed I will, and value it very much."

I turned at once—indeed, I think we all did—to my Aunt Kezia's rules. They were written, as she said, on the first page, in her neat, clear handwriting, which one could read almost in the dark. This is what she had written.

"Put the Lord first in everything.

"Let the approval of those who love you best come second.

"Judge none by the outside, till you have seen what is within.

"Never take compliment for earnest.

"Never put off doing a right or kind thing.

"If you doubt a thing being right, it is safe not to do it.

"If you know a thing to be right, go on with it, though the world stand in your way.

"'If sinners entice thee, consent thou not.'

"'If any man sin, we have an Advocate with the Father.' Never wait to confess sin and be forgiven.

"In all that is not wrong, put the comfort of others before your own.

"Think it possible you may be mistaken.

"Test everything by the Word of God.

"Remember that the world passeth away."

Flora was the first of us to speak.

"Thank you, indeed, Aunt Kezia, for taking so much trouble for us. If we govern ourselves by your rules, we can hardly go far wrong."

I tried to say something of the same sort, but I am afraid I bungled it.

"I cannot tell when we shall meet again, my lassies," saith my Aunt Kezia. "Only it seems likely to be some time first. Of course, if things fall out ill, and Mrs. Desborough counts it best to remove from London, or to send you elsewhere, you must be ruled by her, as you cannot refer to your father. Remember, Cary—your grandmother and uncle will stand to you in place of father and mother while you are with them. Your father sends you to them, and puts his authority into their hands. Don't go to think you know better—girls so often do. A little humility and obedience won't hurt you, and you need not be afraid there will ever be too much of them in this world."

"But, Aunt!" said I, in some alarm, "suppose Grandmamma tells me to do something which I know you would not allow?"

"Follow your rule, Cary : set the Lord always before you. If it is anything which He would not allow, then you are justified in standing out. Not otherwise."

"But how am I to know, Aunt?" It was a foolish question of mine, for I might have known what my Aunt Kezia would say.

"What do you think the Bible was made for, Cary?"

" But, Aunt, I can't go and read through the Bible every time Grandmamma gives me an order."

" You must do that first, my dear. The Bible won't jump down your throat, that is certain. You must be ready beforehand. You will learn experience, children, as the time goes on—ay, whether you choose or no. But there are two sorts of experience—sweet and bitter: and 'they that will not be ruled by the rudder must be ruled by the rock.' Be ruled by the rudder, lassies. It is the wisest plan."

My Aunt Kezia said more, but it does not come back to me as that does. And the next morning we said good-bye, and went out into the wide world.

I cannot profess to tell the whole of our journey. We slept the first night at Kendal—and a cold bleak journey it was, by Shap Fells—the second at Bolton, the third at Bakewell, the fourth at Leicester, the fifth at Bedford, and on the Saturday evening we reached London.

I believe Annas was very much diverted at some of my speeches during the journey. When I cried, after we had passed Bolton, and were going over a moor, that I did not know there was heather in the South, she said, " You have been a very short time in coming to the South, Cary."

"What do you mean, Annas? " said I.

" Only that a Midland man would think we were still in the North," said she.

" What, is this not the South? " said I. " I thought everything was South after we passed Lancaster."

“England is a little longer than that,” said Annas, laughing. “No, Cary: we do not get into the Midlands on this side of Derby, nor into the South on this side of Bedford.”

So I had to wait until Friday before I saw the South. When I did, I thought it very flat and very woody. I could scarcely see anything for trees; only[1] there were no hills to see. And how strange the talk sounded! They seemed to speak all their *u*'s as if they were *e*'s, and their *a*'s the same. Annas laughed when I said that “take up the mat” sounded in the South like “teek ep the met.” It really did, to me.

“I suppose,” said Flora, “our words sound just as queer to these people.”

“O Flora, they can’t!” I cried.

Because we say the words right; and how can that sound queer ?

It was nearly six o’clock when the chaise drew up before the door of my Uncle Charles’s house in Bloomsbury Square. These poor Southerners think, I hear, that Bloomsbury Square is one of the wonders of the world. The world must be very short of wonders, and so I said.

“O Cary, you are a bundle of prejudices!” laughed Annas.

Flora—who never can bear a word of disagreement— turned the discourse by saying that Mr. Cameron had told her Bloomsbury came from Blumond’s bury, the town of some man called Blumond.

---

[1] Southerners are respectfully informed that the use of *only* for *but* is a Northern peculiarity.

And just then the door opened, and I felt almost terrified of the big, grand-looking man who stood behind it. However, as it was I who was the particularly invited guest, I had to jump down from the chaise, after a boy had let down the steps, and to tell the big man who I was and whence I came: when he said, in that mincing way they have in the South, as if they must cut their words small before they could get them into their mouths, that Madam expected me, and I was to walk up-stairs. My heart went pit-a-pat, but up I marched, Annas and Flora following; and if the big man did not call out my name to another big man, just the copy of him, who stood at the top of the stairs, so loud that I should think it must have been heard over half the house. I felt quite ashamed, but I walked straight on, into a grand room all over looking-glasses and crimson, where a circle of ladies and gentlemen were sitting round the fire. We have not begun fires in the North. I do think they are a nesh [1] lot of folks who live in the South.

Grandmamma was at one end of the circle, and my Aunt Dorothea at the other. I went straight up to Grandmamma.

"How do you, Grandmamma?" said I. This is my cousin, Flora Drummond, and this is our friend, Annas Keith. Fa——Papa, I mean, and Aunt Kezia, sent their respectful compliments, and begged that you would kindly allow them to tarry here for a night on their way to the Isle of Wight."

[1] Sensitive, delicate.

Grandmamma looked at me, then at Flora, then at Annas, and took a pinch of snuff.

"How dusty you are, my dear!" said she. "Pray go and shift your gown. Perkins will show you the way."

She just gave a nod to the other two, and then went back to her discourse with the gentleman next her. Those are what Grandmamma calls easy manners, I know: but I think I like the other sort better. My Aunt Kezia would have given the girls a warm grasp of the hand and a kiss, and told them they were heartily welcome, and begged them to make themselves at home. Grandmamma thinks that rough and coarse and country-bred: but I am sure it makes me feel more as if people really were pleased to see me.

I felt that I must just speak first to my Aunt Dorothea; and she did shake hands with Flora and me, and courtesied to Annas. Then we courtesied to the company, and left the room, I telling the big man that Grandmamma wished Perkins to attend us. The big man looked over the banisters, and said, " Harry, call Perkins." When Perkins came, she proved, as I expected, to be Grandmamma's waiting-maid; and she carried us off to a little chamber on the upper floor, where was hardly room for anything but two beds.

Flora, I saw, seemed to feel strange and uncomfortable, as if she were somewhere where she had no business to be; but Annas behaved like one to the manner born, and handed her gloves to Perkins with the air of a princess—I do not mean proudly, but easily, as if she knew just what to do, and did it, without any feeling of awkwardness.

We had to wait till the trunks were carried up, and Perkins had unpacked our tea-gowns; then we shifted ourselves, and had our hair dressed, and went back to the withdrawing room. Perkins is a stranger to me, and I was sorry not to see Willet, Grandmamma's old maid: but Grandmamma never keeps servants long, so I was not surprised. I don't believe Willet had been with her above six years, when I left Carlisle.

Annas sat down on an empty chair in the circle, and began to talk with the lady nearest to her. Flora, apparently in much hesitation, took a chair, but did not venture to talk. I knew what I had to do, and I felt as if my old ways would come back if I called them. I sat down near my Aunt Dorothea.

"That friend of yours, Cary, is quite a distinguished-looking girl," said my Aunt Dorothea, in a low voice. "Really presentable, for the country, you know."

I said Annas came of a high Scots family, and was related to Sir James De Lannoy, of the Isle of Wight. I saw that Annas went up directly in my Aunt Dorothea's thermometer.

"De Lannoy!" said she. "A fine old Norman line. Very well connected, then? I am glad to hear it."

Flora, I saw, was getting over her shyness—indeed, I never knew her seem shy before—and beginning to talk a little with her next neighbour. I looked round, but could not see any one I knew. I took refuge in an inquiry after my Uncle Charles.

"He is very well," said my Aunt Dorothea. "He is away somewhere—men always are. At the Court, I dare say."

How strange it did sound! I felt as if I had come into a new world.

"I hope that is not your best gown, child?" said my Aunt Dorothea.

"But it is, Aunt—my best tea-gown," I answered.

"Then you must have a better," replied she. "It is easy to see that was made in the country."

"Certainly it was, Aunt. Fanny and I made it."

My Aunt Dorothea shrugged her shoulders, gave me a glance which said plainly, "Don't tell tales out of school!" and turned to another lady in the group.

At Brocklebank we never thought of not saying such things. But I see I have forgotten many of my Carlisle habits, and I shall have to pick them up again by degrees.

When we went up to bed, I found that Grandmamma had asked Annas to stay in London. Annas replied that her father had given her leave to stay a month if she wished it and were offered the chance, and she would be very pleased: but that as Flora was her guest, the invitation would have to include both. Grandmamma glanced again at Flora, and took another pinch of snuff.

"I suppose she has some Courtenay blood in her," said she. "And Drummond is not a bad name—for a Scotswoman. She can stay, if she be not a Covenanter, and won't want to pray and preach. She must have a new gown, and then she will do, if she keep her mouth shut. She has a fine pair of shoulders, if she were only dressed decently."

" I am glad," said I, "for I know what that means. Grandmamma likes Annas, and will like Flora in time. Don't be any shyer than you can help, Flora; that will not please her."

" I do not think I am shy," said Flora; "at least, I never felt so before. But to-night—— Cary, I don't know what it looked like! I could only think of a great spider's web, and we three poor little flies had to walk straight into it."

" I wonder where Duncan and Angus are to-night," said Annas; " I hope no one is playing spider there."

Flora sighed, but made no answer.

Our new gowns had to be made in a great hurry, for Grandmamma had invited an assembly for the Thursday night, and she wished Flora and me to be decently dressed, she said. I am sure I don't know how the mantua-maker managed it, for the cloth was only bought on Monday morning; I suppose she must have had plenty of apprentices. The gowns were sacques of cherry damask, with quilted silk petticoats of black trimmed with silver lace. I find hoops are all the mode again, and very large indeed—so big that when you enter a door you have to double your hoop round in front, or lift it on one side out of the way. The cap is a little scrap of a thing, scarce bigger than a crown-piece, and a flower or pompoon is stuck at the side; stomachers are worn, and very full elbow ruffles;

velvet slippers with high heels. Grandmamma put a little grey powder in my hair, but when Flora said she was sure that her father would disapprove, she did not urge her to wear it. But she did want us both to wear red ribbons mixed with our white ones. I did not know what to do.

"I did not know Mrs. Desborough was a trimmer," said Annas, in the severest tone I ever heard from her lips.

"What shall we do?" said I.

"I shall not wear them," said Flora. "Mrs. Desborough is not my grandmother; nor has my father put me in her care. I do not see, therefore, that I am at all bound to obey her. For you, Cary, it is different. I think you will have to submit."

"But only think what it means!" cried I.

"It means," said Annas, "that you are indifferent in the matter of politics."

"If it meant only that," I said, "I should not think much about it. But surely it means more, much more. It means that I am disloyal; that I do not care whether the King or the Elector wins the day; or even that I do care, and am willing to hide my belief for fashion's or money's sake. This red ribbon on me is a lie; and an acted lie is no better than a spoken one."

My Aunt Dorothea came in so immediately after I had spoken that I felt sure she must have heard me.

"Dear me, what a fuss about a bit of ribbon!" said she. "Cary, don't be a little goose."

"Aunt, I only want to be true!" cried I. "It is

my truth I make a fuss about, not my ribbons. I will wear a ribbon of every colour in the rainbow, if Grandmamma wish it, except just this one which tells falsehoods about me."

"My dear, it is so unbecoming in you to be thus warm!" said my Aunt Dorothea. "Enthusiasm is always in bad taste, no matter what it is about. You will not see half-a-dozen ladies in the room in white ribbons. Nobody expects the Prince to come South."

"But, Aunt, please give me leave to say that it will not alter my truthfulness, whether the Prince comes to London or goes to the North Pole!" cried I. "If the Elector himself——"

"'Sh-'sh!" said my Aunt Dorothea. "My dear, that sort of thing may be very well at Brocklebank, but it really will not do in Bloomsbury Square. You must not bring your wild, antiquated Tory notions here. Tories are among the extinct animals."

"Not while my father is alive, please, Aunt."

"My dear, we are not at Brocklebank, as I told you just now," answered my Aunt Dorothea. "It may be all very well to toast the Chevalier, and pray for him, and so forth—(I am sure I don't know whether it do him any good): but when you come to living in the world with other people, you must do as they do.—Yes, Perkins, certainly, put Miss Courtenay a red ribbon, and Miss Drummond also.—My dear girls, you must."

"Not for me, Mrs. Charles, if you please," said Flora, very quietly: "I should prefer, if you will allow it, to remain in this room."

My Aunt Dorothea looked at her, and seemed puzzled what to do with her.

"Miss Keith," said she, "do you wear the red?"

"Certainly not, Madam," replied Annas.

"Well!" said my Aunt Dorothea, shrugging her shoulders, "I suppose we must say you are Scots girls, and have not learnt English customs.—You can let it alone for Miss Drummond, Perkins.—But that won't do for you, Cary; you must have one."

"Aunt Dorothea, I will wear it if you bid me," said I: "but I shall tell everybody who speaks to me that my red ribbon is a lie."

"Then you had better have none!" cried my Aunt Dorothea, petulantly. "That would be worse than wearing all white. Cary, I never knew you were so horribly obstinate."

"I suppose I am older, Aunt, and understand things better now," said I.

"Dear, I wish girls would stay girls!" said my Aunt Dorothea. "Well, Perkins, let it alone. Just do up that lace a little to the left, that the white ribbon may not show so much. There, that will do.—Cary, if your Grandmamma notices this, I must tell her it is all your fault."

Well, down-stairs we went, and found the company beginning to come. My Aunt Dorothea, I knew, never cares much about anything to last, but I was in some fear of Grandmamma. (By the way, I find this house is Grandmamma's, not my Uncle Charles's, as I thought.) There was one lady there, a Mrs. Francis, who was here the other evening when we came, and she spoke kindly to us, and began to talk with Annas and Flora. I rather shrank into a corner by the window, for I did not want Grandmamma to see me. People were chattering away on all sides of me; and very droll it was to listen first to one and then to another.

I was amusing myself in this way, and laughing to myself under a grave face, when all at once I heard three words from the next window. Who said " By no means !" in that soft velvet voice, through which ran a ripple of silvery laughter? I should have known that voice in the desert of Arabia. And the next moment she moved away from the window, and I saw her face.

We stood fronting each other, Cecilia and I. That she knew me as well as I knew her, I could not doubt for an instant. For one moment she hesitated whether to speak to me, and I took advantage of it. Dropping the lowest courtesy I could make, I turned my back upon her, and walked straight away to the other end of the room. But not before I had seen that she was superbly dressed, and was leaning on the arm of Mr. Parmenter. Not, also, before I caught a fiery flash gleaming at me out of the tawny eyes, and knew that I had made an enemy of the most dangerous woman in my world.

But what could I have done else ? If I had accepted Cecilia's hand, and treated her as a friend, I should have felt as though I were conniving at an insult to my father.

At the other end of the room, I nearly ran against a

handsome, dark-haired girl in a yellow satin slip, who to my great astonishment said to me,—

"Well played, Miss Caroline Courtenay! I have been watching the little drama, and I really compliment you on your readiness and spirit. You have taken the wind out of her Ladyship's sails."

"Hatty!" I cried, in much amazement. "Is it you?"

"Well, I fancy so," said she, in her usual mocking way. "My beloved Cary, do tell me, *have* you brought that delicious journal? Do let me read to-night's entry!"

"Hatty!" I cried all at once. "You——"

"Yes, Madam?"

If she had not on my best purple scarf—my lost scarf, that my Aunt Kezia could not find! But I did not go on. I felt it was of no earthly use to talk to Hatty.

"Seen it before, haven't you?" said Hatty, in her odious teasing way. "Yes, I thought I had better have it: mine is so shabby; and you are only a little Miss—it does not matter for you. Beside, you have Grandmamma to look after you. You shall have it again when I have done with it."

I had to bite my tongue terribly hard, but I did manage to hold it. I only said, "Where are you staying, Hatty?"

"At Mrs. Crossland's, in Charles Street, where I shall be perfectly delighted to see my youngest sister."

"Oh! Not with the Bracewells?"

"With the Bracewells, certainly. Did you suppose they had pitchforked me through the window into Mrs. Crossland's drawing-room?"

“But who is Mrs. Crossland?”

“A friend of the Bracewells,” said Hatty, with an air of such studied carelessness that I began to wonder what was behind it.

“Has Mrs. Crossland daughters?” I asked.

“One—a little chit, scarce in her teens.”

“Is there a Mr. Crossland?”

“There isn’t a Papa Crossland, if you mean that. There is a young Mr. Crossland.”

“Oh!” said I.

“Pray, Miss Caroline, what do you mean by ‘Oh’?” asked Hatty, whose eyes laughed with fun.

“Oh, nothing,” I replied.

“Oh!” replied Hatty, so exactly in my tone that I could not help laughing. “Take care, her Ladyship may see you.”

“Hatty, why do you call Cecilia ‘her Ladyship’?”

“Well, it doesn’t know anything, does it?” replied Hatty, in her teasing way. “Only just up from the country, isn’t it? Madam, Mr. Anthony Parmenter as was (as old Will says) is *Sir* Anthony Parmenter; and Miss Cecilia Osborne as was, is her Ladyship.”

“Do you mean to say Cecilia has married Mr. Parmenter?”

“Oh dear, no! she has married Sir Anthony.”

“Then she jilted our father for a title? The snake!”

“Don’t use such charming language, my sweetest; her Ladyship might not admire it. And if I were you, I would make myself scarce; she is coming this way.”

“Then I will go the other,” said I, and I did.

To my astonishment, as soon as I had left her, what should Hatty do but walk up and shake hands with Cecilia, and in a few minutes they and Mr. Parmenter were all laughing about something. I was amazed beyond words. I had always thought Hatty pert, teasing, disagreeable; but never underhand or mean. But just then I saw a good-looking young man join them, and offer his arm to Hatty for a walk round the room; and it flashed on me directly that this was young Mr. Crossland, and that he was a friend of Mr.—I mean Sir Anthony—Parmenter.

When we were undressing that night, I said,—

"Annas, can a person do anything to make the world better?"

"What person?" asked she, and smiled.

"Well, say me. Can I do anything?"

"Certainly. You can be as good as you know how to be."

"But that won't make other people better."

"I do not know that. Some other people it may."

"But that will be the people who are good already. I want to mend the people who are bad."

"Then pray for them," said Annas, gravely.

Pray for Cecilia Osborne! It came upon me with a feeling of intense aversion. I could not pray for her!

Nor did I think there would be a bit of good in praying for Hatty. And yet—if she were getting drawn into Cecilia's toils—if that young Mr. Crossland were not a good man—I might pray for her to be kept safe. I thought I would try it.

But when I began to pray for Hatty, it seemed unkind to leave out Fanny and Sophy. And then I got to Father and my Aunt Kezia; and then to Maria and Bessy; and then to Sam and Will; and then to old Elspie; and then to Helen Raeburn, and my Uncle Drummond, and Angus, and Mr. Keith, and the Laird, and Lady Monksburn—and so on and on, till the whole world seemed full of people to be prayed for.

I suppose it is so always—if we only thought of it!

Grandmamma never noticed my ribbons—or rather my want of them.

It really is of no use my trying to keep to dates. I have begun several times, and I cannot get on with it. That last piece, dated the 23rd, took me nearly a week to write; so that what was to-morrow when I began, was behind yesterday before I had finished. I shall just go right on without any more pother, and put a date now and then when it is very particular.

Grandmamma has an assembly every week,—Tuesday is her day[1]—and now and then an extra one on Thursday or Saturday. I do not think anything would persuade her to have an assembly, or play cards, on a Friday. But on a Sunday evening she always has her rubber, to Flora's horror. It does not startle me, because I remember it always was so when I lived with her at Carlisle: nor Annas, because she knew people did such things in the South. I find Grand-

---

[1] The assemblies on a lady's visiting day required no invitations. The rooms were open to any person acquainted with members of the family.

mamma usually spends the winter at the Bath : but she has not quite made up her mind whether to go this year or not, on account of all the tumults in the North. If the royal army should march on London (and Annas says of course they will) we may be shut up here for a long while. But Annas says, if we heard anything certain of it, she and Flora would set off at once to "the island," as she always calls the Isle of Wight.

Last Tuesday, I was sitting by a young lady whom I have talked with more than once; her name is Newton. I do not quite know how we got on to the subject, but we began to talk politics. I said I could not understand why it was, but people in the South did not seem to care for politics nearly so much as I was accustomed to see done. Half the ladies in the room appeared to be trimmers; and many more wore the red ribbon alone. Such people, with us, would never be received into a Tory family.

"We do not take things so seriously as you," said she, with a diverted look. "That with us is an opinion which with you is an enthusiasm. I suppose up there, where the sun never shines, you have to make some sort of noise and fuss to keep yourselves alive."

"'The sun never shines!'" cried I. "Now, really, Miss Newton! You don't mean to say you believe that story?"

"I am only repeating what I have been told," said she. "I never was north of Barnet."

"We are alive enough," said I. "I wonder if you are. It looks to me much more like living, to make beds and boil puddings and stitch shirts, than to sit on a sofa in a satin gown, flickering a fan and talking rubbish."

"Oh, fie!" said Miss Newton, laughing, and tapping me on the arm with her fan. "That really will not do, Miss Courtenay. You will shock everybody in the room."

"I can tell you, most whom I see here shock me," said I. "They seem to have no honour and no honesty. They think white and they wear red, or the other way about, just as it happens. If the Prince were to enter London on Monday, what colour would all these ribbons be next Tuesday night?"

"The colour of yours, undoubtedly," she said, laughing.

"And do you call that honesty?" said I. "These people could not change their opinions and feelings between Monday and Tuesday: and to change their ribbons without them would be simply falsehood."

"I told you, you take things so seriously!" she answered.

"But is it not a serious thing?" I continued. "And ought we to take serious things any way but seriously? Miss Newton, do you not see that it is a question of *right*—not a question of taste or convenience? Your allegiance is not a piece of jewellery, that you can give to the person you like best; it is a debt, which you can only pay to the person to whom you owe it. Do you not see that?"

"My dear Miss Courtenay," said Miss Newton, in a low voice, "excuse me, but you are a little too warm. It is not thought good taste, you know, to take up any subject so very decidedly as that."

"And is right only to be thought a matter of taste?" cried I, quite disregarding her caution. "Am I to rule my life, as I do my trimmings, by the fashion-book? We have not come to that yet in the North, I can assure you! We are a sturdy race there, Madam, and don't swallow our opinions as we do pills, of whatever the apothecary likes to put into them. We prefer to know what we are taking."

"Do excuse me," said Miss Newton, with laughter in her eyes, and laying her hand upon my arm; "but don't you see people are looking round?"

"Let them look round!" cried I. "I am not ashamed of one word that I have spoken."

"Dear Miss Courtenay, I am not objecting to your words. Every one, of course, has his opinions: yours, I suppose, are your father's."

"Not a bit of it!" cried I; "they are my own!"

"But young ladies of your age should not have strong opinions," said she. She is about five years older than I am.

"Will you tell me how to help it?" said I. "I must go through the world with my eyes shut, if I am not to form opinions."

"Oh yes, moderately," she replied.

"Shut my eyes moderately?" I asked; "or, form opinions moderately?"

"Both," answered Miss Newton, laughing.

"Your advice is worse than wasted, my dear Miss Newton," said a voice behind us. "That young person will never do anything in moderation."

“You know better, Hatty!” said I.

“And, as your elder sister, my darling, let me give you a scrap of advice. Men never like contentious, arguing women. Don’t be a little goose.”

I don’t know whether I am a goose or a duck, but I am afraid I could have done something to Hatty just then which I should have found agreeable, and she would not. That elder-sister air of hers is so absurd, for she is not eighteen months older than I am ; I can stand it well enough from Sophy, but from Hatty it really is too ridiculous. But that was nothing, compared with the insult she had offered, not so much to me, as through me to all womanhood. “Men don’t like!” Does it signify three halfpence what they like? Are women to make slaves of themselves, considering what men fancy or don’t fancy? Men, mark you! Not, your father, or brother, or husband : that would be right and reasonable enough : but, *men !*

“Hatty,” I said, after doing battle with myself for a moment, “I think I had better give you no answer. If I did, and if my words and tones suited my feelings, I should scream the house down.”

She burst out laughing behind her fan. I walked away at once, lest I should be tempted to reply further. I am afraid I almost ran, for I came bolt against a gentleman in the corner, and had to stop and make my apologies.

“Don’t run quite over me, Cary, if it suit you,” said somebody who, I thought, was in Cumberland.

CHAPTER IX.

DIFFICULTIES.

> " And 't was na for a Popish yoke
> That bravest men came forth
> To part wi' life and dearest ties,
> And a' that life was worth."
> —*Jacobite Ballad.*

PHRAIM HEBBLETHWAITE!" I cried out.

" I believe so," he said, laughing.

" Where did you come from ? "

" From a certain place in the North, called Brockle-bank."

" But what brought you to London ? " I cried.

" What brought me to London ? " he repeated, in quite a different tone,—so much softer. " Well, Cary, I wanted to see something."

" Have you been to see it ? " I asked, more to give myself time to cool down than because I cared to know.

" Yes, I have been to see it," he said, and smiled.

" And did you find it as agreeable as you expected ? "

" Quite. I had seen it before, and I wanted to know if it were spoiled."

" Oh, I hope it is not spoiled ! " said I.

" Not at all," said he, his voice growing softer and softer. " No, it is not spoiled yet, Cary."

"Do you expect it will be?" I was getting cooler now.

"I don't know," he answered, very gravely for him, for Ephraim is not at all given to moroseness and long faces. "God grant it never may!"

I could not think what he meant, and I did not like to ask him. Indeed, I had not much opportunity, for he began talking about our journey, and Brocklebank, and all the people there, and I was so interested that we did not get back to what Ephraim came to see.

There is a new Vicar, he says, whose name is Mr. Liversedge, and he has quite changed things in the parish. The people are divided about him; some like him, and some do not. He does not read his sermons, which is very strange, but speaks them out just as if he were talking to you; and he has begun to catechise the children in an afternoon, and to visit everybody in the parish; and he neither shoots, hunts, nor fishes. His sermons have a ring in them, says Ephraim; they wake you up. Old John Oakley complains that he can't nap nigh so comfortable as when th' old Vicar were there; and Mally Crosthwaite says she never heard such goings on—why, th' parson asked her if she were a Christian!—she that had always kept to her church, rain and shine, and never missed once! and it was hard if she were to miss the Christmas dole this year, along o' not being a Christian. She'd always thought being Church was plenty good enough—none o' your low Dissenting work: but, mercy on us, she didn't know what to say to this here parson, that she didn't! A Christian, indeed! The parson was a Christian, was he? Well, if so, she didn't make much 'count o' Christians, for all he was a parson. Didn't he tell old John he couldn't recommend him for the dole, just by reason he rapped out an oath or two when his grand-daughter let the milk-jug fall?—and if old Bet Donnerthwaite had had a sup too much one night at the ale-house, was it for a gentleman born like the parson to take note of that?

"But he has done worse things than that, Cary," said Ephraim, with grave mouth and laughing eyes.

"What? Go on," said I, for I saw something funny was coming.

"Why, would you believe it?" said Ephraim. "He called on Mr. Bagnall, and asked him if he felt satisfied with the pattern he was setting his flock."

"I am very glad he did!" said I. "What did Mr. Bagnall say?"

"Got into an awful rage, and told it to all the neighbourhood—as bearing against Mr. Liversedge, you understand."

"Well, then, he is a greater simpleton than I took him for," said I.

"I am rather afraid," said Ephraim, in a hesitating tone, "that he will call at the Fells: and if he say anything that the Squire thinks impertinent or inter-fering, he will make an enemy of him."

"Oh, Father would just show him the door," said I, "without more ado."

"Yes, I fear so," replied Ephraim. "And I am sure

he is a good man, Cary. A little rash and incautious, perhaps; does not take time to study character, and so forth; but I am sure he means to do right."

"It will be a pity," said I. "Ephraim, do you think the Prince will march on London?"

"I have not a doubt of it, Cary."

"Oh!" said I. I don't quite know whether I felt more glad or sorry. "But you will not stay here if he do?"

"Yes, I think I shall," said he.

"You will join the army?"

"No, not unless I am pressed."

I suppose my face asked another question, for he added with a smile, "I came to keep watch of—*that.* I must see that it is not spoiled."

I wonder what *that* is! If Ephraim would tell me, I might take some care of it too. I should not like anything he cared for to be spoiled.

As I sat in a corner afterwards, I was looking at him, and comparing him in my own mind with all the fine gentlemen in the chamber. Ephraim was quite as handsome as any of them; but his clothes certainly had a country cut, and he did not show as easy manners as they. I am afraid Grandmamma would say he had no manners. He actually put his hand out to save a tray when Grandmamma's black boy, Cæsar, stumbled at the tiger-skin mat: and I am sure no other gentleman in the room would have condescended to see it. There are many little things by which it is easy to tell that Ephraim has not been used to the best society. And yet, I could not help feeling that if I were ill and wanted to be helped upstairs, or if I were wretched and wanted comforting, it would be Ephraim to whom I should appeal, and not one of these fine gentlemen. They seemed only to be made for sunshine. He would wear, and stand rain. If Hatty's "men" were all Ephraims, there might be some sense in caring for their opinions. But these fellows—I really can't afford a better word —these " chiels with glasses in their e'en," as Sam says, who seem to have no opinions beyond the colour of their coats and paying compliments to everything they see with a petticoat on—do they expect sensible women to care what *they* think? Let them have a little more sense themselves first—that's what *I* say!

I said so, one morning as we were dressing: and to my surprise, Annas replied,—

" I fancy they have sense enough, Cary, when there are no women in the room. They think we only care for nonsense."

" Yes, I expect that is it," added Flora.

I flew out. I could not stand that. What sort of women must their mothers and sisters be?

· " Card-playing snuff-takers and giddy flirts," said Annas. " Be just to them, Cary. If they never see women of any other sort, how are they to know that such are?"

" Poor wretches! do you think that possible. Annas?" said I.

" Miserably possible," she said, very seriously. " In every human heart, Cary, there is a place where the man or the woman dwells inside all the frippery and mannerism; the real creature itself, stripped of all disguises. Dig down to that place if you want to see it."

"I should think it takes a vast deal of digging!"

"Yes, in some people. But that is the thing God looks at: that is it for which Christ died, and for which Christ's servants ought to feel love and pity."

I thought it would be terribly difficult to feel love or pity for some people!

My Uncle Charles has just come in, and he says a rumour is flying that there has been a great battle near Edinburgh, and that the Prince (who was victorious) is marching on Carlisle. Flora went very white, and even Annas set her lips: but I do not see what we have to fear—at least if Angus and Mr. Keith are safe.

"Charles," said Grandmamma, "where are those white cockades we used to have?"

"I haven't a notion, Mother."

Nor had my Aunt Dorothea. But when Perkins was asked, she said, "Isn't it them, Madam, as you pinned in a parcel, and laid away in the garret?"

"Oh, I dare say," said Grandmamma. "Fetch them down, and let us see if they are worth anything."

So Perkins fetched the parcel, and the cockades were looked over, and pronounced useable by torchlight, though too bad a colour for the day-time.

"Keep the packet handy, Perkins," said Grandmamma.

"Shall I give them out now, Madam?" asked Perkins.

"Oh, not yet!" said Grandmamma.   "Wait till we see how things turn out.   White soils so soon, too: we had much better go on with the black ones, at any rate, till the Prince has passed Bedford."

It is wicked, I suppose, to despise one's elders.   But is it not sometimes very difficult to help doing it?

I have been reading over the last page or two that I writ, and I came on a line that set me thinking.   Things do set me thinking of late in a way they never used to do.   It was that about Ephraim's not being used to the best society.   What is the best society?   God and the angels; I suppose nobody could question that.   Yet, if an angel had been in Grandmamma's rooms just then, would he not have cared more that Cæsar should not fall and hurt himself, and most likely be scolded as well, than that he should be thought to have fine easy manners himself?   And I suppose the Lord Jesus died even for Cæsar, black though he be.   Well, then, the next best society must be those who are going to Heaven: and Ephraim is one of them, I believe.   And those who are not going must be bad society, even if they are dressed up to the latest fashion-book, and have the newest and finest breeding at the tips of their fingers.   The world seems to be turned round.   Ah, but what was that text Mr. Whitefield quoted?   "Love not the world, neither the things that are in the world.   If any man love the world, the love of the Father is not in him.   For all that is in the world, the lust of the flesh, and the lust of the eyes, and the pride of life, are not of the Father, but are of the world."   Then must we turn the

world round before we get things put straight?   It
looks like it.   I have just been looking at another text,
where St. Paul gives a list of the works of the flesh;[1]
and I find, along with some things which everybody
calls wicked, a lot of others which everybody in "the
world" does, and never seems to think of as wrong.
"Hatred, variance, emulations, . . . envyings, . . .
drunkenness, revellings, and such like:" and he says,
"They which do such things shall not inherit the kingdom of God."   That is dreadful.   I am afraid the world
must be worse than I thought.   I must take heed to
my Aunt Kezia's rules—set the Lord always before me,
and remember that this world passeth away.   I suppose
the world will laugh at me, if I be not one of its people.
What will that matter, if it passeth away ?   The angels
will like me all the better: and they are the best society.

And I was thinking the other night as I lay awake,
what an awful thing it would be to hear the Lord
Jesus, the very Man who died for me, say, "Depart
from Me!"   I think I could stand the world's laughter,
but I am sure I could never bear *that.*   Christ could
help and comfort me if the world used me ill; but who
could help me, or comfort me, when He had cast me
out ?   There would be nothing to take refuge in—not
even the world, for it would be done with then.

Oh, I do hope our Saviour will never say that to me!

I seem bound to get into fights with Miss Newton.
I do not mean quarrels, but arguments.   She is a

Gal. v 19-21.

pleasant, good-humoured girl, but she has such queer ideas. I dare say she thinks I have. I do not know what my Aunt Kezia would say to her. She does not appear to see the right and wrong of things at all. It is only what people will think, and what one likes. If everybody did only what they liked,—is that proper grammar, I wonder? Oh, well, never mind!—I think it would make the world a very disagreeable place to live in, and it is not too pleasant now. And as to people thinking, what on earth does it signify what they think, if they don't think right? If one person thinking that two and two make three does not alter the fact, why should ten thousand people thinking so be held to make any difference? How many simpletons does it take to be equal to a wise man? I wonder people do not see how ridiculous such notions are.

We hear nothing at all from the North—the seat of war, as they begin to call it now. Everybody supposes that the Prince is marching southwards, and will be here some day before long. It diverts me exceedingly to sit every Tuesday in a corner of the room, and watch the red ribbons disappearing and the white ones coming instead. Grandmamma's two footmen, Morris and Dobson, have orders to take the black cockade out of their hats and clap on a white one, the minute they hear that the royal army enters Middlesex.

November 22nd.

The Prince has taken Carlisle! It is said that he is marching on Derby as fast as his troops can come.

Everybody is in a flutter. I can guess where Father is, and how excited he will be. I know he would go to wait on his Royal Highness directly, and I should not wonder if a number of the officers are quartered at Brocklebank—were, I should say. I almost wish we were there! But when I said so to Ephraim, who comes every Tuesday, such a strange look of pain came into his eyes, and he said, "Don't, Cary!" so sadly.

I wonder what the next thing will be!

After I had written this, came one of Grandmamma's extra assemblies—Oh, I should have altered my date! it is so troublesome—on Thursday evening, and I looked round, and could not see one red ribbon that was not mixed with white. A great many wore plain white, and among them Miss Newton. I sat down by her.

"How do you this evening, Miss Newton?" I mischievously asked. "I am so delighted to see you become a Tory since I saw you last Tuesday."

"How do you know I was not one before?" asked she, laughing.

"Your ribbons were not," said I. "They were red on Tuesday."

"Well, you ought to compliment me on the suddenness of my conversion," said she: "for I never was a trimmer. Oh, how absurd it is to make ribbons and patches mean things! Why should one not wear red and white just as one does green and blue?"

"It would be a boon to some people, I am sure," said I.

"Perhaps we shall, some day, when the world has become sensible," said Miss Newton.

"Can you give me the date, Madam?"

It was a strange voice which asked this question. I looked up over my shoulder, and saw a man of no particular age, dressed in gown and cassock.[1] Miss Newton looked up too, laughing.

"Indeed I cannot, Mr. Raymond," said she. "Can you?"

"Only by events," he answered. "I should expect it to be after the King has entered His capital."

I felt, rather than saw, what he meant.

"I am a poor hand at riddles," said Miss Newton, shaking her head. "I did not expect to see you here, Mr. Raymond."

"Nor would you have seen me here," was the answer, "had I not been charged to deliver a message of grave import to one who is here."

"Not me, I hope?" said Miss Newton, looking graver.

"Not you. I trust you will thank God for it. And now, can you kindly direct me to the young lady for whom I am to look? Is there here a Miss Flora Drummond?"

I sprang up with a smothered cry of "Angus!"

"Are you Miss Drummond?" he asked, very kindly.

---

[1] A clergyman always wore his cassock at this time. Whitefield was very severe on those worldly clergy who laid it aside, and went "disguised"—namely, in the ordinary coat—to entertainments of various kinds.

"Flora Drummond is my cousin," I answered. "I will take you to her. But is it about Angus?"

"It is about her brother, Lieutenant Drummond. He is not killed—let me say so at once."

We were pressing through the superb crowd, and the moment afterwards we reached Flora. She was standing by a little table, talking with Ephraim Hebblethwaite, who spoke to Mr. Raymond in a way which showed that they knew each other. Flora just looked at him, and then said, quietly enough to all appearance, though she went very white—

"You have bad news for some one, and I think for me."

"Lieutenant Drummond was severely wounded at Prestonpans, and has fallen into the hands of the King's troops," said Mr. Raymond, gently, as if he wished her to know the worst at once. "He is a prisoner now."

Flora clasped her hands with a long breath of pain and apprehension. "You are sure, Sir? There is no mistake?"

"I think, none," he replied. "I have the news from Colonel Keith."

"If you heard it from him, it must be true," she said. "But is he in London?"

"Yes; and he ran some risk, as you may guess, to send that message to you."

"Duncan is always good," said Flora, with tears in her eyes. "He was not hurt, I hope? Will you see him again?"

" He said he was not hurt worth mention." (I began to wonder what size of a hurt Mr. Keith would think worth mention.) " Yes, I shall see him again this evening or to-morrow."

" Oh, do give him the kindest words and thanks from me," said Flora, commanding her voice with some difficulty. " I wish I could have seen him ! Let me tell Annas—she may wish "—— and away she went to fetch Annas, while Mr. Raymond looked after her with a look which I thought half sad and half diverted.

" Will you tell me," I said, " how Mr. Keith ran any risk ? "

" Why, you do not suppose, young lady, that London is in the hands of the rebels ? "

" The rebels!—Oh, you are a Whig; I see. But the Prince is coming, and fast. Is he not ? "

" Not just yet, I think," said Mr. Raymond, with an odd look in his eyes.

" Why, we hear it from all quarters," said I; " and the red ribbons are all getting white."

Mr. Raymond smiled. " Rather a singular transformation, truly. But I think the ribbons will be well worn before the young Chevalier reviews his army in Hyde Park."

" I will not believe it !" cried I. " The Prince must be victorious! God defends the right !"

" God defends His own," said Mr. Raymond. " Do you see in history that He always defends the cause which you account to be right ? "

No; I could not say that.

"How can you be an opponent of the Cause?" I cried—I am afraid, shifting my ground.

He smiled again. "I can well understand the attraction of the Cause," said he, "to a young and enthusiastic nature. There is something very enticing in the son of an exiled Prince, come to win back what he conceives to be the inheritance of his fathers. And in truth, if the Old Pretender were really the son of King James,—well, it might be more difficult to say what a man's duty would be in that case. But that, as you know, is thought by many to be at best very doubtful."

"You do not believe he is?" cried I.

"I do not believe it," said Mr. Raymond.

I wondered how he could possibly doubt it.

"Nor is that all that is to be considered," he went on. "I can tell you, young lady, if he were to succeed, we should all rue it bitterly before long. His triumph is the triumph of Rome—the triumph of persecution and martyrdom and agony for God's people."

"I know that," said I. "But right is right, for all that! The Crown is his, not the Elector's. On that principle, any man might steal money, if he meant to do good with it."

"The Crown is neither George's nor James's, as some think," said Mr. Raymond, "but belongs to the people."

Who could have stood such a speech as that?

"The people!" I cried. "The mob—the rabble—the Crown is theirs! How can any man imagine such a thing?"

"You forget, methinks, young lady," said Mr. Raymond, as quietly as before, "that you are one of those of whom you speak."

"I forget nothing of the kind," cried I, too angry to be civil. "Of course I know I am one of the people. What do you mean? Am I to maintain that black beetles are cherubim, because I am a black beetle? Truth is truth. The Crown is God's, not the people's. When He chose to make the present King—King James of course, not that wretched Elector—the son of his father, He distinctly told the people whom He wished them to have for their king. What right have they to dispute His ordinance?"

I was quite beyond myself. I had forgotten where I was, and to whom I was talking—forgotten Mr. Raymond, and Angus, and Flora, and even Grandmamma. It seemed to me as if there were only two parties in the world, and on the one hand were God and the King, and on the other a miserable mass of silly nobodies called The People. How could such contemptible insects presume to judge for themselves, or to set their wills up in opposition to the will of him whom God had commanded them to obey?

The softest, lightest of touches fell on my shoulder. I looked up into the grave grey eyes of Annas Keith. And feeling myself excessively rude and utterly extinguished,—(and yet, after all, right)—I slipped out of the group, and made my way into the farthest corner. Mr. Raymond, of course, would think me no gentlewoman. Well, it did not much matter what he thought; he was only a Whig. And when the Prince were actually

come, which would be in a very few days at the furthest
—then he would see which of us was right. Meantime,
I could wait. And the next minute I felt as if I could
not wait—no, not another instant.

" Sit down, Cary. You look tired," said Ephraim
beside me.

" I am not a bit tired, thank you," said I, " but I
am abominably angry."

" Nothing more tiring," said he. " What about? "

" Oh, don't make me go over it ! I have been talking
to a Whig."

" That means, I suppose, that the Whig has been
talking to you. Which beat ? I beg pardon—you did,
of course."

" I was right and he was wrong, if you mean that,"
said I. " But whether he thinks he is beaten——"

" If he be an Englishman, he does not," said Ephraim.
" Particularly if he be a North Country man."

" I don't know what country he comes from," cried I.
" I should like to make mincemeat of him."

" Indigestible," suggested Ephraim, quite gravely.

" Ephraim, what are we to do for Angus? " said I, as
it came back to me : and I told him the news which
Mr. Raymond had brought. Ephraim gave a soft
whispered whistle.

" You may well ask," said he. " I am afraid, Cary,
nothing can be done."

" What will they do to him ? "

His face grew graver still.

" You know," he said, in a low voice, " what they

did to Lord Derwentwater. Colonel Keith had better lie close."

"But that Whig knows where he is!" cried I. "He—Ephraim, do you know him?"

"Know whom, Cary?"

"Mr. Raymond."

"Is he your Whig?" asked Ephraim, laughing. "Pray, don't make him into mincemeat; he is one of the best men in England."

"He need be," said I; "he is a horrid Whig! What do you, being friends with such a man?"

"He is a very good man, Cary. He was one of my tutors at school. I never knew what his politics were before to-night."

We were silent for a while; and then Grandmamma sent for me, not, as I feared, to scold me for being loud-spoken and warm, but to tell me that one of my lappets hung below the other, and I must make Perkins alter it before Tuesday. I do not know how I bore the rest of the evening.

When I went up at last to our chamber, I found it empty. Lucette, Grandmamma's French woman, who waits on her, while Perkins is rather my Aunt Dorothea's and ours, came in to tell me that Perkins was gone to bed with a headache, and hoped that we would allow her to wait on us to-night, when she was dismissed by the elder ladies.

"Oh, I want no waiting at all," said I, " if somebody will just take the pins out of my head-dress carefully. Do that, Lucette, and then I shall need nothing else. I cannot speak for the other young ladies."

Lucette threw a wrapping-cape over my shoulders, and began to remove the pins with deft fingers. Grandmamma had not yet come upstairs.

"Mademoiselle Agnès looks *charmante* to-night," said she: "but then she is always *charmante*. But what has Mademoiselle Flore? So white, so white she is! I saw her through the door."

I told her that Flora's brother had been taken prisoner.

"Ah, this horrible war!" cried she. "Can the *grands Seigneurs* not leave alone the wars? or else fight out their quarrels their own selves?"

"Oh, the Prince will soon be here," said I, "and then it will all be over."

"All be over? Ah, *sapristi!* Mademoiselle does not know. The Prince means the priests: and the priests mean—*Bon!* have I not heard my grandmother tell?"

"Tell what, Lucette? I thought you were a Papist, like all Frenchwomen."

"A Catholic—I? Why then came my grandfather to this country, and my father, and all? Does Mademoiselle suppose they loved better Spitalfields than Blois? Should they then leave a country where the sun is glorious and the vines *ravissantes*, for this black cold place where the sun shine once a year? *Vraiment! Serait-il possible?*"

I laughed. "The sun shines oftener in Cumberland, Lucette. I won't defend Spitalfields. But I want to know what your grandmother told you about the priests."

"The priests have two sides, Mademoiselle. On the one

is the confessional: you must go—you shall not choose.
You kneel; you speak out all—every thought in your
heart, every secret of your dearest friend. You may not
hide one little thought. The priest hears you hesitate?
The questions come:—Mademoiselle, terrible questions,
questions I could not ask, nor you understand. You
learn to understand them. They burn up your heart,
they drag down to Hell your soul. That is one side."

"Would they see me there twice!" said I.

"Then, if not so, there is the other side. The chains,
the torture-irons, the fire. You can choose, so: you
tell, or you die. There is no more choice. Does
Mademoiselle wonder that we came?"

"No, indeed, Lucette. How could I? But that
was in France. This is England. We are a different
sort of people here."

"You—yes. But the Church and the priests are
the same everywhere. Everywhere! May the good
God keep them from us!"

"Why, Lucette! you are praying against the Prince,
if it be as you say!"

"Ah! would I then do harm to *Monseigneur le
Prince?* Let him leave there the priests, and none
shall be more glad to see him come than I. I love the
right, always. But the priests! No, no."

"But if it be right, Lucette?"

"The good God knows what is right. But, Mademoiselle, can it be right to bring in the priests and the
confessions?"

"Is it not God who brings them, Lucette? We

only bring the King.   If the King choose to bring the priests——"

"Ah! then the Lord will bring the fires.   But the Lord bring the priests!   The Lord shut up the *prêches* and set up the mass?   The Lord burn His poor servants, and clothe the servants of Satan in gold and scarlet?   The Lord forbid His Word, and set up images?   *Comment*, Mademoiselle!   It would not be possible."

"But, Lucette, the King has the *right!*"

"The Lord Christ has the right," said Lucette, solemnly.   "Is it not 'He whose right it is'?   Mademoiselle, He stands before the King!"

We heard Grandmamma saying good-night to my Uncle Charles at the foot of the stairs, and Lucette ran off to her chamber.

I felt more plagued than ever.   What *is* right?

Just then Annas and Flora came up; Annas grave but composed, Flora with a white face and red eyes.

"O Cary, Cary!"   She came and put her arms round me.   "Pray for Angus; we shall never see him again.   And he is not ready—he is not ready."

"My poor Flora!"   I said, and I did my best to soothe her.   But Annas did better.

"The Lord can make him ready," she said.   "He healed the paralytic man, dear, as some have it, entirely for the faith of them that bore him.   And surely the daughter of the Canaanitish woman could have no faith herself."

"Pray for him, Annas!" sobbed Flora.   "You have more faith than I."

" I am not so hard tried—yet," was the grave reply.

" You do not think Mr. Keith in danger?" said I.

" I think the Lord sitteth above the water-floods, Cary; and I would rather not look lower. Not till I must, and that may be very soon."

" Annas," said I, " I wish you would tell me what right is. I do get so puzzled."

" What puzzles you, Cary? Right is what God wills."

" But would the Prince not have the right, if God did not will him to succeed?"

" The Lawgiver can always repeal His own laws. We in the crowd, Cary, can only judge when they be repealed by hearing Him decree something contrary to them. And there are no precedents in that Court. ' Whatsoever the Lord pleased, that did He.' We can only wait and see. Until we do see it, we must follow our last orders."

" My Father says," added Flora, " that this question was made harder than it need have been, by the throwing out of the Exclusion Bill. The House of Commons passed it, but the Bishops and Lord Halifax threw it out; if that had been passed, making it impossible for a Papist to be King, then King James would never have come to the throne at all, and all the troubles and persecutions of his reign would not have happened. That, my Father says, was where they went wrong."

" Well," said I, " it does look like it. But how queer that the Bishops should be the people to go wrong!"

Annas laughed.

" You will find that nothing new, Cary, if you

search," said she. "'They that lead thee cause thee
to err' is as old a calamity as the Prophets. And where
priests or would-be priests are the leaders, they very
generally do go wrong."

"I wish," said I, "there were a few more 'Thou
shalt nots' in the Bible."

"Have you finished obeying all there are?"

I considered that question with one sleeve off.

"Well, no, I suppose not," I said at length, pulling
off the other.

Annas smiled gravely, and said no more.

Glorious news! The Prince is at Derby. I am sure
there is no more need to fear for Angus. His Royal
Highness will be here in a very few days now: and
then let the Whigs look to themselves!

Grandmamma has bought some more white cockades.
She says Hatty has improved wonderfully; her cheeks
are not so shockingly red, and she speaks better, and has
more decent manners. She thinks the Crosslands have
done her a great deal of good. I thought Hatty looking not at all well the last time she was here; and
so grave for her—almost sad. And I am afraid the
Crosslands, or somebody, have done her a great deal of
bad. But somehow, Hatty is one of those people whom
you cannot question unless she likes. Something inside
me will not put the questions. I don't know what it is.

I wish I knew everything! If I could only understand myself, I should get on better. And how am I
going to understand other people?

CHAPTER X.

SPIDERS' WEBS.

" Why does he find so many tangled threads,
   So many dislocated purposes,
   So many failures in the race of life ?"
                    —REV. HORATIUS BONAR, D.D.

E had a grand time of it last night, to celebrate
the Prince's entry into Derby. I did not see
one red ribbon. Grandmamma is very much
put out at the forbidding of French cambrics ; she says
nobody will be able to have a decent ruffle or a respectable handkerchief now : but what can you expect of
these Hanoverians ? And I am sure she looked smart
enough last night. We had dancing—first, the minuet,
and then a round—" Pepper's black," and then " Dull
Sir John," and a country dance, " Smiling Polly."
Flora would not dance, and Grandmamma excused
her, because she was a minister's daughter: Grandmamma always says a clergyman when she tells people :
she says minister is a low word only used by Dissenters,
and she does not want people to know that any guest
of hers has any connection with those creatures. " However, thank Heaven ! (says she) the girl is not my grand-

daughter!" I don't know what she would say if I were
to turn Dissenter. I suppose she would cut me off
with a shilling. Ephraim said so, and I asked him what
it meant. Shillings are not very sharp, and what was
I to be cut off? Ephraim seemed excessively amused.

"You are too good, Cary," said he. "Did you think
the shilling was a knife to cut you off something? It
means she will only leave you a shilling in her will."

"Well, that will be a shilling more than I expect,"
said I: and Ephraim went off laughing.

I asked Miss Newton, as she seemed to know him,
who Mr. Raymond was. She says he is the lecturer at
St. Helen's, and might have been a decent man if that
horrid creature Mr. Wesley had not got hold of him.

"Oh, do you know anything about Mr. Wesley,
or Mr. Whitefield?" cried I. "Are they in London
now?"

If I could hear them again!

"I am sure I cannot tell you," said Miss Newton,
laughing. "I have heard my father speak of them
with some very strong language after it—that I know.
My dear Miss Courtenay, does everything rouse your
enthusiasm? For how you can bring that brilliant
light into your eyes for the Prince, and for Mr. Wesley,
is quite beyond me. I should have thought they were
the two opposite ends of a pole."

"I don't know anything about Mr. Wesley," I said,
"and I have only heard Mr. Whitefield preach once
in Scotland."

"You have heard him?" she asked.

“ Yes, and liked him very much,” said I.

Miss Newton shrugged her shoulders in that little French way she has. “ Why, some people think him the worse of the two,” she said. “ I don’t know anything about them, I can tell you—only that Mr. Wesley makes Dissenters faster than you could make tatting-stitches.”

“ What does he do to them ? ” said I.

“ I don’t know, and I don’t want to know,” said she. “ If he had lived in former times, I am sure he would have been taken up for witchcraft. He is a clergyman, or they say so ; but I really wonder the Bishops have not turned him out of the Church long ago.”

“ A clergyman, and makes people Dissenters ! ” cried I. “ Why, Mr. Whitefield quoted the Articles in his sermon.”

“ They said so,” she replied. “ I know nothing about it ; I never heard the man, thank Heaven ! but they say he goes about preaching to all sorts of dreadful creatures—those wild miners down in Cornwall, and coal-heavers, and any sort of mobs he can get to listen. Only fancy a clergyman—a gentleman—doing any such thing ! ”

I thought a moment, and some words came to my mind.

“ Do you think Mr. Wesley was wrong ? ” I said. “ ‘ The common people heard Him gladly.’ And I suppose you would not say that our Lord was not a gentleman.”

“ Dear Miss Courtenay, forgive me, but what very

odd things you say! And—excuse me—don't you know it is not thought at all good taste to quote the Bible in polite society?"

"Is the Bible worse off for that?" said I. "Or is it the polite society? The best society, I suppose, ought to be in Heaven: and I fancy they do not shut out the Bible there. What think you?"

"Are you very innocent?" she answered, laughing; "or are you only making believe? You must know, surely, that religion is not talked about except from the pulpit, and on Sundays."

"But can we all be sure of dying on a Sunday?" I answered. "We shall want religion then, shall we not?"

"Hush! we don't talk of dying either—it is too shocking!"

"But don't we do it sometimes?" I said.

Miss Newton looked as if she did not know whether to laugh or be angry—certainly very much disturbed.

"Let us talk of something more agreeable, I beg," said she. "See, Miss Bracewell is going to sing."

"Oh, she will sing nothing worth listening to," said I.

"I suppose you think only Methodist hymns worth listening to," responded Miss Newton, rather sneeringly.

I don't like to be sneered at. I suppose nobody does. But it does not make me feel timid and yield, as it seems to do many: it only makes me angry.

"Well," said I, "listen how much this is worth."

Amelia drew off her gloves with a listless air which I believe she thought exceedingly genteel. I cannot undertake to describe her song: it was one of those queer lackadaisical ditties which always remind me of those tunes which go just where you don't expect them to go, and end nowhere. I hate them. And I don't like the songs much better. Of course there was a lady wringing her hands—why do people in ballads wring their hands so much? I never saw anybody do it in my life—and a cavalier on a coal-black steed, and a silvery moon; what would become of the song-writers if there were no moon and no sea?—and " she sat and wailed," and he did something or other, I could not exactly hear what; and at last he, or she, or both of them (only that would not suit the grammar) " was at rest," and I was thankful to hear it, for Amelia stopped singing.

" How sweet and sad !" said Miss Newton.

" Do you like that kind of song? I think it is rubbish."

She laughed with that little deprecating air which she often uses to me. I looked up to see who was going to sing next: and to my extreme surprise, and almost equal pleasure, I saw Annas sit down to the harp.

" Oh, Miss Keith is going to sing !" cried I. " I should like to hear hers."

" A Scottish ballad, no doubt," replied Miss Newton.

There was a soft, low, weird-like prelude : and then came a voice like that of a thrush, at which every other in the room seemed to hush instinctively. Each word was clear.

This was Annas's song.

"She said,—'We parted for a while,
But we shall meet again ere long ;
I work in lowly, lonely room,
And he amid the foreign throng :
But here I willingly abide,—
Here, where I see the other side.

"'Look to those hills which reach away
Beyond the sea that rolls between ;
Here from my casement, day by day,
Their happy summits can be seen :
Happy, although they us divide,—
I know he sees the other side.

"'The days go on to make the year—
A year we must be parted yet—
I sing amid my crosses light,
For on those hills mine eyes are set ;
You say, those hills our eyes divide ?
Ay, but he sees the other side !

"'So these dividing hills become
Our point of meeting, every eve ;
Up to the hills we look and pray
And love—our work so soon we leave ;
And then no more shall aught divide—
We dwell upon the other side.'"

"Pretty !" said Miss Newton, in the tone which people use when they do not think a thing pretty, but fancy that you expect them to say so : "but not so charming as Miss Bracewell's song."

"Wait," said I ; "she has not finished yet."

The harp was speaking now—in a sad low voice, rising gradually to a note of triumph. Then it sank low again, and Annas's voice continued the song.

"She said,—'We parted for a while,
    But we shall meet again ere long;
I dwell in lonely, lowly room,
    And he hath joined the heavenly throng :
Yet here I willingly abide,
For yet I see the Other Side.

"'I look unto the hills of God
    Beyond the life that rolls between ;
Here from my work by faith each day
    Their blessed summits can be seen :
Blessed, although they us divide,—
I know he sees the Other Side.

"'The days go on, the days go on,—
    Through earthly life we meet not yet ;
I sing amid my crosses light,
    For on those hills mine eyes are set :
'Tis true, those hills our eyes divide—
Ay, but he sees the Other Side !

"'So the eternal hills become
    Our point of meeting, every eve ;
Up to the hills I look and pray
    And love—soon all my work I leave :
And then no more shall aught divide—
We dwell upon the Other Side.'"

I turned to Miss Newton with my eyes full, as Annas
rose from the harp. The expression of her face was a
curious mixture of feelings.

"Was ever such a song sung in Mrs. Desborough's
drawing-room!" she cried. "She will think it no
better than a Methodist hymn. I am afraid Miss Keith
has done herself no good with her hostess."

"But Grandmamma would never——" I said, hesitatingly. "Annas Keith's connections are——"

"I advise you not to be too sure what she 'would never,'" answered Miss Newton, with a little capable nod. "Mrs. Desborough would scarce be civil to the Princess herself if she sang a pious song in her drawing-room on a reception evening."

"But it was charming!" I said.

Miss Newton shrugged her shoulders. "The same things do not charm everybody," said she. "It seemed to me no better than that Methodist doggrel. The latter half, at least; the beginning promised better."

When we went up to bed, Annas came to me as I stood folding my shoulder-knots, and laid a hand on each of my shoulders from behind.

"Cary, we must say 'good-bye,' I think. I scarce expected it. But Mrs. Desborough's face, when my song was ended, had 'good-bye' in it."

"O Annas!" said I. "Surely she would never be angry with you for a mere song! Your connections are so good, and Grandmamma thinks so much of connections."

"If my song had only had a few wicked words in it," replied Annas, with that slight curl of her lip which I was learning to understand, "I dare say she would have recovered it by to-morrow. And if my connections had been poor people,—or better, Whigs,—or better still, disreputable rakes—she might have got over that. But a pious song, and a sisterly connection of spirit with Mr. Whitefield and the Scottish Covenanters No, Cary, she will not survive that. I never yet knew a worldly woman forgive that one crime of crimes—

Q

Calvinism. Anything else! Don't you see why, my dear? It sets her outside. And she knows that I know she is outside. Therefore I am unforgivable. However absurd the idea may be in reality, it is to her mind equivalent to *my* setting her outside. She is unable to recognise that she has chosen to stay without, and I am guilty of nothing worse than unavoidably seeing that she is there. That I should be able to see it is unpardonable. I am sorry it should have happened just now; but I suppose it was to be."

"Are you going to tell her so?" I asked, wondering what Annas meant.

"I expect she will tell me before to-morrow is over," said Annas, with a peculiar smile.

"But what made you choose that song, then? I thought it so pretty."

"I chose the one I knew, to which I supposed she would object the least," replied Annas. "She asked me to sing."

When we came down to breakfast, the next morning, I felt that something was in the air. Grandmamma sat so particularly straight up, and my Aunt Dorothea looked so prim, and my Uncle Charles fidgetted about between the fire and the window, like a man who knew of something coming which he wanted to have over. My Aunt Dorothea poured the chocolate in silence. When all were served, Grandmamma took a pinch of snuff.

"Miss Keith!"

"Madam!"

"Do you think the air of the Isle of Wight wholesome at this season of the year?"

"So much so, Madam, that I am inclined to propose we should resume our journey thither."

Grandmamma took another pinch.

"I will beg you, then, to make my compliments to Sir James, and tell him how much entertained I have been by your visit, and especially by your performance on the harp. You have a fine finger, Miss Keith, and your choice of a song is unexceptionable."

"I thank you for the compliment, Madam, which I shall be happy to make to Sir James."

There was nothing but dead silence after that until breakfast was over. When we were back in our room, I broke down. To lose both Annas and Flora was too much.

"O Annas! why did you take the bull by the horns?" I cried.

She laughed. "It is always the best way, Cary, when you see him put his head down!"

Annas and Flora are gone, and I feel like one shipwrecked. I wander about the house, and do not know what to do. I might read, but Grandmamma has no books except dreary romances in huge volumes, which date, I suppose, from the time when she was a girl at school; and my Uncle Charles has none but books about farming and etiquette. I have looked up and mended all my clothes, and cannot find any sewing to do. I wrote to Sophy only last week, and they will not expect another letter for a while. I wish something pleasant would happen. The only thing I can think of to do is to go in a chair to visit Hatty and the Bracewells, and I am afraid that would be something unpleasant. I have not spoken to Mr. Crossland, but I do not like the look of him ; and Mrs. Crossland is a stranger, and I am tired of strangers. They so seldom seem to turn out pleasant people.

Just as I had written that, as if to complete my vexation, my Aunt Dorothea looked in and told me to put on my cherry satin this evening, for Sir Anthony and my Lady Parmenter were expected. If there be a creature I particularly wish not to see, he is sure to come! I wish I knew why things are always going wrong in this world! There are two or three people that I would give a good deal for, and I am quite sure they will not be here; and I should think Cecilia dear at three-farthings, with Sir Anthony thrown in for the penny.

I wish I were making jumballs in the kitchen at Brocklebank, and could have a good talk with my Aunt Kezia afterwards! Somehow, I never cared much about it when I could, and now that I cannot, I feel as if I would give anything for it. Are things always like that? Does nothing in this world ever happen just as one would like it in every point?

In my cherry-coloured satin, with white shoulder-knots, a blue pompoon in my hair, and my new hoop (I detest these hoops; they are horrid), I came down to the withdrawing room, and cast my eye round the chamber. Grandmamma, in brocaded black silk, sat where she always does, at the side of the fire, and my Uncle Charles—who for a wonder was at home—and my Aunt Dorothea were receiving the people as they came in. The Bracewells were there already, and Hatty, and Mr. Crossland, and a middle-aged lady, who I suppose was his mother, and Miss Newton, and a few more whose faces and names I know. Sir Anthony and my Lady Parmenter came in just after I got there.

What has come over Hatty? She does not look like the same girl. Grandmamma can never talk of her glazed red cheeks now. She is whiter almost than I am, and so thin! I am quite sure she is either ill, or unhappy, or both. But I cannot ask her, for somehow we never meet each other except for a minute. Several times I have thought, and the thought grows upon me, that somebody does not want Hatty and me to have a quiet talk with each other. At first I thought it was Hatty who kept away from me herself, but I am beginning to think now that somebody else is doing it. I do not trust that young Mr. Crossland, not one bit. Yet, why he should wish to keep us apart, I cannot even imagine. I made up my mind to get hold of Hatty and ask her when she were going home; I think she would be safer there than here. But it was a long, long while before I could reach her. So many people seemed to be hemming her in. I sat on an ottoman in the corner, watching my opportunity, when all at once a voice called me back to something else.

“Dear little Cary, I have been so wishing for a chat with you.”

Hatty used to say that you may always know something funny is coming when you see a cat wag her tail. I had come to the conclusion that whenever one person addressed me with endearing phrases, something sinister was coming. I looked up this time: I did not courtesy and walk away, as I did on the last occasion. I wanted to avoid an open quarrel. If she had sought me out after that, I could not avoid it. But to speak to me as if nothing had happened!—how could the woman be so brazen as that?

I looked up, and saw a large gold-coloured fan, most beautifully painted with birds of all the hues of the rainbow, from over which those tawny eyes were glancing at me; and for one moment I wished that hating people were not wicked.

“For what purpose, Madam?” I replied.

“Dear child, you are angry with me,” she said, and the soft, warm, gloved hand pressed mine, before I could draw it away. “It is so natural, for of course you do not understand. But it makes me very sorry, for I loved you so much.”

O serpent, how beautiful you are! But you are a serpent still.

“Did you?” I said, and my voice sounded hard and cold to my own ears. “I take the liberty of doubting whether you and I give that name to the same thing.”

The light gleamed and flashed, softened and darkened,

then shot out again from those wonderful, beautiful eyes.

"And you won't forgive me?" she said, in a soft sad voice. How she can govern that voice, to be sure!

"Forgive you? Yes," I answered. "But trust you? No. I think never again, my Lady Parmenter."

"You will be sorry some day that you did not."

Was it a regret? was it a threat? The voice conveyed neither, and might have stood for both. I looked up again, but she had vanished, and where she had been the moment before stood Mr. Raymond.

"A penny for your thoughts, Miss Courtenay."

"You shall have my past thoughts, if you please," said I, trying to speak lightly. "I would rather not sell my present ones at the price."

He smiled, and drew out a new penny. "Then let me make the less valuable purchase."

Even Mr. Raymond was a welcome change from *her*.

"Then tell me, Mr. Raymond," said I, "do things ever happen exactly as one wishes them to do?"

"Once in a thousand times, perhaps," said he. "I should imagine, though, that the occasion usually comes after long waiting and bitter pain. Generally there is something to remind us that this is not our rest."

"Why?" I said, and I heard my soul go into the word.

"Why not?" answered he, pithily. "Is the servant so much greater than his Lord that he may reasonably look for things to be otherwise? Cast your mind's eye over the life of Christ our Master, and see on how many occasions matters happened in a way which you would suppose entirely to His liking? Can you name one?"

I thought, and could not see anything, except when He did a miracle, or when He spent a night in prayer to God.

"I give you those nights of prayer," said Mr. Raymond. "But I think you must yield me the miracles. Unquestionably it must have given Him pleasure to relieve pain; but see how much pain to Himself was often mixed in it!—'Looking up to Heaven, He sighed' ere He did one; He wept, just before performing another; He cried, 'How long shall I be with you, and suffer you!' ere he worked a third. No, Miss Courtenay, the miracles of our Divine Master were not all pleasure to Himself. Indeed, I should be inclined to venture further, and ask if we have no hint that they were wrought at a considerable cost to Himself. He 'took our infirmities, and bare our sicknesses'; He knew when 'virtue had gone out of Him.' That may mean only that His Divine knowledge was conscious of it; but taking both passages together, is it not possible that His wonderful works were wrought at personal expense—that His human body suffered weakness, faintness, perhaps acute pain, as the natural consequence of doing them? You will understand that I merely throw out the hint. Scripture does not speak decisively; and where God does not decide, it is well for men to be cautious."

"Mr. Raymond," I exclaimed, "how can you be a Whig?"

" Pardon me, but what is the connection ? " asked he, ooking both astonished and diverted.

" Don't you see it ?   You are much too good for one."

Mr. Raymond laughed.   " Thank you ; I fear I did not detect the compliment.   May I put the counter question, and ask how you came to be a Tory ?"

" Why, I was born so," said I.

" And so was I a Whig," replied he.

" Excuse me !" came laughingly from my other hand, in Miss Newton's voice.   " The waters are not quite so smooth as they were, and I thought I had better be at hand to pour a little oil if necessary.   Mr. Raymond, I am afraid you are getting worldly.   Is that not the proper word ? "

" It is the proper word for an improper thing," said Mr. Raymond.   " On what evidence do you rest your accusation, Miss Theresa ? "

" On the fact that you have twice in one week made your appearance in Mrs. Desborough's rooms, which are the very pink of worldliness."

" Have I come without reason ? "

" You have not given it me," said the young lady, laughing.   " You cannot always come to tell one of the guests that his (or her) relations have been taken prisoner."

I looked up so suddenly that Mr. Raymond answered my eyes before he replied to Miss Newton's words.

" No, Miss Courtenay, I did not come with ill news.   I suppose a man may have two reasons at different times for the same action ? "

"Where is our handsome friend of the dreadful name?" asked Miss Newton.

"Mr. Hebblethwaite?   He told me he could not be here this evening."

"That man will have to change his name before anybody will marry him," said Miss Newton.

"Then, if he takes my advice, he will continue in single blessedness," was Mr. Raymond's answer

"Now, why?"

"Do you not think it would be preferable to marrying a woman whose regard for you was limited by the alphabet?"

"Mr. Raymond, you and Miss Courtenay do say such odd things!   Is that because you are religious people?"

Oh, what a strange feeling came over me when Miss Newton said that!   What made her count me a "religious person"?   Am I one?   I should not have dared to say it.   I should like to be so; I am afraid to go further.   To reckon myself one would be to sign my name as a queen, and I am not sufficiently sure of my royal blood to do it.

But what had I ever said to Miss Newton that she should entertain such an idea?   Mr. Raymond glanced at me with a brotherly sort of smile, which I wished from my heart that I deserved (for all he is a Whig!), and was afraid I did not.   Then he said,—

"Religious people, I believe, are often very odd things in the eyes of irreligious people.   Do you count yourself among the latter class, Miss Theresa?"

"Oh, I don't make any profession," said she. "I have but one life, and I want to enjoy it."

"That is exactly my position," said Mr. Raymond, smiling.

"Now, what do you mean?" demanded she. "Don't the Methodists label everything 'wicked' that one wants to do?"

"'One' sometimes means another," replied Mr. Raymond, with a funny look in his eyes. "They do not put that label on anything I want to do. I cannot answer for other people."

"I am sure they would put it on a thousand things that I should," said Miss Newton.

"Am I to understand that speaks badly for them? —or for you?"

"Mr. Raymond! You know I make no profession of religion. I think it is much better to be free."

The look in Mr. Raymond's eyes seemed to me very like Divine compassion.

"Miss Theresa, your remark makes me ask two questions: Do you suppose that 'making no profession' will excuse you to the Lord? Does your Bible read, 'He that maketh no profession shall be saved'? And also—Are you free?"

"Am I free? Why, of course I am!" she cried. "I can do what I like, without asking leave of priest or minister."

"God forbid that you should ask leave of priest or minister! But I can do what I like, also. What the

Lord likes, I like. No priest on earth shall come between Him and me."

"That sounds very grand, Mr. Raymond. But just listen to me. I know a young gentlewoman who says the same thing. She is dead against everything which she thinks to be Popery. Submit to the Pope?—no, not for a moment! But this dear creature has a pet minister, who is to her exactly what the Pope is to his subjects. She won't dance, because Mr. Gardiner disapproves of it; she can't sing a song, of the most innocent sort, because Mr. Gardiner thinks songs naughty; she won't do this, and she can't go there, because Mr. Gardiner says this and that. Now, what do you call that?"

"Human nature, Miss Theresa. Depend upon it, Popery would never have the hold it has if there were not in it something very palatable to human nature. Human nature is of two varieties, and Satan's two grand masterpieces appeal to both. To the proud man, who is a law unto himself, he brings infidelity as the grand temptation : 'Ye shall be as gods'—'Yea, hath God said?'—and lastly, 'There is no God.' To the weaker nature, which demands authority to lean on, he brings Popery, offering to decide for you all the difficult questions of heart and life with authority— offering you the romantic fancy of a semi-goddess in its worship of the Virgin, in whose gentle bosom you may repose every trouble, and an infallible Church which can set everything right for you. Now just notice how far God's religion is from both. It does not say, 'Ye shall be as gods;' but, 'This Man receiveth sinners': not, 'Hath God said?' but, 'Thus saith the Lord.' Turn to the other side, and instead of your compassionate goddess, it offers you Jesus, the God-man, able to succour them that are tempted, in that He Himself hath suffered being tempted. Infallibility, too, it offers you, but not resident in a man, nor in a body of men. It resides in a book, which is not the word of man, but the Word of God, and effective only when it is interpreted and applied by the living Spirit, whose guidance may be had by the weakest and poorest child that will ask God for Him."

"We are not in church, my dear Mr. Raymond!" said Miss Newton, shrugging her shoulders. "If you preach over the hour, Mrs. Desborough will be sending Cæsar to show you the clock."

"I have not exceeded it yet, I think," said Mr. Raymond.

"Well, I wish you would talk to Eliza Wilkinson instead of me. She says she has been—is 'converted' the word? I am ill up in Methodist terms. And ever since she is converted, or was converted, she does not commit sin. I wish you would talk to her."

"I am not fit to talk to such a seraph. I am a sinner."

"Oh, but I think there is some distinction, which I do not properly understand. She does not wilfully sin; and as to those little things which everybody does, that are not quite right, you know,—well, they don't count for anything.   She is a child of God, she says, and therefore He will not be hard upon her for little nothings.   Is that your creed, Mr. Raymond ? "

" Do you know the true name of that creed, Miss Theresa ? "

" Dear, no ! I understand nothing about it."

Mr. Raymond's voice was very solemn : " ' So hast thou also them that hold the doctrine of the Nico-laitanes, *which thing I hate.*' ' Turning the grace of our God into lasciviousness.'   Antinomianism is the name of it.   It has existed in the Church of God from a date, you see, earlier than the close of the in-spired canon.   Essentially the same thing survives in the Popish Church, under the name of mortal and venial sins ; and it creeps sooner or later into every denomina-tion, in its robes of an angel of light.   But it belongs to the darkness.   Sin !   Do we know the meaning of that awful word ?   I believe none but God knows rightly what sin is.   But he who does not know something of what sin is can have very poor ideas of the Christ who saves from sin.   He does not save men *in* sin, but *from* sin : not only from penalty,—from *sin*.   Christ is not dead, but alive.   And sin is not a painted plaything, but a deadly poison.   God forgive them who speak lightly of it ! "

I do not know what Miss Newton said to this, for at that minute I caught sight of Hatty in a corner, alone, and seized my opportunity at once.   Threading my way with some difficulty among bewigged and belaced gentlemen, and ladies with long trains and fluttering fans, I reached my sister, and sat down by her.

"Hatty," said I, "I hardly ever get a word with you How long do you stay with the Crosslands?"

"I do not know, Cary," she answered, looking down, and playing with her fan.

"Do you know that you look very far from well?"

"There are mirrors in Charles Street," she replied, with a slight curl of her lip.

"Hatty, are those people kind to you?" I said, thinking I had better, like Annas, take the bull by the horns.

"I suppose so. They mean to be. Let it alone, Cary; you are not old enough to interfere—hardly to understand."

"I am only eighteen months younger than you," said I. "I do not wish to interfere, Hatty; but I do want to understand. Surely your own sister many be concerned if she see you looking ill and unhappy."

"Do I look so, Cary?"

I thought, from the tone, that Hatty was giving way a little.

"You look both," I said. "I wish you would come here."

"Do you wish it, Cary?" The tone now was very unlike Hatty.

"Indeed I do, Hatty," said I, warmly. "I don't half believe in those people in Charles Street; and as to Amelia and Charlotte, I doubt if either of them would see anything, look how you might."

"Oh, Charlotte is not to blame; thoughtlessness is her worst fault," said Hatty, still playing with her fan.

"And somebody is to blame?   Is it Amelia?"

"I did not say so," was the answer.

"No," I said, feeling disappointed; "I cannot get you to say anything.   Hatty, I do wish you would trust me.   Nobody here loves you except me."

"You did not love me much once, Cary."

"Oh, I get vexed when you tease me, that is all," said I.   "But I want you to look happier, Hatty, dear."

"I should not tease you much now, Cary."

I looked up, and saw that Hatty's eyes were full of tears.

"Do come here, Hatty!" I said, earnestly.

"Grandmamma has not asked me," she replied.

"Then I will beg her to ask you.   I think she will. She said the other day that you were very much improved."

"At all events, my red cheeks and my plough-boy appetite would scarcely distress her now," returned Hatty, rather bitterly.   "Mr. Crossland is coming for me—I must go."   And while she held my hand, I was amazed to hear a low whisper, in a voice of unutterable longing,—"Cary, pray for me!"

That horrid Mr. Crossland came up and carried her off.   Poor dear Hatty!   I am sure something is wrong. And somehow, I think I love her better since I began to pray for her, only that was not last night, as she seemed to think.

This morning at breakfast, I asked Grandmamma if she would do me a favour.

"Yes, child, if it be reasonable," said she. "What would you have?"

"Please, Grandmamma, will you ask Hatty to come for a little while? I should so like to have her; and I cannot talk to her comfortably in a room full of people."

Grandmamma took a pinch of snuff, as she generally does when she wants to consider a minute.

"She is very much improved," said she. "She really is almost presentable. I should not feel ashamed, I think, of introducing her as my grand-daughter. Well, Cary, if you wish it, I do not mind. You are a tolerably good girl, and I do not object to give you a pleasure. But it must be after she has finished her visit to the Crosslands. I could not entice her away."

"I asked her how long she was going to stay there, Grandmamma, and she said she did not know."

"Then, my dear, you must wait till she do." [1]

But what may happen before then? I knew it would be of no use to say any more to Grandmamma: she is a perfect Mede and Persian when she have once declared her royal pleasure. And my Aunt Dorothea will never interfere. My Uncle Charles is the only one who dare say another word, and it was a question if he would. He is good-natured enough, but so careless that I could not feel at all certain of enlisting him. Oh dear! I do feel to be growing so old with all my

---

[1] The use of the subjunctive with *when* and *until*, now obsolete, was correct English until the present century was some thirty years old.

cares! It seems as if Hatty, and Annas, and Flora, and Angus, and Colonel Keith, and the Prince,—I beg his pardon, he should have come first,—were all on my shoulders at once. And I don't feel strong enough to carry such a lot of people.

I wish my Aunt Kezia was here. I have wished it so many times lately.

When I had written so far, I turned back to look at my Aunt Kezia's rules. And then I saw how foolish I am. Why, instead of putting the Lord first, I had been leaving Him out of the whole thing. Could He not carry all these cares for me? Did He not know what ailed Hatty, and how to deliver Angus, and all about it? I knelt down there and then (I always write in my own chamber), and asked Him to send Hatty to me, and better still, to bring her to Him; and to show me whether I had better speak to my Uncle Charles, or try to get things out of Amelia. As to Charlotte, I would not ask her about anything which I did not care to tell the town crier.

The next morning—(there, my dates are getting all wrong again! It is no use trying to keep them straight) —as my Uncle Charles was putting on his gloves to go out, he said,—

"Well, Cary, shall I bring you a fairing of any sort?"

"Uncle Charles," I said, leaping to a decision at once, "do bring me Hatty! I am sure she is not happy. Do get Grandmamma to let her come now."

"Not happy!" cried my Uncle Charles, lifting his

eyebrows. "Why, what is the matter with the girl? Can't she get married? Time enough, surely."

Oh dear, how can men be so silly! But I let it pass, for I wanted Hatty to come, much more than to make my Uncle Charles sensible. In fact, I am afraid the last would take too much time and labour. There, now, I should not have said that.

"Won't you try, Uncle Charles? I do want her so much."

"Child, I cannot interfere with my mother. Ask Hatty to spend the day. Then you can have a talk with her."

"Uncle, please, will you ask Grandmamma?"

"If you like," said he, with a laugh.

I heard no more about it till supper-time, when my Uncle Charles said, as if it had just occurred to him (which I dare say it had),—"Madam, I think this little puss is disappointed that Hatty cannot come at once. Might she not spend the day here? It would be a treat for both girls."

Grandmamma's snuff-box came out as usual. I sat on thorns, while she rapped her box, opened it, took a pinch, shut the box with a snap, and consigned it to her pocket.

"Yes," she said, at last. "Dorothea, you can send Cæsar with a note."

"Oh, thank you, Grandmamma!" cried I.

Grandmamma looked at me, and gave an odd little laugh.

"These fresh girls!" she said, "how they do care about things, to be sure!"

"Grandmamma, is it pleasanter not to care about things?" said I.

"It is better, my dear. To be at all warm or enthusiastic betrays under-breeding."

"But — please, Grandmamma — do not well-bred people get very warm over politics?"

"Sometimes well-bred people forget themselves," said Grandmamma. "But it is more allowable to be warm over some matters than others. Politics are to some degree an exception. We do not make exhibitions of our personal affections, Caroline, and above all things we avoid showing warmth on religious questions. We do not talk of such things at all in good society."

Now—I say this to my book, of course, not to Grandmamma—is not that very strange? We are not to be warm over the most important things, matters of life and death, things we really care about in our inmost hearts: but over all the little affairs that we do not care about, we may lose our tempers a little (in an elegant and reasonable way) if we choose to do so. Would it not be better the other way about?

CHAPTER XI.

CARY IN A NEW CHARACTER.

"God has a few of us whom He whispers in the ear."
—BROWNING.

I FEEL more and more certain that something is wrong in Charles Street. The invitation is declined, not by Hatty herself, but in a note from Mrs. Crossland: "Miss Hester Courtenay has so sad a catarrh that it will not be safe for her to venture out for some days to come." [1]

"Why, Cary, that is a disappointment for you," said my Uncle Charles, kindly. "I think, Madam, as Hester cannot come, Mrs. Crossland might have offered a counter-invitation to Caroline."

"It would have been well-bred," said Grandmamma. "Mrs. Crossland is not very well connected. She was the daughter or niece of an archdeacon, I believe; rather raised by her marriage. I am sorry you are disappointed, child."

This was a good deal for Grandmamma to say, and I thanked her.

[1] Our forefathers thought colds a much more serious affair than we do. They probably knew much less about them.

Well, one thing had failed me; I must try another. At the next evening assembly I watched my chance, and caught Charlotte in a corner.   I asked how Hatty was.

"Hatty?" said Charlotte, looking surprised.   "She is well enough, for aught I know."

"I thought she had a bad catarrh?" said I.

"Didn't know she had one.   She is going to my Lady Milworth's assembly with Mrs. Crossland."

I felt more sure of ill-play than ever, but to Charlotte I said no more.   The next person whom I pinned to the wall was Amelia.   With her I felt more need of caution in one sense, for I did not know how far she might be in the plot, whatever it was.   That no living mortal with any shadow of brains would have trusted Charlotte with a secret, I felt as sure as I did that my ribbons were white, and not red.

"Emily," I said, "why did not Hatty come with you to-night?"

"I did not ask," was Amelia's languid answer.   I do think she gets more and more limp and unstarched as time goes on.

"Is she better?"

"What is the matter with her?"   Amelia's eyes betrayed no artifice.

"A catarrh, I understand."

"Oh, you heard that from Miss Newton.   The Newtons asked her for an assembly, and Mrs. Crossland did not want to give up my Lady Milworth, so she sent word Hatty had a catarrh, I believe.   It is all nonsense."

"And it is not telling falsehoods?" said I.

"My dear, I have nothing to do with it," said Amelia, fanning herself. "Mrs. Crossland may carry her own shortcomings."

I felt pretty sure now that Amelia was not in the plot.

"Will you give a message to Hatty?" I said.

"If it be not too long to remember."

"Tell her I wanted her to spend the day, and my Aunt Dorothea writ to ask her to come, and Mrs. Crossland returned answer that she had too bad a catarrh, and must keep indoors for some days."

"Did she—to Mrs. Desborough?" said Amelia, with a surprised look. "I rather wonder at that, too."

"Emily, help me!" I said. "These Crosslands want to keep Hatty and me apart. There is something wrong going on. Do help us, if you ever cared for either of us."

Amelia looked quite astonished and puzzled.

"Really, I knew nothing about it! Of course I care for you, Cary. But what can I do?"

"Give that message to Hatty. Bid her, from me, break through the snares, and *come.* Then we can see what must be done next."

"I will give her the message," said Amelia, with what was energy for her. "Cary, I have had nothing to do with it, if something be wrong. I never even guessed it."

"I don't believe you have," said I. "But tell me one thing, Emily: are they scheming to make Hatty marry Mr. Crossland?"

"Most certainly not!" cried Amelia, with more warmth than I had thought was in her. "Impossible! Why, Mr. Crossland is engaged to Marianne Newton."

" Is Miss Marianne Newton a friend of yours ? "

" Yes, the dearest friend I have."

" Then you will be on my side.   Keep your eyes and ears open, and find out what it is.   I tell you, something is wrong.   Put yourself in the breach ; help Miss Marianne, if you like ; but, for pity's sake, save Hatty!"

" But what makes you suppose that what is wrong nas anything to do with Mr. Crossland !"

" I do not know why I fancy it ; but I do.   I cannot let the idea go.   I do not like the look of him.   He does not look like a true man."

" Cary, you have grown up since you came to London."

" I feel like somebody's grandmother," said I.   " But I think I have been growing to it, Amelia, since I left Brocklebank."

" Well, you certainly are much less of a child than you were.   I will do my best, Cary."   And Amelia looked as if she meant it.

" But take no one into your confidence." said I.— " least of all Charlotte."

" Thank you, I don't need that warning !" said Amelia, with her languid laugh, as she furled her fan and turned away.   And as I passed on the other side I came upon Ephraim Hebblethwaite.

All at once my resolution was taken.

" Come this way, Ephraim," said I ; " I want to show you my Uncle Charles's new engravings."

I lifted down the large portfolio, with Ephraim's help, —I don't think Ephraim would let a cat jump down by itself if he thought the jump too far,—set it on a little table, and under cover of the engravings I told him the whole story, and all my uneasiness about Hatty. He listened very attentively, but without showing either the surprise or the perplexity which Amelia had done.

"If you suspect rightly," said he, when I had finished my tale, "the first thing to be done is to get her out of Charles Street."

"Do you think me too ready to suspect?" I replied.

"No," was his answer; "I am afraid you are right."

"But what do they want to do with her. or to her?" cried I, under my breath.

"Cary," said Ephraim, gravely, "I am very glad you have told me this. I will go so far as to tell you in return that I too have my suspicions of young Crossland, though they are of rather a different kind from yours. You suspect him, so far as I understand you, of matrimonial designs on Hatty, real or feigned. I am afraid rather that these appearances are a blind to hide something deeper and worse. I know something of this man, not enough to let me speak with certainty, but just sufficient to make me doubt him, and to guide me in what direction to look. We must walk carefully on this path, for if I mistake not. the ground is strewn with snares."

"What do you mean?" I cried, feeling terrified.

"I would rather not tell you till I know more. I will try to do that as soon as possible."

"I never thought of anything worse," said I, "than

that knowing, as he is likely to do, that Hatty will some day have a few hundreds a year of her own, he is trying to inveigle her to marry him, and is not a man likely to be kind to her and make her happy."

"He is certainly likely to make her very unhappy," replied Ephraim. "But I do not believe that he has any intentions of marriage, towards Hatty or anybody else."

"But don't you think he may make her think so? Amelia told me he was engaged in marriage with a gentlewoman she knows."

"I am sorry for the gentlewoman. Make her think so? Yes, and under cover of that, work out his plot. I would advise Miss Bracewell to beware that she is not made a catspaw."

I told Ephraim what I had said to Amelia.

"Then she is put on her guard: so far, well."

"Ephraim, have you heard anything more of Angus?"

"Nothing but what you know already."

"Nor, I suppose, of Colonel Keith? I wish I knew what he is doing."

"He has not had much chance of doing anything yet," said Ephraim, rather drily. "A sick-bed is not the most favourable place for helping one's friends out of prison."

"Has Colonel Keith been ill?" cried I.

"Mr. Raymond did not tell you?"

"He never told me a word. I do not know what he may have said to Annas."

"A broken arm, and a fever on the top of it," said Ephraim. "The doctor talks of letting him go out to-morrow, if the weather suit."

"O Ephraim!" cried I. "But where is he?"

"Don't tell any one, if I tell you. Remember, Colonel Keith is a proscribed man."

"I will do no harm to Annas's brother, trust me!" said I.

"He is at Raymond's house, where he and I have been nursing him."

"In a fever!"

"Oh, it is not a catching fever. Think you either of us would have come here if it were?"

"Ephraim, is Mr. Raymond to be trusted?" said I. "I am sure he is a good man, but he is a shocking Whig. And I do believe one of the queerest things in this queer world is the odd notions that men take of what it is their duty to do."

"Have you found that out?" said he, looking much diverted.

"I am always finding things out," I answered. "I had no idea there was so much to be found. But, don't you see, Mr. Raymond might fancy it his duty to betray Colonel Keith? Is there no danger?"

"Not the slightest," said Ephraim, warmly. "Mr. Raymond would be much more likely to give up his own life. Don't you know, Cary, that Scripture forbids us to betray a fugitive? And all the noblest instincts of human nature forbid it too."

"I know all one's feelings are against it," said I,

"but I did not know that there was anything about it in the Bible."

"Look in the twenty-third of Deuteronomy," replied Ephraim, "the fifteenth verse. The passage itself refers to a slave, but it must be equally applicable to a political fugitive."

"I will look," I answered. "But tell me, Ephraim, can nothing be done for Angus?"

"If it can, it will be done," he made answer.

He said no more, but from his manner I could not but fancy that somebody was trying to do something.

I never had two letters at once, by the same post, in my life: but this morning two came—one from Flora, and one from my Aunt Kezia. Flora's is not long: it says that she and Annas have reached the Isle of Wight in safety, and were but three hours a-crossing from Portsmouth; and she begs me, if I can obtain it, to send her some news of Angus. My Lady De Lannoy was extreme kind to them both, and Flora says she is very comfortable, and would be quite happy but for her anxiety about my Uncle Drummond and Angus. My Uncle Drummond has not writ once, and she is very fearful lest some ill have befallen him.

My Aunt Kezia's letter is long, and full of good counsel, which I am glad to have, for I do find the world a worse place than I thought it, and yet not in the way I expected. She warns me to have a care lest my tongue get me into trouble; and that is one of the dangers I find, and did not look for. Father is well, and all other friends : and I am not to be surprised if I should hear of Sophy's marriage. Fanny gets on very well, and makes a better housekeeper than my Aunt Kezia expected. But I have spent much thought over the last passage of her letter, and I do not like it at all :—

"Is Hatty yet in Charles Street? We have had but one letter from the child in all this time, and that was short and told nothing. I hope you see her often, and can give us some tidings. Squire Bracewell writ to your father a fortnight gone that he was weary of dwelling alone, and as the Prince's army is in retreat, he thinks it now safe to have the girls home. If this be so, we shall soon have Hatty here. I have writ to her, by your father's wish, that she is not to tarry behind."

I cried aloud when I came to this : " The Prince in retreat from Derby ! Uncle Charles, do you know anything of it ? Sure, it can never be true ! "

"Nonsense ! " he made answer. "Some silly rumour, no doubt."

" But my Uncle Bracewell writ it to my Aunt Kezia, and he dwells within fifteen miles," I said.

My Uncle Charles looked much disturbed.

" I must go forth and see about this," answered he.

"With your catarrh, Mr. Desborough ! " cried my Aunt Dorothea.

For above a week my Uncle Charles has not ventured from the door, having a bad catarrh.

"My catarrh must take care of itself," he made

answer. "This is serious news. Dobson, have you heard aught about the Prince being in retreat?"

Dobson, who was setting down the chocolate pot, looked up and smiled.

"Yes, Sir, we heard that yesterday."

"You idiot! why did you not tell me?" cried my Uncle Charles. "In retreat! I cannot believe it."

"Run to the coffee-house, Dobson," said Grandmamma, "and ask what news they have this morning."

So Dobson went off, and has not yet returned. My Aunt Dorothea laughs all to scorn, but my Uncle Charles is uneasy, and I am sure Grandmamma believes the report. It is dreadful if it is true. Are we to sit down under another thirty years of foreign oppression?

Before Dobson could get back, Mrs. Newton came in her chair. She *is* a very stout old lady, and she puffed and panted as she came up the stairs, leaning on her black footman, with her little Dutch pug after, which is as fat as its mistress, and it panted and puffed too. Her two daughters came in behind her.

"Oh, my dear—Mrs. Desborough! My—dear creature! This is—the horridest news! We must—go back to our—red ribbons and—black cockades! Could I ever have—thought it! Aren't you—perfectly miserable? Dear, dear me!"

"Ma is miserable because red does not suit her," said Miss Marianne. "I can wear it quite well, so I don't need to be."

"Marianne!" said her sister, laughing.

" Well, you know, Theresa, you don't care two pins whether the Prince wins or loses. Who does ? "

" The Prince and my Lord Tullibardine," said Miss Newton.

" Oh, of course, those who looked to the Prince to make their fortunes are disappointed enough. I don't."

" I rather thought Mr. Crossland *did*," said Miss Newton, with a mischievous air.

" Well, I hope there are other people in the world beside Mr. Crossland," said Miss Marianne.

" All right, my dear," replied her sister. " If you don't care, I am sure I need not. I am not in love with Mr. Crossland—not by any means. I never did admire the way in which his nose droops over his mouth. He has fine teeth—that is a redeeming point."

" Is it ? I don't want him to bite me," observed Miss Marianne.

Miss Newton went off into a little (subdued) burst of silvery laughter, and I sat astonished. Was this the sort of thing which girls called love ?—and was this the way in which fashionable women spoke of the men whom they had pledged themselves to marry ? I am sure I like Mr. Crossland little enough ; but I felt almost sorry for him as I listened to the girl who professed to love him.

Meanwhile, Grandmamma and Mrs. Newton were lamenting over the news—as I supposed : but when I began to listen, I found all that was over and done with. First, the merits of Puck, the fat pug, were being dis- cussed, and then the wretchedness of being unable to

buy or wear French cambrics, and the whole history of
Mrs. Newton's last cambric gown: they washed it, and
mended it, and ripped it, and made it up again.   And
then Grandmamma's brocaded silk came on, and how
much worse it wore than the last : and when I was just
wondering how many more gowns would have to be
taken to pieces, Mrs. Newton rose to go.

"Really, Mrs. Desborough, I ought to make my
apologies for coming so early.   But this sad news, you
know,—the poor Prince!   I could not bear another
minute.   I knew you would feel it so much.   I felt as
if I must come.   Now, my dear girls."

" Ma, you haven't asked Mrs. Desborough what you
came for," said Miss Marianne.

" What I——Oh!" and Mrs. Newton turned back.
"This absurd child!   Would you believe it, she gave
me no peace till I had asked if you would be so good
as to allow your cook to give mine her receipt for
Paradise pudding.   Marianne dotes on your Paradise
puddings.   Do you mind?   I should be so infinitely
obliged to you."

" Dear, no!" said Grandmamma, taking a pinch of
snuff, just as Dobson tapped at the door.   "Dobson,
run down and tell Cook to send somebody over to
Mrs. Newton's with her receipt for Paradise pudding.
Be sure it is not forgotten."

" Yes, Madam," said Dobson.   "If you please,
Madam, the army is a-going back ; all the coffee-houses
have the news this morning."

" Dear, it must be true, then," said Grandmamma,

taking another pinch. " What a pity !—Be sure you do not forget the Paradise pudding."

"Yes, Madam. They say, Madam, the Prince was nigh heart-broke that he couldn't come on."

"Ah, I dare say. Poor young gentleman !" said Mrs. Newton. " Dear Mrs. Desborough, do excuse me, but where did you meet with that lovely crewel fringe on your curtains ? It is so exactly what I wanted and could not get anywhere."

" I got it at Cooper and Smithson's—Holborn Bars, you know," said Grandmamma. "This is sad news, indeed. But your curtains, my dear, have an extreme pretty trimming."

"Oh, tolerable," said Mrs. Newton, gathering up her hoop.

Away they went, with another lament over the Prince and the news; and I sat wondering whether everybody in this world were as hollow as a tobacco-pipe. I do think, in London, they must be.

Then my thoughts went back to my Aunt Kezia's letter.

" Grandmamma," I said, after a few minutes' reflection, " may I have a chair this afternoon ? I want to go and see Hatty."

Grandmamma nodded. She had come, I think, to an awkward place in her tatting.

" Take Cæsar with you," was all she said.

So after dinner I sent Cæsar for the chair, and, dressed in my best, went over to Charles Street to see Hatty. I sent in my name, and waited an infinite time in a cold room before any one appeared. At last Charlotte bounced in—I cannot use another word, for it was just what she did—saying,—

"O Cary, you here? Emily is coming, as soon as she can settle her ribbons. Isn't it fun? They are all coming out in red now."

"I don't think it is fun at all," said I. "It is very sad."

"Oh, pother!—what do you and I care?" cried she.

"You do not care much, it seems," said I: but Charlotte was off again before I had finished.

A minute later, the door opened much more gently, and Amelia entered in her calm, languid way. But as soon as she saw me, her eyes lighted up, and she closed the door and sat down.

Amelia spoke in a hurried whisper as she kissed me.

"One word, before any one comes," she said. "Insist on seeing Hatty. Don't go without it."

"Will they try to prevent me?" I replied.

Before she could answer, Mrs. Crossland sailed in, all over rose-coloured ribbons.

"Why, Miss Caroline, what an unexpected pleasure!" said she, and if she had added "an unwelcome one," I fancy she would have spoken the truth. "Dear, what was Cicely thinking of to put you in this cold room? Pray come upstairs to the fire."

"Thank you," said I, and rose to follow her.

The room upstairs was warm and comfortable, but Hatty was not there. A girl of about fourteen, in a loose blue sacque, which looked very cold for the weather, came forward and shook hands with me.

"My daughter," said Mrs. Crossland. "Annabella, my dear, run up and ask Miss Hester if she feels well enough to come down. Tell her that her sister is here."

"Allow me to go up with Miss Annabella, and perhaps save her a journey," said I. "Messages are apt to be returned and to make further errands."

"Oh, but—pray do not give yourself that trouble," said Miss Annabella, glancing at her mother.

"Certainly not. I cannot think of it," answered Mrs. Crossland, hastily. "Poor Miss Hester has been suffering so much from toothache—I beg you will not disturb her, Miss Caroline."

I suppose I was rude: but how could I help it?

"Why should I disturb her more than Miss Crossland?" I replied. "Sisters do not make strangers of each other."

"Oh, she does not expect you : and indeed, Miss Caroline,—do let me beg of you,—Dr. Summerfield did just hint yesterday—just a hint, you understand,— about small-pox. I could not on any account let you go up, for your own sake."

"Is my sister so ill as that?" I replied. "I think we might have expected to be told it sooner. Then, Madam, I shall certainly go up. Miss Crossland, will you show me the way?"

I do not know whether Mrs. Crossland thought me bold and unladylike, but if she had known how every bit of me was trembling, she might perhaps have changed that view.

"O Miss Caroline, how can you? I could not allow Annabella to do such a thing. Think of the danger!—Annabella, come back! You shall not go into an infected air."

"Pardon me, Madam, but I thought you proposed yourself to send Miss Annabella. Then I will not trouble any one. I can find the way myself."

And resolutely closing the door behind me, up-stairs I walked. I did not believe a word about Hatty having the small-pox: but if I had done, I should have done the same. I heard behind me exclamations of—"That bold, brazen thing! She will find out all. Annabella, call Godfrey! call him! That hussy must not——"

I was upstairs by this time. I rapped at the first door, and had no answer; the second was the same. From the third I heard the sound of weeping, and a man's voice, which I thought I recognised as that of Mr. Crossland.

"I shall not allow of any more hesitation," he was saying. "You must make your choice to-day. You have given me trouble enough, and have made far too many excuses. I shall wait no longer."

"Oh, once more!—only once more!" was the answer, interrupted by heartrending sobs,—in whose voice I rather guessed than heard.

Neither would I wait any longer. I never thought about ceremony and gentility, any more than about the possible dangers, known and unknown, which I might be running. I opened the door and walked straight in.

Mr. Crossland stood on the hearth, clad in a queer long black gown, and a black cap upon his head. On a chair near him sat a girl, her head bowed down in her hands upon the table, weeping bitterly. Her long dark hair was partly unfastened, and falling over her shoulder: what I could see of her face was white as death. Was this white, cowed creature our once pert, bright Hatty?

"What do you want?" said Mr. Crossland, angrily, as he caught sight of me. "Oh, I beg pardon, Miss Caroline. Your poor sister is suffering so much to-day. I have been trying to divert her a little, but her pain is so great. How very good of you to come! Was no one here to show you anywhere, that you had to come by yourself?"

The bowed head had been lifted up, and the face that met my eyes was one of the extremest misery. She held out her arms to me with a low, sad, wailing cry—

"O Cary, Cary, save me! Cannot you save me?"

I walked past that black-robed wretch, and took poor Hatty in my arms, drawing her head to lie on my bosom.

"Yes, my dear, you shall be saved," I said,—I hope, God said through me. "Mr. Crossland, will you have the goodness to leave my sister to me?"

If looks had power to kill, I think I should never have spoken again in this world. Mr. Crossland turned on his heel, and walked out of the room without another word. The moment he was gone, I made a rush at the door, drew out the key (which was on the outside), locked it, and put the key on the table. Then I went back to Hatty.

"My poor darling, what have they done to you?"

Somehow, I felt as if I were older than she that day

But she could not tell me at first. "O Cary, Cary!' seemed to be all that she could say. I rang the bell, and when somebody tried the door, I asked the unknown helper to send Miss Amelia Bracewell.

" I beg your pardon, Madam, I dare not," answered a girl's voice. "Nobody is allowed to enter this chamber but my mistress and Fa——and my master."

It seemed as if an angel must be helping me, and whispering what to do. Perhaps it was so.

" Will you be so good as to take a message to the black servant who came with me?" I said.

" Certainly, Madam."

"Then please to tell him that I wish to speak with him at the door of this room."

" Madam, forgive me, but I dare not bring any one here."

I tore a blank leaf out of a book on the table. I had a pencil in my pocket. " Give him this, then; and let no one take it from you. You shall have a guinea to do it."

" Gemini !" I heard the girl whisper to herself in amazement.

I wrote hastily :—" Beg my Uncle Charles to come

this moment, and bring Dobson. Tell him, if he ever loved either me or Miss Hester, he will do this. It is a matter of life and death."

"Promise me," I said, unlocking the door to give it to her, "that this piece of paper shall be in my black servant's hands directly, and that no one else shall see it."

I spoke to a young girl, apparently one of the lower servants of the house. Her round eyes opened wide.

"Please do it, Betty!" sobbed poor Hatty. "Do it, for pity's sake!"

"I'll do it for yours, Miss Hester," said the girl, and her kindly, honest-looking face reassured me. She hid the paper in her bosom, and ran down. I locked the door again, and went back to Hatty.

"O Cary, dear, God sent you!" she sobbed. "I thought I must give in."

"What are they trying to make you do, Hatty?"

To my amazement, she replied,—"To be a nun."

"To be what?" I shrieked. "Are these people Papists, then?"

"Not to acknowledge it. I had not an idea when we came—nor the Bracewells, I am sure."

"And did they want all three of you to be nuns?"

"No—only me, I believe. I heard Father Godfrey saying to the Mother that neither Charlotte nor Amelia would answer the purpose: but what the purpose was, I don't know."

"Who are you talking about? Who is Father Godfrey?—Mr. Crossland?"

"Yes.   He is a Jesuit priest."

"You mean his mother, then, by '*the* Mother'?"

"Oh, she is not his mother.   I don't think they are related."

"What is she?"

"The Abbess of a convent of English nuns at Bruges."

"And is that poor little girl, Miss Annabella, one of the conspirators?"

"She is the decoy.   I think her wits have been terrified out of her; she only does as she is told."

"Hatty," I said, "you do not believe the doctrines of Popery?"

"I don't know what I believe, or don't believe," she sobbed.   "If you can get me out of here and back home, I shall think there is a God again.   I was beginning to doubt that and everything else."

A voice came up the stairs, raised rather loudly.

"You must pardon me, Madam, but I am quite sure both my nieces are here," said my Uncle Charles's welcome tones.

I rushed to the door again.

"This way, Uncle Charles!" I cried.   "Hatty, where is your bonnet?"

"I don't know.   They took all my outdoor things away."

"Tie my scarf over your head, and get into the chair.   As my Uncle Charles is here, I can walk very well."

He had come up now, and stood looking at Hatty's

white, miserable face. If he had seen it a few minutes earlier, he would have thought the misery far greater.

"Well, this is a pretty to-do!" cried my Uncle. "Hatty, child, these wretches have used you ill. Why on earth did you stay with them?"

"At first I did not want to get away, Uncle," she said, "and afterwards I could not."

We went downstairs. Mrs. Crossland was standing in the door of the drawing-room, with thin, shut-up lips, and a red, angry spot on either cheek. Inside the room I caught a glimpse of Annabella, looking wofully white and frightened. Mr. Crossland I could nowhere see.

"Madam," said my Uncle Charles, sarcastically, "I will thank you to give up those other young ladies, my nieces' cousins. If they wish to remain in London, they can do so, but it will not be in Charles Street. Did you not tell me, Cary, that their father wished them to come home?"

"My Aunt Kezia said that he intended to write to them to say so," I answered, feeling as though it were about a year since I had received my Aunt Kezia's letter.

"Really, Sir!" Mrs. Crossland began, "the father of these gentlewomen consigned them to my care——"

"And I take them out of your care," returned my Uncle Charles. "I will take the responsibility to Mr. Bracewell."

"I'll take all the responsi-what's-its-name," said Charlotte, suddenly appearing among us. "Thank you, Mr. Desborough; I'd *rather* not stop here when Hatty is gone. Emily!" she shouted.

Amelia came downstairs with her bonnet on, and Charlotte's in her hand. "You can't go without a bonnet, my dear child."

"Oh, pother!" cried Charlotte, seizing her bonnet by the strings, and sticking it on the top of her head anyhow it liked.

"One word before we leave, Mr. Desborough, if you please," said Amelia, with more dignity than I had thought she possessed. "I have strong reason to believe these persons to be Popish recusants, and the last to whom my father would have confided us, had he known their real character. They have not used any of us so kindly that I need spare them out of any tenderness."

"I thank you, Miss Bracewell," said my Uncle Charles, who also, I thought, was showing qualities that I had not known to be in him. (How scenes like these do bring one's faculties out!) "I rather thought there was some sort of Jesuitry at work. Madam," he turned to Mrs. Crossland, "I am sure there is no necessity for me to recall the penal laws to your mind. So long as these young ladies are left undisturbed in my care, in any way,—*so long*, Madam,—they will not be put in force against you. You understand me, I feel sure. Now, girls, let us go."

So, we three girls walking, and Hatty in the chair, with Dobson and Cæsar as a guard behind, we reached Bloomsbury Square.

"Charles, what is it all about?" said Grandmamma, taking a bigger pinch than usual, and spilling some of it on her lace stomacher.

"A spider's web, Madam, from which I have been freeing four flies. But one was a blue-bottle, and broke some of the threads," said my Uncle Charles, laughing, and patting my shoulder.

"Really!" said Grandmamma. "I am pleased to see you, young ladies. Hester, my dear, are you sure you are quite well?"

"I shall be better now," Hatty tried to say, in a trembling voice,—and fainted away.

There was a great commotion then, four or five talking at once, making impossible recommendations, and getting in each other's way; but at the end of it all we got poor Hatty into bed in my chamber, and even Grandmamma said that rest was the best thing for her. My Aunt Dorothea mixed a cordial draught, which she gave her to take; and as Hatty's head sank on the pillow, she said to my surprise,—

"Oh, the rest of being free again! Cary, I never expected you to be the heroine of the family."

"I think you are the heroine, Hatty."

"Most people would have thought I should be. But I have proved weak as water—yet not till after long suffering and hard pressure. You will never see the old Hatty again, Cary."

"Oh yes, dear!" said I. "Wait a few days, till you have had a good rest, and we have fed you up. You will feel quite different a week hence."

"My body will, I dare say, but *me*—that inside feeling and thinking machine—that will never be the same again. I want to tell you everything."

"And I want to hear it," I replied. "But don't talk now, Hatty; go to sleep, like a good girl. You will be much better for a long rest."

I drew the curtains, and asked Amelia to stay until Hatty was asleep. I knew she would not talk much, and Hatty would not care to tell her things as she would me. Going downstairs, my Uncle Charles greeted me, laughing, with,—

"Here she comes, the good Queen Bess! Cary, you deserve a gold medal."

Grandmamma bade me come to her, and tell her all I knew. She exclaimed several times, and took ever so many pinches of snuff, till she had to call on my Aunt Dorothea to refill the box. At the end of it she called me a good child, and the Jesuits traitors and scoundrels, to which my Uncle Charles added some rather stronger language.

Charlotte seems to have known nothing of what was going on; or, I should rather say, to have noticed nothing. She is such a careless girl in every way that I am scarce surprised. Amelia did notice things, but she had a mistaken notion of what they meant. She fancied that Hatty was in love with Mr. Crossland, and that she, not knowing of his engagement in marriage with Miss Marianne Newton, was very jealous of what she thought his double-dealing. Until after I spoke to her, she had no notion that there might be any sort of Popish treachery. Something which happened soon after that, helped to turn her mind in that direction. But Hatty says she knew next to nothing.

" But," says my Uncle Charles, " how could a Jesuit priest marry anybody? It seems to be all in a muddle."
That I cannot answer.

Hatty is better to-day, after a quiet night's rest. She still looks wofully ill, and Grandmamma will not let her speak yet. Now that Grandmamma is roused about it, she is very kind to Hatty and me also. I do hope, now, that things have done happening ! The poor Prince is a fugitive somewhere in Scotland, and everybody says " the rebellion is quashed." They did not call it a rebellion until he turned back from Derby. My Uncle Bracewell has writ to my Uncle Charles again with news, and has asked him to see Amelia and Charlotte sent off homeward. Hatty will tarry here till we can return together.

At last our poor Hatty has told her story : and a sad, sad story it is. It seems that Mr. Crossland was pretending to make court to her at first, and she believed in him, and loved him. At that time, she says, she would not have brooked a word against him ; and as to believing him to be the wretch he has turned out, she would as soon have thought the sun created darkness. There was no show of Popery at all in the family. They went to church like other people, and talked just like others. From a word dropped by Miss Theresa Newton, Hatty began to think that Mr. Crossland's heart was not so undividedly her own as she had hoped; and she presently discovered that he was not to be trusted on that point. They had a quarrel, and he professed penitence, and promised to give up Miss Marianne; and for a while Hatty thought all was right again. Then, little by little, Mrs. Crossland (whose right name seems to be Mother Mary Benedicta of the Annunciation—what queer names they do use, to be sure!)—well, Mrs. Crossland began to tell Hatty all kinds of strange stories about the saints, and miracles, and so forth, which she said she had heard from the Irish peasantry. At first she told them as things to laugh at; then she began to wonder if there might be some truth in one or two of them; there were strange things in this world! And so she went on from little to little, always drawing back and keeping silence for a while if she found that she was going too fast for Hatty to follow.

"I can see it all now, looking back," said Hatty "It was all one great whole; but at the time I did not see it at all. They seemed mere passing remarks, bits of conversation that came in anyhow."

Hatty felt sure that Mrs. Crossland was a concealed Papist long before she suspected the young man. And when, at last, both threw the mask off, they had her fast in their toils. She was strictly warned never to talk with me except on mere trifling subjects; and she had to give an account of every word that had been said when she returned. If she hid the least thing from them, she was assured it would be a terrible sin.

"But you don't mean to say you believed all that rubbish?" cried I.

"It was not a question of belief," she answered. "I loved him. I would have done anything in all the world to win a smile from him; and he knew it. As to belief—I do not know what I believed: my brain felt like a chaos, and my heart in a whirl."

"And now, Hatty?" said I. I meant to ask what she believed now: but she answered me differently.

"Now," she said, in a low, hopeless voice, "the shrine is deserted, and the idol is broken, and the world feels a great wide, empty place where there is no room for me—a cold, hard place that I must toil through, and the only hope left is to get to the end as soon as possible."

Oh, I wish Flora or Annas were here! I do not know how to deal with my poor Hatty. Thoughts which would comfort me seem to fall powerless with her; and I have nobody to counsel me. I suppose my Aunt Kezia would say I must set the Lord before me; but I do not see how to do it in this case. I am sure I have prayed enough. What I want is an angel to whisper to me what to do again; and my angel has gone back into Heaven, I suppose, for I feel completely puzzled now. At any rate, I do hope things have done happening.

CHAPTER XII.

BOUGHT WITH A PRICE.

Host. "Trust me, I think 'tis almost day."
Julia. "Not so; but it hath been the longest night
That e'er I watched, and the most heaviest."
—SHAKSPERE.

 AM writing four days later than my last sentence, and I wonder whether things have finished beginning to happen.

Grandmamma's Tuesday was the day after I writ. The Newtons were there,—at least Mrs. Newton and Miss Theresa,—and ever so many people whom I knew and cared nothing about. My Lady Parmenter came early, but did not stay long; and very late, long after every one else, Ephraim Hebblethwaite. Mr. Raymond I did not see, and have not done so for several times.

I was not much inclined to talk, and I got into a corner with some pictures which I had seen twenty times, and turned them over just as an excuse for keeping quiet. All at once I heard Ephraim's voice at my side:

"Cary, I want to speak to you. Go on looking at those pictures: other ears are best away. How is Hatty?"

"She is better," I said; "but she is not the old Hatty."

"I don't think the old Hatty will come back," he said. "Perhaps the new one may be better. Are the Miss Bracewells gone home?"

"They start to-morrow," said I.

"Cary, I am going to ask you something. Don't show any surprise. Are you a brave girl?"

"I hardly know," said I, resisting the temptation to look up and see what he meant. "Why?"

"Because a woman is wanted for a piece of work, and we think you would answer."

"What piece of work?—and who are 'we'?" I asked, turning over some views of Rome with very little notion what they were.

"'We' are Colonel Keith, Raymond, and myself."

"And what 'piece of work'?" I asked again.

"To attempt the rescue of Angus."

"How?—what am I to do?"

"Did you ever try to personate anybody?"

"Well, we used to act little pieces sometimes at Carlisle, I and the Grandison girls and Lucretia Carnwath. There has never been anything of the sort here."

"Did they think you did it well?"

"Lucretia Carnwath and Diana Grandison were thought the best performers; but once they said I made a capital housemaid."

"Were you ever a laundress?"

"No, but I dare say I could have managed it."

"Are you willing to try?"

T

"I am ready to do anything, if it will help Angus. I don't see at present how my playing the laundress is to do that."

"You will not play it on a mock stage in a drawing-room, but in reality. Neither you nor I are to do the hardest part of the work ; Colonel Keith takes that."

"What have I to do ?"

"To carry a basket of clothes into the prison, and bring it out again."

"I hope Angus will not be in the basket," said I, trying to smother my laughter ; "I could not carry him."

"Oh, no !" replied Ephraim, laughing too. "Now listen."

"I am all attention," said I.

"Next Tuesday evening, about nine o'clock, slip out of this room, and throw a large cloak over your dress—one that will quite hide you. You will find me at the foot of the back-stairs. We shall go out of the back-door, and get to Raymond's house. A lady, whom you will find there, will help you to put on the dress which is prepared. Then you and I (who are brother and sister, if you please) will carry the basket to the prison. Just before reaching it, I shall pretend to hear something, and run off to see what is the matter. You will be left alone (in appearance), and will call after me in vain, and abuse me roundly when I do not return, declaring that you cannot possibly carry that heavy basket in alone. Then, but not before, you will descry a certain William standing close by,—who will be Colonel Keith,—and showing surprise at seeing him there, will ask him to help you with the basket. He and you will carry the basket into the prison, and you will stand waiting a little while, during which time he will (with the connivance of a warder in our pay) visit Angus's cell. Presently 'William' will return to you, but it will be Angus and not Keith. You are to scold him for having kept you such an unconscionable time, and, declaring that you will have no more to do with him, to take up the empty basket and walk off. Our warder will then declare that he cannot do with all this row,—you must make as much noise as you can,—and push you both out of the prison door. Angus will follow you, expressing penitence and begging to be allowed to carry the basket, but you are not to let him. A few yards from the prison, I shall come running out of a side street, seize the basket, give Angus a thump or two with it and bid him be off, for I am not going to have such good-for-noughts loitering about and making up to my sister. He will pretend to be cowed, and run away, and you will then abuse me in no measured terms for having left you without protector, in the first place, and for having behaved so badly to your dear Will in the second. When we are out of sight, we may gradually drop our pretended quarrel; and when we reach Mr. Raymond's house, you will return to Caroline Courtenay,. and I shall be Ephraim Hebblethwaite. There is the programme. Can you carry out your part ?—and are you willing ?"

My heart stood still a moment, and then came up and throbbed violently in my throat.

"Could I? Yes, I think I could. But I want to know something first. How far I am willing will depend on circumstances. What is going to become of Colonel Keith in this business?"

"He takes Angus's place—don't you see?"

"Yes, but when Angus has got away, how is *he* to escape?"

"God knoweth. It is not likely that he can."

"And do you mean to say that Colonel Keith is to be sacrificed to save Angus?"

"The sacrifice is his own. The proposal comes from himself."

"And you mean to *let* him?"

"Not if I could do it myself," was the quiet answer.

"I don't want you to do it. Is there nobody else?"

"No one except Keith, Raymond, and myself. Raymond is too tall, and I am not tall enough. Keith and Angus are just of a height."

"And if Colonel Keith cannot escape, what will become of him?"

Silence answered me,—a silence which said far more than words.

"Ephraim, Colonel Keith is worth fifty of Angus."

"I have not spent these weeks at his bedside, Cary, without finding that out."

"And is the worse to be bought with the better?"

"It was done once, upon the hill of Calvary. And 'This is My commandment, that ye love one another as I have loved you.'"

I was silent. I did not like the idea at all.

"You must talk to Keith about it before we leave

the house," said Ephraim. "But I am afraid it will be of no use. We have all tried in vain."

I said no more.

"Well, Cary,—will you undertake it?"

"Ephraim," I said, looking up at last, "I cannot bear to think of sacrificing Colonel Keith. I could do it, I think, for anything but that. It would be hard work, no doubt, at the best; but I would go through with it to save Angus. But cannot it be done in some other way?"

Ephraim shook his head.

"We can see no other way at all. There are only three men who could do it — Colonel Keith, Mr. Raymond, and myself; and Keith is far the best for personal reasons. Beside the matter of height, he has, or at any rate could easily put on, a slight Scots accent, which we should find difficult, and might very likely do it wrong. He is acquainted with all the places and people that Angus is; we are not. And remember, it is not only the getting Angus out of the place that is of consequence: whoever takes his place must personate Angus for some hours, till he can get safely away.[1] Only Keith can do this with any chance of success. As to sacrifice, why, soldiers sacrifice themselves every day, and he is a soldier. I can assure you, it seems to him a natural, commonplace affair. He is very anxious to do it."

"He must be fonder of Angus——" I stopped.

---

[1] How far such a personation is consistent with truth and righteousness may be reasonably questioned. But very few persons would have thought of raising the question in 1745.

"Than we are?" answered Ephraim, with a smile. "Perhaps he is. But I think he has other reasons, Cary."

"What made you think of me?"

"Well, we must have a girl in the affair, and we were very much puzzled whom to ask. If Miss Keith had been here, we should certainly have asked her."

"Annas? Oh, how could she?" I cried.

"She has pluck enough," said Ephraim. "Of course, Miss Drummond would have been the most natural person to play the part, but Keith would not hear of that, and Raymond doubted if she were a suitable person. With her, the Scots accent would be in the way, and rouse suspicion; and I am not sure whether she could manage such a thing in other respects. Then we thought of Hatty and you; but Hatty, I suppose, is out of the question at present."

"Oh yes, quite," said I.

"She would have been the very one, if she had been well and strong. She has plenty of go and dash in her. But Raymond and Keith both wanted you."

"And you did not?" said I, feeling rather mortified that Ephraim should seem to think more of Hatty than of me.

"No, I did not, Cary," he said, in a changed voice. "You think I am paying you a poor compliment. Perhaps, some day, you will know better."

"Does any one in this house know of the rescue plot?"

"Mr. Desborough knows that an attempt may be made, but not that you are in it. Lucette is engaged to keep the coast clear while we get away. And now, Cary, what say you?"

"Yes, Ephraim, I will do it, though I almost wish it were anything else. May God help Colonel Keith!"

"Amen, with all my heart!"

We had no opportunity to say more.

So now I wait for next Tuesday, not knowing what it may bring forth.

It was about a quarter of an hour before the fated moment, when Miss Theresa Newton sat down by me.

"Very serious to-night, Miss Caroline!" said she, jestingly.

I thought I had good cause, considering what was about to happen. But I turned it off as best I could.

"Where is our handsome friend this evening?" said she.

"Have we only one?" replied I.

Miss Newton laughed that musical laugh of hers.

"I should hope we are rather happier. I meant Mr. Hebblethwaite—horrible name!"

"I saw him a little while ago," said I, wondering if he were then at the foot of the back-stairs.

"What has become of the Crosslands? Have you any idea? I have not seen them here now for—ever so long."

"Nor have I. I do not know at all," said I, devoutly hoping that I never should see them again.

"My sister is perfectly in despair. Her intended never comes to see her now. I tell her she had better find somebody else. It is too tiresome to keep on and off with a man in that way. Oh, you don't know anything about it. Your time has not come yet."

" When it do," said I, " I will either be on or off,
if you please. I should not like to be on *and* off, by
any means."

Miss Newton hid her laughing face behind her fan.

" My dear child, you are so refreshing ! Don't
change, I beg of you. It is charming to meet any
one like you."

" I thank you for your good opinion," I replied ;
and, my Aunt Dorothea just then coming up, I re-
signed my seat to her, and dropped the conversation.

For a minute or two I wandered about,—asked
Hatty if she were tired (this was her first evening in
the drawing-room with company), and when she said,
" Not yet," I inquired after Puck's health from Mrs.
Newton, told Miss Emma Page that Grandmamma
had been admiring her sister's dress, and slipped out of
the door when I arrived at it. In my room Lucette
was standing with the cloak ready to throw over me.

" Monsieur Ebaté is at the *escalier dérobé*," said she.
Poor Lucette could get no nearer Hebblethwaite. " He
tell me, this night, Mademoiselle goes on an errand for
the good Lord. May the Lord keep safe His messenger!"

" Mr. Hebblethwaite goes with me," said I. " He
will take all the care of me he can."

" I will trust him for that!" said Lucette, with
a little nod. " He is good man, *celui-là*. But,
Mademoiselle, 'except the Lord keep the city——'
you know."

'" The watchman waketh but in vain.' Yes, Lucette,
I know, in every sense. But how do *you* know that
Mr. Hebblethwaite is a good man ? "

"Ah! I know, I. And I know what makes him stay in London, all same. Now Mademoiselle is ready, and César is at the door, *là-bas.*"

Downstairs I ran, joined Ephraim, who also wore a large cloak over his evening dress, and we went out of the back-door, which was guarded by Cæsar, whose white teeth and gleaming eyes were all I could see of him in the dusk.

" Lucette asked leave to take Cæsar into the affair," said Ephraim. "She promised to answer for him as for herself. Now, Cary, we must step out : there is no time to lose."

"As fast as you please," said I.

In a few minutes, we came to Mr. Raymond's house. I never knew before where he lived. It is in a small house in Endell Street. An elderly woman opened the door, who evidently expected us, and ushered us at once into a living-room on the right hand. Here I saw Mr. Raymond and a lady—a lady past her youth, who had, as I could not help seeing, been extreme beautiful. I thought there was no one else till I heard a voice beside me :

"I fear I am almost a stranger, Miss Cary."

"Mr. Keith!" I did not feel him a stranger, but a very old friend indeed. But how ill he looked! I told him so, and he said he was wonderfully better,—quite well again,—with that old, sweet smile that he always had. My heart came up into my throat.

"Mr. Keith, must you go into this danger?"

"If I fail to go where my Master calls me, how can I look for His presence and blessing to go with me?

They who go with God are they with whom God goes."

" Are you quite sure He has called you ? "

" Quite sure." His fine eyes lighted up.

" Have you thought—— "

" Forgive my interruption. I have thought of every-thing. Miss Cary, you heard the vow which I took to God and Flora Drummond—never to lose sight of Angus, and to keep him true and safe. I have kept it so far as it lay in me, and I will keep it to the end. Come what may, I will be true to God and her."

And looking up into his eyes, I saw—revealed to me as by a flash of lightning—what was Duncan Keith's most precious thing.

" Now, Miss Caroline," said Mr. Raymond, " will you kindly go up with this lady,"—I fancied I heard the shortest possible sign of hesitation before the last two words,—" and she will be so good as to help you to assume the dress you are to wear."

I went upstairs with the beautiful woman, who gave a little laugh as she shut the door.

" Poor Mr. Raymond ! " said she ; " I feel so sorry for the man. Nature meant him to be a Tory, and education has turned him into a Whig. He has the kindest of hearts, and the most unmanageable of con-sciences. He will help us to free a prisoner, but he would not call me anything but ' Mistress ' to save his life."

" And your Ladyship—? " said I, guessing in an instant what she ought to be called, and that she was the wife of a peer—not a Hanoverian peer.

"Oh, my Ladyship can put up with it very well," said she, laughing, as she helped me off with my evening dress. "I wish I may never have anything worse. The man would not pain me for the world. It is only his awful Puritan conscience; Methodist, perhaps. Puritan was the word in my day. When one lives in exile, one almost loses one's native tongue."

And I thought I heard a light sigh. Her Ladyship, however, said no more, except what had reference to our business. When the process was over, I found myself in a printed linen gown, with a linen hood on my head, a long white apron made quite plain, and stout clumsy shoes.

"Now, be as vulgar as you possibly can," said her Ladyship. "Try to forget all your proprieties, and do everything the wrong way. You are Betty Walkden, if you please, and Mr. Heoblethwaite is Joel Walkden, and your brother. You are a washerwoman, and your mistress, Mrs. Richardson. lives in Chelsea. Don't forget your history. Oh! I am forgetting one thing myself. Colonel Keith, and therefore Lieutenant Drummond, as they are the same person for this evening, is Will Clowes, a young gardener at Wandsworth, who is your lover, of whom your brother Joel does not particularly approve. N w then, keep up your character. And remember "—her Ladyship was very grave now—"to call any of them by his real name may be death to all of you."

I turned round and faced her.

"Madam, what will become of Colonel Keith?"

I thought her Ladyship looked rather keenly at me.

"'The sword devoureth one as well as another,'" was her reply. "You know whence that comes, Miss Courtenay."

"Is that all?" I answered. "If any act of mine lead to his death, how shall I answer it to his father and mother, and to Annas?"

"They gave him up to the Cause, my dear, when they sent him forth to join the Prince. A soldier must always do his duty."

"Forgive me, Madam. I was not questioning his duty, but my own."

"Too late for that, Miss Courtenay. My dear, he is ready for death. I would more of us were!"

I read in the superb eyes above me that she was not.

"Forward!" she said, as if giving a word of command.

Somehow, I felt as if I must go. Her Ladyship was right: it was too late to draw back. So Ephraim and I set forth on our dangerous errand.

I cannot undertake to say how we went, or where. It all comes back to me as if I had walked it in a dream: and I felt as if I were dreaming all the while. At last, as we went along, carrying the basket, Ephraim suddenly set it down with "Hallo! what's that?" I knew then that we must be close to the prison, and that he was about to leave me.

"I say, I must see after that. You go on, Bet!" cried Ephraim; and he was off in a minute—in what direction I could not even see.

"Gemini!" cried I, catching up the word I had heard from Mrs. Crossland's Betty. "Joel! I say,

Joel! You bad fellow, can't you come back? How am I to lift this great thing, I should like to know?"

A dark shadow close to the wall moved a little.

"Come now, can't one of you lads help a poor maid?" said I. "It's a shame of Joel to leave me in the lurch like this. Come, give us a hand!"

I was trembling like an aspen leaf. Suppose the wrong man offered to help me! What could I do then?

"Want a hand, my pretty maid?" said a voice which certainly was not Colonel Keith's. "I'm your man! Give us hold!"

Oh, what was I to do! This horrid man would carry the basket, and how could I explain to the warder? How could I know which warder was the right one?

"Now then, hold hard, mate!" said a second voice, which I greeted with delight. "Just you let this here young woman be. How do, Betty? Why, wherever's Joel? He's no call to let the likes o' you carry things o' thisn's."

What had the Colonel done with his Scots accent? I did not hear a trace of it.

"Oh, Will Clowes, is that you?" said I, giving a little toss of my head, which I thought would be in character. "Well, I don't know whether I shall let you carry it."

The next minute I felt how wrong I was to say so.

"Yes, you will," said Colonel Keith, and took the basket out of my hands. I should never have known him, dressed in corduroy, and with a rake over his shoulder. He shouted something, and the great prison door opened slowly, and a warder put his head out.

"Who goes there?"

"Washing for Cartwright's ward."

" Ay, all right. Come within. Cartwright!" shouted the porter.

We went in, and stood waiting a moment just inside the door, till a warder appeared, who desired Colonel Keith to "bring that 'ere basket up, now."

" You can wait a bit, Betty," said the Colonel, turning to me. "Don't be afraid, my girl. Nobody 'll touch you, and Will 'll soon be back."

They say it is unlucky to watch people out of sight. I hope it is not true. True or untrue, I watched him. Yes, Will Clowes might be back soon; but would Duncan Keith ever return any more?

And then a feeling came, as if a tide of fear swept over me,—Was it right of Flora to ask him to make that promise? I have wondered vaguely many a time: but in that minute, with all my senses sharpened, I seemed to *see* what a blunder it was. Is it ever right to ask people for such unconditional pledges to a distinct course of action, when we cannot know what is going to happen? To what agony—nay, even to what wrong-doing—may we pledge them without knowing it! It seems to me that influence is a very awful thing, for it reaches so much farther than you can see. May it not be said sometimes of us all, " They know not what they do"? And then to think that when we come out of that Valley of the Shadow into the clear light of the Judgment Bar, all our unknown sins may burst upon us like a great army, more than we can count or imagine —it is terrible!

O my God, save me from unknown sins! O Christ, be my Help and Advocate when I come to know them!

How I lived through the next quarter of an hour I can never say to anybody. I sat upon a settle near the door of the prison, praying—how earnestly!—for both of those in danger, but more especially for Colonel Keith. At last I saw a man coming towards me with the empty basket, in which he had inserted his head, like a bonnet, so that it rather veiled his face. I remembered then that I was to "make as much noise as I could," and quarrel with my supposed lover.

"Well, you are a proper young man!" said I, standing up. "How long do you mean to keep me waiting, I should like to know? You think I've nothing in the world to do, don't you, now? And Missis 'll say nought to me, will she, for coming home late? Just you give me that basket—men be such dolts!"

"Come, my girl,"—in a deprecating tone—said a voice, which I recognised as that of Angus. I hoped nobody else would.

"I'm not your girl, and I'll not come unless I've a mind, neither!" cried I, loudly, trying to put in practice her Ladyship's advice to be as vulgar as I could. "I'm not a-going to have fellows dangling at my heels as keeps me a-waiting——"

"Come, young woman, you just clear out," said the warder Cartwright. "My word, lad, but she's a spitfire! You be wise, and think better of it. Now then, be off, both of you!"

And he laid his hand on my shoulder, as if to push me through the door, which I pretended to resent very angrily, and Angus flung down the basket and began to strip up his sleeves, as if he meant to fight the warder.

"Now, we can't do with that kind of thing here!" cried another man, coming forward, whom I took to be somewhat above the rest. "Be off at once—you must not offer to fight the King's warders. Turn them out, Cartwright, and shut the door on them."

Angus caught up the basket and dashed through the door, and I followed, making all the noise I could, and scolding everybody. We had only just got outside the gate when Ephraim came running up, and snatched the basket from Angus. There was a few minutes' pretended struggle between them, and then Ephraim chased Angus into a side-street, and came back to me, whom he began to scold emphatically for encouraging such idle ne'er-do-wells as that rascal Clowes. I tried to give him as good as he brought; and so we went on, jangling as we walked, until nearly within sight of Mr. Raymond's door. Then, declaring that I would not speak to him if he could not behave better, and that I was not going to walk in his leading-strings, I marched on with my head held very high, and Ephraim trudged after me, looking as sulky as he knew how. We rapped on the back door, and Mr. Raymond's servant let us in. In the parlour we found Mr. Raymond and her Ladyship.

"I am thankful to see you safe back!" cried the former; and his manner suggested to me the idea that he had not felt at all sure of doing so. "Is all well accomplished?"

"Angus Drummond is out, and Keith is in," replied

Ephraim. "As to the rest, we must leave it for time to reveal. I am frightfully tired of quarrelling; I never did so much in my life before."

"Has Miss Courtenay done her part well?" asked her Ladyship.

"Too well, if anything," said Ephraim. "I was sadly afraid of a slip once. If that fellow had insisted on carrying in the basket, Cary, we should have had a complete smash of the whole thing."

"Why, did you see that?" said I.

"Of course I did," he answered. "I was never many yards from you. I lay hidden in a doorway, close to. Cary, you make a deplorably good scold! I never guessed you would do that part of the business so well."

"I am glad to hear it, for I found it the hardest part," said I.

Her Ladyship came up and helped me to change my dress.

"The Cause owes something to you to-night, Miss Courtenay," said she. "At least, if Colonel Keith can escape."

"And if not, Madam?"

"If not, my dear, we shall but have done our duty. Good-night. Will you accept a little reminder of this evening—and of Lady Inverness?"

I looked up in astonishment. Was this beautiful woman, with her tinge of sadness in face and voice, the woman who had so long stood first at the Court of Montefiascone—the Mistress of the Robes to Queen Clementina, and as some said, of the heart of King James?

My Lady Inverness drew from her finger a small ring of chased gold. " It will fit you, I think, my dear. You are a brave maid, and I like you.   Farewell."

I am not at all sure that my Aunt Kezia would have allowed me to accept it.   Some, even among the Tories, thought my Lady Inverness a wicked woman; others reckoned her an injured and a slandered one.   I gave her what Father calls " the benefit of the doubt," thanked her, and accepted the ring.   I do not know whether I did right or wrong.

To run downstairs, say good-bye to Mr. Raymond, —by the way, would Mr. Raymond have allowed my Lady to enter his house, if he had believed the tales against her? — and hasten back with Ephraim to Bloomsbury Square, took but few minutes.   Lucette let us in; I think she had been watching.

" The good Lord has watched over Mademoiselle," said she, as she took my cloak from me.

Ephraim had gone back to the drawing-room, and I followed.   I glanced at the French clock on the mantel- piece, where a gold Cupid in a robe of blue enamel was mowing down an array of hearts with a scythe, and saw that we had been away a little over an hour. Could that be all?   How strange it seemed!   People were chattering, and flirting fans, and playing cards, as if nothing at all had happened.   Miss Newton was sitting where I had left her, talking to Mr. Robert Page.   Grandmamma sat in her chair, just as usual.   Nobody seemed to have missed us, except Hatty, who said with a smile,—" I had lost you, Cary, for the last half-hour."

"Yes," said I, "something detained me out of the room."

I only exchanged one other sentence in the course of the evening with Ephraim:

"You will let me know how things go on? I shall be very anxious."

"Of course. Yes, I will take care of that."

And then the company broke up, and I helped Hatty to bed, and prayed from my heart for Colonel Keith and Angus, and did not fall asleep till I had heard St. Olave's clock strike two. When I woke, I had been making jumballs in the drawing-room with somebody who was both my Lady Inverness and my Aunt Kezia, and who told me that Colonel Keith had been appointed Governor of the American plantations, and that he would have to be dressed in corduroy.

When I arose in the morning, I could—and willingly would—have thought the whole a dream. But there on my finger, a solid contradiction, was my Lady Inverness's ring.

For four days I heard nothing more. On the Friday, my Uncle Charles told us that rumours were abroad of the escape of a prisoner, and he hoped it might be Angus. My Aunt Dorothea wanted to hear all the particulars. I sat and listened, looking as grave as I could.

"Why, it seems they must have bribed some fellow to carry in a basket of foul clothes, and then to change clothes with the prisoner, and so let him get out. There appears to have been a girl in it as well—a girl and a man. I suppose they were both bribed, very likely.

Anyhow, the prisoner is set free. I only hope it is young Drummond, Cary."

I said I hoped so too.

"But, dear me, what will become of the man that went in?" asked my Aunt Dorothea.

"Oh, he'll be hanged, sure enough," said my Uncle Charles. "Only some low fellow, I suppose, that was willing to sell himself."

"A man does not sell his life in a hurry," said my Aunt Dorothea.

"My dear," replied my Uncle Charles, "there are men who would sell their own mothers and children."

"Oh, I dare say, but not themselves," said she.

"I suppose somebody cared for him," observed Hatty.

I found it hard work to keep silence.

"Only low people like himself," said Grandmamma. "Those creatures will do anything for money."

And then, Cæsar bringing in a note with Mrs. Newton's compliments, the talk went off to something else.

On the Saturday evening there was an extra assembly, and I caught Ephraim as soon as ever I could.

"Ephraim, they have found it out!" I said, in a whisper.

"Turn your back on the room," said he, quietly. "Yes, Cary, they have. There goes Keith's first chance of safety—yet it was a poor one from the beginning."

"Can nobody intercede for him?"

"With whom? The Electress is dead: and they say she was the only one who had much influence with the Elector."

"He has daughters," I suggested.

Ephraim shrugged his shoulders, as much as to say that was a very poor hope.

" Your friend Mr. Raymond, being a Whig," I urged, " might be able to do something."

" I will see," said he. " Do you know that Miss Keith is to be in London this evening ? "

" Annas ? No ! I have never heard a word about it."

" I was told so," said Ephraim, looking hard at an engraving which he had taken up.

I wondered very much who told him.

" She might possibly go to the Princess Caroline. People say she is the best of the family. Bad is the best, I am afraid." [1]

" How did Mr. Raymond come to know my Lady Inverness ? "

" Oh, you discovered who she was, did you ? "

" She told me herself."

" Ah !—I cannot say ; I am not sure that he knew anything of her before Tuesday night. She was our superior officer, and gave orders which we obeyed—that was all."

" I cannot understand how Mr. Raymond could have anything to do with it ! " cried I.

" Nor I, precisely. I believe there are wheels within wheels. Is he not a friend of your uncle, Mr. Drummond ?—an old friend, I mean, when they were young men."

" Possibly," said I ; " I do not know."

Somebody came up now, and drew Ephraim away.

[1] Ephraim does the Princess Caroline an injustice. She was a lily among the thorns.

I had no more private talk with him. But how could he come to know anything about Annas? And where is she going to be?

The next morning Cæsar brought me a little three-cornered note. I guessed at once from whom it came, and eagerly tore it open.

"We arrived in London last night, my dear Caroline, and are very desirous of seeing you. Could you meet me at Mr. Raymond's house this afternoon? Mr. Hebblethwaite will be so good as to call for you, if you can come. Love from both to you and Hester. Your affectionate friend, A. K."

Come! I should think I would come! I only hoped Annas already knew of my share in the plot to rescue Angus. If not, what would she say to me?

I read the note again. "We"—who were "we"? —and "love from *both*." Surely Flora must be with her! I kept wishing—and I could not tell myself why—that Ephraim had less to do with it. I did not like his seeming to be thus at the beck and call of Annas; and I did not know why it vexed me. I must be growing selfish. That would never do! Why should Ephraim not do things for Annas? I was an older friend, it is true, but that was all. I had no more claim on him than any one else. I recognised that clearly enough : yet I could not banish the feeling that I was sorry for it.

When Ephraim came, I thought he looked exceeding grave. I had told Grandmamma beforehand that

Annas (and I thought Flora also) had returned to London, and asked me to go and see them, which I begged her leave to do. Grandmamma took a pinch of snuff over it, and then said that Cæsar might call me a chair.

"Could I not walk, Grandmamma? It is very near."

"Walk!" cried Grandmamma, and looked at me much as if I had asked if I might not lie or steal. "My dear, you must not bring country ways to Town like that. Walk, indeed!—and you a Courtenay of Powderham! Why, people would take you for a mantua-maker."

"But, Grandmamma, please,—if I am a Courtenay, does it signify what people take me for?"

"I should like to know, Caroline," said Grandmamma, with severity, "where you picked up such levelling ideas? Why, they are Whiggery, and worse. I cannot bear these dreadful mob notions that creep about now o' days. We shall soon be told that a king may as well sell his crown and sceptre, because he would be a king without them."

"He would not, Madam?" I am afraid I spoke mischievously.

"My dear, of course he would. Once a king, always a king. But the common people need to have symbols before their eyes. They cannot take in any but common notions of what they see. A monarch without a crown, or a judge without robes, or a bishop without lawn sleeves, would never do for them. Why, they would begin to think they were just men like themselves! They do think so, a great deal too much."

And Grandmamma took two pinches in rapid succession, which proceeding with her always betrays uneasiness of mind.

"Dear, dear!" she muttered, as she snapped her box again, and dropped it into her pocket. "It must be that lamentable mixture in your blood. Whatever a Courtenay could be thinking of, to marry a Dissenter,—a Puritan minister's daughter, too,—he must have been mad! Yet she was of good blood on the mother's side."

I believe Grandmamma knows the pedigree of every creature in this mortal world, up to the seventh generation.

"Was that Deborah Hunter, Grandmamma?"

"What do you know about Deborah Hunter?" returned Grandmamma, pulling out her snuff-box, and taking a third pinch in a hurry, as if the mere mention of a Dissenter made her feel faint. "Who has been talking to *you* about such a creature? The less you hear of her the better."

"Oh, we always knew her name, Madam," said Hatty, "and that she was a presbyter's daughter."

"Well, that is as much as you will know of her with my leave!" said Grandmamma.

I do not know what more she might have said, if my Uncle Charles had not come in: but he brought news that the Prince's army had been victorious at Falkirk, and the Cause is looking up again.

"They say the folks at St. James's are very uneasy," said my Uncle Charles, "and the Elector's son is to be sent against the Prince with a larger army. I hear he set forth for Edinburgh last night."

" What, Fred ? " said Grandmamma.

" Fred ? No,—Will," [1] answered my Uncle Charles.

" That is the lad who was wounded at Dettingen ? " replied she.

" The same," he made answer. " Oh, they are not without pluck, this family, foreigners though they be. The old blood is in them, though there's not much of it."

" They are a pack of rascals ! " said Grandmamma, with another pinch. I thought the box would soon be empty if she were much more provoked.

" Nay, Madam, under your pleasure : the lad is great-grandson to the Queen of Bohemia, and she was without reproach. I would rather have Fred or Will than Oliver."

Grandmamma sat extreme upright, and spoke in those measured tones, and with that nice politeness, which showed that she was excessively put out.

" May I trouble you, Charles, if you please, never to *name* that—person—in *my* hearing again ! "

[1] The Prince of Wales and the Duke of Cumberland. The former distinguished himself by little beyond opposition to his father, and an extremely profligate life. The Jacobite epitaph written on his death, five years later, will show the light in which he and his relatives were regarded by that half of the nation :

> " Here lies Fred,
> Who was alive and is dead.
> Had it been his father,
> I had much rather ;
> Had it been his sister,
> No one would have missed her ;
> Had it been his brother,
> Still better than another :
> But since 'tis only Fred,
> Who was alive and is dead,
> Why, there's no more to be said."

" Certainly, Madam," said my Uncle Charles, with a naughty look at me which nearly upset my gravity. If I had dared to laugh, I do not know what would have happened to me.

"The age is quite levelling enough, and the scoundrels quite numerous enough, without *your* joining them, Mr. Charles Carlingford Desborough ! "

Saying which, Grandmamma arose, and as Hatty said afterwards, " swept from the room "—my Uncle Charles offering her his arm, and assuring her, with a most disconcerting look over his shoulder at us, that he would do his very best to mend his manners.

" Your manners are good enough, Sir," said Grandmamma severely : " 'tis your morals I wish to mend."

When we thought Grandmamma out of hearing, we did laugh : and my Uncle Charles, coming down, joined us,— which I am afraid neither he nor we ought to have done.

" My mother's infinitely put out," said he. " Her snuff-box is empty: and she never gave me my full name but twice before, that I remember. When I am Charles Desborough, she is not pleased; when I am Mr. Charles Desborough, she is gravely annoyed ; but when I become Mr. Charles Carlingford Desborough, matters are desperate indeed. I shall have to go to the cost of a new snuff-box, I expect, before I get forgiven. Yet I have no doubt Oliver was a pretty decent fellow—putting his politics on one side."

" I am afraid, Uncle Charles," said Hatty, " a snuff-box would hardly make your peace for that."

" Oh, that's for you maids, not for her. She is not

a good forgiver," said my Uncle Charles, more gravely. "She takes after her mother, my Lady Sophia. Don't I remember my Lady Sophia!"

And I should say, from the expression of my Uncle Charles's face, that his recollections of my Lady Sophia Carlingford were not among the pleasantest he had.

Hatty is growing much more like herself, with the pertness left out. She looks a great deal better, and can smile and laugh now; but her old sharp, bright ways are gone, and only show now and then, in a little flash, what she was once.

The Crosslands have disappeared—nobody knows where. But I do not think Miss Marianne Newton has broken her heart; indeed, I am not quite sure that she has one.

In the afternoon, Ephraim came, and I went in a chair under his escort to Mr. Raymond's house. Hatty declined to come; she seemed to have a dislike to go out of doors, further than just to take the air in the square, with Dobson behind her. I should not like that at all. It would make me feel as if the constable had me in custody. But Grandmamma insists on it; and Hatty does not seem to feel safe without somebody.

In Mr. Raymond's parlour, I found Annas and Flora, alone. I do not know what to say they looked like. Both are white and worn, as if a great strain had been on their hearts: but Flora is much the more broken down of the two. Annas is more queenly than ever, with a strange, far-away look in the dear grey eyes, that I can hardly bear to see. I ran up to her first thing.

"O Annas, tell me!" I cried, amidst my kisses, "tell me, did I do right or wrong?"

I felt sure she would need no explanation.

"You did right, Cary,"—and the dark grey eyes looked full into mine. "Who are we, to refuse our best to the Master when He calls? But it is hard, hard to bear it!"

"Is there *any* hope of escape?" I asked.

"There is always hope where God is," said Annas. "But it is not always hope for earth."

Flora kissed me, and whispered, "Thank you for Angus!" but then she broke down, and cried like a child.

"Have you heard anything of Angus?" I asked.

"Yes," said Annas, who shed no tears. "He is safe in France, with friends of the Cause."

"In France!" cried I.

"Yes. Did you think he could stay in England? Impossible, except now and then in disguise, for a stolen visit, perhaps, when some years are gone."

"Then if Colonel Keith could escape——"

"That would be his lot. Of course, unless the Prince were entirely successful."

I felt quite dismayed. I had never thought of this.

"And how long do you stay here?" said I.

"Only till I can obtain a hearing of the Princess Caroline. That is arranged by Mr. Raymond, through some friends of his. He and Mr. Hebblethwaite have been very, very good to us."

"I do not know what we should have done without them," said Flora, wiping her eyes.

"And is the day fixed for you to see the Princess?"

"Not quite, but I expect it will be Thursday next. Pray for us, Cary, for that seems the last hope."

"And you have heard nothing, I suppose, from th
Colonel?"

"Yes, I have." Annas put her hand into her bosom, and drew forth a scrap of paper. "You may read it, Cary. It will very likely be the last."

My own eyes were dim as I carried the paper to the window. I could have read it where I was, but I wanted an excuse to turn my back on every one.

"My own dear Sister,—If it make you feel happier, do what you will for my release: but beyond that do nothing. I have ceased even to wish it. I am so near the gates of pearl, that I do not want to turn back unless I hear my Master call me. And I think He is calling from the other side.

"That does not mean that I love you less: rather, if it be possible, the more. Tell our father and mother that we shall soon meet again, and in the meantime they know how safe their boy must be. Say to Angus, if you have the opportunity, that so far as in him lies, I charge him to be to God and man all that I hoped to have been. Thank Miss C. Courtenay and Mr. Hebblethwaite for their brave help: they both played their part well. And tell Flora that I kept my vow, and that she shall hear the rest when we meet again.

"God bless you, every one. Farewell, darling Annas.

"Your loving brother, not till, but beyond, death,

Duncan Keith."

CHAPTER XIII.

STEPPING NORTHWARDS.

" It were to be wished the flaws were fewer
  In the earthen vessel, holding treasure
Which lies as safe in a golden ewer :
  But the main thing is, does it hold good measure ? "
—Browning

I TURNED back to the table, and dropping the letter on it, I laid my head down upon my arms and wept bitterly. He who wrote it had done with the world and the world's things for ever. Words such as these were not of earth. They had come from the other side of the world-storm and the life's fever. And he was nearly there.

I wondered how much Flora understood. Did she guess anything of that unwhispered secret which he promised to tell her in the courts of Heaven? Had she ever given to Duncan Keith what he had given her ?

I rose at last, and returned the letter to Annas.

"Thank you," I said. "You will be glad some day to have had that letter."

"I am glad now," said Annas, quietly, as she restored it to its place. "And ere long we shall be glad together. The tears help the journey, not hinder it."

"How calm you are, Annas!" I said, wondering at her.

"The time for Miss Keith to be otherwise has not come yet," said Mr. Raymond's voice behind me. "I think, Miss Courtenay, you have not seen much sorrow."

"I have not, Sir," said I, turning to him. "I think I have seen—and felt—more in the last six months than ever before."

"And I dare say you have grown more in that period," he made answer, "than in all the years before. You know in what sort of stature I mean."

He left us, and went upstairs, and Ephraim came in soon after. I had no words with Flora alone, and only a moment with Annas. She came with us to the door.

"Does Flora understand?" I whispered, as I kissed Annas for good-bye.

"I think not, Cary. I hope not. It would be far better."

"*You* do?" said I.

"I knew it long ago," she answered. "It is no new thing."

We went back to Bloomsbury Square, where I found in the drawing-room a whole parcel of visitors—Mrs. Newton and her daughters, and a lot of the Pages (there are twelve of them), Sir Anthony Parmenter, and a young gentleman and gentlewoman who were strangers to me. Grandmamma called me up at once.

"Here, child," said she, "come and speak to your cousins. These are my brother's grandchildren—your second cousins, my dear." And she introduced them —Mr. Roland and Miss Hilary Carlingford.

What contrasts there are in this world, to be sure! As my Cousin Hilary sat by me, and asked me if I went often to the play, and if I had seen Mrs. Bellamy,[1] and whether I loved music, and all those endless questions that people seem as if they must ask you when they first make acquaintance with you,—all at once there came up before me the white, calm face of Annas Keith, and the inner vision of Colonel Keith in his prison, waiting so patiently and heroically for death. And oh, how small did the one seem, and how grand the other! Could there be a doubt which was nearer God?

A lump came up in my throat, which I had to swallow before I could tell Hilary that I loved old ballads and such things better than what they call classical music, much of which seems to me like running up and down without any aim or tune to it—and she was giving me a tap with her fan, and saying,—

"Oh, fie, Cousin Caroline! Don't tell the world your taste is so bad as that!"

Suddenly a sound broke across it all, that sent everything vanishing away, present and future, good and ill, and carried me off to the old winter parlour at Brocklebank.

"Bless me, man! don't you know how to carry a basket?" said a voice, which I felt as ready and as glad to welcome as if it had been that of an angel. "Well, you Londoners have not much pith. We Cumberland folks don't carry our baskets with the tips of our fingers—can't, very often; they are a good heft."

"Madam," said Dobson at the door, looking more

---

[1] A noted actress of that day.

uncomfortable than I had ever seen him, "here is a—a person—who———"

"Woman, man! I'm a woman, and not ashamed of it! Mrs. Desborough, Madam, I hope you are well."

What Grandmamma was going to do or say, I cannot tell. She sat looking at her visitor from head to foot, as if she were some kind of curiosity. I am afraid I spoilt the effect completely, for with a cry of "Aunt Kezia!" I rushed to her and threw my arms round her neck, and got a warmer hug than I expected my Aunt Kezia to have given me. Oh dear, what a comfort it was to see her! She was what nobody else was in Bloomsbury Square—something to lean on and cling to. And I *did* cling to her: and if I went down in the esteem of all the big people round me, I felt as if I did not care a straw about it, now that I had got my own dear Aunt Kezia again.

"Here's one glad to see me, at any rate!" said my Aunt Kezia; and I fancy her eyes were not quite dry.

"Here are two, Aunt Kezia," said Hatty, coming up.

"Mrs. Kezia Courtenay, is it not?" said Grandmamma, so extra graciously that I felt sure she was vexed. "I am extreme glad to see you, Madam. Have you come from the North to-day? Hester, my dear, you will like to take your aunt to your chamber. Caroline, you may go also, if you desire it."

Thus benignantly dismissed, we carried off my Aunt Kezia as if she had been a casket of jewels. And as to what the fine folks said behind our backs, either of her or of us, I do not believe either Hatty or I cared a bit. I can answer for one of us, anyhow.

x

"Now sit down and rest yourself, Aunt Kezia," said I, when we reached our chamber. "Oh, how delightful it is to have you! Is Father well? Are we to go home?"

And then it flashed upon me—to go home, leaving Colonel Keith in prison, and Annas and Flora in such a position! Must we do that? I listened somewhat anxiously for my Aunt Kezia's answer.

"It is pleasant to see you, girls, I can tell you. And it is double pleasant to have such a hearty welcome to anybody. Your Father and Sophy are quite well, and everybody else. You are to go home?—ay: but when, we'll see by-and-by. But now I want my questions answered, if you please. I shall be glad to know what has come to you both? I sent off two throddy, rosy-cheeked maids to London, that did a bit of credit to Cumberland air and country milk, and here are two poor, thin, limp, white creatures, that look as if they had lost all the sunshine out of them. What have you been doing to yourselves?—or what has somebody else been doing to you? Which is it?"

"Cary must speak for herself," said Hatty.

"Hatty must speak for herself," said I.

Hatty laughed.

"It is somebody else, with Hatty," I went on, "and I don't quite know how it is with me, Aunt Kezia. I have been feeling for some weeks past as if I had the world on my shoulders."

"Your shoulders are not strong enough for that, child," replied my Aunt Kezia. "There is but one shoulder which can carry the world. 'The government shall be upon His shoulder.' You may well look poor if you have been at that work. Where are Flora and Miss Keith?—and what has become of their brothers, both?"

"Annas and Flora have just come back to London," said Hatty. "But Angus is in dreadful trouble, Aunt; and I do not know where Colonel Keith is—with the Prince, I suppose."

"No, Hatty," said I. "Aunt Kezia, Angus is safe, but an exile in France; and Colonel Keith lies in Newgate Prison, waiting for death."

"What do you know about it?" asked Hatty, in an astonished tone.

My Aunt Kezia looked from one of us to the other.

"You cannot both be right," said she. "I hope you are mistaken, Cary."

"I have no chance to be so," I answered; and I heard my voice tremble. "Colonel Keith bought Angus's freedom with his own life. At least, there is every reason to fear that result, and none to hope."

"Then that man who escaped was Angus?" asked Hatty.

I bowed my head. I felt inclined to burst out crying if I spoke.

"But who told you? and how come you to be so sure it is true?"

"I was the girl who carried the basket into the prison." I just managed to say so much without breaking down, though that tiresome lump in my throat kept teasing me.

"You!" cried Hatty, in more tones than the word

has letters. "Cary, you must be dreaming! When could you have done it?"

"In the evening, on one of Grandmamma's Tuesdays, and I was back before any one missed me, except you."

"Who went with you?—who was in the plot? Do tell us, Cary!"

"Yes, I suppose you may know now," I said, for I could now speak more calmly. "Ephraim took me to the place where I put on the disguise, and forward to the prison. Then Colonel Keith and I carried in the basket, and Angus brought it out. Ephraim came to us after we left the prison, and brought me back here."

"Ephraim Hebblethwaite helped *you* to do *that?*"

I did not understand Hatty's tone. She was astonished, undoubtedly so, but she was something else too, and what that was I could not tell.

My Aunt Kezia listened silently.

"Why, Cary, you are a heroine! I could not have believed that a timid little thing like you——" Hatty stopped.

"There was nobody else," said I. "You were not well enough, you know. I had to do it; but I can assure you, Hatty, I felt like anything but a hero."

"They are the heroes," said my Aunt Kezia, softly, "who feel unlike heroes, but have to do it, and go and do it therefore. Colonel Keith and Cary seem to be of that sort. And there is only one other kind of heroes — those who stand by and see their best beloved do such things, and, knowing it to be God's will, bid them God-speed with cheerful countenance, and cry their own hearts out afterwards, when no one sees them but Himself."

"That is Annas' sort," said I.

"Yes, and one other," replied my Aunt Kezia.

"But Hatty did not know till afterwards," said I.

"Child, I did not mean Hatty. Do Flora and Miss Keith look as white as you poor thin things?"

"Much worse, I think," said I. "Annas keeps up, and does not shed a tear, and Flora cries her eyes out. But they are both white and sadly worn."

"Poor souls!" said my Aunt Kezia. "Maybe they would like to go home with us. Do you know when they wish to go?"

"Annas has been promised a hearing of Princess Caroline, to intercede for her brother," I made answer. "I think she will be ready to go as soon as that is over. There would be no good in waiting." And my voice choked a little as I remembered for what our poor Annas would otherwise wait.

"Cary Courtenay, do you know you have got ten years on your head in six months?"

"I feel as if I were a good deal older," I said, smiling.

"You are the elder of the two now," said my Aunt Kezia, drily. "Not but what Hatty has been through the kiln too; but it has softened her, and hardened you."

"Then Hatty is gold, and I am only clay," I said; and I could not help laughing a little, though I have not laughed much lately.

"There is some porcelain sells for its weight in gold," said my Aunt Kezia.

"Thank you for the compliment, Aunt Kezia."

"Nay, lass, I'm a poor hand at compliments; but I know gold when I see it—and brass, too. You'll be home in good time for Sophy's wedding."

"Aunt Kezia, who does Sophy marry?"

"Mr. Liversedge, the Rector."

"Is not he rather rough?"

"Rough? Not a bit of it. He is a rough diamond, if he be."

"I fancied from what Sam said when he came back to Carlisle——"

"Oh, we had seen nought of him then. He has done more good at Brocklebank than Mr. Digby did all the years he was there. You'll see fast enough when you get back. 'Tis the nature of the sun to shine."

"What do you mean by that, Aunt Kezia?"

"Keep your eyes open—that's what I mean. Girls, your father bade me please myself about tarrying a bit before I turned homeward. I doubt I'm not just as welcome to your grandmother as to you; but I think we shall do best to bide till we see if the others can come with us. Maybe Ephraim may be ready to go home by then, too. 'Tis a bad thing for a young man to get into idle habits."

"O Aunt Kezia, Ephraim is not idle!" I cried.

"Pray, who asked you to stand up for him, Miss?" replied my Aunt Kezia. "'A still tongue makes a wise head,' lass. I'll tell you what, I rather fancy Mrs. Desborough thinks me rough above a bit. If I'm to be stroked alongside of these fine folks here, I shall feel rough, I've no doubt. That smart, plush fellow, with his silver clocks to his silk stockings, took up my basket as if he expected it to bite his fingers. We don't take hold of baskets that road in our parts. I haven't seen a pair of decent clogs since I passed Derby. They are all slim French finnicking pattens down here. How many of those fine lords-in-waiting have you in the house?"

"Three, and a black boy, Aunt."

"And how many maids?"

"I must count. Lucette and Perkins, and the cook-maid, and the kitchen girl, four; and two chamber-maids, six, and a seamstress, seven."

"What, have you a mantua-maker all to yourselves?"

"Oh, she does not make gowns; she only does plain sewing."

"And two cookmaids, and two chambermaids, and two beside! Why, whatever in all the world can they find to do?"

"Lucette is Grandmamma's woman, and Perkins is my Aunt Dorothea's," said I.

"But what have they got to *do?* That's what I want to know," said my Aunt Kezia.

"Well, Lucette gets up Grandmamma's laces and fine things," said I, "and quills the nett for her ruffles, and dresses her hair, and alters her gowns——"

"What's that for?" said my Aunt Kezia.

"When a gown has been worn two or three times," said Hatty, "they turn it upside down, Aunt, and put some fresh trimming on it, so that it looks like a new one."

"But what for?" repeated my Aunt Kezia.

"Why, then, you see, people don't remember that you had it on last week."

" I'll be bound I should ! "

" We have very short memories in London," said Hatty, laughing.

" Seems so !   But why should not folks remember ? I am fairly dumfoozled with it all.   How any mortal woman can get along with four men and seven maids to look after, passes me.   I find Maria and Bessy and Sam enough, I can tell you: too many sometimes. Mrs. Desborough must be up early and down late; or does Mrs. Charles see to things ? "

I began to laugh.   The idea of Grandmamma " seeing to " anything, except fancy work and whist, was so extreme diverting.

" Why, Aunt Kezia, nobody ever sees to anything here," said Hatty.

" And do things get done ? " asked my Aunt Kezia with uplifted eyebrows.

" Sometimes," said Hatty, again laughing.   " They don't do much dusting, I fancy.   I could write my name on the dust on the tables, now and then, and generally on the windows."

My Aunt Kezia glanced at the window, and set her lips grimly.

" If I were mistress in this house for a week," said she, " I reckon those four men and seven maids would scarce send up a round robin begging me to stop another ! "

" Lucette does her work thoroughly," said I, " and so does Cicely, the under chambermaid ; and Cæsar, the black boy, is an honest lad.   I am afraid I cannot say much for the rest.   But really, Aunt, it seemed to me when I came that people hadn't a notion what work was in the South."

" I guess it'll seem so to me, coming and going too," said my Aunt Kezia, in the same tone as before. " No wonder. I couldn't work in silk stockings with silver clocks, and sleeves with lace ruffles, and ever so many yards of silk bundled up of a heap behind me. I like gowns I can live in. I've had this on a bit over three times, Hatty."

" I should think so, Aunt!" said Hatty, laughing something like her old self. " Why, I remember your making it the winter before last. Did not I run the seams ?"

" I dare say you did, child. When you see me bedecked in the pomps and vanities of this wicked world, you may expect to catch larks by the sky falling. At least, I hope so."

" Mademoiselle!" said Lucette's voice at the door, " Madame bids me say the company comes from going, and if Madame and Mesdemoiselles will descend, she will be well at ease."

" That's French lingo, is it ?" said my Aunt Kezia. " Poor lass !"

So down we went to the drawing-room, where we found Grandmamma, my Aunt Dorothea, and my Uncle Charles, who came forward and led my Aunt Kezia to a chair. (Miss Newton told me that ceremony was growing out of date, and was only practised now by nice old-fashioned people ; but Grandmamma likes it, and I fancy my Uncle Charles will keep it up while she lives.)

"Madam," said Grandmamma, "I trust Mr. Courtenay is well, and that you had a prosperous journey."

"He is better than ever he was, I thank you, Madam," answered my Aunt Kezia. "As for my journey, I did not much enjoy it, but here I am, and that is well."

"Your other niece, Miss Drummond, is in Town, as I hear," said Grandmamma. "Dorothea, my dear, it would doubtless be agreeable to Mrs. Kezia if that young gentlewoman came here. Write a line and ask her to tarry with us while Mrs. Kezia stays."

"I thank you, Madam," said my Aunt Kezia.

"If Miss Keith be with her, she may as well be asked too," observed Grandmamma, after she had refreshed her faculties with a pinch of snuff.

My Aunt Dorothea sat down and writ the note, and then, bidding me ring the bell, sent Cæsar with it. He returned with a few lines from Flora, accepting the invitation for herself, but declining it for Annas. I was less surprised than sorry. Certainly, were I Annas, I should not care to come back to Bloomsbury Square.

"Poor white thing!" said my Aunt Kezia, when she saw Flora in the evening. "Why, you are worse to look at than these girls, and they are ill enough."

Flora brings news that Annas is to see the Princess next Thursday, but she has made up her mind to tarry longer in London, and will not go back with us. I asked where she was going to be, and Flora said at Mr. Raymond's.

"What, all alone?" said Hatty.

"Oh, no!" answered Flora; "Mr. Raymond's mother is there."

I did not know that Mr. Raymond had a mother.

Annas had a letter this morning from Lady Monksburn: the loveliest letter, says Flora, that ever woman penned. Mr. Raymond said, when he had read it (which she let him do) that it was worthy of a martyr's mother.

"Is Mr. Raymond coming round?" said I.

"What, in politics?" replied Flora, with a smile. "I don't quite know, Cary. I doubt if he will turr as quickly as you did."

"As I did? What can you mean, Flora?"

"Did you not know you had become of a very cool politician a very warm one?" she said. "I remember, when you first went with me to Abbotscliff, Angus used to tease you about being a Whig: and you once told me you knew little about such matters, and cared less."

I looked back at myself, as it were, and I think Flora must be right. I certainly thought much less of such things six months ago. I suppose hearing them always talked of has made a change in me.

There is another thing that I have been thinking about to-night. What is it in my Aunt Kezia that makes her feel so strong and safe to lean upon—so different from other people? I should never dream of feeling in that way to Grandmamma: and even Father, —though it is pleasant to rely on his strength and kindness, when one wants something done beyond one's own strength,—yet he is not restful to lean on in the same way that she is. Is she so safe to hold by, because she holds by God?

This is Grandmamma's last Tuesday, as Lent begins to-morrow, and I believe she would as soon steal a diamond necklace as have an assembly in Lent. I had been walking a great deal, as I have carried my Aunt Kezia these last few days to see all manner of sights, and I was very tired; so I crept into a little corner, and there Ephraim found me.

By the way, it is most diverting to carry my Aunt Kezia to see things. My Uncle Charles has gone with us sometimes, and Ephraim some other times: but it is so curious to watch her. She is the sight, to me. In the first place, she does not care a bit about going to see a thing just because everybody goes to see it. Then she has very determined ideas of her own about every-thing she does see. I believe she quite horrified my Uncle Charles, one day, when he carried us to see a collection of beautiful paintings. We stopped before one, which my Uncle Charles told us was thought a great deal of, and had cost a mint of money.

"What's it all about?" said my Aunt Kezia.

"'Tis a picture of the Holy Family," he answered "by the great painter Rubens."

"Now, stop a bit: who's what?" said my Aunt Kezia, and set herself to study it. "Who is that old man that hasn't shaved himself?"

"That, Madam, is Saint Joseph."

"Never heard of him before. Oh, do you mean Joseph the carpenter? I see. Well, and who is that woman with the child on her knee? Why ever does not she put him some more clothes on? He'll get his death of cold."

"My dear Madam, that is the Blessed Virgin!"

"I hope it isn't," said my Aunt Kezia, bluntly. "I'll go bail she kept her linen better washed than that. But what's that queer thing sprawling all over the sky?"

"The Angel Gabriel, Madam."

"I hope he hasn't flown in here and seen this," said my Aunt Kezia. "I should say, if he have, he didn't feel flattered by his portrait."

My Aunt Kezia did not seem to care for fine things—smart clothes, jewels, and splendid coaches, or anything like that. She was interested in the lions at the Tower, and she liked to see any famous person of whom my Uncle Charles could tell her; but for Ranelagh she said she did not care twopence. There were men and women plenty wherever you went, and as to silks and laces, she could see them any day over a mercer's counter. Vauxhall was still worse, and Spring Gardens did not please her any better.

But when, in going through the Tower, we came to the axe which beheaded my Lady Jane Grey, she showed no lack of interest in that. And the next day, when my Uncle Charles said he would show us some of the fine things in the City, and we were driving in Grandmamma's coach towards Newgate, my Aunt Kezia wanted to know what the open space was; and my Uncle Charles told her,—"Smithfield."

"Smithfield!" cried she. "Pray you, Mr. Desborough, bid your coachman stop. I would liever see this than a Lord Mayor's Show."

"My dear Madam. there is nothing to see," answered

my Uncle Charles, who seemed rather perplexed.
"This is not a market-day."

"There'll be plenty I can see!" was my Aunt Kezia's
reply; and, my Uncle Charles pulling the check-string,
we alighted. My Aunt Kezia stood a moment, looking round.

"You see, there is nothing to see," he observed.

"Nothing to see!" she made answer. "There are
the fires to see, and the martyrs, and the angels around,
and the devils, and the men well-nigh as ill as devils.
There is the land to see that they saved, and the
Church that their blood watered, and the greatness of
England that they preserved. Aye, and there is the
Day of Judgment, when martyrs and persecutors will
have their reward—and you and I, Mr. Desborough,
shall meet with ours. My word, but there is enough
to see for them that have eyes to see it!"

"Oh!—ah!" said my Uncle Charles.

My Aunt Kezia said no more, except a few words
which I heard her whisper softly to herself,—"'They
shall reign for ever and ever.' 'The noble army of
martyrs praise Thee.'" Then, as she turned back
to the coach, she added, "I thank you, Sir. It was
worth coming to London to look at that. It makes
one feel as if one got nearer to them."

And I thought, but did not say, that I should never
be nearer to them than I had been that winter night,
when Colonel Keith helped me to carry the basket into
the gates of that grim, black pile beyond. He was
there yet. If I had been a bird, to have flown in
and sung to him!—or, better, a giant, to tear away

locks and bars, and let him out! And I could do *nothing*.

But here I am running ever so far from Grandmamma's Tuesday, and the news Ephraim brought.

Annas has seen the Princess Caroline. She liked her, and thought her very gentle and good. But she held out no hope at all, and did not seem to think that anything which she could say would influence her father. She would lay the matter before him, but she could promise no more. However, she appointed another day, about a month hence, when Annas may go to her again, and hear the final answer. So Annas must wait for that.

Ephraim and Annas seem to be great friends. Is it not shockingly selfish of me to wish it otherwise? I do not quite know why I wish it. But sometimes I wonder—no, I won't wonder. It will be all right, of course, however it be arranged. Why should I always want people to care for me, and think of me, and put me first? Cary Courtenay, you are growing horribly vain and selfish! I wonder at you!

It is settled now that we go home the week after Easter Day. We, means my Aunt Kezia, and Flora, and Hatty, and me. I do not know how four women are to travel without a gentleman, or even a servingman: but I suppose we shall find out when the time comes. I said to my Aunt Kezia that perhaps Grandmamma would lend us Dobson.

"Him!" cried she. "Dear heart, but I'd a vast deal liever be without him! He would want all the coach-pockets for his silk stockings, and would take

more waiting on than Prince Charlie himself.   I make
no account of your grand gentlemen in plush, that pick
up baskets with the tips of their fingers! (My Aunt
Kezia cannot get over that.) Give me a man, or a
woman either, with some brains in his head, and some
use in his hands.   These southern folks seem to have
forgotten how to use theirs. I watched that girl Martha
dusting the other day, and if I did not long to snatch
the duster out of her hands and whip her with it ! She
just drew it lazily across the top of the table,—never
troubled herself about the sides,—and gave it one whisk
across the legs, and then she had done.   I'd rather do
my work myself, every bit of it, than have such a pack
of idle folks about me—ay, ten times over, I would !
They don't seem to have a bit of gumption.   They say
lawyers go to Heaven an inch every Good Friday;
but if those lazy creatures get there or anywhere else
in double the time, I wonder!   And just look at the
way they dress ! A good linsey petticoat and a quilted
linen bedgown was good enough for a woman that had
her work to do, when I was young; but now, dear me !
my ladies must have their gowns, and their muslin
aprons of an afternoon, and knots of ribbon in their
hair.   I do believe they will take to wearing white
stockings, next thing ! and gloves when they go to
church ! Eh dear, girls ! I tell you what, this world
is coming to something !"

Later in the evening, Miss Newton came up to me,
with her fan held before her laughing face.

"My dear Miss Courtenay, what curious things
your worthy Aunt does say ! She asked me just now

why I came into the world. I told her I did not
know, and the idea had never before occurred to me :
and she said, ' Well, then, it is high time it did, and
some to spare !' Do all the people in Cumberland ask
you such droll questions ? "

I said I thought not, but my Aunt Kezia did, often
enough.

"Well, she is a real curiosity !" said Miss Newton,
and went away laughing.

BROCKLEBANK FELLS, *April the* 10*th*, 1746.

At least I begin on the 10th, but when I shall finish
is more than I can tell. Things went on happening
so fast after the last page I writ, that I neither had
time to set them down, nor heart for doing it. Prince
William of Hanover (whom the Whigs call Duke of
Cumberland) left Edinburgh with a great army, not
long after I writ ; but no news has yet reached us of
any hostile meeting betwixt him and the Prince. Mr.
Raymond saith Colonel Keith's chances may depend
somewhat upon the results of the battle, which is daily
expected. Nevertheless, he adds, there is no chance,
for the Lord orders all things.

My Aunt Kezia and Mr. Raymond have taken wonderfully to one another. Hatty said to her that she
could not think how they got on when they chanced
on politics.

"Bless you, child, we never do !" said my Aunt
Kezia. "We have got something better to talk about.
And why should two brothers quarrel because one likes
red heels to his shoes and the other admires black ones ?"

Y

"Ah, if that were all, Aunt!" said I. "But how can you leave it there? It seems to me not a matter for opinion, but a question of right. We have to take sides ; and we may choose the wrong one."

"I don't see that a woman need take any side unless she likes," quoth my Aunt Kezia. "I can bake as tasty a pie, and put on as neat a patch, whether I talk of Prince Charles or the Young Pretender. And patches and pies are my business: the Prince isn't. I reckon the Lord will manage to see that every one gets his rights, without Kezia Courtenay running up to help Him."

"But somebody has it to do, Aunt."

"Let them do it, then. I'm glad I'm not somebody."

"But, Aunt Kezia, don't you want people to have their rights ? "

"Depends on what their rights are, child. Some of us would be very sadly off if we got them. I should not like my rights, I know."

"Ah, you mean your deserts, Aunt," said Hatty. "But rights are not just the same thing, are they ? "

"Let us look it in the face, girls, if you wish," saith my Aunt Kezia. "I hate seeing folks by side-face. If you want to see anybody, or understand anything, look right in its face. What are rights ? They are not always deserts,—you are right there, Hatty,—for none of us hath any rights as regards God. Rights concern ourselves and our fellow-men. I take it, every man hath a right to what he earns, and to what is given him,—whether God or man gave it to him,—so long as he that gave had the right over what he gave. Now, as to this question, it seems to me all lies in a nut-shell. If King James be truly the son of the old King (which I cannot doubt), then God gave him the crown of England, of which no man can possibly have any right to deprive him. Only God can do that. Then comes the next question, Has God done that? Time must answer. Without a revelation from Heaven, we cannot find it out any other way."

"But until we do find it out, where are we to stand?"

"Keep to your last orders till you get fresh ones. A servant will make sad blunders who goes contrary to orders, just because he fancies that his master may have changed his mind."

I see that for all practical purposes my Aunt Kezia agrees with Annas. And indeed what they say sounds but reasonable.

It was the second of April when we left London. It had been arranged that we should travel by the flying machine[1] which runs from London to Gloucester, setting forth from the Saracen's Head on Snow Hill. The last evening before we set out, my Aunt Kezia, Hatty, and I, spent at Mr. Raymond's with Annas. His mother is a very pleasant old silver-haired gentlewoman, with a soft, low voice and gentle manner that reminded me of Lady Monksburn.

I felt it very hard work to say farewell to Annas. What might not have happened before we met again? Ephraim was there for the last hour or so, and was

---

[1] Stage-coaches originally bore this hyperbolical name.

very attentive to her. I do think—— And I am rather afraid the Laird, her father, will not like it. But Ephraim is good enough for anybody. And I hope, when he marry Annas, which I think is coming, that he will not quite give over being my friend. He has been more like our brother than anybody else. I should not like to lose him. I have always wished we had a brother.

"No, not good-bye just yet, Cary," said Ephraim, in answer to my farewell. "You will see me again in the morning."

"Oh, are you coming to see us off?"

He nodded; and we only said good-night.

Grandmamma was very kind when we took leave of her. She gave each of us a keepsake—a beautiful garnet necklace to Hatty, and a handsome pearl pin to me.

"And, my dear," said she to Hatty, "I do hope you will try to keep as genteel as you are now. Don't, for mercy's sake, go and get those blowzed red cheeks again. They are so unbecoming a gentlewoman. And garnets, though they are the finest things in the world for a pale, clear complexion, look horrid worn with great red cheeks. Cary, your manners had rather gone back when you came, from what they used to be; but you have improved again now. Mind you keep it up. Don't get warm and enthusiastic over things,—that is your danger, my dear,—especially things of no consequence, and which don't concern you. A young gentlewoman should not be a politician; and to be warm over anything which has to do with religion, as I have many times told you, is exceeding bad taste. You should leave those matters to public men and the clergy. It is their business—not yours. My dears," and out came Grandmamma's snuff-box, " I wish you to understand, once for all, that if one of you ever joins those insufferable creatures, the Methodists, I will cut her off with a shilling! I shall wash my hands of her completely. I would not even call her my grand-daughter again! But I am sure, my dears, you have too much sense. I shall not insult you by supposing such a thing. Make my compliments to your father, and tell him I think you both much improved by your winter in Town. Good-bye, my dears. Mrs. Kezia, I wish you a safe and pleasant journey."

" I thank you, Madam, and wish you every blessing," said my Aunt Kezia, with a warm clasp of Grandmamma's hand, which I am sure she would think sadly countrified. "But might I ask you, Madam, to explain something which puzzled me above a bit in what you have just said ? "

"Certainly, Mrs. Kezia," said Grandmamma, in her most gracious manner.

"Then, Madam, as I suppose the clergy are going to Heaven (and I am sure you would be as sorry to think otherwise as I should), if the way to get there is their business and not yours, where are you going, if you please ? "

Grandmamma looked at my Aunt Kezia as if she thought that she must have taken leave of her wits.

"Madam! I—I do not understand——"

My Aunt Kezia did not flinch in the least. She stood quietly looking into Grandmamma's face, with an air of perfect simplicity, and waited for the answer.

"Of course, we—we are all going to Heaven," said Grandmamma, in a hesitating way. "But it is the business of the clergy to see that we do. Excuse me, Madam; I am not accustomed to—to talk about such subjects."

And Grandmamma took two pinches, one after the other.

"Well, you see, I am," coolly said my Aunt Kezia. "Seems to me, Madam, that going to Heaven is every bit as much my business as going to Gloucester; and I have not left that for the clergy to see to, nor do I see why I should the other. Folks don't always remember what you trust them with, and sometimes they can't manage the affair. And I take the liberty to think they'll find that matter rather hard to do, without I see to it as well, and without the Lord sees to it beside. Farewell, Madam; I shall be glad to meet you up there, and I do hope you'll make sure you've got on the right road, for it would be uncommon awkward to find out at last that it was the wrong one. Good-morrow, and God bless you!"

Not a word came in answer, but I just glanced back through the crack of the door, and saw Grandmamma sitting with the reddest face I ever did see to her, and two big wrinkles in her forehead, taking pinch after pinch in the most reckless manner.

My Aunt Dorothea, who stood in the door, said acidly,—"I think, Madam, it would have been as well to keep such remarks till you were alone with my mother. I do not know how it may be in Cumberland, but they are not thought becoming to a gentlewoman here. Believe me, I am indeed sorry to be forced to the discourtesy of saying so; but you were the first offender."

"Ay," said my Aunt Kezia. "Folks that tell the naked truth generally meet with more kicks than halfpence. But I would have spoken out of these girls' hearing, only I got never a chance. And you see I shall have to give in my account some day, and I want it to be as free from blots as I can."

"I suppose you thought you were doing a good work for your own soul!" said my Aunt Dorothea, sneeringly.

"Eh, no, poor soul!" was my Aunt Kezia's sorrowful reply. "My soul's beyond my saving, but Christ has it safe. And knowing that, Madam, makes one very pitiful to unsaved souls."

"Upon my word, Madam!" cried my Aunt Dorothea. "You take enough upon you! 'Unsaved souls,' indeed! Well, I am thankful I never had the presumption to say that my soul was safe. I have a little more humility than that."

"It would indeed be presumption in some cases," said my Aunt Kezia, solemnly. "But, Madam, if you ask a princess whose daughter she is, it is scarce presuming that she should answer you, 'The King's.' What else can she answer? 'We *know* that we have eternal life.'"

"An apostle writ that, I suppose," said my Aunt Dorothea, in a hard tone.

"They were not apostles he writ to," said my Aunt Kezia. "And he says he writ on purpose that they might know it."

"Now, ladies, 'tis high time to set forth," called my Uncle Charles's voice from the hall; and I was glad to hear it. I and Hatty ran off at once, but I could not but catch my Aunt Kezia's parting words,—

"God bless you, Madam, and I thank you for all your kindness. And when I next see you, I hope *you* will know it."

We drove to Snow Hill in Grandmamma's coach, and took our seats (bespoken some days back) in the flying machine, where our company was two country-women with baskets, a youth that looked very pale and cadaverous, and wore his hair uncommon long, a lady in very smart clothes, and a clergyman in his cassock. My Uncle Charles bade us farewell very kindly, and wished us a safe journey. Mr. Raymond was there also, and he bade God bless us. Somehow, in all the bustle, I had not a right chance to take leave of Ephraim. The coach set forth rather sooner than I expected, while Flora and I were charging Mr. Raymond with messages to Annas; and he had only time to step back with a bow and a smile. I looked for Ephraim, but could not even see him. I was so sorry, and I thought of little else until we got to Uxbridge.

At Uxbridge we got out, and went into the inn to dine at the ordinary, which is always spread ready for the coming of the flying machine on a Wednesday. As I sat down beside my Aunt Kezia, a man came and took the chair on the other side of me.

" Tired, Cary ? " he said, to my amazement.

" Ephraim ! " I cried. " Wherever have you come from ? "

" Did you think I had taken up my abode in London ? " said he, looking diverted.

" But I thought you went after some business," I said, feeling very much puzzled that he should be going home just now, and leaving poor Annas in all her trouble.

" I did," he answered. " Business gets done some time. It would be a sad thing if it did not. Will you have some of this rabbit pie ? "

I accepted the pie, for I did not care what I had.

" Then your business is done ? " I said, in some surprise.

His business could hardly have any connection with Annas, in that case. It must be real business—something that concerned his father.

" Yes, Cary ; my business was finished last night, so I was just in time to come with you." And the look of fun came into his eyes again.

" Oh, I am glad ! " said I. " I wondered how my Aunt Kezia would manage all by herself."

" Had you three made up your minds to be particularly naughty ? " asked he, laughing.

" Now, Ephraim ! " said I.

" Sounded like it," he replied. " Well, Cary, are you glad to go home ? "

" Well, yes—I think—I am," answered I.

" Then certainly I think you are not."

" Well. I am glad for some reasons."

" And not for others. Yes, I understand that. And I guess one of the reasons—you are sorry to leave Miss Keith."

I wondered if he guessed that because he was sorry.

" Yes, I am very sorry to leave her in this trouble. Do you think it likely that Colonel Keith can escape ?"

Ephraim shook his head.

" Is it possible ? "

" ' Possible ' is a Divine word, not fit for the lips of men. What God wills is possible. And it is not often that He lets us see long beforehand what He means to do."

" Then you think all lies with God ?" I said—I am afraid, in a rather hopeless tone.

" Does not everything, at all times, lie with God ? That means hope, Cary, not despair. ' Whatsoever the Lord pleased, that did He.' "

" Oh dear ! that sounds as if—Ephraim, I don't mean to say anything wicked—as if He did not care."

" He cares for our sanctification : that is, in the long run, for our happiness. Would you rather that He cared just to rid you of the pain of the moment, and not for your eternal happiness ? "

" Oh no ! But could I not have both ? "

" No, Cary, I don't suppose you could."

" But if God can do everything, why can He not do that ? Do you never want to know the answers to such questions ? Or do they not trouble you ? They are always coming up with me."

" Far too often. Satan takes care of that."

" You think it is wicked to want the answers ? "

"It is rebellion, Cary. The King is the best judge of what concerns His subjects' welfare."

I felt in a corner, so I ate my pie and was silent.

We slept at Reading, and the next day we dined at Wallingford, and slept at the Angel at Oxford. Next morning, which was Saturday, we were up before the sun, to see as much as we could of the city before the machine should set forth. I cannot say that I got a very clear idea of the place, for when I try to remember it, my head seems a confused jumble of towers and gateways, colleges and churches, stained windows and comical gargoyles—at least that is what Ephraim called the funny faces which stuck out from some of the walls. I don't know where he got the word.

This day's stage was the longest. We dined at Lechlade; and it had long been dark when we rattled into the courtyard of the Bell Inn at Gloucester, where we were to pass the Sunday. Oh, how tired I was! almost too tired to sleep.

On Sunday, we went to church at the Cathedral, where we had a very dull sermon from a Minor Canon. In the afternoon, as we sat in the host's parlour, Ephraim said to me,—

"Cary, did you ever hear of George Whitefield?"

"Oh yes, Ephraim!" I cried, and I felt the blood rush to my cheeks, and my eyes light up. "I heard him preach in Scotland, when I was there with Flora. Have you heard him?"

"Yes, many times, and Mr. Wesley also."

I was pleased to hear that. "And what were you going to say about him?"

"That if you knew his name, it would interest you to hear that he was born in this inn. His parents kept it."

"And he chose to be a field-preacher!" cried I. "Why, that was coming down in the world, was it not?"[1]

"It was coming down, in this world," said he. "But there is another world, Cary, and I fancy it was going up in that. You must remember, however, that he did not choose to be a field-preacher nor a Dissenter: he was turned out of the Church."

"But why should he have been turned out?"

"I expect, because he would not hold his tongue."

"But why did anybody want him to hold his tongue?"

"Well, you see, he let it run to awkward subjects. Ladies and gentlemen did not like him because he set his face against fashionable diversions, and told them that they were miserable sinners, and that there was only one way into Heaven, which they would have to take as well as the poor in the almshouses. The neighbouring clergy did not like him because he was better than themselves. And the bishops did not like him because he said they ought to do their duty better, and look after their dioceses, instead of setting bad examples to their clergy by hunting and card-playing and so forth; or, at the best, sitting quiet in their

---

[1] At this date, an innkeeper stood higher in the estimation of society than at present, and a clergyman considerably lower, unless the latter were a dignitary, or a man whose birth and fortune were regarded as entitling him to respect apart from his profession.

closets to write learned books, which was not the duty they promised when they were ordained. But, as was the case with another Preacher, 'the common people heard him gladly.'"

"And he was really turned out?"

"Seven years ago."

"I wonder if it were a wise thing," said I, thinking.

"Mr. Raymond says it was the most unwise thing they could have done. And he says so of the turning forth under the Act of Uniformity, eighty years ago. He thinks the men who were the very salt of the Church left her then: and that now she is a saltless, soulless thing, that will die unless God's mercy put more salt in her."

"But suppose it do, and the bishops get them turned out again?"

"Then, says Raymond, let the bishops look to themselves. There is such a thing as judicial blindness: and there is such a thing as salt that has lost its savour, and is trodden under foot of men. If the Church cast out the children of God, God may cast out the Church of England. There are precedents for it in the Books of Heaven. And in all those cases, God let them go on for a while: over and over again they grieved His Spirit and persecuted His servants; but at last there always came one time which was the last time, and after that the Spirit withdrew, and that Church, or that nation, was left to the lot which it had chosen."

"Oh, Ephraim, that sounds dreadful."

"It will be dreadful," he answered, "if we provoke it at the Lord's hand."

"One feels as if one would like to save such men," I said.

"Do you?   I feel as if I should like to save such Churches.   It is like a son's feeling who sees his own mother going down to the pit of destruction, and is utterly powerless to hold out a hand to save her.   She will not be saved.   And I wonder, sometimes, whether any much sorer anguish can be on this side Heaven!"

I was silent.

"It makes it all the harder," he said, in a troubled voice, "when the Father's other sons, whose mother she is not, jeer at the poor falling creature, and at her own children for their very anguish in seeing it.   I do not think the Father can like them to do that.   It is hard enough for the children without it.   And surely He loves her yet, and would fain save her and bring her home."

And I felt he spoke in parables.

CHAPTER XIV.

HOW THINGS CAME ROUND.

"They say, when cities grow too big,
  Their smoke may make the skies look dim ;
And so may life hide God from us,
  But still it cannot alter Him.
And age and sorrow clear the soul,
  As night and silence clear the sky,
And hopes steal out like silver stars,
  And next day brightens by and by."
—Isabella Fyvie Mayo.

ON the Monday morning, we left Gloucester on horseback, with two baggage-horses beside those we rode. We dined at Worcester, and lay that night at Bridgenorth. On the Tuesday, we slept at Macclesfield ; on the Wednesday, at Colne ; on the Thursday, at Appleby ; and on Friday, about four o'clock in the afternoon, we reached home.

On the steps, waiting for us, stood Father and Sophy.

I had not been many minutes in the house before I felt, in some inward, indescribable way, that things were changed. I wonder what that is by which we feel things that we cannot know ? It was not the house which was altered. The old things, which I had known from a child, all seemed to bid me welcome home. It was Father and Sophy in whom the change was. It was not like Sophy to kiss me so warmly, and call me "darling." And it was not one bit like Father to stroke my hair, and say so solemnly, "God bless my lassie!" I have had many a kiss and a loving word from him, but I never heard him speak of God except when he repeated the responses in church, or when——

I wondered what had come to Father. And how I did wonder when after supper Sam brought, not a pack of cards, but the big Bible which used to lie in the hall window with such heaps of dust on it, and he and Maria and Bessy sat down on the settle at the end of the hall, and Father, in a voice which trembled a little, read a Psalm, and then we knelt down, and said the Confession, and the General Thanksgiving, and the Lord's Prayer. I looked at my Aunt Kezia, and saw that this was nothing new to her. And then I remembered all at once that she had hinted at something which we should see when we came home, and had bidden us keep our eyes open.

The pack of cards did not come out at all.

The next morning I was the first to come down. I found Sam setting the table in the parlour. We exchanged good-morrows, and Sam hoped I was not very tired with the journey. Then he said, without looking up, as he went on with his work—

"Ye'll ha'e found some changes here, I'm thinking, Miss."

"I saw one last night, Sam," said I, smiling.

"There's mair nor ane," he replied. "There's three things i' this warld that can ne'er lie hidden: ye may try to cover them up, but they'll aye out, sooner or later. And that's blood, and truth, and the grace o' God."

"I am not so sure the truth of things always comes out, Sam," said I.

"Ye've no been sae lang i' this warld as me, Miss Cary," said Sam. "And 'deed, sometimes 'tis a lang while first. But the grace o' God shows up quick, mostly. 'Tis its nature to be hard at wark. Ye'll no put barm into a batch o' flour, and ha'e it lying idle. And the kingdom o' Heaven is like unto leaven: it maun wark. Ay, who shall let it?"

"Is Mr. Liversedge well liked, Sam?" I asked, when I had thought a little.

"He's weel eneuch liked o' them as is weel liking," said Sam, setting his forks in their places. "The angels like him, I've nae doubt; and the lost sheep like him: but he does nae gang doun sae weel wi' the ninety and nine. They'd hae him a bit harder on the sinners, and a bit safter wi' the saints—specially wi' theirsels, wha are the vara crown and flower o' a' the saints, and ne'er were sinners—no to speak o', ye ken, and outside the responses. And he disna gang saft and slippy doun their throats, as they'd ha'e him, but he is just main hard on 'em. He tells 'em gin they're saints they suld live like saints, and they'd like the repute o' being saints without the fash o' living. He did himsel' a main deal o' harm wi' sic-like by a discourse some time gane— ye'll judge what like it was when I tell ye the Scripture it was on: 'He that saith he abideth in Him ought himself also so to walk even as He walked.' And there's a gey lot of folks i' this warld 'd like vara weel to abide, but they're a hantle too lazy to walk. And the minister, he comes and stirs 'em up wi' the staff o' the Word, and bids 'em get up and gang their ways, and no keep sat down o' the promises, divertin' theirsels wi' watching ither folk trip. He's vara legal, Miss Cary, is the minister; he reckons folk suld be washed all o'er, and no just dip their tongues in the fountain, and keep their hearts out. He disna make much count o' giving the Lord your tongue, and aye hauding the De'il by the hand ahint your back. And the o'er gude folks disna like that. They'd liever keep friendly wi' baith."

"Then you think the promises were not made to be sat on, Sam?" said I, feeling much diverted with Sam's quaint way of putting things.

Sam settled the cream-jug and sugar-bowl before he answered.

"I'll tell ye how it is, Miss. The promises was made to be lain on by weary, heavy-laden sinners that come for rest, and want to lay down both theirsels and their burden o' sins on the Lord's heart o' love: but they were ne'er made for auld Jeshurun to sit on and wax fat, and kick the puir burdened creatures as they come toiling up the hill. Last time I was in Carlisle, I went to see a kinsman o' mine there as has set up i' the cabinet-making trade, and he showed me a balk o' yon bonnie new wood as they ha'e getten o'er o' late—the auld Vicar used to ha'e his dining-table on't; it comes frae some outlandish pairts, and they call it a queer name; I canna just mind it the noo—I reckon I'm getting too auld to tak' in new notions."

"Mahogany?"

" Ay, maybe that's it : I ken it minded me o' mud and muggins. Atweel, my cousin tauld me they'd a rare call for siccan wood, and being vara costly, they'd hit o' late in the trade on a new way o' making furniture, as did nae come to sae mickle—they ca' it veneer."

" Oh yes, I know," said I.

" Ay, ye'll hae seen it i' London toun, I daur say ? all that's bad's safe to gang there." I believe Sam thinks all Londoners a pack of thieves. " Atweel, Miss Cary, there's a gran' sicht o' veneered Christians i' this country. They look as spic-span, and as glossy, and just the richt shade o' colour, and bonnily grained, and a' that—till ye get ahint 'em, and then ye see that, saving a thin bit o' facing, they're just common deal, like ither folk. Ay, and it's maistly the warst bits o' the deal as is used up ahint the veneer. It is, sae ! Ye see, 'tis no meant to last, but only to sell. And there's a monie folks 'll gi'e the best price for sic-like, and fancy they ha'e getten the true thing. But I'm thinkin' the King 'll no gi'e the price. His eyes are as a flame o fire, and they'll see richt through siccan rubbish, and burn it up."

" And Mr. Liversedge, I suppose, is the real mahogany ? "

" He is sae : and he's a gey awkward way of seeing ahint thae bits o' veneered stuff, and finding out they're no worth the money. And they dinna like him onie better for 't."

" But I hope he does not make a mistake the other way, Sam, and take the real thing for the veneer ? "

" You trust him for that. He was no born yestre'en.
There's a hantle o' folk makes that blunder, though."

Away went Sam for the kettle. When he brought
it back, he said,—" Miss Cary, ye'll mind Annie Crosthwaite, as lives wi' auld Mally ? "

Ah, did I not remember Annie Crosthwaite ?—poor,
fragile, pretty spring flower, that some cruel hand
plucked and threw away, and men trod on the bemired
blossom as it lay in the mire, and women drew their
skirts aside to keep from touching the torn, soiled
petals? " Yes, Sam," I said, in a low voice.

" Ay, the minister brought yon puir lassie a message
frae the gude Lord—' Yet return again to Me '—and
she just took it as heartily as it was gi'en, and went and
fand rest—puir, straying, lost sheep !—but when she
came to the table o' the Lord, the ninety and nine wad
ha'e nane o' her—she was gude eneuch for Him in the
white robe o' His richteousness, but she was no near
gude eneuch for them, sin she had lost her ain—and
not ane soul i' a' the parish wad kneel down aside o'
her. Miss Cary, I ne'er saw the minister's e'en flash
out sparks o' fire as they did when he heard that ! And
what, think ye, said he? "

" I should like to hear, Sam."

" ' Vara gude,' says he. ' I beg,' he says, ' that none
o' ye all will come to the Table to-morrow. Annie
Crosthwaite and I will gang thither our lane : but
there'll be three,' says he, ' for the blessed Lord Himsel' will come and eat wi' us, and we wi' Him, for He
receiveth sinners, and eateth with them.' And he did
it, for a' they tald him the Bishop wad be doun on

him. 'Let him,' says he, 'and he shall hear the haill story': and not ane o' them a' wad he let come that morn. They were no worthy, he said."

"And did the Bishop hear of it ?"

"Ay, did he, and sent doun a big chiel, like an auld eagle, wi' a' his feathers ruffled the wrang way. But the minister, he stood his ground : 'There were three, Mr. Archdeacon,' says he, as quiet as a mill-tarn, 'and the Lord Himsel' made the third.' 'And how am I to ken that ?' says the big chiel, ruffling up his feathers belike. 'Will ye be sae gude as to ask Him ?' says the minister. I dinna ken what the big chiel made o' the tale to the Bishop, but we heard nae mair on't. Maybe he did ask Him, and gat the auld answer,—'Touch not Mine anointed, and do My prophet no harm.'"

"Still, rules ought to be kept, Sam."

"Rules ought to be kept in ordinar'. But this was bye-ordinar', ye see. If a big lad has been tauld no to gang frae the parlour till his faither comes back, and he sees his little brither drooning in the pond just afore the window, I reckon his faither 'll no be mickle angered if he jumps out of the window and saves him. Any way, I wad nae like to ha'e what he'd get, gin he said,—'Faither, ye bade me tarry in this chalmer, and sae I could nae do a hand's turn for Willie.' Rules are man's, Miss Cary, but truth and souls belang to God."

My Aunt Kezia and Sophy had come in while Sam was talking, and Father and Hatty followed now, so we sat down to breakfast.

"Sam has told you one story, girls," said my Aunt Kezia, "and I will tell you another. You will find

the singers changed when you go to church. Dan
Oldfield and Susan Nixon are gone."

"Dan and Susan!" cried Hatty. "The two best
voices in the gallery!"

"Well, you know, under old Mr. Digby, there
always used to be an anthem before the service began,
in which Dan and Susan did their best to show off.
The second week that Mr. Liversedge was here, he
stopped the anthem. Up started the singers, and told
him they would not stand it. It wasn't worth their
while coming just for the psalms. Mr. Liversedge
heard them out quietly, and then said,—'Do you mean
what you have just said?' Yes, to be sure they meant
it. 'Then consider yourselves dismissed from the
gallery without more words,' says he. 'You are not
worthy to sing the praises of Him before whom multi-
tudes of angels veil their faces. Not worth your while
to praise God!—but worth your while to show man
what fine voices He gave you whom you think scorn to
thank for it!' And he turned them off there and then."

The next time I was alone with Sophy, she said to
me, with tears in her eyes,—"Cary, I don't want you
to reckon me worse than I am. That is bad enough,
in all conscience. I would have knelt down with
Annie Crosthwaite, and so, I am sure, would my Aunt
Kezia; but it was while she was up in London with
you, and Father was so poorly with the gout, I could
not leave him. You see there was nobody to take my
place, with all of you away. Please don't fancy I was
one of those that refused, for indeed it was not so."

"I fancy you are a dear, good Sophy," said I, kissing

her; "and I suppose, if Mr. Liversedge asked you to shake hands with a chimney-sweep just come down the chimney, you would be delighted to do it."

"Well, perhaps I might," said Sophy, laughing. "But that, Cary, I should have done, not for him, but for our Master."

I found that I liked Mr. Liversedge very much, as one would wish to like a brother-in-law that was to be. His whole heart seems to be in his Lord's work : and if, perhaps, he is a little sharp and abrupt at times, I think it is simply because he sees everything quickly and distinctly, and speaks as he sees. I was afraid he would have something of the pope about him, but I find he is not like that at all. He lets you alone for all mere differences of opinion, though he will talk them over with you readily if he sees that you wish it. But let those keen, black eyes perceive something which he thinks sin, and down he comes on you in the very manner of the old prophets. Yet show him that he has made a mistake, and that your action was justified, and he begs your forgiveness in a moment. And I never saw a man who seemed more fitted to deal with broken-hearted sinners. To them he is tenderness and comfort itself.

"He just takes pattern frae his Maister; that's whaur it is," said old Elspie. "Mind ye, He was unco gentle wi' the puir despised publicans, and vara tender to the wife that had been a sinner. It was the Pharisees He was hard on. And that's just what the minister is. Miss Cary, he's just the best blessing the Lord ever sent till Brocklebank!"

"I hardly thought, Elspie," said I, a little mis-chievously, "to hear you speak so well of a Prelatist clergyman."

"Hoot awa', we a' ha'e our bees in our bonnets, Miss Cary," said the old woman, a trifle testily. "The minister's no pairfect, I daur say. But he's as gran' at prayiug as John Knox himsel', and he gars ye feel the loue and loueliness o' Christ like Maister Rutherford did. And sae lang 's he'll do that, I'm no like to quarrel wi' him, if he do ha'e a fancy for lawn sleeves and siccan rubbish. I wish him better sense, that's a'. Maybe he'll ha'e it ane o' thae days."

I cannot understand Hatty as she is now. For a while after that affair with the Crosslands she was just like a drooping, broken-down flower ; all her pertness, and even her brightness, completely gone. Now that is changed, and she has become, not pert again, but hard—hard and bitter. Nobody can do anything to suit her, and she says things now and then which make me jump. Things, I mean, as if she believed nothing and cared for nobody. When Hatty speaks in that way, I often see my Aunt Kezia looking at her with a strange light in her eyes, which seems to be half pain and half hopefulness. Mr. Liversedge, I fancy, is studying her ; and I am not sure that he knows what to make of her.

Yesterday evening, Fanny and Ambrose came in and sat a while. Fanny is ever so much improved. She has brightened up, and lost much of that languid, limp, fanciful way she used to have ; and, instead of writing odes to the stars, she seems to take an interest in her poultry-yard and dairy. My Aunt Kezia says Fanny wanted an object in life, and I suppose she has it now.

When they had been there about an hour, Mr. Liversedge came in. He does not visit Sophy often; I fancy he is too busy; but Tuesday evening is usually his leisure time, so far as he can be said to have one, and he generally spends it here when he can. He and Ambrose presently fell into discourse upon the parish, and somehow they got to talking of what a clergyman's duties were. Ambrose thought if he baptized and married and buried people, and administered the sacrament four times a year, and preached every month or so, and went to see sick people when they sent for him, he had done all that could be required, and might quite reasonably spend the rest of his time in hunting either foxes or Latin and Greek, according as his liking led him.

"You think Christ spent His life so?" asked Mr. Liversedge, in that very quiet tone in which he says his sharpest things, and which reminds me so often of Colonel Keith.

Ambrose looked as if he did not know what to say; and before he had found out, Mr. Liversedge went on,—

"Because, you see, He left me an example, that I should follow His steps."

"Mr. Liversedge, I thought you were orthodox."

"I certainly should have thought so, as long as I quoted Scripture," said the Vicar.

"But, you know, nobody does such a thing," said Ambrose.

"Then is it not high time somebody should?"

“Mr. Liversedge, you will never get promotion, if that be the way you are going on.”

“In which world?”

“‘Which world’! There is only one.”

“I thought there were two.”

Ambrose fidgetted uneasily on his chair.

“I tell you what, my good Sir, you are on the way to preach your church empty. The pews have no souls to be saved, I believe”—and Ambrose chuckled over his little joke.

“What of the souls of the absent congregation?” asked Mr. Liversedge.

“Oh, they’ll have to get saved elsewhere,” answered Ambrose.

“Then, if they do get saved, what reason shall I have to regret their absence? But suppose they do not, Mr. Catterall,—is that my loss or theirs?”

“Why couldn’t you keep them?” said Ambrose.

“At what cost?” was the Vicar’s answer.

“A little more music and rather less thunder,” said Ambrose, laughing. “Give us back the anthem—you have no idea how many have taken seats at All Saints’ because of that. And do you know your discarded singers are there?”

“All Saints’ is heartily welcome to everybody that has gone there,” replied Mr. Liversedge. “If I drive them away by preaching error, I shall answer to God for their souls. But if men choose to go because they find truth unpalatable, I have no responsibility for them. The Lord has not given me those souls; that is plain. If He have given them to another sower of seed, by all means let them go to him as fast as they can."

"Mr. Liversedge, I do believe "—Ambrose drew his chair back an inch—" I do almost think—you must be —a—a Calvinist."

" It is not catching, I assure you, Mr. Catterall."

" But are you ? "

"That depends on what you mean. I certainly do not go blindly over hedge and ditch after the opinions of John Calvin. I am not sure that any one does."

" No, but—you believe that people are—a—are elect or non-elect; and if they be elect, they will be saved, however they live, and if they be not, they must needs be lost, however good they are. Excuse my speaking so freely."

"I am very much obliged to you for it. No, Mr. Catterall, I do not believe anything of the sort. If that be what you mean by Calvinism, I abhor it as heartily as you do."

"Why, I thought all Calvinists believed that!"

" I answer most emphatically, No. I believe that men are elect, but that they are elected ' unto sanctification ': and a man who has not the sanctification shows plainly—unless he repent and amend—that he is not one of the elect."

" Now I know a man who says, rolling the whites of his eyes and clasping his palms together as if he were always saying his prayers, like the figures on that old fellow's tomb in the chancel—he says he was elected to salvation from all eternity, and cannot possibly be lost : and he is the biggest swearer and drinker in the parish. What say you to that? Am I to believe him?"

"Can you manage it?"

"I can't: that is exactly the thing."

"Don't, then. I could not."

"But now, do you believe, Mr. Liversedge,—I have picked up the words from this fellow—that God elected men because He foreknew them, or that He foreknew because He had elected them?"

Ambrose gave a little wink at Fanny and me, sitting partly behind him, as if he thought that he had driven the Vicar completely into a corner.

"When the Angel Gabriel is sent to tell me, Mr. Catterall, I shall be most happy to let you know. Until then, you must excuse my deciding a question on which I am entirely ignorant."

Ambrose looked rather blank.

"Well, then, Mr. Liversedge, as to free-will. Do you think that every man can be saved, if he likes, or not?"

"Let Christ answer you—not me. 'No man can come to Me, except the Father which hath sent Me draw him.'"

"Ah! then man has no responsibility?" And Ambrose gave another wink at us.

"Let Christ answer you again. 'Ye will not come unto Me, that ye might have life.' If they had come, you see, they might have had it."

"But how do you reconcile the two?" said Ambrose, knitting his brows.

"When the Lord commands me to reconcile them,

He will show me how. But I do not expect Him to do either, in this world. To what extent our knowledge on such subjects may be enlarged in Heaven, I cannot venture to say."

"But surely you must reconcile them?"

"Pardon me. I must act on them."

"Can you act on principles you cannot reconcile?"

"Certainly—if you can put full trust in their proposer. Every child does it, every day. You will be a long while in the dark, Mr. Catterall, if you must know why a candle burns before you light it. Better be content to have the light, and work by it."

"There are more sorts of light than one," said my Aunt Kezia.

"That is the best light by which you see clearest," was the Vicar's answer.

"What have you got to see?" asked Ambrose.

"Your sins and your Saviour," was the reply. "And till you have looked well at both those, Mr. Catterall, and are sure that you have laid the sins upon the Sacrifice, it is as well not to look much at anything else."

I think Ambrose found that he was in the corner this time, and just the kind of corner that he did not care to get in. At any rate, he said no more.

Sophy's wedding, which took place this evening, was the quietest I ever saw. She let Mr. Liversedge say how everything should be, and he seemed to like it as plain and simple as possible. No bridesmaids, no favours, no dancing, no throwing the stocking, no fuss of any sort! I asked him if he had any objection to a cake.

" None at all," said he, " so long as you don't want me to eat it. And pray don't let us have any sugary Cupids on the top, nor any rubbish of that sort."

So the cake was quite plain, but I took care it should be particularly good, and Hatty made a wreath of spring flowers to put round it.

The house feels so quiet and empty now, when all is over, and Sophy gone. Of course she is not really gone, because the Vicarage is only across a couple of fields, and ten minutes will take us there at any time. But she is not one of us any longer, and that always feels sad.

I do feel, somehow, very sorrowful to-night—more, I think, than I have any reason. I cannot tell why sometimes a sort of tired, sad feeling comes over one, when there seems to be no cause for it. I feel as if I had not something I wanted : and yet, if anybody asked me what I wanted, I am not sure that I could tell. Or rather, I am afraid I could tell, but I don't want to say so. There is something gone out of my life which I wanted more of, and since we came home I have had none of it, or next to none. No, little book, I am not going to tell you what it is. Only there is a reason for my feeling sad, and I must keep it to myself, and never let anybody know it. I suppose other women have had to do the same thing many a time. And some of them, perhaps, grow hard and cold, and say bitter things, and people dislike and avoid them, not knowing that if they lifted up the curtain of their hearts they would see a grave there, in which all their hopes were buried long ago. Well, God knows best, and will do His best for us all. How can I wish for anything more?

22nd.

When we went up to bed last night, to my surprise Hatty came to me, and put her arms round me.

"There are only us two left now, Cary," she said. "And I know I have been very bitter and unloving of late. But I mean to try and do better, dear. Will you love me as much as you can, and help me? I have been very unhappy."

"I was afraid so, and I was very sorry for you," I answered, kissing her. "Must I not ask anything, Hatty?"

"You can ask what you like," she replied. "I think, Cary, that Christ was knocking at my door, and I did not want to open it; and I could not be happy while I knew that I was keeping Him outside. And at last—it was last night, in the sermon—He spoke to me, as it were, through that closed door; and I could not bear it any longer—I had to rise and open it, and let Him in. And before that, with Him, I kept everybody out; and now I feel as if, with Him, I wanted to take everybody in."

Dear Hatty! She seems so changed, and so happy, and I am so thankful. But my prospect looks very dark. It ought not to do so, for I let Him in before Hatty did; and I suppose some day it will be clearer, and I shall have nobody but Him, and shall be satisfied with it.

25th.

You thought you knew a great deal of what was going to happen, did you not, Cary Courtenay?

Such a wise girl you were!   And how little you did know!

This evening, Esther Langridge came in, and stayed to supper.   She said Ephraim had gone to the Parsonage on business, and had promised to call for her on his way home.   He came rather later than Esther expected. (We have only seen him twice since we returned from London, except just meeting at church and so forth: he seemed to be always busy.)   He said he had had to see Mr. Liversedge, and had been detained later than he thought.   He sat and talked to all of us for a while, but I thought his mind seemed somewhere else.   I guessed where, and thought I found myself right whei after a time, when Father had come in, and Ambrost with him, and they were all talking over the fire, Ephraim left them, and coming across to my corner, asked me first thing if I had heard anything from Annas.

I have not had a line from her, nor heard anything of her, and he looked disappointed when I said so.   He was silent for a minute, and then he said,—

"Cary, what do you think I have been making up my mind to do?"

"I do not know, Ephraim," said I.   I did not see how that could have to do with Annas, for I believed he had made up his mind on that subject long ago.

"Would you be very much surprised if I told you that I mean to take holy orders?"

"Ephraim!" I was very, very much surprised.   How would Annas like it?

"Yes, I thought you would be," said he.   "It is no

new idea to me.   But I had to get my father's consent, and smooth away two or three difficulties, before I thought it well to mention it to any one but the Vicar. He will give me a title.   I am to be ordained, Cary, next Trinity Sunday."

"Why, that is almost here!" cried I.

"Yes, it is almost here," he replied, with that far-away look in his eyes which I had seen now and then.

Then Annas had been satisfied, for of course she was one of the difficulties which had to be smoothed away.

"I shall hope to see more of my friends now," he went on, with a smile.   "I know I have seemed rather a hermit of late, while this matter has been trembling in the balance.   I hope the old friend will not be further off because he is the curate.   I should not like that."

"I do not think you need fear," said I, trying to speak lightly.   But how far my heart went down! The future master of the Fells Farm was a fixture at Brocklebank: but the future parson of some parish might be carried a hundred miles away from us.   A few months, and we might see him no more.   Just then, Father set his foot on one of the great logs, and it blazed and crackled, sending a shower of sparkles up the chimney, and a ruddy glow all over the room.   But my fire was dying out, and the sparkles were gone already.

Perhaps it was as well that just at that moment a rather startling diversion occurred, by the entrance of Sam with a letter, which he gave to Flora.

"Here's ill tidings, Sir!" said Sam to Father.   "Miss Flora's letter was brought by ane horseman, that's ridden fast and far; the puir beastie's a' o'er foam, and himsel's just worn out.   He brings news o' a gran' battle betwixt the Prince and yon loon they ca' Cumberland,—ma certie, but Cumberland's no mickle beholden to 'em!—and the Prince's army's just smashed to bits, and himsel' a puir fugitive in the Highlands.   Ill luck tak' 'em!—though that's no just becoming to a Christian man, but there's times as a chiel disna stop to measure his words and cut 'em off even wi' scissors.   'Twas at a place they ca' Culloden, this last week gane: and they say there's na mair chance for the Prince the now than for last year's Christmas to come again."

Father, of course, was extreme troubled by this news, and went forth into the hall to speak with the horseman, whom Sam had served with a good supper. Ambrose followed, and so did my Aunt Kezia, for she said men knew nought about airing beds, and it was as like as not Bessy would take the blankets from the wrong chest if she were not after her.   Hatty was not in the room, and Flora had carried off her letter, which was from my Uncle Drummond.   So Ephraim and I were left alone, for, somewhat to my surprise, he made no motion to follow the rest.

"Cary," he said, in a low tone, as he took the next chair, "I have had news, also."

It was bad news—in a moment I knew that.   His tone said so.   I looked up fearfully.   I felt, before I heard, the terrible words that were coming.

"Duncan Keith rests with God!"

Oh, it was no wonder if I let my work drop, and hid my face in my hands, and wept as if my heart were breaking.   Not for Colonel Keith.   He should never see evil any more. For Annas, and for Flora, and for the stricken friends at Monksburn, and for my Uncle Drummond, who loved him like another son,—and—yes, let me confess it, for Cary Courtenay, who had just then so much to mourn over, and must not mourn for it except with the outside pretence of something else.

"Did you care so much for him, Cary?"

What meant that intense pain in Ephraim's voice? Did he fancy——And what did it matter to him, if he did? I tried to wipe away my tears and speak.

"Did you care so little?" I said, as well as I could utter. "Think of Annas, and his parents, and—— And, Ephraim, we led him to his death—you and I!"

"Nay, not so," he answered. "You must not look at it in that light, Cary. We did but our duty. It is never well to measure duties by consequences. Yes, of course I think of his parents and sister, poor souls! It will be hard for them to bear. Yet I almost think I would change with them rather than with Angus, when he comes to know. Cary, somebody must write to Miss Keith: and it ought to be either Miss Drummond or you."

I felt puzzled. Would he not break it best to her himself? If all were settled betwixt them, and it looked as if it were, was he not the proper person to write?

"You have not written to her?" I said.

"Why, no," he answered. "I scarce like to intrude myself on her. She has not seen much of me, you know. Besides, I think a woman would know far better how to break such news. Men are apt to touch a wound roughly, even when they wish to act as gently as possible. No, Cary—I am unwilling to place such a burden on you, but I think it must be one of you."

Could he speak of Annas thus, if——I felt bewildered.

"Unless," he said, thoughtfully, looking out of the window, where the moon was riding like a queen through the somewhat troubled sky, "unless you think —for you, as a girl, can judge better than I—that Raymond would be the best breaker. Perhaps you do not know that Raymond is not at home? My Lady Inverness writ the news to him, and said she had not spoken either to Mrs. Raymond or Miss Keith. She plainly shrank from doing it. Perhaps he would help her to bear it best."

"How should he be the best?" I said. "Mrs. Raymond might——"

"Why, Cary, is it possible you do not know that Raymond and Miss Keith are troth-plight?"

"Troth-plight! Mr. Raymond! Annas!"

I started up in my astonishment. Here was a turning upside down of all my notions!

"So that is news to you?" said Ephraim, evidently surprised himself. "Why, I thought you had known it long ago. Of course I must have puzzled you! I see, now."

"I never heard a word about it," I said, feeling as though I must be dreaming, and should awake by-and-by. "I always thought——"

"You always thought what?"

"I thought you cared for Annas," I forced my lips to say.

"You thought I cared for Miss Keith?" Ephraim's

tone was a stronger negative than any words could have been. "Yes, I cared for her as your friend, and as a woman in trouble, and a woman of fine character: but if you fancied I wished to make her my wife, you were never more mistaken. No, Cary; I fixed on somebody else for that, a long while ago—before I ever saw Miss Keith. May I tell you her name?"

Then we were right at first, and it was Fanny. I said, "Yes," as well as I could.

"Cary, I never loved, and never shall love, any one but you."

I cannot tell you, little book, either what I said, or exactly what happened after that. I only know that the moaning wind outside chanted a triumphal march, and the dying embers on my hearthstone sprang up into a brilliant illumination, and I did not care a straw for all the battles that ever were fought, and envied neither Annas Keith nor anybody else.

"Well, Hatty! I did not think you were going to be the old maid of the family!" said my Aunt Kezia.

"I did not, either, once," was Hatty's answer, in a low tone, but not a sad one. "Perhaps I was the best one for it, Aunt. At any rate, you and Father will always have one girl to care for you."

We did not see Flora till the next morning. I knew that my Uncle Drummond's letter must be that in which he answered the news of Angus's escape, and I did not wonder if it unnerved her. She let me read it afterwards. The Laird and Lady Monksburn had plainly given up their son for ever when they heard what he had done. And knowing what I knew, I felt it was best so. I had to tell Flora my news :—to see the light die suddenly out of her dear brown velvet eyes,—will it ever come back again? And I wondered, watching her by the light of my own new-born happiness, whether Duncan Keith were as little to her as I had supposed.

I knew, somewhat later, that I had misunderstood her, that we had misinterpreted her. Her one wish seemed to be to get back home. And Father said he would take her himself as far as the Border, if my Uncle Drummond would come for her to the place chosen.

When the parting came, as we took our last kiss, I told her I prayed God bless her, and that some day she might be as happy as I was. There was a moment's flash in the brown eyes.

" Take that wish back, Cary," she said, quietly. " Happy as you are, the woman whom Duncan Keith loved can never be, until she meet him again at the gates of pearl."

" That may be a long while, dear."

" It will be just so long as the Lord hath need of me," she answered: " and I hope, for his sake, that will be as long as my father needs me. And then——Oh, but it will be a blithe day when the call comes to go home !"

THE FELLS FARM, *September 25th.*

Five months since I writ a word ! And how much has happened in them—so much that I could never find time to set it down, and now I must do it just in a few lines.

I have been married six weeks. Father shook his head with a smile when Ephraim first spoke to him, and said his lass was only in the cradle yesterday: but he soon came round. It was as quiet a wedding as Sophy's, and I am sure I liked it all the better, whatever other people might think. We are to live at the Fells Farm during the year of Ephraim's curacy, and then Father thinks he can easily get him a living through the interest of friends. Where it will be, of course we cannot guess.

Flora has writ thrice since she returned home. She says my Uncle Drummond was very thankful to have her back again : but she can see that Lady Monksburn is greatly changed, and the Laird has so failed that he scarce seems the same man. Of herself she said nothing but one sentence,—

"Waiting, dear Cary,—always waiting."

From Angus we do not hear a word. Mr. Raymond and Annas are to be married when their year of mourning is out. I cannot imagine how they will get along —he a Whig clergyman, and she a Tory Presbyterian! However, that is their affair. I am rather thankful 'tis not mine.

My Aunt Dorothea has writ me one letter—very kind to me—(it was writ on the news of my marriage), but very stiff toward my Aunt Kezia. I see she cannot forgive her easily, and I do not think Grandmamma ever will.

Grandmamma sent me a large chest from London, full of handsome presents,—a fine set of Dresden tea china (which travelled very well — only one saucer broke); a new hoop, so wide round that methinks I shall never dare to wear it in the country; a charming piece of dove-coloured damask, and a petticoat, to wear with it, of blue quilted satin; two calico gowns from India, a beautiful worked scarf from the same country, six pair pearl-coloured silk stockings, a new fan, painted with flowers, most charmingly done, a splendid piece of white and gold brocade, and a superb set of turquoise and pearl jewellery. I cannot think when or how I am to wear them; they seem so unfit for the wife of a country curate.

"Oh, wait till I am a bishop," says Ephraim, laughingly; "then you can make the Dean's lady faint away for envy of all your smart things. And as to the white and gold brocade, keep it till the King comes to stay with us, and it will be just the thing for a state bed for him."

"I wonder what colour it will be!" said I. "Which king?"

Ephraim makes me a low bow — over the water bottle.[1]

I must lay down my pen, for I hear a shocking smash in the kitchen. That girl Dolly is so careless! I don't believe I shall ever have much time for writing now.

LANGBECK RECTORY, UNDER THE CHEVIOTS,
August the 28th, 1747.

Nearly a whole year since I writ one line!

Our lot is settled now, and we moved in here in

---

[1] The recognised Jacobite way of answering :—"The King *over the water.*"

May last. I am very thankful that the lines have fallen to me still in my dear North—I have not pleasant recollections of the South. And I fancy—but perhaps unjustly—that we Northerners have a deeper, more yearning love for our hills and dales than they have down there. We are about midway between Brocklebank and Abbotscliff, which is just where I would have chosen to be, if I could have had the choice. It is not often that God gives a man all the desires of his heart; perhaps to a woman He gives it even less often. How thankful I ought to be!

My Aunt Kezia was so good as to come with us, to help me to settle down. I should not have got things straight in twice the time if she had not been here. Sophy spent the days with Father while my Aunt Kezia was here, and just went back to the Vicarage for the night. Father is very much delighted with Sophy's child, and calls him a bouncing boy, and a credit to the family; and Sophy thinks him the finest child that ever lived, as my Aunt Kezia saith every mother hath done since Eve.

The night before my Aunt Kezia went home, as she and I sat together,—it was not yet time for Ephraim to come in from his work in the parish, for he is one of the few parsons who do work, and do not pore over learned books or go a-hunting, and leave their parishes to take care of themselves—well, as my Aunt and I sat by the window, she said something which rather astonished me.

" Cary, I don't know what you and Ephraim would say, but I am beginning to think we made a mistake."

"Do you mean about the Chinese screens, Aunt?" said I. "The gold lacquer would have gone very well with the damask, but——"

"Chinese screens!" saith my Aunt, with a hearty laugh. "Why, whatever is the girl thinking about? No, child! I mean about the Prince."

"Aunt Kezia!" I cried. "You never mean to say we did wrong in fighting for our King?"

"Wrong? No, child, for we meant to do right. I gather from Scripture that the Lord takes a deal more account of what a man means than of what he does. Thank God it is so! For if a man means to come to Christ, he does come, no matter how: ay, and if a man means to reject Christ, he does that too, however fair and orthodox he may look in the eyes of the world. Therefore, as to those matters that are in doubt, and cannot be plainly judged by Scripture, but Christian men may and do lawfully differ about them, if a man honestly meant to do God's will, so far as he knew it, I don't believe he will be judged as if he had not cared to do it. But what I intend to say is this—that it is plain to me now that the Lord hath repealed the decree whereby He gave England to the House of Stuart. There is no right against Him, Cary. He doeth as He will with all the kingdoms of the world. Maybe it's not so plain to you—if so, don't you try to see through my eyes. Follow your own conscience until the Lord teaches yourself. If our fathers had been truer men, and had passed the Bill of Exclusion in 1680, the troubles of 1688 would never have come, nor those of 1745 neither. They ate sour grapes, and set our teeth on edge—ay, and their own too, poor souls! It was the Bishops and Lord Halifax that did it, and the Bishops paid the wyte, as Sam says. It must have been a bitter pill to those seven in the Tower, to think that all might have been prevented by lawful, constitutional means, and that they—their Order, I mean—had just pulled their troubles on their own heads."

"Aunt Kezia," I cried in distress, "you never mean to say that Colonel Keith died for a wrongful cause?"

"God forbid!" she said, gravely. "Colonel Keith did not die for that Cause. He died for right and righteousness, for truth and honour, for faithfulness, for loyalty and love—no bad things to die for. Not for the Prince—only for God and Flora, and a little, perhaps, for Angus. God forbid that I should judge any true and honourable man—most of all that man who gave his life for those we love. Only, Cary, the Cause is dead and gone. The struggle is over for ever: and we may thank God it is so. On the wreck of the old England a new England may arise—an England standing fast in the liberty wherewith Christ hath made her free, free from priestly yoke and priest-ridden rulers, free not to revolt but to follow, not to disobey, but to obey. If only—ah! *if only* she resolve, and stand to it, never to be entangled again with the yoke of bondage, never to forget the lessons which God has taught her, never again to eat the sour grapes, and set the children's teeth on edge. Let her once begin to think of the tiger's beauty, and forget its deathly claws —once lay aside her watchword of 'No peace with Rome' —and she will find it means no peace with God, for His scourge has always pursued her when she has truckled to His great enemy.   Eh, but men have short memories, never name short sight.   Like enough, by a hundred years are over, they'll be looking at Roman sugarsticks as the Scarlet Woman holds them out, and thinking that she is very fair and fine-spoken, and why shouldn't they have a few sweets?   Well! it is well the government of the world isn't in old Kezia's hands, for if it were, some people would find themselves uncommonly uncomfortable before long."

"You don't mean me, I hope?" I said, laughing.

"Nay, child, I don't mean you, nor yet your husband. Very like you'll not see it as I do.   But you'll live to see it—if only you live long enough."

Well, my Aunt Kezia may be right, though I do not see it.   Only that I do think it was a sad blunder to throw out the Bill of Exclusion.   It had passed the Commons, so they were not to blame.   But one thing I should like to set down, for any who may read this book a hundred years hence, if it hath not been tore up for waste-paper long ere that—that we Protestants who fought for the Prince never fought nor meant to fight for Popery.   We hated it every bit as much as any who stood against him.   We fought because the contrary seemed to us to be doing evil that good might come.   But I won't say we may not live to be thankful that we lost our cause.

It has been a warm afternoon, and I sat with the window open in the parlour, singing and sewing; Ephraim was out in the parish.   I was turning down a hem when a voice in the garden spoke to me,—

"An't like you, Madam, to give a drink of whey to a poor soldier?"

There was a slight Scots accent with the words.

"Whence come you?" I said.

"I fought at Prestonpans," he answered. He looked a youngish man, but very ragged and bemired.

"On which side?" I said, as I rose up. Of course I was not going to refuse him food and drink, howevei that might be, but I dare say I should have made it a little more dainty for one of Prince Charlie's troops than for a Hanoverian, and I felt pretty sure he was the former from his accent.

I fancied I saw a twinkle in his eyes.

"The side you are on, Madam," said he.

"How can you know which side I am on?" said I. "Come round to the back door, friend, and I will find you a drink of whey."

"I suppose," said my beggar, looking down at himself, "I don't look quite good enough for the front door. But I am an officer for all that, Madam."

"Sir, I beg your pardon," I made answer. "I will let you in at the front"—for when he spoke more, I heard the accent of a gentleman.

"Pray don't give yourself that trouble, Cousin Cary."

And to my utter amazement, the beggar jumped in at the window, which was low and easily scaled.

"Angus!" I almost screamed.

'At your service, Madam."

"When did you leave France ? Where are you come from ? Have you been to Abbotscliff? Are——"

"Halt ! Can't fight more than three men at once. And I won't answer a question till I have had something to eat.   Forgive me, Cary, but I am very nearly starving."

I rushed into the kitchen, and astonished Caitlin by laying violent hands on a pan of broth which she was going to serve for supper. I don't know what I said to her. I hastily poured the broth into a basin, and seizing a loaf of bread and a knife, dashed back to Angus.

"Eat that now, Angus.   You shall have something better by-and-by."

He ate like a man who was nearly starving, as he had said.   When he had finished, he said,—

"Now! I left France a fortnight since.   I have not been to Abbotscliff. I know nothing but the facts that you are married, and where you live, which I learned by accident, and I instantly thought that your house, if you would take me in, would be a safer refuge than either Brocklebank or Abbotscliff. Now tell me something in turn.   Are my father and Flora well ? "

"Yes, for anything I know."

"And all at Brocklebank ? "

"Quite."

"And the Keiths?   Has Annas bagged her pheasant ? "

"What do you mean, Angus ? "

"Why, is she Mrs. Raymond ? I saw all that. I suppose Duncan got away without any difficulty ? "

"Annas is Mr. Raymond's wife," I said.   "But,

Angus, I cannot think how it is, but—I am afraid you do not understand."

" Understand what ? "

" Is it possible you do not know what price was paid for your ransom ? "

Angus rose hastily, and laid his hand on my arm.

" Speak out, Cary ! What do I not know ? "

"Angus, Colonel Keith bought your life with his own."

In all my life I never saw a man's face change as the face of Angus Drummond changed then. It was plainly to be read there that he had never for a moment understood at what cost he had been purchased. A low moan of intense sorrow broke from him, and he hid his face upon the table.

" I think he paid the price very willingly, Angus," I said, softly. " And he sent Annas a last message for you—he bade you, to the utmost of what your opportunities might be, to be to God and man what he hoped to have been."

" O Duncan, Duncan ! " came in anguish from the white lips. "And I never knew—I never thought——"

Ah, it was so like Angus, " never to think."

He lifted his head at last, with the light of a settled purpose shining in his eyes.

" To man I can never be what he would have been. I am a proscribed fugitive. You harbour me at a risk even now. But to God ! Cary, I have been a rebel: but I never was a deserter from that service. God helping me, I will enlist now. If my worthless life have cost the most precious life in Scotland, it shall not have been given in vain."

"There was Another who gave His life for you, Angus," I could not help saying.

"Ay, I have been bought twice over," was the trembling answer. "God help me to live worthy of the cost!"

We all keep the name of Duncan Keith in our inmost hearts—unspoken, but very dear. But I think it is dearest of all in a little house in the outskirts of Amsterdam, where, now that my Uncle Drummond has been called to his reward, our Flora keeps home bright for a Protestant pastor who works all the day through in the prisons of Amsterdam, among the lowest of the vile; who knows what exile and imprisonment are; and who, once in every year, as the day of his substitute's death comes round, pleads with these prisoners from words which are overwhelming to himself,—"Ye are not your own; for ye are bought with a price."

Many of those men and women sink back again into the mire. But now and then the pastor knows that a soul has been granted to his pleadings,—that in one more instance, as in his own case, the price was not paid in vain.

THE END.